Once Lost

Ber Carroll

First published in 2015 by Killard Publishing

Copyright © Ber Carroll 2015

Layout by Working Type Studio

The moral right of the author has been asserted.

National Library of Australia

Cataloguing-in-Publication data:

Carroll, Ber, 1971–

Once Lost / Ber Carroll

ISBN 978-0-9924721-2-2

Font: Garamond 12.5

Other titles by Ber Carroll

Executive Affair
Just Business
High Potential
The Better Woman
Less Than Perfect
Worlds Apart

For Rob, Conor and Ashling

Chapter 1

Louise

It's unexpectedly beautiful, this room I will be working in for the next twelve months: white walls, polished floor, spacious, serene, and full of natural light. Skylights overhead showcase the deep blue sky — startling against all the white — and the view from the window includes a rippling corner of Sydney Harbour I am not yet familiar with.

'She's over here.' Tom Clifford, the curator, leads the way to one of the large work benches. There, stripped from its frame, lies my project, my raison d'être, and I can't quite contain my gasp of dismay.

'Oh ...'

For a while we both gaze at the portrait, a young woman whose pale hair and skin jump out from the comparatively dark background. Her hair, a frizz of tiny curls, and her mouth, with its slight smirk, inject a playful note into the otherwise formal setting. She's wearing a magenta gown with frilled cuffs made of the same white lace as the ruffled neckline. Her figure seems voluptuous under the stiff bodice of the gown, but her hands and fingers are slender. She has one flaw. Correction, it is the canvas that has the flaw, not the girl. It's quite badly damaged. In the worst possible place: the face. It looks as though it's been poorly repaired around the right eye and a good part of the cheek area below. The effect is rather like a large tea stain. Unfortunately, it draws the eye and detracts from the beautiful colours and detail in the rest of the work.

Tom sighs softly beside me. My first impressions of him are that he's mild-mannered and a little bit vague, but has the potential to be pernickety when it comes to things he cares about. His hair is grey, his face youthful. I estimate his age as late forties, which is relatively young for the profession: the curators I worked with in London were dinosaurs, museum relics in themselves.

'Analiese has completed a full examination of the work.' He gestures to the lever arch folder lying on the tabletop next to the painting. 'Everything is documented both in hard copy and on the collection database … You'll find that her notes are meticulous.'

Analiese is my predecessor and now the mother of a two-week-old baby girl. Apparently the baby arrived early, before Analiese had begun her maternity leave, and almost before she got to the hospital. Gabriella, the flamboyant frame conservator who works in the room next door, filled me in on all the details a few minutes ago, as soon as Tom had made introductions.

'The pains came from nowhere. Bang. One minute Analiese was quietly working on the painting, the next she was howling in pain. The ambulance got stuck in the lunchtime traffic on the way here, and we all thought the gallery was about to give birth to its first bambina.'

Gabriella went on to assure me that the ambulance had eventually arrived, and that Analiese's baby, Stella, was in fact born in transit to the hospital.

'She is *our* bambina, little Stella. She belong to all of us. She love the gallery so much she want to be born here.'

The warmth in Gabriella's voice, the unbridled affection for both Analiese and her baby, was so genuine and heartfelt that for a moment I felt quite inadequate as her replacement.

Gabriella is working on the frame of what is now my painting. From what I've heard (when Tom steered Gabriella away from the subject of baby Stella to request a brief update on her part of the project) and from what I could observe for myself (only one corner of the ornate frame remained fully intact: the others were either broken or extensively damaged), the frame is in even worse condition than the painting. Gabriella has weeks, if not months, of intricate moulding and reconstruction to make it structurally sound.

Now, with Tom looking over my shoulder, I flick through Analiese's folder, quickly scanning her photos and notes.

'All the testing is complete,' he informs me. 'Analiese was about to begin surface cleaning the work. If everything had gone to plan, she would have had that stage completed and you could have started on the varnish removal. But the baby had other ideas!'

So, one to two weeks of surface cleaning, followed by a couple of months removing the varnish, onto which hundreds of years of dust, smoke and grime has attached itself. Then the real work: repairing the terrible damage as unobtrusively as I possibly can, before inpainting and revarnishing.

Tom clears his throat. 'Do you mind if I leave you to it? I have an important meeting …'

His voice trails away. Clearly he feels guilty about abandoning me so soon on my first morning.

Making sure my smile is warm enough to dispel his doubts, I reply, 'I'll be fine. I'll spend most of today reading these notes, I imagine.'

'Excellent. Peter or Heidi should be able to help with any queries.'

I nod. Peter and Heidi seemed friendly and helpful — though not quite as forthcoming as Gabriella — when Tom introduced me earlier. I will work alongside them, if such thing is possible in this enormous room.

Tom departs, and I pull up a swivel chair, Analiese's notes on my knees. For the rest of the morning I am absorbed. There's lots of technical information to take in, but by far the most surprising and compelling fact is that the artist who created this painting is unknown. The work is believed to be from the late 1700s, and is being restored in preparation for an exhibition of portraits from that era. It came into the possession of the gallery three years ago, donated by the executor of a deceased estate, who recognised the considerable skill of the artist but could not sell the painting due to the extensive damage. Analiese's notes suggest that the painting originates from Europe, most likely The Netherlands, as this is where the deceased's ancestors lived before they migrated to Australia after World War II. It's hoped that as the piece is restored, more information will come to light.

Reading takes its toll, and eventually the letters and words begin to blur and make no sense. I set down the folder and press my fingers into my temples, moving them in small slow circles until the tension has eased. When I stop, it feels as though the girl in the painting has been assessing me, her one and only eye overcompensating for the missing one, seeing deeper and wider, bearing witness. It's such a shame that the worst of the damage is to her face. If only it was in a less conspicuous place: her dress, for instance, or, better still, some-where in the background. Then again, the damage is so confronting that it absolutely must be dealt with. That's a good thing, because I know only too well how damage, if not brutally evident, can be underestimated and brushed aside.

It's ironic, really, this anonymous work being assigned to me. I can see how it will play out: months and months of painstaking research, hope creeping in despite my best efforts to keep it at bay, the crushing sense of defeat as every clue, every lead, ends in nothing, absolutely nothing. Maybe I should confess to Tom that I don't have a very good track record when it comes to things like this.

I stand and walk towards the window, which runs the full length of the wall, bathing the room in light. Looking down, I see Sydney buzzing below me: cars, trucks, ferries, and lots and lots of people. I like this city, with its blue water and skies. Though I've lived here less than a week, I've already been wooed by its beauty and glamour, and the startling sky that makes me want to reach up and scrape away a colour sample to preserve for darker, gloomier days. The sun catches off the water and the glass windows of the skyscrapers, and everything glitters. I can see greenery, both in the foreground and background, and I know this city can breathe, that it's open and airy and has somehow escaped that boxed-in, contained feeling that other cities have. Yes, this a good place to visit ... to live ... to stay.

Is this where you are? I whisper under my breath.

Chapter 2

Emma

Today is Louise's first day in her new job, and even though I should be concentrating on my *own* job, I can't stop thinking about her. Of course it's night-time in Sydney now, so Louise isn't at work: she's fast asleep, and her first day is over and done with. To be honest, the time difference is as bloody hard to comprehend as the fact that I won't see her for twelve months.

'Emma?'

Katie, the graduate we hired last month, interrupts my train of thought. She's a nice enough girl, but she can't make a decision to save her fuckin' life. All day she shadows me, asking questions at every available opportunity, her neediness so blatant that I'm almost embarrassed for her. I'll put up with it for another few weeks, give her the opportunity to grow into some semblance of independence. But if she doesn't improve, I'll have to tell her straight: *For fuck's sake, Katie, stand on your own two feet.* I bet she'll cry. It never ceases to amaze me how easily my female colleagues burst into tears. A blip in their carefully laid plans: watery eyes. The slightest confrontation: bawling

7

their faces off. I'm not a crier. No matter how confronting the situation, or how loud someone is shouting at me, or how sad or stupid or disappointed I feel, I don't cry. *Criers are die-ers,* Jamie and I used to sneer. Stop. Don't think about Jamie. Not here. Work is one of the few places where I can almost fool myself into forgetting about him.

'Emma, sorry, I just need to know where to find that document, the one that … sorry …'

I'll have to tell Katie to stop apologising, too. It's constant with her, like a nervous twitch she can't control. Sorry, sorry, sorry … Sorry is a futile word, Katie. It can't change outcomes, or retract words. It rectifies nothing, absolutely nothing. It wastes all our time. Now, what did you want?

'I had a look … I just can't seem to find … sorry …'

I shoot her a smile to calm her down, to let her know that even though she has interrupted me yet again, and even though she should really be able to locate this file without my help, my patience is still — somehow — not at its end.

Opening the appropriate window on my laptop, I click down through the drives and folders until I've reached the document she's after.

'Here.' I tear off a post-it note. 'I'll write down where it is. Alright?'

'Thanks,' she mutters, her eyes downcast, before repeating, 'Sorry.'

Katie has trouble meeting my eyes on most days. I suspect I look and sound coarse to her, coming from one of those scary suburbs her mother would have warned her to avoid. My hair is very short, its natural mousey colour dyed a bright defiant blonde. My ears are pierced, three times. I have a tattoo — a Celtic knot — on the inside of my wrist, and I chew a lot of gum, a habit I took up when I stopped smoking. Then there's the swearing, but I'm trying to cut that out

— for Isla's sake. And as if all that's not enough, there's the blotching on my neck. I do my best to cover it up, but it's there, an ominous shadow above the collar of my blouse, another unwelcome reminder of Jamie.

Poor Katie. It's not just me making her feel uncomfortable, it's the job too. At university she was smart, one of the best in her class. Here in this office, she knows nothing, she's dumb, and she's beginning to realise that taking verbatim notes in lecture theatres, sipping over-priced coffee in the university canteen, and buying a cashmere scarf in this season's colours to combat the biting wind that rips through campus have left her totally ill-prepared for the working world.

Katie, still looking uncertain, goes back to her desk. I'm only three years older than her but she has this way of making me feel ancient.

Where was I before this latest interruption? Yes, Louise. I can't begin to imagine her new workplace, the windows and light, the feel of the place, but I can see her dark hair and sweeping fringe, her slight figure arched over whatever painting she's working on. For such a diminutive thing, she's been a big part of my life. Louise has always been there, even during those times she's been physically apart from me. She spent two years training in London, but she was home every other weekend, sharing the sophistication and making me feel like I lived in London, too. Then she went to New York, filling in for someone on maternity leave. She wasn't able to come home as frequently, only once every few months, but she phoned and emailed and sent touristy postcards that still cling to my fridge door. I regret that I didn't go to visit her in New York. I didn't have the money but the wasted opportunity still grates on me, makes me feel useless, hopeless. The truth of it is, I've never lived fuckin' anywhere but here. Though we grew up side by side — next-door neighbours — in that extraordinarily ugly block of flats, Louise has managed to travel, while my life has been confined to the same desolate suburb. Now she's in Sydney, quite literally on the other side of the world. She's not planning to come home during this contract — another maternity one, apparently. It's too far away, and the flights are too expensive.

My desk phone rings, redirecting my attention from Sydney and the cost of flights.

'The repairs and maintenance account is over budget …' It's Brendan, my boss, his sanctimonious tone filling my ear.

Hello, Emma. How are you today, Emma?

I'm fine, thank you, Brendan.

'It's just timing, that's all,' I tell him. 'It should even out over the next few months.'

He doesn't listen. 'Can you do a full analysis? By the end of the day would be good.'

'Yeah. Alright.'

Yes, Brendan. Three bags full, Brendan. I detest you, Brendan.

Opening a series of windows on my computer, I begin the analysis straight away. I'm fast, a whiz, even if I say so myself. Brendan isn't the type to acknowledge my skills and experience, so I'm left to sing my own praises.

It's ready in a few minutes, Brendan's analysis, but I hold off sending it. He can wait. I dabble with the heading, changing the font a number of times: REPAIRS. This leads me back to Louise, as everything seems to do today. I'm a self-confessed ignoramus when it comes to her job and the elite world of fine art. I think of her work as repairs and restoration, despite the fact that she insists on calling it *conservation*. 'We do as little as possible, Emma. As little as we can get away with. We try not to compromise the integrity of the piece.' Conservation, restoration, the distinction is lost on me. In school, I never had any interest in drawing or painting, and could think of nothing more boring than spending an afternoon in the National Art Gallery. It was the same with English, History, Geography: fuckin' tedious, all of them. Maths was the only subject I tolerated, so no surprises I've ended up an accountant of sorts. (I'm not qualified. My below-average Leaving Certificate results ruled out tertiary education.)

Oh, how I wish I could go back in time and give that teenage me a slap across the face. If I had a second chance at school, I would take more interest in bloody *everything*, not just art. Boredom isn't learning about world history or the great poets or what lies beneath the earth's core. Boredom is seeing your salary go into your bank account month after month, year after year, without any significant increase. Boredom is having a boss who never *ever* listens to a word you say. Boredom is not progressing in your job because all the promotions go to graduates, even inept ones like Katie. This is why I take a great interest in Isla's schoolwork. We read together every night, and do simple maths using apples and oranges and cutlery. When she's older, we'll watch documentaries together and take tours of historic parts of the city, the aim being to extend her well beyond the constraints of the school curriculum, to light the fire of learning early, so that it keeps smouldering through those self-destructive teenage years. And if she ever protests that she's bored, I'll tell her what boredom truly is.

For fuck's sake, Isla! You don't want to end up like Mammy, d'you?

Except I won't use the F word. Not around Isla.

I glance at the clock on my laptop: 3pm. Right about now, Eddie should be picking up my little girl from school. They'll walk home together, her small soft hand ensconced in his big calloused one. At home he'll make a snack for her, some fruit and biscuits. She's allowed two biscuits only, but I know he gives her more if she asks. Eddie is kind to Isla, like another father to her, just like Louise is another mother.

This is what I'm worried about. Louise meeting someone in Sydney, settling down. I can't bear the thought that she might not return, and that I'll be left behind here forever. But it's a possibility, isn't it? She's young, passionate about what she does — which is a point of attractiveness in its own right — and she's got one of those faces that makes you turn for a second look. Louise isn't pretty. Neither am I. Our faces have a hint of toughness that can't be disguised by any amount of make-up or blusher, and our bodies seem to have angles that can't be softened with fashion or accessories.

'We're interesting,' Louise has maintained. 'I'd have that any day rather than prettiness.'

Of course the art world values 'interesting' above 'beautiful'. But in the *real* world, I'd choose beauty, prettiness, in a heartbeat. This shallow attitude would disappoint Louise, but it wouldn't surprise her. If she were here, she'd roll her eyes and tut at me. If she were here, she would call around to my place tonight, and we'd eat dinner with Eddie before he leaves for his shift, and then we'd put Isla to bed, Louise reading with her instead of me, and finally we'd station ourselves on the couch for a night of feel-good-by-comparison reality TV.

'Twelve months will fly,' she assured me before she left.

It hasn't even been twelve days, and already it feels like forever. It sounds melodramatic, needy — and there was I, only moments ago, accusing Katie of being hopelessly clingy! — but this time I feel I have truly lost Louise.

Needy, sad, abandoned, aimless.

It strikes me that this is how Louise must have felt — and still feels — about her mother.

Chapter 3

Louise

By the time I get to the last property on my list, my expectations are pretty low. I've learned that 'perfectly located' and 'neat and tidy' are the most blatantly abused terms in the shared accommodation ads on the internet, and I've established that many of the bedrooms advertised barely qualify as such, because surely fitting a bed that one has enough room to actually walk around is a basic requirement. Even more irritating is the fact that I've been scrutinised from head to toe every time, with possible flatmates assessing if *I'm* worthy of their tiny, badly located, less-than-clean abodes.

According to the ad, this apartment comes with a resident thirty-year-old male. To be honest, sharing with a man isn't my preference. I only made this appointment as a backup if all the others failed to deliver, which they have, so here I am.

A few minutes later, I have been buzzed in, taken the stairs to the second floor, and am being greeted by Joe, the thirty-year-old male in question. He's average height, and his gaze is open and friendly, a nice change from the critical and frankly suspicious receptions I've had so far today.

'Hi. I'm Louise.'

'Dublin?' he enquires.

Despite myself I'm impressed. 'That didn't take you long.'

He grins. 'My mother's from Howth. She's been in Australia more than thirty years, but she sounds like she arrived yesterday. I have cousins and aunts and uncles there — the Flynns. Don't suppose you know them?'

'Err … No.'

I'm smiling, a welcome surprise at the end of such a frustrating afternoon. I like Joe in that certain way that comes purely from instinct and is rarely wrong. Something about him feels familiar, as though he's someone I already know, not someone I'm meeting for the first time. Maybe it's the Irish in him, that classic combination of dark hair, clear skin and warm eyes he must have inherited from his mother.

'Let me show you around.'

The apartment, from what I can see, appears to be genuinely 'neat and tidy', and the bedroom he leads me to, while not large, is big enough, and has a generous rectangular window framing an outlook of red rooftops and gum trees.

'I can remove the bed if you have your own,' he offers.

'I don't. I have no furniture at all, so this is great.'

'The lease is a minimum six months.'

'That's fine …'

'You work in the city?'

'At the Sydney City Art Gallery.' My chin rises of its own accord. 'I'm a conservator.'

Despite my best efforts, the defensiveness is always there; it seems I can't adopt a nonchalant tone, like everyone else does, when I say what I do for a living. It's as though my brain doesn't believe I've managed to get this far.

His smile is wry. 'A conservator and a writer. Interesting combination.'

So he's a writer. What kind? Novelist? Journalist? Copywriter?

He moves on before I can ask.

The kitchen is small but clean and renovated, the balcony is surprisingly spacious — I can see myself spending time out here — and the living area has two beige sofas, a flat-screen TV, a bookshelf that covers an entire wall yet still overflows, and a square dining table with four matching chairs. The bathroom, like the kitchen, is small and freshly renovated. Would it be awkward sharing this bathroom, putting my toiletries next to his, waiting for my turn to shower in the mornings?

'I don't take long showers,' he supplies, reading my mind as proficiently as he read my accent earlier on.

We leave the bathroom and hover where we started off, in the small hallway. The tour is evidently complete.

He smiles a crooked smile. 'So, are you interested?'

'Yes, yes I am.'

I already know that I can live here with him, that we're compatible, and that we won't grate on each other. And this is really jumping ahead, but I am quite sure that if I move in here, Joe and I will become friends.

'Would you like an application form?' he asks.

'Yes, please.'

I leave clutching the form. Outside, a bus swings by, proving that there is indeed public transport on hand. I pause to look up at the building, with its clean blonde brick, and my eyes pick out Joe's apart-ment on the second floor. There's the balcony, the outdoor table and chairs, some healthy plants, and a slice of the hot late afternoon sun. It's perfect. And Joe seems like the perfect flatmate.

'Just email me a copy of the completed form and I'll ring you to confirm when you can move in,' he said before I left.

He seems as sure of me as I am of him. With any luck, I'll be able to check out of my current accommodation — a budget motel on the corner of two extremely noisy streets — in a couple of days.

Walking down the street, towards the bus stop, I acknowledge one misgiving. I wish he wasn't a writer. There's also the floor-to-ceiling bookshelf in the living area, evidence that he not only writes but reads extensively, too.

Writing, books, words. Everywhere.

It's the only fault I can find. In every other way, Joe and his apart-ment are ideal.

Four days later I'm standing outside Joe's door with all my worldly belongings: a suitcase, resting by my legs, and a sports bag, still weigh-ing heavily on my shoulder.

'Is that all you have?' he asks, looking surprised.

I'm sweating and red in the face from exertion. 'Compact but deceivingly heavy.'

'Here.' He lifts the bag away from my aching shoulder. 'You should have buzzed me to come down and help.'

The thought had occurred to me, particularly after struggling up the first flight of stairs, but it felt presumptuous, so I'd persevered.

Now, with my head lolling to one side from the strain of the bag, I wonder at my own stupidity.

Joe has also taken charge of the suitcase, choosing to lift and carry it rather than use the wheels. Being small and slight, I don't have much natural strength, and it's one thing about men that fascinates me, the inherent and seemingly effortless power to lift and lug and, on occasion, strike out. I follow him, closely watching as he exerts his strength.

'Thanks.'

'Next time, please ask,' he says, depositing my bags on the bed and casting me a look that suggests he has already worked out that asking for help is difficult for me.

'Okay,' I reply in a voice that sounds oddly meek and not like me at all.

He hesitates by the door, and I notice then what he's wearing: a grey T-shirt that looks as though it's been washed many times, teamed with well-worn jeans. Are these his writing clothes? When does he write? Monday to Friday? Nine to five? Maybe he's one of those writers who stay up all night and go about like the walking dead during the daylight hours. I guess I'll soon find out.

'Can I make you a tea or coffee?'

'No, thanks,' I smile.

He closes the door behind him, and I'm left alone in my new room. I sit on the bed, and try to restore my equilibrium. As my face cools down and my heart stops racing, I breathe in the room around me, its serenity and cleanness and space. The cream walls, the soft wool carpet, the daylight streaming through the window, all bring a deal of gratefulness, because another kind of room is never very far from the fore of my mind: a fifth-floor room with dull walls, stained old-fashioned carpet, and a small window that always — for safety's sake — remained locked. A room, already too small for one, which had to mould and stretch itself to accommodate two. I was about six or seven when my mother left Simon's bed and moved into mine. There wasn't enough space — or money, for that matter — for two beds, so I slept on a thin mattress on the floor. Every room since has been luxurious by comparison. The various places in Dublin after Simon died. The bedsit in London. The loft-style apartment in New York, paid for by the gallery. This place, with its double bed and clean, pure light.

Slowly, I begin to unpack, placing underwear and socks neatly into drawers, hanging jackets and skirts and trousers for work. T-shirts, shorts and jeans, my hanging-around clothes, folded on shelves. A few textbooks, a crystal paperweight (a graduation gift from Emma), and some stationery for the desk. There's too much storage space: hangers, shelves and drawers that I cannot fill. Obviously this room is used to being inhabited by someone with more possessions — more substance — than me.

I leave my most treasured items until last. The picture frame: her beguiling smile, the tilt of her head, the sun glinting on her copper-brown hair. Though the photograph is slightly out of focus, I like it more than any of the others because it catches her in a moment when she seems genuinely happy. I place the frame on the bedside dresser, the same place it has been in London, New York and everywhere else.

Then there's the box, which contains more photographs, a few personal letters dated before I was born, a notebook with shopping and other lists in her sloping handwriting. Though it goes everywhere with me, I don't open the box very often. Even when I was young and knew nothing at all about conservation, I somehow understood that the more frequently I opened it and fingered through its contents, the more fragile and insubstantial those contents would become. This is all I have of her, and I have used all my skills, my knowledge, my expertise, to keep everything in pristine condition.

Of course the photograph in the picture frame is the exception. Constantly displaying that moment of happiness and exposing it to UV light has faded and yellowed the colours. I know I should store it away, or at least rotate it with the other photographs, but I can't. Something about it gives me hope. It was just a random moment in a hard, disappointing life. An illusion, if anything. Nevertheless, it suggests that a happy ending was within her grasp.

Chapter 4

Emma

Eddie does most of the cooking, and I can smell the sausages as soon as I open the front door. Slamming the door shut on the damp cold evening outside, I unfurl my scarf. Isla barges out from the kitchen and launches herself at my legs before I can get my coat off.

'Mammmyyyyy ...' she squeals.

Every evening I come home to this movie-star reception, and it never fails to lift my heart. No matter how bad my day has been, how innately bored or disheartened or unappreciated I feel, hearing the excitement in her voice, seeing the sheer delight on her face, is like a magic tonic.

I drink her in: pigtails crooked after a day at school, tracksuit pants that are a little too small on her, a smear of food — jam? — on her milky-white face. She's bloody beautiful, my daughter, and it never ceases to amaze me that she came from me, that I'm capable of making something, *someone*, so exquisite.

Bending down to kiss her, I ask, 'What didya learn at school today?'

'Red Robot. He used to be Robber Red, but he got sent to jail ...'

'Interesting ... And what sound does he make again?'

'Rrrrr ...' Isla snarls.

'Good girl.'

Hand in hand, we proceed to the kitchen. Eddie is in his work gear: navy blue overalls, steel-capped boots and a fluoro yellow vest. Dinner is sausages, mashed potato and beans, and he's in the process of serving it up. Time is of the essence. We have half an hour before he leaves for his shift, so not a minute can be wasted.

I sit down, a steaming plate of food in front of me. The food warms me, as does the heat from the stove and the closeness between the three of us. This is what matters, I tell myself. At the end of the day, if you can't come home to this, you have nothing. Even though it's only for thirty minutes, it sustains me for much, much longer than that.

'How was work?' Eddie enquires between mouthfuls.

He generally waits a while before asking this question, allowing me the opportunity to talk about it first. It's important, he maintains. It's what I do all day long, and if he doesn't know about it, then he doesn't know *me*. So if I don't start talking of my own accord, he asks.

'The same,' I reply, my tone noncommittal though I know Eddie will coax until I've told him everything.

'The graduate, she's settling in alright?'

'Katie? Yeah, suppose so, even though she's so fu—' I swallow the swearword from the tip of my tongue. 'So ... *indecisive* ... I have this crazy urge to shake her.'

'What is inde ... inde ...' Isla struggles to repeat the word.

'Indecisive is someone who can't make decisions, who can't seem to make up their mind and get on with the job.' I direct my next comment to Eddie, rolling my eyes in the process. 'What do they teach them at bl—' Another swearword down the hatch. 'At university? To ask questions all day long?' Immediately, I realise that this may be giving the wrong message to Isla and quickly qualify what I have just said. 'Not that there's anything wrong with asking questions, love. You just have to make sure they are *sensible* questions, and that you don't already know the answers. Alright?'

She nods, and then enquires gravely, 'Do you really want to shake her?'

'No. Of course not. That was just a joke.'

I need to watch what I say in front of her these days. Not just the swearing; everything else too.

Another time, maybe at the weekend when we have a moment alone and Isla's not hanging on my every word, I'll tell Eddie how I overheard Brendan talking to Katie today, and how he had a note of respect in his voice that's never there when he speaks to me. I'll tell Eddie how irrationally hurt I felt. Come to think of it, I was genuinely at risk of shaking *him*, Brendan, taking him firmly by the shoulders, shaking until his hair was ruffled and his tie askew and he finally noticed, *really* noticed, my existence.

We continue to eat, our conversation wandering round everything from work, to school, to a TV program that Eddie wants me to record tonight.

Then, suddenly, our time is almost up. Eddie wolfs the last of his dinner, rinses his plate under the tap, his stubble grizzling my skin as he kisses me farewell.

'I'm off.'

'Alright. See ya.'

Eddie is thirty-two, eight years older than me. He's had two other significant relationships, and as a result he knows what he wants from life: a family and home. Mum says I've struck gold with Eddie, and this is one of those few occasions when she's actually right. Inside his rough-and-ready exterior there's something shiny and good and lasting. He came at the right time in my life, and apparently I came at the right time in his. He says he wouldn't have been ready if I'd met him earlier, just ask his exes. As if I would!

Eddie is lingering, a twinkle in his eye.

'Are you going to do it tonight?' Isla asks breathlessly.

He cocks an eyebrow. 'D'you think I should?'

'Yes. Yes. *Yes.*' Her voice ascends with each affirmation, the last a shriek.

'Alright.'

He steps towards the window, slides it back fully, and then pauses for dramatic effect. As the cold air rushes into the kitchen, he puts one hand on the sill and swings himself over to the other side. And with that he's gone, into the dark, and we're left with the open window and the startling draught. We're laughing so hard you'd swear he'd never done it before.

Isla closes the window and I start to clear up. I begin a game, trying to come up with as many Red Robot words as I can.

'Rock ... Rabbit ... Right ... Rap ... Rich ... Rag ...'

Isla sings each one after me.

When we run out of words, her little face puckers. 'What day is it, again?'

'Wednesday.'

She counts on her fingers. 'Two days until the weekend.'

'Yes,' I say with false cheeriness.

We both hate the weekends. Well, every second one anyway. Like her, I count down on my fingers, my dread increasing as it gets closer and closer.

'Rightio, Miss Red Robot … Time to *rub* you clean, and *read* you a story, and put you to sleep in your *room* …'

Her laugh is restrained, and I know I haven't succeeded in distracting her.

Suddenly, Jamie looms between us, as menacing as he is invisible.

'Time for bed,' I chirp, as though the mere movement from one room to another is enough to make him disappear from our lives.

The weekend foists itself upon us, and once again the flat is hollow without Isla. Gone is her sing-song voice, musical laughter and frequent crescendos of 'Mammy'. Her absence creates a pause. The tempo of our lives won't resume until her return.

Every second weekend, two days and two infinitely long nights, she is in his care. I use the term 'care' loosely, because keeping a child up past her bedtime is not caring for her. Feeding her greasy junk food isn't caring either, and neither is having your drunk, drug-using friends in the flat when she's there. I know that the sheets she will sleep in have not been changed in weeks. I know that when she wakes in the morning she will have to switch on the TV and wait for hours until he remembers her and stumbles out of bed. I know all this for a fact because *she has told me so.* When she was younger and without the language skills to recount what her weekend had been like, I had to draw my own conclusions from her bloodshot eyes and clinginess and tantrums when she got home to me. That was harder. At least now we can speak about it and I can assure her that it isn't normal, and that most people — most *fathers* — don't live like that.

'I hope he dumps her at his mother's house again,' I mutter to Eddie, who's trying to talk me out of this dark mood I'm in.

'Maybe he will. Look, Emma, try to distract yourself, otherwise you'll go crazy.'

'Don't ask me to switch off. I *can't*. I know Jamie. I can't fuckin' *trust* him. Not for one single moment. That's what's so fuckin' hard.'

'I know it's not easy,' Eddie says calmly, 'but you need to find something to do other than worrying yourself sick. You need to find some other way of occupying yourself on these weekends.'

My helplessness bubbles into misdirected anger. *No, Eddie, it is not easy.* It's downright heartbreaking, that's what it is. Bloody hell, the most difficult part of being a parent is not childbirth — though at the tender age of eighteen, it was a horrendous shock — nor the sleepless nights that go on for years afterwards, nor the constant demands, negotiation and complaints that seem to come hand-in-hand with children of any age. The hardest part, for me, has been giving my child over to someone I don't trust. A minute is too long. Two days and nights? No parent in the world should be asked to do that.

Eddie squeezes my shoulder. 'Do something nice. Go and have a look around the shops. Or get your nails done.'

He's anxious to get going. Saturday is a working day for him, even better than weekdays because he gets paid double time. We're saving for a house of our own, and every extra euro that goes into our bank account brings him inordinate satisfaction, happiness even. As he sets off for work, he holds his cheerfulness in check, because he understands the depth of my misery.

After the door shuts — he saves the window exits for Isla — I spend some time staring at my fingernails. They're uneven and dry. It's been a long time since I had a manicure: my birthday last year. Isla came too and we sat in the salon like spoiled princesses, acting as if we did extravagant things like this all the time, when in fact it was our first time ever. Afterwards we went for a milkshake, cupping the tall pale-pink tumblers with our freshly painted hot-pink nails.

Instead of taking Eddie's advice and slipping on my jacket to go out, I use my jagged-ended, dry fingers to tap out my mother's number on the phone.

'Emma!' she exclaims. 'I was just this minute thinking of you. How are you, love?'

My mother can drive me crazy more rapidly and profoundly than anyone else in the universe, yet — other than Louise — she's always the one I go to when I'm down, or in trouble. I can't lie to her. I can't pretend to be happy when I'm not, and neither can she. If we were each able to gloss over our feelings, hide what we really thought, perhaps we would bicker less than we do.

'Depressed.'

I don't need to explain any further. Mum knows how painful these weekends are for me. In an ironic shift of time and responsibility, she herself used to feel similar pain and worry when *I* was with Jamie.

'Please, Emma, he's bad news,' she would plead as I was headed out the door to meet him. 'You can do so much better.'

Did I listen? No, of course not. I knew he was no good, but I craved the danger of being with him in the same way he craved the danger of alcohol and drugs. I felt so alive, buzzing with the excitement of living on the edge, not for one minute imagining I would fall over that edge and get pregnant, or that one day my own daughter — thanks to me — would be exposed to the very same Jamie-brand danger.

'God love us,' Mum says now. 'If he were living with you, Family Services would be trying to protect her from him, but because you're apart they don't seem to care. It's completely backward, that's what it is.'

She's right. It is backward, and it is wrong, *so fuckin' wrong*. Jamie was oblivious to Isla for the first year of her life, barely aware of her existence. Then some stupid bloody counsellor suggested that he should see his daughter more regularly, forge a proper relationship with her. She was treating Isla like a pawn, like some sort of step in his recovery program instead of an incredibly vulnerable toddler. Of course I fought the weekend custody hard, but Jamie's mum, Sue, weighed in, so respectable and full of guarantees, and the counsellor, unfortunately, seemed to have a lot of influence with the court.

'It's a terrible system,' Mum laments again, 'and I know you've tried as hard as you can to make them see sense. All we can do is pray, love, that's all we can do.'

Three years ago, after Dad died from a sudden heart attack, my mother became religious. Amidst the dank stairwells and hallways of her block of flats, the perpetual smell and litter and dirt, and the drug deals happening virtually outside her front door, she found the pure, shining presence of God. Before she started quoting from the bible, my mother used to have a wicked turn of phrase. Before she started praying, she used to figure things out for herself, and yeah, she made many mistakes, but at least she wasn't forever abdicating responsibility to a higher being. Even though we disagreed more violently back then, I prefer that sharper, less-devout version of my mother. But in a completely contradictory fashion, I do like the way she fosters Isla's spirituality, and that she sometimes takes her to Mass and has instilled in her the ritual of praying before she sleeps at night. At times like this, when she's with her father, Isla needs someone to watch over her and keep her safe. She needs God, no bloody doubt about it.

I talk to Mum for another ten minutes or so, chit-chatting about Isla and Eddie, the dismal weather and a morning tea she's hosting after tomorrow morning's Mass. We get through the conversation without snapping at each other. This in itself is testament to how utterly despondent and helpless I feel, and perhaps testament to Mum's empathy, too.

Later on, I decide to do my nails after all, rubbing oil into the cuticles, pushing back the frayed skin, filing and shaping, buffing until they look shiny and healthy. Two coats of pale pink gloss later and they're finished. Then I busy myself making a cup of tea, after which I send Louise a text: *Home alone. Call me if you're at a loose end. Need cheering up.*

A mindless TV show later, I decide to call it a night. Though I take my time checking the door and windows, washing my face and brushing my teeth, Louise hasn't replied by the time I turn out the light.

In the darkness, I do exactly what my mother and my daughter do before they fall asleep at night: I pray. My mother prays for world peace and the safety and health of her family. Isla's prayers are recitals from her prayer book. My prayers are the brutal kind.

Please, God, just make him go away. Let him fall out with one of his shady friends and have to go on the run. Or have him meet some woman from another city, preferably another country, and move away permanently. Or — forgive me for this — let him die. An overdose, car accident, serious illness, I don't care. Anything to get him out of our lives forever. Amen.

Chapter 5

Louise

My shoulders and neck ache from the strain. All morning, I've been bent over the painting, cleaning it, millimetre by millimetre, using a mild alkaline solution. Everything about this painting is delicate. Nothing can be rushed, so it has taken me two weeks to get this far. Once this first layer of dirt has been dealt with, I can move on to the varnish removal, which is even more painstaking. Non-professionals find it startling that the whole process takes so long. I find it equally startling that something so important, so very delicate, should be rushed.

Heidi appears at my elbow. 'Time for cake,' she announces excitedly.

My colleagues seem to have a fetish for cake. On my first afternoon they surprised me with strawberry sponge cake. After two slices, I felt resoundingly welcome. And last week we had chocolate mud cake for Peter's birthday. It was a bit too rich for my liking, but this did not deter me from having a second helping, just like everyone else. Today Analiese is meant to be popping in with the baby, and the cake is in her honour.

Following Heidi to the staff kitchen, I wash my hands at the sink.

Peter is standing nearby, already scoffing cake, catching the crumbs with his plate.

'Oh,' Heidi drools. 'It's hummingbird cake, my favourite.'

Gabriella slices and deftly transfers the piece to a plate, which she proffers to Heidi. 'I don't know what's happened to Analiese. She texted twenty minutes ago to say she was in the car park. What on earth is she doing?'

'She'd better hurry,' Peter grins. 'Or there'll be none left.'

Gabriella waves the sticky knife at him. 'You've had your share. Keep away.'

As Gabriella is serving me, Analiese and an oversized pram finally appear at the doorway.

'Sorry, sorry.' She's clearly flustered. 'I needed to change her nappy, and then she started fretting so I fed her. And then there wasn't room for my pram in the lift, and I had to wait for the next one …'

Gabriella drops the knife, the clatter startling all of us, including the baby, who lets out a sharp cry. Enveloping Analiese in a hug, Gabriella's hands then rise to clasp either side of her face. 'Oh, you poor thing. Sit down. *I* will mind the bambina. Would you like coffee? Peter, make yourself useful and get this new mother some coffee.'

Analiese is not what I expected. She's short, like me, and has dark curly hair, a little longer than mine. I had married her meticulous notes to a thin, sparing personality, but she's not sparing at all. Every-thing about her is generous — her smile, her figure, her honesty.

'You must be Louise. Sorry I wasn't here to hand over as planned. And that I haven't even *phoned* to see if you have any questions. The last few weeks have been a blur.'

I smile in return, and nod at the baby, whom Gabriella is presently extracting from the pram. 'You've clearly had your hands full.'

Heidi takes over cake-dispensing responsibilities, allocating an extra large piece to the guest of honour. Meanwhile, Peter has come through in the coffee department. Analiese looks touched by their attentiveness.

'This is such a treat. Coffee *and* cake. I don't think I've managed to finish a cup of coffee since Stella was born. As for cake, I don't have the time to *buy* it, let alone bake it ...' She fills her mouth with a bite, some of the icing lodging on her lip. 'Oh, it's heavenly ...'

Her gratitude conjures up memories of Emma when Isla was a newborn. The glazed look in Emma's eyes, the dark roots growing through her highlighted hair, her jerky movements as she tried to settle the baby in her arms, and how she burst into tears when I offered to take Isla for a walk so she could enjoy the luxury of a shower without straining to hear if the baby was wailing in the background. We were so young, both of us. Analiese is older, so much more mature and accomplished than Emma was, but as I watch her I realise that all first-time mothers, no matter what age or background, battle with sleep deprivation, the uncertainty of each day and night, the anxiety about whether or not they are doing things the right way.

Analiese begins to speak about the painting. Between spoonfuls of cake and sips of coffee, she enquires about where I am up to in the project, my opinion on how we should deal with the damage to the face, and if any new information about the origin of the painting has come to light. Heidi and Peter join in, while Gabriella concentrates solely on Stella, rocking her in her arms and murmuring to her in Italian. Though Analiese is clearly engaged in the conversation, her eyes intermittently flick in the direction of her baby daughter, assuring herself that she's happy and safe. Analiese, like Emma, is a good mother. Over the years, I've done my fair share of mother-watching, and I'm familiar with the on-tap hugs, the resignation and rolled eyes, the prouder-than-proud smiles. I've noticed how mothers sweep their children out of danger's way, and how they hoist them on their hip, even when they are too big and heavy. Even the reprimands and discipline are evidence that the mothers care.

Stella lets out a wail and Analiese instantly jumps up and goes to her, lifting her out of Gabriella's arms and propping her on her shoulder.

A good mother comforts, chides and praises, but more than anything, she protects. A good mother *always* knows where her children are. She never leaves her children for longer than necessary, and she knows, sometimes before her child knows, when she is needed.

For many years after my mother left, I truly believed that if I cried hard enough or behaved badly enough, she would react the same way as other mothers, and come rushing in with a cuddle or a scolding. And so I howled and screamed and acted out, time after time. As a young teenager, I smoked, drank and got into all sorts of trouble with Emma and Jamie, but my mother still didn't come. She was a no show at my hospital bed when I had appendicitis, a no show at my graduation ceremony and a no show at Simon's funeral.

Nothing, it seemed, was strong enough to draw my mother back to me.

Chapter 6

Emma

When Louise's mother disappeared, Ann-Marie — my mum — stepped in. She fed Louise dinner a few nights a week, bought her clothes when she grew out of her old ones, and even supplied her with a training bra and sanitary pads. Sometimes, when Simon was motivated enough to find a few hours' casual work, my mother would 'break into' their flat, vacuuming quickly, stealthily cleaning the kitchen and bathroom but not going overboard for fear he'd suspect. It was my mother who kept Family Services abreast of what was happening, my mother who oversaw Louise's homework (*Just do it in our place, love, and have done with it*), and my mother who had the hideous task of treating Louise's hair for nits in secondary school (*But you're fifteen years of age, I thought we were past this ... Maybe you should keep your hair shorter, love*). My mother, for all her faults, was there for Louise in every way she could be. Mum was like one of those glue-on patches, trying her best to cover and fill the nonstop holes, those times when Louise needed a mother and no one else would do.

Jamie drops Isla off at six, as agreed. Although he is pathologically unreliable, her drop-off time seems to be hardwired into his addled brain. I scoop her into my arms, and by the time I stand up he's already gone, his hands stuffed deep in the pockets of his parka, his soft-soled shoes soundless on the footpath.

The first thing I do with Isla, other than that hug at the door, is wash her. I fill the bath, strip off her clothes, and scrub her from head to toe. While I'm shampooing her hair, I ask her how it was.

'Alright,' she replies, in a non-committal tone that reminds me of her father.

'What time didya go to bed? Was it late?'

'I don't think so.'

'Did he have other people around?'

'No, it was just me and Daddy. We watched a movie.'

'You did?'

'Yes.' Isla's small face is suddenly earnest. 'Daddy is trying very hard to be good.'

Is he? Well, that's bloody news to me, and to be honest, I don't quite know how I feel about it. You see, if Jamie cleans up his act, I have no hope of stopping these visits, or of him disappearing from our lives. And if he *doesn't* clean up his act, Isla continues to be in danger, but there's always the hope that he'll eventually self-destruct and go away. Can you see my dilemma?

All I want, really, is what's best for my daughter. Louise's mother, or rather her mother's absence, has made me very conscious of my own mothering. Isla's wellbeing, education, happiness, safety, I take them all very seriously. Even when I'm tired and grumpy, I try to rise above my own feelings and do my best for her. Even when we're laughing and being silly, I'm thinking to myself, *humour is good, I'm teaching her how to see the funny side of things, that's an important lesson.*

Wrapping Isla in a fluffy towel, I sit her down on the side of the bath and blow-dry her hair. Every now and then I direct the warm air at her face to make her giggle.

'Are ya hungry?'

'Starving.'

A small hesitation on my part. 'Did you have lunch?'

She shakes her head. 'I had a sausage roll for breakfast. That's all.'

Jamie is always forgetting to feed her. For a start, I don't think he realises how much children eat: breakfast, morning tea, lunch, afternoon tea, dinner, milk before bed. More significantly, and more worrying, is the fact that I suspect he doesn't have much food in his flat. A weekly grocery shop would not be part of his routine.

Eddie, who actually enjoys grocery shopping and anything to do with food, has a roast chicken crackling in the oven for tonight's dinner. He understands how important it is to me that Isla has a hearty meal when she returns from these weekends. As we leave the bathroom, Isla's hand in mine, the smell from the kitchen, chicken juices and gravy, wafts up the stairs.

'Eddie's preparing a feast,' I say brightly. I must be holding Isla's hand too tightly because she wriggles it free. 'Sorry, love. I'm just *really* happy to have you back.'

I vividly remember my mother clutching Louise's hand in the school yard. It must have been early on, maybe Louise's first day back at school. I remember feeling a pang of jealousy that my mother was holding Louise's hand, not mine, and then feeling rather ashamed of myself because Louise was obviously scared and upset and that was why my mother was gripping her hand so hard. As Mum and Louise stood there in the yard, the wind whipping their hair, they both looked so pale and bereft and frightened that they *could* have been mother and daughter. If I had that moment back again, I would rush forward and take Louise's other hand. I would obliterate that momentary misplaced jealousy, and replace it with a show of solidarity.

Eddie feeds us, and it is indeed a feast. His cooking is plain — his repertoire consists of traditional dishes only — but he excels at what he does. The chicken is succulent, the potatoes are golden brown, and the vegetables have a slight crunch. While we eat, he chats easily to Isla, drawing information without her realising what he's doing. He's wonderful with her. Present in every possible way.

At school, missing fathers were par for the course, but a missing mother was another matter altogether. We came up with all sorts of stories, each one more far-fetched than the last, to try to explain it. She must have got hit by a car and died, unidentified, on the side of the road. Or maybe she knocked her head and lost her memory, forgetting where she lived and that she had an eight-year-old daughter waiting at home. Or perhaps she'd been captured and taken prisoner, locked in the cellar of some lunatic's house.

Nobody, not even the most cynical of us, could accept that Louise's mother had simply walked out.

We were only eight years old, but we knew that mothers, even the crossest and most disillusioned ones, didn't do that.

Chapter 7

Louise

Joe has left his phone behind. It rings intermittently throughout the morning, singing out to me from where it lies on the dining table. I studiously ignore it.

According to the White Pages, there are 273 'J Mitchells' in New South Wales, 166 in Victoria, 120 in Queensland, and another couple of hundred scattered across the other states. This stage of the search is going to take longer than I anticipated, albeit not as long as the UK and America. Why, oh why can't these stupid phone directories state a first name rather than a mere initial? It would make life so much easier all round. It would save me making all those unnecessary calls, and save those on the other end from receiving them.

Now the home phone is ringing. Whoever is trying to contact Joe is certainly persistent. Sighing, I slide my laptop off my knees, carefully putting it on the sofa next to me, before going to answer the phone.

'Hello.'

'Oh, hello.' The voice, female — Irish? — sounds surprised to hear me. 'I'm looking for Joe, who's *obviously* not around. You must be Louise, the new flatmate.'

'Yes,' I confirm.

'It's Mary Connelly here, Joe's mother,' she supplies in a rush. 'I've been trying to get hold of him all morning.'

'He left his phone behind,' I explain, feeling guilty now that I didn't answer it the first time and save her all those calls.

'Is he at the gym?'

'Err ... I'm not sure.'

Now that I think about it, I'm not certain that Joe came home last night. If he did, I didn't hear him.

'Can you give him a message for me?'

'Yes, of course.'

'Tell him Samuel is home, and we're all getting together tomorrow afternoon, about two. Tell him I expect him to be here *on time*. And if he's been staying out all night drinking and womanising, tell him I'm *not* impressed.'

'Yes, Mrs Connelly,' I say meekly.

'It's Mary.'

'Yes, Mary, I'll pass on the message.'

I put down the phone and return to my laptop, a grin creeping across my face. Mary sounds like the proverbial Irish mother, deeply involved in her family, her authority unquestionable despite her children being adults, their good behaviour and manners still of paramount importance, and her offspring never too old or accomplished for a good scolding.

Joe is in trouble with his mum.

I'm positively giggling now, as I copy all the J Mitchells in the White Pages to an Excel spreadsheet so that I can easily categorise and sort them, depending on the information I gather. Each time I go through this process, I learn something new, and I'm becoming more and more efficient at it. If I were any good with words, I could write a how-to book on this subject: *Finding a missing mother in ten easy steps.* Except that I haven't found her.

The phone rings again, and this time I answer immediately.

'Louise, it's Mary again.'

'Hello, Mary,' I say, not at all surprised.

'You must think me terribly rude. Of course, you must come tomorrow, too. You're here without your family, and Joe says you don't know a soul, and I'd love to meet you …'

'Really, Mary, that's very kind of you but there's no need—'

'There's every need. You'd be doing me a favour. Some female company, a chance to reminisce about home—'

'But I—'

'Remember, tell Joe it's two o'clock. *Sharp.*'

Mary, quite evidently, is an old hand at claiming the last word. I'm left with the dialling tone in my ear, and the feeling that I've been whipped into line by a woman I haven't even met.

Thankfully, all the phones, home and mobile, stay quiet for the next hour or so, and the only telephonic activity is my outward calls, as one by one I work through the names on my spreadsheet. Progress is slow, some numbers ringing out, many of the people answering needing to be convinced that my enquiries are genuine and that I'm not some prankster trying to steal their identity. I speak to twenty-five people, and not one of them is Janet, or has a Janet in the house. To say that the task is time-consuming would be the understatement of the century, but I am used to it, so I plod along.

Last week, Joe handed me a book and insisted I read it.

'Best book I've read this year.' His expression implied that he would like me to open the book and begin reading it right there and then.

'Thanks, Joe, but I'm not a reader.'

'Everyone is a reader,' he exclaimed in a shocked tone.

'Not me.'

After a few moments of silence, his gaze alternating between me and the apparently brilliant book lying unclaimed on the coffee table, he finally asked, 'But if you don't read, *what do you do with your time?*'

I shrugged and laughed, and didn't answer his question.

The truth is I watch TV, like everyone else, and I surf the net. Sometimes, if the mood takes me, I can while away an hour or two sketching.

But more than anything, I spend my time searching. Trawling through phone directories, electoral rolls, registries of births, deaths and marriages.

I wonder how he would have reacted if I'd responded more honestly. 'I search, Joe, and trust me, that sucks up more time than any other conceivable pastime. You know that sense of unease when you've lost something *really* important? I live with that every day of my life, and the process of searching seems to settle the uneasiness, and makes me feel as if I'm doing something constructive. Maybe one day, when I've nowhere left to search, or — being optimistic — when I've actually *found* her, I can waste some time on a book.'

Joe writes books, hence his obsession with them. His first two novels were on the shelves of the bookshop I happened across during the week. Okay, so I didn't exactly stray into the bookshop, I went in there with the specific intention of checking if his books were in stock. They were. Only a couple of copies, on the second shelf from the top, not at eye level, which even *I* understand is bad. Before leaving the shop, I moved his books down a shelf and faced the covers outwards. Of course, it was only a matter of time before one of the shop assistants noticed and returned them, spine out, to their designated place in the alphabet. Still, though, my small act made me feel good.

I like Joe, a lot. And though I protested about accepting Mary's invitation to lunch, and still feel a little railroaded into going, I'm curious to meet his family. Because families, like mothers, are a source of fascination to me. The different personalities and dynamics. The openness, affection and acceptance, co-existing with undercurrents of discontent, age-old grudges and rivalries.

I find everything about families utterly compelling, especially how much they are taken for granted.

While one part of my brain is focused on my spreadsheet and the data I'm collecting as I work my way through the phone list, another part is already imagining Mary Connelly with her husband and their three strapping sons, standing outside their solid, single-level house. A grassy fenced backyard, a kitchen big enough to accommodate a thick, wooden, no-nonsense dining table, and — it goes without saying — at least four bedrooms: one for Mary and her husband, Richie, and one for each of the boys.

A close family. Everything shared.

Except, of course, the bedrooms.

Chapter 8

Emma

Mum has two spots of colour on her cheeks when she opens the door. She's excited about something. Not only can I tell from her face, but I can hear it in her voice, which sounds breathless and jittery.

'A sight for sore eyes.'

She speaks in clichés, my mother. If Isla and I are not a 'sight for sore eyes', we're 'rays of sunshine on a gloomy day'. Jamie was 'bad news' but I've 'struck gold' with Eddie. Rather like the clichés, my mother's view of life is simple. Sometimes, more often than I care to admit, I envy her this.

Before Isla and I go inside, I can't help throwing another glance in the direction of Louise's old flat. The door looks worn and neglected, and seems to imply that it is empty inside, which it is not. A sullen woman and her equally sullen ten-year-old son are the new tenants. The flat has had a string of occupants since Louise and Simon. Mum hasn't liked any of them.

It's always a relief to shut the door on the sour-smelling corridor. Mum's apartment has changed little over the years. I remember the day the patterned maroon carpet was fitted — I was nine or ten and couldn't stop marvelling at the plush feeling underfoot. It's far from plush these days. I remember the curtains being hung, and the time we had an extra few cupboards built in the kitchen. Home renovations were rare, so the times when they did occur stand out in my memory. Everything has more or less stayed the same for the last ten years. Except for Dad. His absence has been the only change. A huge, unwelcome alteration.

Mum puts on the kettle without asking if I want tea. She makes a glass of orange cordial for Isla, and whips out some cream biscuits from one of the cupboards. My brief glance establishes that the cupboard in question looks rather bare, and this observation brings a jab of sadness with it.

'How's Eddie?'

She always enquires about Eddie before she asks about me or Isla. It's a reassurance of sorts. If Eddie is well and happy, then all else must be good.

'He's grand. Working hard, as usual.'

She nods approvingly.

I stir my tea with a teaspoon that should have been thrown out years ago. The plastic handle is warped — it must have fallen against a hot kettle or one of the rings on the cooker. Mum finds it hard to throw things out. No matter how battered and damaged, if the item is functioning it's a waste to let it go. Warped cutlery, cracked plates and mugs, blackened roasting dishes, she keeps everything, and the cupboards — other than the food ones, it seems — are bulging at the seams.

'And how's school?' Mum's gaze switches to Isla, who is always next on her welfare enquiry list.

Isla has nibbled around the edges of her biscuit and is regarding her handiwork. 'We've nearly finished the alphabet, Nan. We're up to Walter Walrus.'

'That's wonderful.'

'Wonderful is a Walter Walrus word,' Isla points out after a moment's thought.

'Yes, it is. You're a clever clogs, Isla.'

'It's clever cat,' I correct Mum dryly, and she laughs as though that's the funniest thing she's heard in years. Her laughter sounds girlish, at odds with the rest of her. Mum hasn't weathered the years particularly well. The lines on her face are etched deeper than they are on other women her age. This, I strongly suspect, is due to me.

I sip my tea, which is strong and bitter, how Mum and I like it, one of the few things we have in common. We make small talk about all the usual stuff, while I wait for her to reveal whatever it is that has caused the tell-tale brightness on her cheeks. Has she met another man? Some kindly old fellow at the church? Or maybe she's simply wound up about some impending breakfast, afternoon tea, or other fundraising event. There's always something going on, money being raised for this or that good cause.

'I've got something for you,' she announces. 'A surprise.'

'I didn't know it was my birthday.'

'I'm your mother. I don't need to wait for birthdays. And when I saw this, I simply couldn't resist ...'

What is it? Some clothes? A scarf, handbag or earrings that she was particularly taken with? We don't have the same taste, Mum and I, so I brace myself to be polite no matter how awful this unexpected gift might be.

She skips away to her bedroom, and returns with an envelope. I shoot her a questioning glance before I open it.

Beginner's ballet.

'Is this for Isla?' I enquire, turning over the gift voucher to see if I can garner any further information from the small print on the back.

'It's for you.'

'*Me?*' I splutter.

Even as I'm thinking she's lost the plot, I read the word 'adult' on the voucher.

Beginner's ballet for adults.

'Mum, I—'

'It's something you've always wanted to do,' she exclaims, wringing her hands in excitement.

Yeah, I did want to do ballet. I remember asking, begging.

'That was when I was six or seven, Mum,' I point out as gently as I can. 'I think we've missed the boat on this one.'

'Dad and I didn't have the money back then,' Mum continues, obliviously. 'And it broke our hearts. So when I saw this class being advertised, and realised that they actually take *adults*, well I simply had to put your name down. You can go on either Wednesday night or Saturday morning. Of course, I'll mind Isla for you.'

This is a bad idea. I do not want to go to a beginner's ballet class with other adults either on a Wednesday *or* a Saturday. I cannot think of anything more humiliating or pathetic, or anything that could even come close as a waste of time and money.

But Mum looks inordinately pleased with herself and I realise how much it hurt her to say no to me back then, when I was little more than Isla's age. Speaking of Isla, she's watching all this with wide eyes.

'Thanks, Mum,' I say with difficulty.

It's preposterous. I will feel like a complete fuckin' fool, prancing around on my tiptoes. Please, *please* don't tell me I have to wear a tutu!

I'll go for one reason only.

Mum is so giddy and excited that I simply cannot bear to disappoint her. I've let her down so many times before. Now that I'm older, and know that I'm the cause of those lines on her face, that slight shake in her hand, the fact that she looks older than she should, I don't have it in me to let her down ever again.

Chapter 9

Louise

I'm wrong on a number of counts. Mary Connelly's house has three bedrooms, not four. Apparently, Joe and Dan (older by two years) used to share a room. Joe tells me this while laughing as he recounts the time Dan threw a steel-capped boot at him in bed, to stop him snoring. When his mother heard Joe's yelp of pain, she barged into the room, and after assessing what had happened, whacked Dan with the same boot so he would know *exactly* how much it hurt.

The garden, the living area, everything about the house is more compact than I imagined. The kitchen has been renovated, the bathroom hasn't. The deck at the back is new and modern, but the front of the house looks tired. It's not the perfect house by any stretch of the imagination, and I feel even more jealous because of this fact.

After introductions and a quick tour, we station ourselves outside on the new deck, drinking beer while listening to Samuel, the youngest brother, who has just returned from overseas, recount some of his adventures. It's obvious that Samuel is being selective about which experiences to share: nights spent huddled on benches in European train stations, emergencies regarding lack of money and food, bizarre misunderstandings with the locals in Vietnam. Yes, Samuel is heavily censoring, probably for his mother's benefit. Following the furtive glances and smirks he darts to Joe, and to Dan, who is manning the barbecue, I guess that Samuel will relay the uncensored version to his brothers in the not-too-distant future. All three brothers have the same dark hair, clear skin, and strong, wiry physiques. Dan is ever so slightly shorter, and it's easy to pick Samuel as the youngest, as his face is plumper.

Mary, when she is not fussing with the food preparation, tuts intermittently as she hears of all the near-misses and potential disasters.

'I'm better off not hearing some of this.'

Her husband, Richie, is in agreement. 'It's a wonder you got home safely at all.'

They are an odd-looking couple. Mary, short and round with coiffed blonde hair, Richie tall and lean like his sons, his grey hair cut in a surprisingly trendy style. Mary looks traditional, and Richie is one of those modern-looking older men. In fact, Mary and Richie's differences seem to be reflected in the contrasting décor throughout their house.

'You'll have to settle down now, Samuel, and get a job,' Richie comments, a serious note to his tone.

'What kind of work do you want to do?' I ask Samuel.

He shrugs. 'I don't know ... I *really* haven't got a clue.'

Mary has no such doubts about her youngest son's future career. 'He has an honours degree in communications,' she states, pride evident with each word. 'He'll do something media-related, I expect.' She swings around to address Dan. 'You might be able to get him a start at the newspaper, Dan.'

'I'll look into it, Mum,' he replies in a non-committal tone.

'Off the record,' Joe interjects with a snigger.

'No comment, eh, Dan?' Samuel adds cheekily.

Dan rolls his eyes at them, and I get the impression that this particular in-joke has been doing the rounds a long time.

Going by their comments, and Mary's reference to the newspaper, I assume that Dan is a journalist of some kind. Add that to Joe, an author, and Samuel, with a communications degree, and it's very clear that the Connolly family has a particular affinity with the written word. For the first time since I got out of Joe's car, I feel out of place, awkward.

'So you're all writers?' I ask.

Joe grins. 'Of some description. That's what happens when your father is an English teacher and your mother's a librarian.'

'Oh. It's in your blood then.'

I catch Dan looking at me. A brief, questioning glance. He must have heard something in my tone that the others didn't. Thank goodness he's distracted by his mother, who goes over to survey his handiwork and declares the meat ready to eat (quite obviously, Dan doesn't have the requisite authority to make such an announcement). Suddenly there's a flurry of activity, with plates being filled and passed around, drinks being replenished, and everyone finding a seat at the heavy wooden outdoor table, which is exactly like the no-nonsense table I imagined would be in the kitchen.

'Tell us about your family,' Mary says when the activity has died down and everyone is quietly eating. 'What do they do for a living? Are they arty like you?'

I glance down at my food while I consider what to say. There is no breezy reply to this question. Either I tell the truth, or a bare-faced lie. Both options seem equally extreme.

I opt for the truth. 'I have no family. It's just me.'

Having told them the truth, I eat a forkful of steak.

Mary, when I look at her again, seems perturbed. 'Your mother and father …' Her voice trails away in a question.

I swallow the steak, and take a quick drink from my bottle of beer.

'Simon, my stepfather, died when I was twenty.'

There's a pause. No one is eating now. No one except me. If it weren't for the conversation topic, I would be really enjoying this meal.

'And your mother?'

Surprisingly, it's Dan, not Mary, who has asked this oh-so-predictable question.

I look at Dan, then at Mary and Joe and Samuel and Richie. This lovely, welcoming family in their lovely, albeit not-perfect house. It seems wrong, sacrilegious, to bring up the sadder-than-sad circumstances of my family, or lack thereof. But I can see that this meal cannot progress, that no one will appreciate the meat Dan has cooked so beautifully or the salads Mary has prepared with such love, unless I satisfy their curiosity.

'My mother left when I was eight.' My tone is practical but Mary sounds stricken.

'Where is she, your mother?'

'I don't know.' I shrug, and even manage to smile. 'I'm still looking for her.'

Chapter 10

Emma

'Excuse me, Emma?'

It's Katie. She's been getting better. More self-sufficient. This is the first time she's interrupted me today and it's almost lunchtime. Well done, Katie.

'Yeah?' I look up from the report I'm proofreading for tomorrow's board meeting. I've found three mistakes so far, and circled them in red. One is a typo, embedded deep in the text and difficult to spot unless you're a veteran like me. The other two are more serious: numbers that haven't been updated since last month. I'm glad I found them before Brendan saw the report. He's a stickler when it comes to the monthly reports, and would be furious if our department produced anything that was less than perfect for the board. Pity he's not a stickler when it comes to all the behind-the-scenes work that we do here, the day-to-day processes and procedures that make this report possible. It's all image with Brendan. It's all about the over-engineered glossy package the board will see tomorrow.

'Emma, as I'm not going to be here next week, I thought I should check what you want done before I go … what you see as a priority.'

What? Is Katie taking time off? *Next week?* Why is this news to me?

'Backtrack a minute. Where are you going next week?'

Katie flicks her long sandy hair over her shoulder. 'You know, I'm going on that leadership course …'

No, I *don't* know, Katie. This is the first I've heard of it.

I must be frowning, because she rushes to explain. 'Someone from marketing pulled out at the last minute, so there was an unexpected vacancy. Brendan said he'd planned to send me on the course later in the year, but it made sense to do it now … given the vacancy …'

Yes, it makes perfect sense, Katie. The only thing is that you've been here barely a month. I, on the other hand, have been working for Brendan for four years, and yet it has never occurred to him to send *me* on such a course, now or later in the year or fuckin' ever at all.

My face is getting red. I can feel the colour creeping up from my neck. Anger. Mortification. And — more pitiful — hurt.

'Can't you see I'm busy? This could have waited, Katie. You can't just interrupt me whenever you see fit. I have work to do.'

Her face crumples, and I feel terrible.

'Sorry. I'm sorry, Emma. I'll talk to you about it later. Sorry.'

She backs away, apologising with each step. I should be the one who's apologising. It's not Katie's fault that Brendan sees leadership potential in her. It's not her fault that I'm virtually invisible to him.

The report blurs in front of me. It takes me a while to gather myself. When I do, I resume proofreading, using a ruler as I scrutinise each line. On page six, halfway down, there's another typo. I circle it, but my hand must be shaky because the circle is distorted and messy.

Once finished, I correct all the errors online, print a fresh copy, staple the pages together, knock on Brendan's door, and thrust the report into his hand without meeting his eyes. If I catch his eye, it'll be all over. Four years of being overlooked. The injustice, the helplessness and my mounting anger would come out in an unintelligible torrent, and I could lose my job as well as my hard-fought-for dignity.

'Sorry for snapping,' I say, stopping by Katie's desk on my way back to my own. 'You can come to me any time, any time at all.'

'Okay.' Her eyes aren't trusting, and I really can't blame her.

Feeling hugely remorseful, I perch on the side of her desk and try to start a conversation. 'Guess what I'm doing next Wednesday night?'

'What?'

'Ballet.'

Her blue eyes blink. 'You're a ballet dancer?'

'Do I *look* like a ballet dancer?' I snort.

We get the giggles, both of us. The thought of the tutu gets me every time. Heads pop over partitions, curious at the laughter.

'My mother had this hare-brained idea,' I explain, lowering my voice. 'She paid upfront for twelve classes, so I'm obliged to go. I can't think of anything more fuck ... I mean more ridiculous ... I suppose you did ballet when you were a kid?'

'Me?' Katie shakes her head. 'No.'

Funny, I would have thought that ballet classes were par for the course in a family like hers. Soft pink leotards and sparkling tutus in her already crammed wardrobe, being dropped off to lessons in the family Mercedes, glittery end-of-year concerts with indulgent accolades from her parents.

'Actually, I did want to do ballet,' she elaborates, looking slightly bashful. 'But Mum said I was too big-boned. Dancers have a more *delicate* physique, at least in her view, so she enrolled me in basketball instead.' She casts a disdainful look down at herself. 'I suppose she was right ... My thighs would've looked horrific in a leotard!' Then she laughs. 'And I turned out to be a decent enough basketball player.'

She expects me to laugh too but I'm not amused. It's cruel telling a child they're the wrong shape. Cruel to have them believe their bodies are anything but perfect. Please God, I'll never limit Isla in such a way, stop her from doing anything she wants to do, or make her feel she's not good enough. Please God, even if her thighs *are* big, she'll never know it because I've succeeded in making her feel beautiful and confident ... I'm sounding like *my* mother now, with all this 'Please God' business.

Fishing a packet of chewing gum from my trouser pocket, I hold it out as a peace offering. 'Want some?'

She helps herself, popping it in her mouth. 'Thanks ... Where are the ballet classes being held?' she enquires with heightened — frankly suspicious — interest.

'Oh. Just local to me. Probably in some dingy hall or other.'

I'm sorry that her mother said she was too 'big-boned', and even more sorry that I snapped at her earlier on, but suddenly I feel rather proprietary about these ballet classes. Imagine if I turned up next Wednesday night and found Katie standing at the barre, with thighs considerably smaller than mine, I suspect, and already bombarding the poor instructor with questions.

'Better get back to work.' I stand up, and send her a brisk smile before striding towards my desk.

I can't help feeling mean, not giving her the details of the class when she is so obviously interested in it.

But competing with Katie at work is more than enough. Competing with her at ballet class would be taking things a step (no pun intended) too far.

Chapter 11

Louise

I have a searing headache by midmorning. So much so that I have to down tools and go outside to get some air. Unfortunately, headaches are something of a professional hazard for me. It's the combined effect of the close, detailed work and the residual smell of the solvent I'm using to remove the varnish. The gallery spends a lot of money on fume extraction, and we're told to take regular breaks, but the latter is easier said than done. Progress is very slow, and it's natural to want to keep at the job until you can see that you've made some headway. Ever tried to remove a sticker from a pane of glass using your fingernail? It can take forever, but something keeps you there, picking away at those gluey fragments.

Clutching a takeaway coffee, I cross the road to Hyde Park. It's a hot, airless day, and I sit under the shade of one of the fig trees that line the main walking avenues. Some lunchtimes I wear my runners and go for a walk. There's plenty to see: the Archibald Fountain, Sandringham Gardens and ANZAC War Memorial within the park; the Supreme Court, St Mary's Cathedral and the Australian Museum along the boundaries.

My coffee tastes good. I'm yet to have a bad coffee in Sydney. In fact, the coffee here is better than the coffee in London or New York. Who would have thought? My phone rings and vibrates in my handbag, muffled yet insistent.

'Hello?'

'Louise, it's Dan.'

Dan? I quickly search my headache-afflicted brain for a Dan. There's one in the photography department, I think.

'Joe's brother,' the voice prompts, and immediately I have an image: the barbecuing journalist.

'Oh, yes, Dan, hello.'

'Joe gave me your number.'

'I assumed that,' I say drily.

'I hope you don't mind … I asked him because I think I can help you.'

'Help me?' I seem to be a step behind in this conversation. I take a sip of coffee in the hope that it will somehow help me catch up.

'Find your mother.'

Oh. Now I understand. That kind of help.

'I don't work that far from you,' he continues after a heavy silence. 'I'm in Park Street. Maybe we can meet for a coffee. Or a drink after work.'

A drink sounds like the better option. Dutch courage. For some reason I find everything about this call quite unsettling.

We agree on a place and time — outside the gallery, Thursday at 6pm — and I hang up, scared, nervous, warily excited.

Never, in all the years I've been looking for my mother, has anyone offered to help.

Is this a sign that things are about to change? That this time my search is going to be successful? Quite suddenly, I have the strongest feeling that she *is* in this city, and that it's only a matter of weeks before we're reconciled. Once all the tears and recriminations have passed, we could meet for lunch. She'd wait for me outside work and we'd walk through this park with linked arms and wide, happy smiles.

Reality intrudes as my phone beeps, a diary reminder popping up: there's a department meeting in ten minutes.

Draining the rest of my coffee quickly, I leave my fig tree and hurry back to work. The foyer of the gallery is dark and cool but my thoughts are still outside in the burning sunshine. I feel confused, off-kilter, as I take the lift.

My head is in such chaos I cannot even tell if I still have the headache.

Sydney sizzles over the next three days, and the media declares it the warmest week on record. This I can believe. Our apartment isn't air-conditioned. Joe maintains that there's only a week or two like this each summer and it's not worth the cost of installing air-conditioning. This morning, after a hot, restless night, I accused him of being one of those horrible penny-pinching landlords, hiding behind the guise of a struggling novelist.

At least the gallery is properly air-conditioned: it has to be, as excessive heat and humidity can damage the artworks. We've had record numbers through the doors, tourists seeking reprieve from the blistering heat. At lunchtime I join the tourists ambling through the Picasso exhibition that opened last week. My first walk-through was a hurried one before the exhibition opened to the public. Today I can take my time. The technique is exquisite, but I try to blot this out so I can respond to the work purely on an instinctual level. Sometimes it's better to know nothing at all about art, I often say to Emma. I truly mean this, even though she thinks I'm just trying to make her feel better about her ignorance. When we first look at a piece of art, we shouldn't be analysing the technique or the supposed uniqueness or even the materials used. We should be looking for one thing only: an emotional connection.

The sun has dropped by the time I leave work, taking away the scorching, relentless heat and leaving behind a balmy evening. Dan is waiting outside, as arranged. He's wearing a blue shirt — open at the neck, the sleeves rolled up to his elbows — and charcoal trousers. His skin is a shade darker than Joe's, a light golden colour that's particularly attractive against the blue of his shirt. There's a slight sheen of perspiration on his forehead.

'Maybe we should go for a swim instead of a drink,' is the first thing he says to me.

'Once you can find a corner of the harbour that doesn't have any sharks!'

The city has been setting records in relation to shark sightings as well as the heat. Apparently, the warm water has been luring the sharks closer to shore. We both laugh, and I forget how anxious I've been about this meeting, how the thought of it has kept me awake at night every bit as much as the heat has.

We talk about the circling sharks and other deadly Australian creatures as we walk through the park and some streets, the names of which I am beginning to remember. We end up in an enormous outdoor pub, pulsing with people and music. Dan takes on the crowd at the bar, while my lightning-quick eyes spot a group preparing to leave. I negotiate — through gestures, nods and smiles — permission to take their table, and I'm perched on a stool with a smug smile by the time Dan returns with two bottles of beer.

'I'm impressed.' He nods at the table and flashes an approving grin.

'I'm well trained. This place is virtually empty compared to the pubs in Dublin.'

He laughs again, and so do I.

Then there's silence. I know what's coming, and I can feel my mirth draining away.

'Tell me about your mother,' he invites.

'There's not much to tell. She was there one day, gone the next.' Suddenly, my mouth is dry, and I take a long drink from my bottle. 'She took her purse and some clothes. She didn't leave a note.'

The facts are basically that. Quite straightforward, really. The complexity was in the feelings, *my* feelings. The terrible confusion I felt in those first few days. What had just happened? What had I done to cause it? Was Simon to blame? Had he done something to her? Could I trust him? Maybe this was all a horrible dream, the people and the setting distorted yet chillingly realistic. Or maybe Mum had made a simple mistake, forgotten to tell us something, a missing fact that would explain everything. Or maybe it was the police who had made the mistake, who had neglected to follow up an important lead, or missed some other vital piece of evidence. The confusion was followed by hurt, embarrassment and shame. Nobody else's mother had done this. Why had mine? It had something to do with me, any fool could see that. Standing in the school yard, hanging onto Ann-Marie's hand for dear life, everyone knowing my name and the terrible thing my mother had done to me: *See that girl over there? She's the one whose mother ran away from her.*

The confusion and shame morphed into anger, and by the time I reached my teens, rebellion. If she didn't care about me, then I didn't care either. If she could do what she wanted — with no thought for other people's feelings — then so could I. Emma seemed to feel everything to the same degree as I did, even though her own mother was very much present. We clung to each other, first as nervous little girls who had lost their trust in grown-ups, later as reckless teenagers who thought — wrongly — that the worst thing possible had already happened, so why not push the limits as far as we could?

'Were there domestic problems?' Dan asks now.

'You could say so, yes.'

Memories flash behind my eyes. Screaming arguments. Shattered crockery, picture frames, dreams. Long periods of hostile silence, strangely more bleak and ominous than the shouting.

'And you think she's here, in Sydney?'

'I have no idea, really.' My beer is almost empty, and yet I'm still desperately thirsty. I wet my lips. 'I know she's not in Ireland: the police searched extensively for her. And I know she's not in England. That's where she grew up, so it made sense to look there before anywhere else.'

'Is her family still in England?'

'There's an uncle, Bob. He has a farm in Dorset. My grandparents died a long time ago.'

I managed to track Bob down when I was working in London. He was astounded to meet me, to find out that Janet had a daughter, and he had a grand-niece. My mother ran away from home when she was sixteen, and apparently my grandparents never got over the heartbreak. Unhappiness and bitterness ate at them until their health deteriorated. My mother, by Bob's account, had wrecked her parents' lives before going on to wreck mine.

'I can't believe she left you, too,' he said, shaking his grizzly head in disbelief.

Dan is still asking questions. 'So how did you know for certain that your mother didn't return to Dorset, or another part of England?'

'I hired a private investigator.' The investigator — Kenneth Duckworth, such an English-sounding name — cost an absolute fortune, all my savings. He tried, really tried, and was as disappointed as I was when we didn't find a trace of her. 'He thought she must have gone overseas. He suggested America and Australia as two of the more likely destinations.'

Dan looks doubtful, and I really can't blame him.

'Did she ever mention Australia?' he probes. 'Can you recall any special connection she might have had with this country?'

He's a good journalist. He knows what questions to ask, how to peel back the layers. The problem is that very little lies beneath.

'Only that I seem to remember her saying something once when *Home and Away* was on the telly: "I want to go there some day." I'm sure that's what she said, or the gist of it anyway. But maybe she wasn't being serious. Or maybe I misheard her. It's all so long ago now.'

I laugh, embarrassed by the sheer flimsiness of this 'connection'. But flimsy or not, it's all I have to go on: Kenneth's best guess on immigration patterns in the 1990s, and the vague memory of a comment my mother may or may not have made while watching an Australian soap opera. Pathetic.

'How about America? Any connections there? Friends? Family?'

'Not that I know of.' No American friends or family, not even a tenuous connection with a particular TV show. 'I took up an assignment in New York last year, specifically so I could investigate the possibility of her being somewhere in America. I trawled through all the phone directories and whatever online records I could get access to, but found no trace of her whatsoever.'

Dan takes a while to think. 'So you take on assignments in countries where you think she might be ...' He offers this as a statement of fact rather than a question.

'Yes. My work is good like that. There aren't very many of us — conservators, that is — so contract positions are often filled with international candidates.' I emit another short, bitter laugh. 'Going to a new country isn't a problem, it's where to start when I get there. Getting my head around the different records and processes and laws. And it doesn't help that everyone everywhere is completely obsessed with privacy.'

He takes my hand. Just like that. As though it's the most natural thing in the world. 'It must be really difficult. Living with this.'

The understanding, the *knowing*, in his eyes is every bit as astonishing as his touch. If I hadn't seen his larger-than-life mother for myself, I would think that she had absconded just like mine did. I nod, unable to speak. My mouth feels as though it's on fire.

We stay like this for a few moments, my hand loosely in his, the music swelling around us.

'I'll get you another one of those.' He nods at my drink, lets go of my hand and slides off his stool.

Though he has disappeared into the crowd, his empathy is still here. It comforts me for a short while. Until I begin to resent it.

'Tell me how you can help.' I'm abrupt when he returns with two more beers. I pick up the bottle he has assigned to me, gulping almost half of it down.

'I'm an investigative journalist. I know how to access information, particularly in this country. I have contacts in government departments, and access to newspaper records and community notices and any number of other resources where your mother's name might turn up.'

I look at him through narrowed eyes. 'What's in it for you?'

'First and foremost, the satisfaction of helping you out …'

'And?'

'And I wouldn't be entirely honest if I didn't admit that I'm intrigued by the story.'

I'm stunned. 'You want to write about it?'

'Maybe. I don't know yet. Would you let me write about it?'

I pause. 'Maybe.'

Our eyes meet. Dan Connelly. Brother to Joe and Samuel. Son of Mary and Richie. Investigative journalist, working in Park Street. Knows what questions to ask, how to get to the bottom of things. Shows extraordinary empathy. I can't help wondering if the empathy is part and parcel of his nature, or if he learnt it on the job, from all the sad, hopeless cases he's investigated over the years.

His gaze doesn't waver. His brown eyes are soft, evoking trust.

Do I have a problem with the possibility of him writing an article about this? No, none that I can think of. In fact, I would love a fresh perspective: a clear clinical analysis of the ambiguity I've lived with all these years.

If I put aside everything that I know about Dan Connelly so far — his family, his profession, his personality — and rely solely on my instincts and nothing more, when I look into those warm and quite lovely eyes of his, I feel an unmistakeable attraction. Rather like the elusive pull I sometimes feel when I first look at a work of art.

An emotional connection.

Chapter 12

Emma

Wednesday is one work disaster after another. The day starts with a system crash, and we're offline for three hours. I use this time to catch up on filing and some other admin. It turns out that I would have been better off using the down time to investigate why we've unexpectedly exceeded our credit limit, but of course the bank doesn't call to advise me of this fact until five minutes after the system comes back online! Had I known earlier, I could have met with Caroline (who takes care of treasury duties) and with Brendan (our relationship with the bank, just like the board, seems to be of disproportionate importance to him). Instead, the entire afternoon is taken up with these meetings, mollifying the bank, who want to charge a small fortune for the breach, and Brendan, who wants to know where our internal controls 'broke down', and Caroline, who is completely mortified by the magnitude of the error found in her cashflow projection. Before I know it, it's time to go home. A system crash and a credit emergency. That's the sum of my day.

As I put on my anorak and brace myself for the miserable evening outside, I'm cranky and frustrated and cannot think of anything worse than a ballet class for beginners. So I decide not to go.

I call Mum while I'm waiting for the bus.

'It's me. You don't need to babysit after all.'

'Why?'

'I'm not going.'

'What's wrong? Are you feeling sick?'

'No. Yes. Sick of work.'

She adopts the coaxing tone I know all too well. 'The dancing will take your mind off it.'

'I'll go on Saturday, Mum.'

'Oh, Emma. For goodness sake, can't you just—'

'Sorry, I have to go.' I hang up before she can guilt me into changing my mind.

I should call Eddie to let him know I'm coming home after all, but I'm not in the mood to make any more calls, and it feels so much easier to get from A to B without fielding any more questions on why I don't want to dance this evening. I never wanted to dance — these classes weren't my idea — but everyone seems to have forgotten this fact.

The rain becomes more insistent, pinging off the road, puddles swelling along the kerbside. Of course the bus is late. When it finally comes into view I notice that it's travelling rather fast. In fact, it looks like the driver is away in his own little world. A few of my fellow commuters realise this too, and we stick out our arms and jump up and down to get his attention. Visibly startling as he finally notices us, he pulls the steering wheel with a sudden jerk, and the bus proceeds to spray dirty rain water over those of us standing closest to the kerbside before it comes to an abrupt halt. Oh, for fuck's sake! I'm soaked from head to toe, streams of water running down my face. I don't know whether to laugh or cry.

Of course Eddie is surprised to see me. They're already eating dinner. Isla's face is animated, her eyes bright. While I've been inwardly seething at how my entire working day was hijacked, and how I'll have to pay to have my suit dry-cleaned due to that stupid, day-dreaming bus driver, Isla and Eddie have been eating and chin-wagging.

'What happened to dancing?' he asks.

'I decided today wasn't the right day for it. Pirouetting across a room just might push me over the edge.'

'We would have waited if we knew you were coming.'

'Sorry. I should have called to let you know.'

I wrap my arms around Isla in her chair, kissing the top of her head. She tolerates my embrace for a few seconds before wriggling free.

'Have you cancelled Ann-Marie?' Eddie checks.

'Yeah, I spoke to her.'

'Sit.' He stands up from his meal and goes to the stovetop. 'It should still be warm. Here.'

I love how he feeds me, how he always makes me sit before he sets my meals down in front of me. The love in this routine of his, the nurturing, *the sheer romance* — all the flowers or chocolates in the world couldn't come close to it. Even though my pants are still damp and I'd rather have a shower and a change of clothes before eating, I sit down at the table.

Dinner is a bowl of steaming spaghetti bolognaise.

Eddie pours some chilled water into a glass and gives it to me along with a glossy flyer.

'What's this?' I ask.

'A house I thought might be good for us.'

'Oh, Eddie.'

I know from a quick glance at the pictures that we can't afford it. Three bedrooms, a nice kitchen with white cabinets and dark countertop, a neat square of grass out the back. Modest as this house is, it's way out of our reach.

'It's a buyer's market,' he declares, excitement causing his usually steady voice to gather momentum. 'And it's a nice estate. There are a few houses for sale there, but I think this is the best of them. It's practically brand new.'

I shake my head sadly. 'It's nobody's market. The banks aren't lending any money.'

A few years ago, the bank wouldn't have made half the fuss they did today about an accidental credit breach. But if commercial credit lines are tough at the moment, personal loans and mortgages are tougher again.

'If the price dropped another twenty, we'd almost have enough for a deposit.'

I say nothing. This is his dream. I'll leave the banks to shatter it.

Isla takes the brochure, her head tilting to one side as she examines the pictures.

'You can't climb out the window. The sink's in the way.' She doesn't sound impressed by this particular shortcoming.

Eddie and I share a fond look before we laugh. She is such a blessing, my daughter. Now I sound like Mum again.

'Well, we can't possibly buy it so,' Eddie says matter-of-factly.

We laugh again, all three of us, though Isla doesn't really get the joke.

The system crash, the credit crisis, the drenching at the bus stop, all those things happened to another person. This is my real life: this homely kitchen, wholesome food and heart-warming laughter.

Once I have this, I can work at any job, live in any old place. 'This' being Eddie and Isla.

When Eddie has gone to work (much to Isla's disappointment, he used the traditional means of departure: the doorway), and Isla is bathed and put to bed, the phone rings.

It's Louise.

'Hey, it's me.' Her voice is bouncy, happy. She sounds like she's a million miles away from here.

'Hello, stranger.' I've had a shower at this point, and I'm in my favourite fleecy pyjamas and fluffy slippers. I curl up on the couch with the phone, settling in for a long talk. 'How're things?'

'Great. The weather's been incredible. Actually, a little too hot, if anything.'

'It's pissing rain here.' My tone is deeply sarcastic. 'Just in case you care.'

She laughs. There's glee in that laughter. Bitch.

'How's Isla?'

'She's grand. Still loving school.'

'I miss her,' Louise says in a more serious tone. 'I bought her a soft toy yesterday, a koala bear with an Australian-flag T-shirt and an akubra. Gimmicky but cute. She might think it's too babyish, though.'

'She'll love it,' I say firmly, adjusting the cushions behind my back to make myself more comfortable. 'She misses you too, Lou. She keeps asking about you. I blue-tacked a map onto her bedroom wall so she could see how far apart Dublin and Sydney are, but she can't comprehend the distance.'

'Sometimes I can't either.' Louise laughs again. 'And how's Eddie?'

Louise is like my mother in that respect, always asking about Isla and Eddie before me. Isla and Eddie are my barometer, I suppose: I can't be happy unless they are. Sometimes I think they're all that I am, the sum of me, and without them I'd be nothing at all.

'Yeah, grand. Determined to be a home-owner. Showed me a brochure tonight of a house in Clondalkin. As if we could afford it.'

'Maybe …' Louise begins.

'No fuckin' chance … Shit, there I go again. I'm trying to stop swearing.'

'Isla?'

'Yeah. I don't want her growing up and talking like I do … Anyhow, so what've you been up to?'

'The usual. Working. Actually, I really like this job. Lovely people, an interesting project … And, of course, I'm spending all my spare time looking at phone directories and the like … Actually, Joe's brother, Dan, is helping me.'

I feel my hackles rise. 'How do you mean "helping"?'

'He's a journalist … he has contacts.'

'Are you seeing him?'

She snorts, as though I'm being absurd. 'No, I'm not *seeing* him, at least not in the way you mean.'

I'm not put off by that sardonic tone of hers. If anything, it makes me only more suspicious. 'You like him, don't ya?'

'Of course I like him,' she exclaims. 'I like *all* the family. I've told you about the mother, Mary, haven't I? Well, she has offered to help, too. She works at the local library, and she's familiar with the resources people use to research their family history and so on.'

'Isn't family genealogy a completely different thing?'

'Yes, but some of the resources might be of use.'

It has been a long time since Louise has been so optimistic. This worries me.

'It's nice of them to help,' I say with some difficulty.

'Yes, it is. I feel very touched. They're such a genuinely lovely family, Em. You'd like them.'

I feel jealous, insanely envious of this 'lovely family' who have taken it upon themselves to help her. And I feel inadequate, as though I have somehow let her down. Quite suddenly, I'm berating myself for not having helped her in a more practical way. Instead of being a shoulder to cry on and a sounding board, I should have taken a more active role in the search, trawled through the internet and library records, like this Mary, this woman who hardly *knows* Louise.

'I'd better go,' she says. 'I'm late for work. This time difference is a nightmare, isn't it?'

'The nightmare is that I'm stuck here in this miserable weather while you're complaining of being too fuckin' hot.'

'You'd better start a swear jar.' With one final laugh, a laugh that has sunshine and blue skies and hope in it, she hangs up.

Distractedly, I pick up the remote and turn up the volume of the TV. There's a show on that Louise likes: *Secret Millionaire*. I forgot to tell her about the ballet classes. We could have laughed our heads off at that. And I also forgot to mention how Jamie is supposedly turning over a new leaf, and how nervous that makes me feel. Louise is the only one who gets how I feel about Jamie. She witnessed the ugliest moments of our relationship, and understands how precarious the current situation is.

I hug one of the cushions to my body. The truth is, I don't just need Eddie and Isla to feel whole. I need Louise, too.

From the sounds of it, she's settling in well. Her job is going great, she seems to have made friends with this entire Connolly clan, and I can't remember the last time she sounded so hopeful.

I'm happy for her, I really am. It hurts only because in recent years I suspect she has needed me less than I need her.

Chapter 13

Louise

Dan kissed me yesterday. I was so stunned I didn't respond, either to push him away or to return the kiss. It lasted only a few seconds, his mouth warm and surprisingly soft as it moved against mine, which felt cold and limp by comparison.

'Sorry,' he said, pulling away. 'You obviously don't feel the same way. Now I've wrecked things.'

I didn't answer, didn't know what to say. Though we were standing in the middle of a crowded pub, it felt as if we were completely alone, not a soul nor a sound around us.

I raised my bottle of beer (the one he had thrust into my hands moments before he kissed me), and gulped it back. I noticed that he was doing the same, attempting to extinguish the excruciating awkwardness with alcohol.

'Thanks for your help today,' I said, trying to get things back on an even keel. 'I don't know what I'd have done without you.'

Before the pub, Dan and I had been at the local Australian Electoral Commission office. The office had access to the country-wide electoral roll. The system was easy to use, the search engine surprisingly fast, and there were four different terminals available, only one of which was being used when we walked in. The only negative was all the stupid rules, which were displayed in large, impossible-to-miss signs above each terminal. Terminals were not allowed to be used for stretches of time longer than forty-five minutes, and if other people were waiting, this reduced to a time limit of just fifteen minutes. According to the rules, one was not allowed to use the roll for private investigations or genealogy enquiries. Why else, I ask you, would one need to consult the electoral roll? Just to look oneself up? For the fun of it? The last rule — the most important one, it seemed, given all the bold lettering — was that photocopying or printing or taking photographs of the roll were all strictly prohibited.

'Pretend you're not with me,' I hissed to Dan. 'You work from the top of the list, and I'll work from the bottom. Try not to make it too obvious you're directly copying from it.'

When the receptionist behind the desk wasn't looking, I tore a sheet of paper from my pad and passed it to him. He had his own pen in his shirt pocket.

The search threw up over a hundred listings.

Middle name Elizabeth, I wrote on my pad for Dan to see, so he would know to eliminate entries with middle names that were different. Of course entries without a middle name would have to be included.

Someone came in and stationed themselves at the last available terminal. Luckily, no other members of the public appeared until we were almost finished, by which time the first terminal had been vacated.

Dan, like me, took care to write slowly, in stops and starts, so it wasn't obvious we were 'copying' from the list. The Janet Elizabeth Mitchells were scattered all over the country — New South Wales and Queensland claiming the majority. My progress was slower than Dan's because I'm simply not good at transcribing, even less so, it seems, when I have to pretend I'm doing something else entirely. I kept my writing pad close to his left arm so he could tell where I was at. It was a strangely intimate forty-five minutes — with quite a few surreptitious glances and smiles while we pretended to be total strangers. He gave me a discreet nod when we had all the names covered between us and carrying through with the charade, he left before me. I followed a few minutes later, and outside we grinned at each other like two kids who had got away with something very naughty. Going for a drink had been his suggestion.

He took another long drink from his beer. 'What are you going to do next?'

'I'll cross-check the street addresses with my phone directory spreadsheet,' I replied, pleased that my voice sounded matter-of-fact, with no signs of the turmoil from his kiss, 'and identify the Janet Mitchells I haven't yet contacted. Then I'll write to them, and hope that they have the courtesy to respond.'

'Of course, this all assumes that your mother didn't get married.'

'Yes.' I winced inwardly. He'd hit a sore spot.

I really don't know what I'll do if I find out my mother is married, or — more disturbingly — if she has other children: children who are part of her life. Of course, the possibility has crossed my mind, many times, and just the thought of it is enough to make my eyes glaze over with jealousy, and my knees weaken with hurt. Sometimes, if I'm feeling negative, I imagine the happy, carefree lives these fictional children would have. I imagine my mother, looking slightly older but as beautiful as ever, throwing back her head with a tinkling laugh at these perfect children, whom she hates to be parted from, even for short periods of time.

'She didn't marry Simon.' My voice came out sounding unduly harsh. 'And she didn't marry my father, so I'm not sure marriage is her thing.'

He frowned. 'You haven't said much about your father. Don't you want to track him down, too?'

I shrugged. 'I couldn't even if I wanted to. I don't know the first thing about him — not even his name.'

According to my birth certificate, my father is a blank, another piece of missing information in my life. But at least it has always been that way, so I can't claim to miss him. And I had Simon anyway. Not the perfect father-figure, granted, but at least he stuck around.

'Going back to Simon ...' Dan said.

'Yes?'

'I know this sounds terrible, and I don't want to upset you, but how can you be sure he didn't murder her? I mean, they had quite a volatile relationship, didn't they?'

I shook my head. 'You're forgetting that she took some of her clothes. She went of her own free will, Dan.'

'Simon could have staged that,' he argued. 'It would have been easy to go through her wardrobe, make it look like she was leaving him.'

'Yes, but the police were all over Simon. They questioned him a million times. And he was too messed up back then to lie. He could barely remember his own name, let alone some kind of elaborate cover-up.'

'Maybe someone else murdered her then,' Dan suggested.

'She wasn't murdered, Dan.'

'How can you be so sure?'

For a moment I considered telling him. Why I was so sure. But the shame of it clammed me up.

'I just know, that's all.'

He finished the rest of his beer. 'So what else could it be? Drugs? Depression? Debt?'

'I've considered all those possibilities. Problem is I have nothing tangible to go on. Nothing to suggest that she was addicted to drugs, or that she was sadder than most other mums, or that she was a secret gambler. Nothing stands out. I wish it did.' I gestured to his empty bottle. 'I'll get the next one. As a thank you for today.'

His help was becoming something I relied on, looked forward to, even.

The bar was heaving with people, and it was ages before I got served.

'Sorry it took so long,' I apologised when I finally got back.

We smiled at each other, and then it hit me like a punch to the stomach: how attractive his smile was, and his eyes too, and the muscles knotted across his shoulders, which — now that I thought about it — had caught my attention more than once as he hunched over the terminal at the AEC office. And how attractive I found his intelligence, the fact that he knew exactly what questions to ask and how he obviously, and with great care, retained the answers I supplied. But more than anything, how attractive it was that he was so helpful, so intrinsically obliging, because that quality, entirely on its own, could quite easily make me fall in love with him.

As I handed him his beer, I found myself doing exactly as he had done earlier on: kissing him. His lips were still warm. They tasted of beer now. There was a millisecond — I think I startled him as much as he had startled me — before he responded, but within a few moments I felt like I'd been kissing Dan Connolly all my life.

'I do feel the same way,' I said, just to clarify when we finally stopped kissing.

We grinned at each other with all the surprise and shyness and delight that come with a new relationship, and I could almost hear Emma sniggering in my ear. From thousands of miles away, ever before I had realised it myself, she had intuitively known just how much I liked Dan Connolly.

Then again, Emma knows me better than I know myself.

Chapter 14

Emma

The doorbell rings. Nausea swells inside me.

'Ready?' My voice sounds squeaky, nervous, and I hate it because I know I should sound cheerful and confident, for Isla's sake.

She nods. Her small hand slips into mine and holds on tightly. I pick up her backpack on the way to the door.

'Hi, Jamie.' I force out a greeting.

'Hi,' he mutters. We're long past the days of sparkling conversation.

'Her bag has all her stuff. She seems to have a slight sniffle. Keep an extra eye on her, especially tonight.'

'Alright,' he replies, sniffing himself.

I bend down and hug Isla, breathing in her smell, getting one last fix of her small, warm body.

'See ya Sunday. Tell Daddy if your cold gets worse.' I lower my voice to whisper in her ear. 'Don't forget to say your prayers.'

I misjudge the distance between me and Jamie as I straighten. Quite suddenly, I'm closer to him than I've been for years. His eyes seem to be unusually enlarged, but other than that he seems sober.

Maybe it's the purple semicircles beneath his eyes that are making them seem so out of proportion. Is he still good-looking? It's hard to say. His face is far too pale. He has some unattractive marks around his hairline, small gouges that might not have stood out so much had he more colour in his face. He's thin to the point of being gaunt. It's difficult for me to be objective, to assess him purely on how he looks today without searching for traces of that drop-dead gorgeousness that used to make my seventeen-year-old heart race with anticipation. Taking a step back to a safer distance, I decide that he is still attractive, though I suspect a stranger would not come to the same conclusion.

As Isla puts her hand in his, he sniffs again and rubs his nose with the back of his other hand.

'We might go to that new play centre,' he says.

He doesn't normally make plans to go places with Isla. More often than not, she's cooped up in that awful flat of his for the duration of their time together. The odd walk to the park, or the closest chipper for dinner, or a visit to his mother, is about as fancy as it gets. Does this mean he's still 'trying to be good'?

Isla brightens at the mention of the play centre. She has already been: one of the kids in her class had a birthday party there. It has a foam pit and a flying fox, and after the party she couldn't decide which one was her favourite.

She tugs at his hand excitedly. 'Really, Daddy?'

'Yeah, why not?' He smiles down at her, and the tenderness in that smile brings back a thousand memories.

They set off down the road, my daughter and her father, hand in hand.

Jamie walks like an old man. His gait is uneven. His shoulders droop and look weak.

Isla walks and skips next to him.

I have a lump in my throat as I watch.

An uneasy night's sleep and then it's Saturday. I'm even less in the mood for ballet than last time. The only thing that propels me out the door is the unbearable emptiness. Eddie has already left for his twelve-hour double-pay shift. Without him, and especially without Isla, the flat is hollow and somehow mocking. Ballet, rather strangely, seems like the lesser evil.

A mature woman, at least sixty years old, walks into the church hall ahead of me. She's in full regalia: pink leotard, tutu, her silver hair scraped into a severe ballet bun. I smother a snigger.

I'm relieved to note that most of the other beginners are dressed much as I am — black T-shirt and leggings — except for ballet slippers, the pale-pink ribbons criss-crossing at their ankles. I'll have to buy a pair before the next class. For now my bare feet will have to do.

The instructor, Miss Sophia, isn't exactly young either. Early fifties, dyed jet-black hair, eyes heavily outlined in kohl and mascara.

'Welcome, Emma.' The make-up on her face cracks as she smiles. Her thick country accent takes me by surprise. 'Have you any experience of ballet?'

'No.'

'Well, this is where you belong — our beginners' class. We're going to start with some warm-ups at the barre.' She raises her arms and claps three times. The class, about ten of us in total, immediately jump to attention and line up at the barre. I avoid looking at myself in the wall-length mirror, training my eyes on Miss Sophia as she presses some buttons on her iPod, which is perched in a sound dock system on the timber floor.

Clear, crisp piano notes fill the hall, immediately transforming the ambience from dull and church-like to something more enchanting.

'Shoulders back. Chins up. Show me your beautiful necks, ladies. Feet in first position ... Demi-plié ... Heels on the ground, ladies ... Again, demi-plié ... nice and smoothly, now ...'

Concentrating fiercely, I bend my knees outwards, in line with my feet, in what I now know is a demi-plié.

'Straight back, Emma ...'

Oh, she's talking to *me*. I jerk my shoulders back.

'Feet in *first position*.'

My feet *are* in first. Okay, so maybe they've gone ever so slightly out of position. This actually hurts.

'Good, everyone. Now, arabesque ...'

From a quick check of what the others are doing, I establish that an arabesque is supporting your weight on one leg while the other leg is extended behind you. The classic ballerina pose.

'Straight knee, Emma ...'

By the end of the class, I've learnt second position, third position, and a handful of new French words, including grand jeté (this is a splits in the air, and — at least in my book — physically impossible) and pas de cheval (which means step of the horse). I've risked a few glances in the mirror and, feeling sheepish, tried to adjust my posture. I have chatted with Trish, one of the other women. Trish is about my age, maybe a couple of years older, and she has two little girls. Like me, she seems prone to sniggering, and when we were doing the pas de cheval we could hardly contain ourselves.

The hour and a half has flown. I emerge into the grey afternoon feeling as though I've been away somewhere for an extended time, somewhere different — more exotic — than the church hall.

As I get on the bus home, my neck feels elongated from all that stretching. I'm definitely standing taller.

I wonder if any of the other passengers — a collection of old people and teenagers plugged into their iPods — notice my extraordinary gracefulness, and then I laugh at myself for being so bloody stupid.

Chapter 15

Louise

Dan examines my bedroom in the same way he might examine a crime scene for clues. He picks things up, turns them over in his hand, before putting them back down. Some things he leaves as is, touching them briefly before moving on.

'You're a minimalist,' he states, as though it's a personality flaw.

'And you're very *tactile*, I see,' I say tartly. I'm sitting on the bed, one knee hugged to my body, my chin resting on it. One of the bedside lamps provides mood lighting. 'Feel free to turn on the main light if you want to get a closer look at anything.'

He throws back his head and laughs.

Dan, I've noticed, is difficult to offend. He's been hardened by his family — by his brothers, and the rough and tumble of an all-boy household, and by his mother, who takes no prisoners. It's one of the things I like about him. Memories of a house where everyone was on tenterhooks, where it was easier to say nothing at all than risk saying the wrong thing, are etched deep in my psyche.

He pauses in front of the pair of sketches I've mounted on the wall.

One is of a piano, the other of a cello. The pair is slightly abstract, some of the dimensions and shading exaggerated. For some reason, I've always liked them more than the other stuff in my portfolio.

'You did these?'

'Years ago. When I was in college.'

'Can you play music?'

'God, no.'

Drawing. That's about it, Dan. No other hidden talents here. Far from it, in fact.

Now he picks up the frame with my mother's photograph. I suck in my breath. *Be careful with that. Please.*

He looks from the photo to me and then back again, searching for a resemblance.

'I know.' I shrug. 'We're not very alike.'

He tilts his head in an assessing manner. 'Well, you're both beautiful.'

I roll my eyes at him. 'Oh, stop it.'

He puts down the frame with extraordinary gentleness, as though he now understands how precious it is, and climbs onto the bed next to me, his hands interlacing with mine and pushing me backwards so that I'm fully lying down. 'You don't think you're beautiful?'

'I think you're trying to seduce me, that's what I think.'

He scatters kisses on my face. 'No comment.'

He's making me laugh, even as his kisses and the feeling of his body pressing on mine are turning me on.

Finally, he finishes kissing my nose and my eyes and various other parts of my face, and his mouth moves over mine. The mood immediately changes from playful to serious. This, after all, is the reason why he's here, in my bedroom. It's been five days since I first kissed Dan

Connolly. We've found excuses to meet every day since, and we've kissed in cafés, outside shop fronts, on park benches. Long kisses that have undoubtedly caused onlookers to tut, snigger or smile, depending on how they are disposed towards public displays of affection.

With no one but ourselves looking on now, and nothing to restrain the rapidly mounting sexual tension, things are moving quickly. Dan raises my arms and slips off my T-shirt. I do the same with him. His bare chest is well built, muscular, but I already know this; he fills his business shirts and T-shirts very nicely. The contours of his torso, the smattering of dark hair, the flat stomach below, I feast my eyes before exploring with my hands, skimming his warm, naked skin.

If anyone here is physically beautiful, it's him. Of course I don't say this out loud. It's a thought that temporarily lodges in my mind. Then his fingers brush my nipples, followed by the flick of his tongue, and I'm incapable of holding onto any more thoughts.

Afterwards, we lie still and silent, his arm around my shoulders, one of his legs twisted around one of mine.

My eyes are closed — in fact I'm half-asleep — when he asks, 'Where did you get this?'

I know, without opening my eyes, what he's referring to: the white scarring on my left thigh.

'A car accident. When I was eighteen.'

He takes that in for a while.

'And the tattoo?'

The Celtic knot, on the inside of my wrist.

'Emma and I got matching tattoos when we were sixteen.'

'Emma?'

'My friend ...' I smile as I correct myself. 'My *best* friend, for as long as I can remember.'

I open one eye to leer at the naked body lying next to me. 'Any noteworthy scars or tattoos I should know about?'

He laughs. 'Remarkably, no. You'd think I'd have more to show for all the times I got into scraps with my brothers, and the times Mum whacked me with the wooden spoon—'

'Don't forget the steel-capped boot,' I remind him of the anecdote I heard on the day of the barbecue.

'Yes,' He laughs. 'The steel-capped boot. God, that hurt. Mum was so upset afterwards. Her temper just got the better of her.'

I can see the scene. Mary's fury. Her immediate remorse. All of them laughing about it, eventually. Now it's one of their family stories.

When Simon was in hospital and we both felt compelled to make bedside conversation, we would sometimes stumble upon the past, the memory of something particularly discomfiting. A silence would ensue, a horrible awkwardness, before one or the other of us would change the topic of conversation. I can't help wondering, listening to Dan, if any of those memories could have been deemed humorous. If hindsight, and time, could trivialise them, throw up a funny side that wasn't apparent at the time. No. What am I thinking? My memories and Dan's memories are of a different ilk. If the steel-capped boot was Mary's worst moment as a parent, a time when she completely lost control and reason, that was pretty mild.

We hear a sound: the turn of a key, followed by a door — quite obviously the front door of the apartment — opening and slamming shut again. Joe. Damn. Damn. *Damn.* It's unheard of, him coming home this early on a Saturday night. Half the time he doesn't come home at all.

Frantically, I look around for my clothes. Some are on the bed, some on the floor.

Dan doesn't seem quite so panicked. Rather the opposite.

'Time to come clean,' he says cheerfully.

We get dressed, exchanging sheepish glances as we yank on our T-shirts and get into our jeans.

As we're about to go out and explain ourselves to Joe, Dan stops and pulls me close to him, his fingers brushing my face.

'If I could draw half as well as you can, I'd sketch your face to show you how beautiful you truly are. I'd shade under your cheekbones so that you could see how perfectly sculpted they are. I'd capture the line of your mouth, the cynicism and yet the vulnerability in it.' His fingers move to touch my fringe. 'I would labour over this, striving to get the angle just right. How it half-hides your eyes. How it tells me this girl has attitude, she's no pushover.'

With that, Dan takes my hand in his and pulls me after him as he opens the door of my bedroom and sweeps into the living area, as though he's the one who lives here and I'm the tagger-on.

Joe is astounded to see us together, to find out we're a couple.

I'm every bit as astounded as Joe, albeit for different reasons.

I don't think anyone has said anything quite so lovely to me before. And it's not just what Dan said, but the way he said it. The analogy with sketching. My language.

Chapter 16

Emma

Brendan calls me into his office just before lunchtime on Monday.

'I've put your name down for one of those courses,' he informs me without bothering to ask how my weekend was. He's not one for small talk, unless he's speaking to one of the revered board members, or the bank manager, or someone else important. The rest of us are spoken to in staccato, with instructions delivered in bullet points, and no padding or niceties whatsoever.

'What course?' I ask, frowning in confusion.

'One of those leadership courses. You said you wanted to do one, didn't you?'

Yeah, I did. After Katie went off on her course, I made a point of commenting to Brendan that I would like to do one, too. I waited until I had my initial indignation under control, and for the right opportunity to present itself, and then I said that I had never been on such a course and would love the chance to expand my skill-set, blah, blah, blah. Even though I made my point quite clearly (and, to my credit, without a trace of the resentment I felt in regard to Katie being nominated before me) I didn't think Brendan was listening, *really listening*, and now I'm surprised on two counts: not only did he *hear*, but he's also *done* something about it. For a brief moment I wonder if I've misjudged him.

'When is it?' I ask, inordinately pleased, excited even.

'Next month. It runs for six days, Monday to Saturday.'

Saturday? That could be tricky.

I see it then, the slight smirk on his face.

He thrusts a folder at me. 'You need to fill out the preliminary questionnaires and hand them in to Human Resources.'

Back at my desk, I leaf through the contents of the folder. The dates are on the second page. As luck would have it, the Saturday in question is the one Saturday of the year when Mum is away on retreat. Eddie, of course, will be working. It's not one of Jamie's weekends to have Isla, and there's no way on earth I would ask him: I don't want my little girl with him a minute longer than she has to be. They might be watching movies together these days and going to new play centres, but I *know* him. This won't last.

So Jamie isn't an option.

Maybe I could ask his mother? Sue adores Isla, spoils her rotten. But if I ask Sue to take Isla, she wouldn't be able to stop herself from mentioning it to Jamie. Then Jamie would drop in to visit, and Isla would end up with him after all. Sue is lovely — very ladylike and warm — and I'm genuinely fond of her. The only problem with Sue is that she's blind when it comes to Jamie. In her mind, he's just going through a bad phase. She doesn't seem to get that he's twenty-six now, or that this 'phase' has lasted more than ten years. Her son isn't dabbling in drugs, he's addicted to them. No, it's a bad idea to ask anything of Sue. However much I like her, however much she adores

Isla, Sue is another avenue to Jamie, and I'm trying to close off as many of those as I can.

Of course Brendan doesn't know about Sue or Jamie. All he knows is that I have a young daughter and a partner who works shifts. Enough to bring out the nasty, that'll-show-you smirk I saw on his face.

Regardless of the fact that I have nobody to mind Isla, and so I'm not sure how I can manage to attend this stupid course, I begin to fill out one of the preliminary questionnaires.

What is your leadership style? Autocratic, Democratic, Delegative.

Brendan is Delegative. We're given free rein. The less detail we bother him with, the better. Lazy would be a better word.

Katie will be Democratic one day. I can see her consulting her staff regularly … probably too regularly.

Me? I don't know what my style is. None of the above.

I'm a nothing.

'This is it,' says Eddie.

I'm holding one of his hands, Isla the other, and the three of us line up to study the house: red-brick and pebble-dash exterior, a tiled shelter over the front door (I like this particular feature), windows a little bigger than those on your normal semi (yeah, I quite like the windows, too). There's nothing else to distinguish this house from all the others on the estate, except the For Sale board in the front garden. Actually, not even that is unique. A quick glance around confirms that a few of the neighbouring properties are on the market, too.

'It doesn't look brand new,' I point out in a critical tone.

It's true. The house has an old-style look. No cutting-edge architecture or bespoke materials here. It's obvious that the builder used the cheapest design and materials possible, and it already looks dated.

'Let's go inside,' says Eddie, undeterred by my cynicism.

The front door, painted in a nice black gloss, is slightly ajar, and Eddie knocks before pushing it in.

'There you are,' the agent exclaims, pumping Eddie's hand, then mine, before ruffling Isla's hair, completely oblivious to her chagrin.

'Sorry we're a bit late,' Eddie apologises with a rueful smile. 'We came on public transport.'

It took over an hour to get here. Two overcrowded buses, a maze of traffic-clogged roads. To be honest, I feel a bit disoriented. I've never been in this part of Dublin before.

'Oh, that's alright,' the agent replies breezily. 'Sure, I knew you were on your way.'

Already, I can see a rapport between Eddie and this agent. I know they talked on the phone yesterday to arrange this viewing, but somehow that businesslike exchange has morphed into a camaraderie which seems to imply that this is not a one-off viewing but rather the start of something more involved.

'Have a look around. Take your time.'

We walk through the narrow hallway to the kitchen/living area. It's bright, and though it's a small enough area (not much bigger than the space we have now), it feels surprisingly roomy. The kitchen countertop is laminate, the appliances are a low-end brand, but the overall look is classic: black and white and stainless-steel. I'm drawn to the sink, and the large window that looks out onto the back garden. A vase of purple wildflowers has been placed on the windowsill and I breathe in their faint, earthy scent. Isla, I'm surprised to see, has already slipped outside. She's standing smack in the middle of the compact garden, swinging her head from one side to the other, as though assessing what she could do in this space. The garden is overlooked by houses on all sides, but still that patch of grass seems precious, like an oasis, and I feel an unexpected surge of longing as I stand there watching Isla. I can imagine myself living here, my hands in a sink of sudsy water, washing up while keeping half an eye on my daughter as she potters about outside. I'd make some changes: a flower bed, some herbs in pots, and a swing for Isla. Thoughts like these are dangerous, and I shake my head to rid myself of them.

Eddie goes outside, too. He opens the shed door, sticks his head inside for a few seconds, and then, like Isla, plants himself in the centre of the garden, his hands stuffed in his pockets, his eyes looking upwards as he examines the back of the house.

Eventually, they come inside, hand in hand, their eyes bright.

'We shouldn't have come here,' I say quietly, turning around from the window.

Eddie shrugs. 'We're only looking.'

But we're not only looking, we're *coveting*. We want this house, all three of us. We've never wanted anything so badly.

Upstairs has three bedrooms. The master bedroom has a small walk-in-robe and an even smaller en-suite. The fittings in the en-suite and the main bathroom are inexpensive, but have the same clean, classic look as the kitchen. Eddie indulges Isla as she picks out which of the other two bedrooms would be hers. He shouldn't lead her on, get her hopes up. Angry, I stalk back downstairs on my own.

'How long has it been on the market?' I snap at the agent.

'Three months,' he replies, his gaze skittering away from mine.

'Are they prepared to negotiate on the price?'

'They've already adjusted the price twice.' He clears his throat. 'They need to sell.'

My eyes narrow. 'Why do they need to sell?'

Eddie and Isla come downstairs in time to hear his response.

'Because the couple can't afford the mortgage. If they don't sell, the bank will.'

'They've hardly lived here.'

'That's the way it happens sometimes. A mortgage can be a harsh reality.'

'Well, we can't afford it either,' I state venomously. 'Sorry for wasting your time.'

Eddie says nothing. Disappointment is written all over his face. I can't even bear to look at Isla. I feel like a bitch, I really do, but someone needed to bring us all back down to earth.

For once, public transport is startlingly efficient, both of our buses arriving within minutes, whizzing us along the unfamiliar roads until we're back to where we really belong.

By the time I open the door of our flat, the house, the whole afternoon, already feels like it was nothing more than a dream.

Chapter 17

Louise

Simon died four years ago today. He was dying for weeks (years, really, if you start the clock from the moment he received his first diagnosis). A long, angry illness, yet the end was curiously peaceful. His body expelled a breath and never thought to take the next one in. As I sat by his bedside, held his once-strong hand in mine, Simon slipped away from this world. He didn't stomp out, or slam the door, or yell one last rebuke; he merely slipped away. Strange that a man once so loud and violent could pass on so quietly, so unobtrusively.

I'm busy at work today. As well as working on the painting, I have a number of meetings to attend, file notes to update, and I really need to get started on the research side of this project. Tom has been pressing for updates at the weekly staff meetings. He's indicated that he would like more of my time to be spent uncovering the origin of the painting. The problem is that I have practically nothing to go on. Analiese wrote to the family of the deceased estate (via the executor) but they haven't replied. Without the family's input, it's very hard to imagine who this girl might be or who painted her so exquisitely.

'Louise, I have a treat for you.'

It's Gabriella. Her booming voice reaches me well before she does. This morning she's wearing one of her signature dresses, with colours as loud as her voice.

The 'treat' is cranberry and almond biscotti, sealed in a zip-lock sandwich bag.

'For your morning tea, eh?' she says, beaming.

'They look absolutely delicious. Did you make them?'

She cackles. 'No, no. They are leftover from the family dinner yesterday.'

Leftover Italian biscuits, cake for every conceivable occasion — I'm going to be two sizes larger by the time I finish this project.

I thank Gabriella again, and she heads towards Heidi's workspace at the other end of the room to distribute more biscotti.

For the next hour or so I dab away at the canvas. Swab after swab of cotton wool. White and soft before becoming stained with years and years of grime. I'm working on the girl's face, and the lighter colours of her skin are more durable than the darker ones over much of the rest of the painting, which means progress is slightly faster. It would be easy to assume the opposite, that white is more fragile, but beneath the purity there's strength and resilience. I've always liked the thought of this.

The painting's varnish is not only discoloured; it's uneven too, especially in this facial area. There are scattered retouchings, another issue to deal with. But despite all these challenges, my progress is evident: there is a rough line indicating where I am up to, everything above it bright and clean, everything below now looking even more soiled in comparison.

I take an early break for morning tea, mindful of the meeting I have straight afterwards. As I sip my coffee and nibble on the mouth-watering biscotti, my thoughts return to Simon. My memories of him are conflicting, to say the least. When he wasn't roaring and being argumentative, his voice could be astonishingly soft. When he wasn't drunk and unsteady, he could be deft with his hands, chopping meat and vegetables for dinner, sewing a button onto my school uniform (before I learned how to do it myself).

Despite all his faults, all his contradictions, Simon was all that I had. She left me with him, dumped me on him, and he wasn't even my father. It was hugely presumptuous on her part. Presumptuous and ill-thought-out. Quite immature, really.

My phone beeps with a text. It's from Dan. *Free for lunch?*

Working in such close proximity makes it easy to have lunch together. We don't arrange it in advance, it's more a spur of the moment thing, one of us texting the other around midmorning to assess the lay of the land. More often than not we're both free, and we buy takeaway rolls at the closest sandwich shop before finding a spot in the park to eat. After we've eaten, if we're not in a rush, we walk. I'm getting to know Dan more through these spur-of-the-moment lunch dates than through the evening and weekend time we spend together. That lunch hour is so finite. Every second seems to count. We talk non-stop.

Sorry. Can't do today.

Today is one of those rare days when I can't afford to take a full lunch break. Generally, my days at the gallery are steady and relatively calm, and I can't really complain that today is extra busy.

Lonely sandwich on my own, then. His reply makes me smile. Draining my coffee, I rinse the cup in the kitchenette, turning it upside down until my next caffeine fix. Then, armed with a pen and pad, I head for my meeting.

'I'm going to coerce the executor into giving me the family's phone number,' I inform Tom and my colleagues.

There are eight of us sitting around the meeting table. We're discussing the logistics of the upcoming exhibition, and the preparatory work needed for each particular piece. Over a hundred pieces will be displayed and, as one would expect, they're in varying states of readiness. My painting has the dubious status of needing the most work done to it.

'Maybe you should write to them again,' Tom suggests. Writing is the preferred means of communication in our business. Keeping records is vital to what we do. But sometimes written communication simply doesn't work. Some people — me, for instance — respond better to verbal contact.

I compromise with Tom. 'I'll phone *and* write.'

He nods his approval. 'I think it's time to ask the opinion of some experts, too.'

'Yes.' I rattle off names of known experts around the world, and Tom and the others add a few extra. It goes without saying that we would all prefer to wait until the painting is fully cleaned before seeking expert advice, but the lack of response from the family and the absence of any other leads have necessitated a deviation from this.

After the meeting, I take some updated photographs and forward them to the various experts, with a covering note explaining who I am, and how the painting came into the possession of the gallery. Hopefully, one of experts will recognise the style of the artist. Or maybe they have seen this girl somewhere else, even in some other form. You never know.

Next on my list is the executor.

'My main interface with the family is Mrs Karen Brooks,' he tells me in his plummy voice. 'She is the deceased's daughter.'

'Yes, I see that from the paperwork. I'm looking for a contact number, please.'

'I'm afraid I'm not at liberty to pass it on. Privacy laws, you understand.'

'The disclosure of Mrs Brooks' phone number in this instance is *directly* related to the administration of her father's estate, and the painting that formed part of that estate,' I inform him snippily. 'In addition, I believe that a *reasonable person*, as defined by the privacy laws you refer to, would expect the gallery to have access to Mrs Brooks' phone number in the circumstances.'

There's a pause.

'I suppose you're correct,' he says eventually.

I *know* I'm correct. I'm a veritable expert on privacy laws and their irritating restrictions.

He asks me to wait while he looks up the number. A few moments later I have it written in my file, and I thank him in a slightly less clipped tone of voice.

Unfortunately, after all that effort, Karen Brooks doesn't answer her phone. It rings through to voicemail. I listen to her voice — mature, articulate, a little bit posh — and hang up without leaving a message. I'll keep trying until I speak to her. I don't like leaving messages. I hate to think of the person on the other end analysing *my* voice and forming impressions of me.

The rest of the day speeds along, but every time I write or type the date it feels as though there's a sudden pause and memories rush in. Simon stumbling through the door, drunk. Simon, his head in his hands, his body heaving with silent sobs, unaware of me watching from the doorway. Simon, a cigarette defiantly hanging from his mouth, refusing to listen when I told him that one day he would get lung cancer. Simon, a distorted adult reflection of my own confusion and sense of abandonment.

I miss him, and I'm glad that today is busy because otherwise I might feel sadder, more melancholy.

I know he was far, far from perfect. He was inherently lazy, and didn't contribute anyway near enough money — or even love — to keep our household running. He had no ambition, no interest in anything but the short-term hit of nicotine and the oblivion of alcohol. He was violent towards my mother. Not physically violent, as far as I can remember, but verbally, behaviourally. Roaring at her, smashing furniture and anything he could lay his hands on. She retaliated in kind. Maybe she even instigated the arguments. He was never violent towards me, and that makes me question my mother's part in their arguments. After she left, he continued to drink, but he never completely lost control of his temper. The worst I can accuse him of is shouting at me, and being extraordinarily grumpy the morning after. What does that say about him? About her? About them together?

In the hospital, towards the end, I asked him outright. 'Why did you stay with me?'

'Because someone had to,' he croaked. 'And look at you now, going to university, ready to conquer the world ...' With the little strength he had left, he squeezed my hand. 'Staying with you is one of the few things I can be proud of ...'

In a weird way, I was proud too, that *I* had stayed, because it had been a conscious decision on my part. Natasha, my social worker, asked me regularly if I wanted to move into a foster home or some other supervised accommodation. No, I didn't want to move out. I didn't want to leave Ann-Marie and Emma next door. I didn't want to leave the very place my mother might return to some day. And, for reasons that were harder to explain, I didn't want to leave Simon. So I covered up the extent of his drinking, skirted around his dark moods, and became quite hysterical at the suggestion of moving out. Natasha, God bless her, would always back off.

Then along came the cancer. I was sixteen when he was first diagnosed, twenty when he died. These were our best years. The cancer changed him. Or maybe it was the chemo that brought about the change, poisoning the badness in him as it endeavoured to poison those abnormal cells. Fighting for his life, he let go of his vices one by one: the cigarettes, the booze and, finally, his temper. What lay beneath was a vulnerable, humble and loyal man, as good a father figure as any.

If I ever find her, this will be one of the first things I will tell her. *You missed the best of him. You should have stuck around.*

Chapter 18

Emma

I can't get that fuckin' house out of my head. Last night I even dreamt about it. We were sitting in our black-and-white kitchen, Eddie, Isla and me, eating one of Eddie's roast dinners. Rain thrashed the kitchen window, thunder cracked overhead, but we were unperturbed. We laughed and joked while we ate. It felt so cosy and right. It felt like our *home*, and when I woke this morning it took me a few moments to realise I wasn't in the house, I was in our dingy two-bed flat in the same inner-city suburb I've always lived in.

At work, the house continues to monopolise my thoughts. I find myself on the real estate agent's website, taking one of those virtual tours. The kitchen and living area from a few different angles. The bedrooms and upstairs: I scrutinise the photos, hitting pause a few times because I was a little bit distracted when we were looking around this part of the house. All the bedrooms have built-in wardrobes. There's additional storage in the closet outside the bathroom, as well as some space in the attic. Why the hell does storage suddenly seem so vitally important?

After taking three virtual tours, I find myself on a mortgage website, putting numbers into one of those online calculators, establishing how much we can borrow, and what the repayments would look like over twenty years: too high. Thirty years? Almost achievable. If everything went right, and there were no major financial hiccups. I'd be fifty-four when the house would be paid off. The same age as my mother, who, incidentally, has rented all her life and has never owned a property.

'Emma?'

I jump at the sound of Katie's voice, and fumble with my mouse to close down the mortgage calculator.

'Do you have the month-end file?' she asks tentatively. 'I can't find it anywhere.'

'Yeah, I do.' The file is sitting on my desk. 'I'm working on it at the moment.' Well, I *would* be working on it, if I weren't strangely mesmerised by real estate and mortgage websites this morning.

'Can I take the bank reconciliation?'

'Yeah, alright.'

Her long fair hair shielding her face, she opens the lever-arch folder, and carefully extracts the reconciliation. She's a nice girl, Katie. A good worker in a slow, solid way that I'm getting more used to, and appreciative of. It seems to take her a while to grasp things, but once she understands them she rarely makes an error. And she seems genuinely eager to help. Obliging, that's the word.

'Katie, d'you ever babysit?'

'Sometimes. For my aunt.' She laughs self-consciously, tucking her hair behind one ear. 'I love babies, but I'm a bit hopeless with them. Can't seem to settle them when they're crying. Luckily, my cousins are a bit older now.'

Alright. So she babysits her cousins occasionally. And seems to prefer older children. Should I ask? I don't want to make her feel uncomfortable, or to feel obliged to say yes just because I'm her boss.

'You need someone to watch Isla?' she guesses while I'm still in the throes of deciding whether to ask.

'Yeah,' I reply meekly.

'When?'

'This is the problem. It's a daytime gig, a Saturday. I'm sure you'd prefer to go shopping, or hang out with your friends.'

'What Saturday are we talking about?'

I tell her the Saturday in question, and the reason: the leadership course.

'Eddie will be there in the morning. You wouldn't need to come until noon.'

'I can do it.' For once Katie seems decisive.

But I'm not. 'Are you sure?'

'Yes. Seriously, it's not a problem. It'll be fun. But I should probably meet Isla before I spend the entire day with her.'

Yeah, that would make sense.

'Maybe you could come around for dinner one night after work?'

'Perfect,' she says, smiling that lovely smile of hers before taking off with the bank reconciliation.

I'm left feeling a bit off-kilter. I can do the leadership course. That's good, *very good*, as the solution does not involve Jamie. But Katie coming to my flat is not so good. I can't imagine what she'll make of it. If only we lived in that house. Then I wouldn't have any second thoughts about inviting her around.

Maybe this is what spurs me to pick up the phone.

'I'd like to see a contract for the house, please.' From my tone, you'd swear I do this kind of thing all the time.

'Well, we don't usually give out the contract until an offer has been made,' the agent says, sounding a bit flummoxed.

Really?

'You see, the offer is made subject to contract and inspection, etcetera,' he explains kindly. 'There's plenty of opportunity to examine the contract at that point ...'

'Oh.'

'Do you want to make an offer on the house?'

'No, I do not.' We haven't even had mortgage approval, for God's sake.

'Well, then ...'

'I just want a copy of the contract,' I insist, somewhat belligerently. 'Are you saying I can't have it?'

'I'll send it via courier,' he relents. 'It will get to you within the hour.'

There's no urgency, we both know this, but I reel off my work address anyhow.

I thank him, he thanks me, and it's a done deal.

'There's a slab of concrete in there,' the receptionist jokes when I go to her desk to collect the package a couple of hours later. So much for *within the hour*. 'It weighs a ton.'

I feel like joking back that it really is part of a house, in a way. But I don't.

The contract spends the rest of the day on my desk, undisturbed in its package. Then it gets the bus home with me, sitting on my lap like a young child.

'Look what I got today.' It lands on the kitchen table with an almighty thump.

Eddie looks alarmed. 'What is it?'

'A small forest ... The contract for that house.'

'But ...'

He doesn't need to say it. I was the one who said we couldn't afford it. I was the one who flounced out of the house. And we haven't even got mortgage approval, not to mention putting an offer in.

I shake my head, every bit as bewildered as he is. 'I don't know what came over me. I just felt this overwhelming need to have it.'

Chapter 19

Louise

'You'll have some tea?'

Though Mary phrases it as a question, she is making a statement. I can't help smiling: it's such an Irish thing to do.

She bounces around the kitchen, filling the kettle, assembling cups and saucers, laying out plates, and — almost as a grand finale — whisking away a tea-towel to reveal a tray of freshly baked muffins.

Dan smacks his lips. 'What have you got there, Mum?'

Mary glares at him. 'Hands off. These are for Louise, not you.'

I laugh. I'm beginning to think that I must have a sign on my forehead saying, 'Waif: please feed.'

'They're like horses, all of them,' Mary says, casting another disparaging glare at Dan, who is pretending to look hurt. 'I'm worn out from feeding them. Years and years of buying trolleys of food at the supermarket, only to have an empty pantry by the end of the day. And with Samuel back home, it's as bad as ever ... Dan, carry this out to the table for me ... No, Louise, you don't need to do a thing. Just go and sit down ...'

Feeling a bit like a princess, I do as I'm told, sitting at one corner of the large outdoor table as Dan treks back and forth to the kitchen. Eventually, everything has been transported, including Mary, who pours the tea before she finally sits down.

'I've been looking through the cemeteries for your mother,' she begins, and then, clearly horrified by her choice of phrasing, slaps her hand over her mouth. 'I'm sorry, Louise. I didn't mean to sound so completely tactless.'

I smile reassuringly. 'It's okay. I've been doing this long enough to be desensitised by now.'

The police who initially investigated my mother's disappearance, as well as the private investigator I hired later on, centred a good deal of their efforts on death records, funeral notices and cemetery websites. The irony is that it's easier to find someone if they're dead. Privacy laws seem to lose their power.

'What I meant to say is that I've been looking through some online cemetery indexes,' Mary makes another start, speaking more carefully this time. 'There are various websites on the net, some state-based, others Australia-wide. As a matter of fact, I found the state-based ones more up to date. They have a summary of the inscriptions, and if you want more details you can click on an actual image of the headstone … It's quite amazing.'

I came across similar websites in the US, and spent many hours trawling through their records. Not every cemetery contributed to the online websites, and most of the records were at least a year or two behind. So the fact that I didn't find any record of my mother's death was completely inconclusive. I assume it's a similar situation here in Australia.

'Thanks, Mary.' I know from experience how much time it takes to navigate through all those sites and records, and I feel overcome with gratitude. The fact that the result is likely to prove nothing is beside the point.

'No problem.' Mary smiles, then confides, 'Without meaning to sound ghoulish, I quite enjoyed it. Finding the best websites, sifting through all the information, narrowing it down ...'

I know what she means. This kind of investigation work can be totally absorbing, addictive even. 'Any Janet Mitchells in there?'

'A dozen or so, but I eliminated more than half of them from their year of birth, or year of death, or other details on the inscription that didn't seem to match. I have five possibilities. I've printed out all the details for you.' She swishes her hand in the direction of the house. 'They're inside, on the hall table in a special file. Don't leave without them. My head is like a sieve.' She glares at Dan again, clearly holding him and his brothers responsible for her memory deficiencies.

Once again, I thank her. Her helpfulness and kindness, like Dan's, leaves me feeling both touched and humbled. I'm not sure we'll get anywhere, not if my track record is anything to go by, but it's comforting not to be in this alone, to know that this time there will be someone else who can comprehend the pain and disappointment of each dead end.

And there's no chance I'll forget the 'special file'; I'm scrupulous when it comes to this. I will add these new Janet Mitchells to my spreadsheet, and based on the inscription details — if a spouse or children are named on the monument — I will endeavour to contact the family left behind, and eliminate that particular Janet Mitchell from my enquiries. That's what I do: find Janet Mitchells, then eliminate them.

Mary pats my hand. 'Sorry, love. This is all a bit morbid, isn't it?'

'It's part of the process.' My reply is matter-of-fact.

Picking up my cup of tea, which I'd all but forgotten, I take a sip. The tea is cool. Mary, watching me closely, asks if I want a top up.

'Yes, please.' After she pours more tea, she once again finds my hand to give it a weirdly reassuring pat. And maybe this is why I confide in her. 'I don't think my mother is dead, so I'm able to go through this side of things without getting upset. I see it as closing off a particular avenue of enquiry. That's all.'

'How can you be sure?' Dan leans forward, suddenly in journalist mode. He's been uncharacteristically quiet until now. 'I know you're adamant that she wasn't murdered, but what if she died some other way? Accidents happen. Illnesses. It's been a long time.'

I shrug as I look from him to Mary. 'I think I would know if she had died. I would feel it, somehow. I can't really explain how, or why, but I'm *very sure* I'd know.'

A ruckus inside the house interrupts the contemplative mood outside.

Mary cocks her head. 'It's Richie and Samuel. They're back. And disagreeing about something, from the sounds of it. Dan, go in and sort them out, would you?'

Dan rolls his eyes before getting up from his seat.

'I'm sorry you have to go through this,' Mary says when he's gone, the sudden gravity in her tone leading me to believe she got rid of Dan in order to speak to me alone. 'The uncertainty must be terrible. If she died, God forbid, you could at least go through the grieving process. But you're stuck in between, in no-man's land, not knowing either way … How can you move on?'

She's so forthright she almost takes my breath away. Most people keep their thoughts to themselves, choosing what to say and the moment to say it, if they say anything at all. But Mary seems to have no such filter. Then again, most people just don't get my situation, what it really feels like, and I think she does. We live in a world of absolutes. If we don't know something, we have infinite resources to access in order to find out whatever it is we need to know. Mary has got to the heart of it, just as Dan did. They see that the uncertainty and ambiguity are more damaging and debilitating than any grief.

'You don't move on,' I murmur, even though I'm not sure she was seeking a reply.

Unresolved loss, that's what Natasha, my social worker, called it. A state of existence where there are no certainties, absolutes, or sense of control. The police insisted that it's not actually a crime to go missing. Natasha disagreed. It *is* a crime, a *moral* crime, she said.

'You're a good girl.' Mary squeezes my hand. 'I can't think of a better daughter. I'm sure she would be very proud if she could see you today.'

I laugh bitterly. If I had been such an outstanding daughter, I don't think my mother would have walked out the door and left me with a man who wasn't even my father.

'You *are* good, Louise,' Mary insists. 'You're a worthy and accomplished young woman. And you and Dan together, I couldn't be happier ...' She makes a snorting sound. 'He had his heart broken by the other one ...'

The other one?

'The last girlfriend,' Mary elaborates when she sees the question on my face. 'She was one of those high-flying types. Hated coming around here, and did everything she could to avoid our family get-togethers. We were all delighted when she dumped him.'

Perhaps I should feel a little jealous of this high-flying ex, but I don't. In fact, it's all I can do not to laugh at the idea of someone trying to stay aloof amidst this family.

We smile at each other, and though nothing is said it's as if Mary knows exactly what I'm thinking. As we sit in silence, the noise from the kitchen increases, Dan's voice as loud as the other two.

Mary shakes her head. 'They're arguing about the car. Now that Samuel is home, he thinks he can take it whenever he fancies and Richie is getting annoyed.' Her sigh has an air of inevitability. 'I'd better go in …'

She goes inside, and her voice, with its high, commanding pitch, adds to the fracas. Forthright, feisty, Mary isn't one to stand back for long. She's in there, in the thick of it, firing on all fronts. Why am I smiling? Because their arguing is endearing, in a way. There's passion rather than aggression. Honesty rather than secrecy. Love instead of contempt. The argument is a product of their closeness, not of their distance from one another. All these factors make it different from the arguments between my mother and Simon.

In the car on the way home, Dan shoots me a sideways glance. 'Sorry about my family. We're shouters. It's how we communicate, and I know it can be very startling for outsiders.'

I smile at him. 'I like your family.'

To be truthful, I more than like the O'Connollys; I'm becoming dangerously attached to them.

Dan slows at some lights. 'What were you and Mum talking about out there?'

I smirk. 'Your ex-girlfriend, amongst other things.'

He groans. 'She didn't bring up Heather, did she?'

'Yup. I heard that you were dumped.'

He grins before resorting to his favourite cop-out. 'No comment.'

Chapter 20

Emma

Eddie is making beef and red-wine casserole for dinner, and we're having lemon-and-lime tart and ice-cream for dessert. I bought the tart in the patisserie on my way home from work yesterday. I've never gone to this patisserie before, their stuff is far too expensive, and I just hope this flimsy-looking tart is worth the bloody exorbitant price. This visit from Katie has been stressing me out. Over the past few days I've been seeing everything through her eyes: the frayed carpet in the hallway, the dated kitchen, the mouldy grout in the bathroom. I've cleaned and scoured, bought a new mat for the hall, fresh flowers to brighten up the kitchen, and a special mould solution for the bathroom tiles (which didn't work). Eddie has arranged to start his shift an hour later than usual, and Isla has tried really hard to keep her room tidy. I think we're ready, or as ready as we can be without transplanting ourselves to a different house in a different suburb.

Katie chatters away as we walk from the bus stop, and doesn't seem to notice that I'm a little on the quiet side. I'm nervous, and more preoccupied with studying her expression as we walk past depressing blocks of flats, neglected housing estates and — to my mortification — a burnt-out car. The council and politicians claim that they're regenerating the area, moving people out of the flats and into houses, building parks and cycleways, and planting trees. They're trying, even I can see that. Every now and then a new playground appears, and the small children get wildly excited and want to go there every day, and everything is wonderful until the play equipment gets bashed and covered with graffiti, and the mothers see their children with syringes in their hands, at which point the 'new' playground is a no-go zone, just like everywhere else around here. I think that one day the politicians will succeed and the area will become regenerated, but quite frankly I don't care enough to wait around. It will be years and years, and I'll be so disillusioned by then that no amount of new greenery or cultural centres or village-like set-ups will make up for the bleakness that went before.

Katie seems relaxed. She's still doing most of the chatting, talking about her nephew, who's Isla's age, and — using Katie's words — 'a bit mental'. She glances at the burnt-out car and frowns briefly, but other than that she doesn't seem to notice anything untoward. I'm coming to the realisation that she's considerably less critical than me.

'We're here,' I say grimly.

I quicken my pace so that Katie doesn't have the opportunity to absorb the building's less-than-grand façade. My keys are ready, and I have the door open and Katie inside before she can catch her breath.

'Mammyyyyy …' Isla hurls herself down the hall and latches onto my legs.

'Hi, pet … This is Katie … Katie works with me …'

'Hello, Isla.' Katie's smile is casual and not too over-the-top. Since I've become a mother, I've noticed that children find fake, teeth-baring smiles quite scary. Katie's smile is perfectly pitched, but Isla can't appreciate this because her face is lodged in my thighs. 'I've heard all about you from your mum.'

Caught between intrigue and shyness, Isla risks a peek at the visitor. Other than my mother, and Louise when she's around, we don't have many people calling to our home. 'Hi, Katie,' she manages after a long pause, and then, beset with another attack of shyness, she retreats into my legs once more.

Eddie is next to be introduced. He's wearing his best jeans and the shirt I bought him for Christmas. My heart melts with gratitude. If he were less in tune with me, he would have fronted up in his work clothes. But he knows how stressed out I've been — in his opinion, unnecessarily so — and he's done his best to make a good impression. He shakes Katie's hand, and we all proceed to the kitchen.

'Eddie is the cook around here,' I say awkwardly. 'I hope you like casserole.'

Just like Isla isn't used to visitors, I'm not used to playing hostess. I sound false, as though I'm acting. Which I am, really.

'Casserole's my favourite,' Katie replies. Something tells me that she would say this even if it weren't. She has lovely manners.

'My favourite dinner is spaghetti,' Isla chirps in a more forthcoming tone.

'That's my second favourite,' Katie says.

Isla is clearly delighted by this, and decides to establish if they have any other likes or dislikes in common.

'What's your favourite colour?'

'Green.'

'Mine's red. Favourite drink?'

'Coke.'

'Me too!' Isla squeals, before adding sadly, 'But Mammy doesn't let me have it very often. It makes me hyper.' Then she brightens. 'Daddy lets me have it when I'm in his house ... He lets me eat and drink anything I want.'

I sigh inwardly. Katie doesn't know anything about Jamie, and I wasn't planning on telling her. So much for that.

'Isla spends every second weekend with her father,' I say in a business-like tone. 'What would you like to drink, Katie? We have red wine, white wine, beer ...'

'A Coke is fine, if you have it.' Katie shoots Isla a sympathetic smile.

Eddie gets some glasses from the cupboard while I extract the litre bottle of Coke from the fridge.

'You don't drink alcohol?' I ask conversationally as I pour the Coke, relenting and putting a smidgeon in one of the glasses for Isla.

'No.' Katie shrugs. 'I don't like the taste of it.'

She really is from a different planet. Around here *all* the young people drink alcohol. It doesn't matter if they don't like the taste, they drink it anyway, congregating on street corners with cans of lager. Having said that, Katie must have encountered peer pressure even in her own circles, and must have had to stick to her guns. She's very self-possessed, Katie. She's her own person. I like that.

Eddie, conscious of the time, asks if anyone is hungry. Yes, we all chorus, and then Isla and Katie say, 'Jinx' and then 'Double jinx' and then we laugh again.

The casserole is cooked beautifully. Eddie has excelled himself, made me so proud of him. Katie takes small ladylike bites, chewing slowly, never speaking with food in her mouth yet managing to converse with everyone. I see Eddie making an effort not to fork the food into his mouth too quickly, and Isla mimicking the way Katie handles her cutlery. Me too. We're all trying to rise to her standard.

The lemon-and-lime tart is a hit, and Katie says she will buy one for a girls'-night-in she's hosting next week. After dinner, Eddie excuses himself to get ready for work, Isla invites Katie to 'play' in her room, and I begin cleaning up.

It went well. I'm pleased.

Scraping the leftovers into the bin, I immerse the plates in the sink. Eddie is the cook, I'm the washer-upper; these are our roles. The water stings my hands — it's a bit too hot — and I run the cold tap for a short burst. Our new house has a dishwasher, stainless steel like the other appliances. Except it's not our new house, and I absolutely *must* stop thinking of it like that.

I hear the front door open and shut. That's Eddie slipping out to work in his overalls. I'll thank him when he comes home. Most mornings I don't wake when he climbs into bed next to me. It's usually about 4 am when he gets in, and if I wake — even just to give him a sleepy smile or a quick hug — it's hard to get back to sleep. Tomorrow I'll wake. Just to thank him. For the meal. For wearing a shirt. For everything.

Finishing the washing up, I grab a clean tea-towel and begin drying. What are the girls doing? Playing dolls? Dressing up? I can hear Isla's voice imparting instructions. Poor Katie, being ordered around by a five-year-old. She's been lovely: so accommodating and easy to have around, the perfect guest.

'What's going on here?' I enquire, sticking my head around the bedroom door once the dishes are done.

'We're playing teachers,' Isla informs me in a tone that implies she's the teacher and Katie's the student.

Katie grins gamely.

'Now, Katie, please tell me two Sammy Snake words ...' Isla continues in her bossiest voice.

Later, when I judge that Katie has had enough of Isla's lessons, I insist on calling her a taxi.

'I can get the bus home,' Katie protests.

'No, you can't.' I sound every bit as bossy as Isla now. 'Not at this time of night. Not around here.'

When Katie has been dispatched safely in a taxi, I get Isla ready for bed in quick-smart time. We're late, for a school night. I berate myself for not winding things up earlier. I don't like sending Isla to school tired. Bright and fresh and clean, that's how I like my daughter to front up each morning.

'Do you like Katie?' I ask, giving her hair a fast run through with her princess comb.

'I do, Mammy. She's very nice and very pretty.'

I like Katie too, though it has taken me quite a while to realise it. In fact, I want Isla to grow up to be just like Katie. I want her to go to university, and to secure a graduate placement in a blue-chip company, just as Katie has. I want her to prefer Coke to alcohol, and to have immaculate table manners. If Isla turns out anything like Katie, I'll feel that I have mothered her successfully.

Isla's face puckers in a frown. 'I just don't know why you want to shake her.'

'What?'

'You said to Eddie that you wanted to shake Katie. You did. I remember it.'

Oh God, so I did. It had been a bad day at work. I didn't really know her back then. A terrible, terrible thought occurs to me.

'You didn't tell Katie I said that, did you?'

Isla's face drops. 'Sorry, Mammy … It just came out.'

Oh fuck!

'Sorry, Mammy,' Isla says again, looking very woebegone.

'It's not your fault, love. Quick, into bed now.'

After a quick search for Koala, the toy bear Louise sent from Australia, Isla finally climbs into bed. It would make a lovely photo, Isla with Koala squashed against her face. Tomorrow night, when I'm not so distracted, I'll take a shot and send it to Louise.

'Night, love. Straight to sleep now.'

My tone gives no hint of the fact that I'm cringing inside. Fuck! Fuck! Fuck! Me and my big mouth. What will Katie think? I imagine I'll get a text before the night is out, cancelling the babysitting, and I really can't bloody blame her.

Chapter 21

Louise

Rejections are coming from all angles. Every day at work, at least one email from the art experts, expressing their disappointment that the artist's technique is not one they recognise, and wishing me luck with my further investigations. And, to balance things out not so nicely, when I get home from work in the evening, there is often at least one letter waiting on the dining table — where Joe tends to leave my mail — from one of the Janet Mitchells I've written to, stating that she isn't my mother, and kindly wishing me luck with my search. They all sound so hopeful, the art experts and the Janet Mitchells (who, incidentally, all seem to have such pretty handwriting in their letters), as though it's only a matter of time before I find what I'm looking for. It would be nice to somehow tap into their hopefulness, because I feel pretty despondent now.

My phone rings, taking my attention away from the latest sorry-can't-help-you email from Jacquie, an expert based in Amsterdam.

'Louise, it's Analiese.'

I'm surprised. I haven't seen or heard from Analiese since the day she came in with baby Stella, the day we had the hummingbird cake, the thought of which makes me smile.

'Hi, Analiese.' My voice is warm, my frustrations temporarily forgotten. 'How are you? How's the baby?'

'We're fine.' There's a rather long pause, and I wonder why she has phoned. Finally, she asks, 'How's the painting coming along?'

So she's calling to find out about her old project. She's curious to know what progress I've made.

'Well, she's looking decidedly cleaner, our girl.' As I speak, I look over at the portrait, appraising it with fresh eyes. 'The colours have come up beautifully. And the brush technique is every bit as exquisite as we thought. No luck on finding out who she is, though, or who painted her. At this rate she'll be nothing more than an *unknown* in the exhibition.'

Analiese contemplates my response, and there's another long pause.

'The family?' she asks eventually. 'Any leads from them?'

'No. They haven't replied to your letter, and I've tried to call the woman — Karen Brooks — countless times but she never answers her phone. I'm beginning to think she's some kind of recluse.'

Analiese sounds thoughtful. 'Maybe. Some people live in their own little world, oblivious to everything and everyone else. Sometimes I'd like to be that way, less tuned in. It would be easier, I think.'

Analiese seems to be in an odd mood. Not that I know her well enough to establish what is or isn't odd behaviour. I'm going purely by instinct.

I'm not sure if Analiese is expecting a response or not, but either way a baby begins wailing in the background before I need to think of one. Stella. Once again, I find that I'm smiling. Something about this mother-baby duo is uplifting. Maybe because they remind me of Emma and Isla.

Analiese is not as charmed as I am by the sound of her baby crying. Her sigh seems to have a touch of the despondence I was feeling before she called and somehow cheered me up.

'I can't believe she's awake again … That was barely twenty minutes … I'd better go, Louise. Thank you. Sorry if I interrupted while you were in the middle of something important — I really should have asked if you were free. And I hope you don't think I'm interfering …'

'Not at all,' I say firmly because she sounds like she needs reassurance. 'Happy to talk anytime.'

Dan is waiting at our usual lunchtime meeting spot. He's talking on his phone, and doesn't see me approach. Today he's wearing a white shirt and a patterned tie, a touch more formal than his usual work attire. He must have had an important meeting. He turns to the side, staring into the middle distance, and my eyes scan his profile, the solid shoulders beneath his shirt, tapering to his slim belted hips. He — in a completely different way from Analiese and Stella — is a living, breathing antidote for despondence. Just seeing him is enough to banish any lingering feelings of failure from all those rejection letters.

I'm close by the time he notices me. He smiles and rolls his eyes, indicating that he's been trying to wind up the call.

'Yes … Yes, I know it's a risk but …'

With his free hand he pulls me close.

'Yes, certainly.' Now that free hand of his is stroking the side of my face. 'I don't foresee any major problems, try not to worry …' His tone becomes even more officious as his thumb brushes my lips. Playing him at his own game, I give his thumb a playful nip. He feigns a look of pain, before removing his hand, sweeping it down to rest on my waist. 'Actually, John, I'd better go. I have someone waiting to see me … And she's beginning to look very impatient …' Clearly John, whoever he is, finds this as amusing as Dan does, and they share a chuckle at my expense.

'Impatient?' I arch my brows when he finally hangs up.

He slides both arms around me. 'You can't wait to have me to yourself. Admit it.'

'No comment, Mister Big-Head Journalist.'

It's all too easy, this jokey lovey-dovey act that we do.

Hand in hand, we cross the street to our favourite sandwich shop. We've done this often, and now I could order for Dan, and he could order for me. I don't know where this comfortableness has sprung from, but deep down it makes me uneasy. A few minutes later, clutching our lunches in their brown paper bags, we amble towards our preferred spot in the park, under one of the huge fig trees, away from the main drag — it's one of the few relatively private corners of this vast public area.

'Something occurred to me this morning,' Dan says out of the blue. 'Something about your mother.'

Whilst Dan and I have already established certain rituals in our relationship, our conversations are anything but routine. They fly in all directions, from the practical to the philosophical, to the deeply personal (things I haven't shared with anyone else, and revelations from him which feel similarly sacred). Dan's brain, I've discovered, is always on the move, always pondering the next thing. I'm less fluid than he is.

'What about my mother?' I ask, cagily.

'Her middle name. I wonder if she goes by it.'

'Elizabeth? You mean she could be going around as Elizabeth Mitchell instead of Janet Mitchell?'

'I don't know.' He sits down on the grass and begins to unwrap his sandwich. 'But it's a possibility, isn't it? Lots of people go by their second name. There's no paperwork involved, not too many questions asked. In fact, I was talking to someone this morning, a colleague I've known for years, and I found out by chance that the name he goes by is in fact his second name. That's what made me think of your mother. Actually, I was annoyed I hadn't thought of it earlier. It's so obvious.'

Dan has a point. As he says, it would be easy, a change of identity without any paperwork or questions. But the thought of it is enough to make me feel exhausted. Elizabeth Mitchell is a whole new person.

I kneel on the grass next to him, and then sit back on my heels, frowning to let him know I am not pleased with where this is heading. 'Are you suggesting I start a new search, for Elizabeth Mitchell?'

'I'm suggesting that you *concurrently* search for Elizabeth and Janet.' His tone is mollifying.

'Oh, come on, Dan. There's no such thing as concurrent when it comes to this. It's a *whole new search*. And I don't think I have the energy.'

'Of course you do,' he states, calm as anything. '*We* do. Let's go back to the AEC office. Lunchtime tomorrow.'

'Dan …'

'We can pretend not to know one another again. I found that quite a turn-on, actually …'

Somehow he's made me smile. I too have fond memories of that afternoon in the AEC office, all the more because Dan kissed me in the pub afterwards. It feels like so much longer than a few weeks ago.

He takes a bite from his sandwich, and prompts me to do the same. The conversation moves on — with suspicious ease — to an exposé he is working on for the newspaper. Apparently the John he was speaking to earlier is the source, and is suffering from cold feet. Then we talk about Samuel, who's doing a few weeks' contract work at the newspaper thanks to Dan. Samuel is the new office boy — for want of a better role description — but has already made the powers that be aware that this is a first step only, and he wants to go to the top, the very top.

Dan laughs. 'I got him to do some photocopying this morning, just to put him in his place.'

'Oh, don't be mean to him,' I implore.

I can't help feeling protective of Samuel. In fact, I feel protective of all of them, the entire Connolly clan.

By the time Dan walks me back to the gallery, he has worked some kind of magic and I'm already resigned to adding Elizabeth Mitchell to my search. Dan is dangerous that way. He can talk me into things. He knows when to push and when to step back, just as easily as he seems to be able to gauge my mood.

'See you later tonight.' He kisses me thoroughly on the lips and then he's gone, back to the newspaper, no doubt to sort out John's cold feet, or perhaps to find some other menial task that will put Samuel in his place.

I watch him go, a solitary figure with swinging arms, until he joins the busy footpath and melts into the crowd.

I'm resigned, but that doesn't mean I'm not mad at him.

Because when it comes down to it, Elizabeth Mitchell means nothing more than another flood of rejections.

Chapter 22

Emma

I smother a yawn, and briefly fantasise about my usual Saturday morning sleep-in. My warm squashy bed exchanged for this hard plastic seat. I must be bloody mad. My fellow leadership students are visibly more perky than I am, sitting on the edge of their seats, bright-eyed and hanging on the instructor's every word. A few of them are taking notes — they have been madly jotting things down all week — even though it's clear the instructor is only warming up. Another yawn rises from deep inside me. Perhaps I don't have the stamina to be a leader. Ha, ha. To be honest, I'm finding this course a little dry, and more than a little unrealistic. It's great in theory, establishing what a good leader is, examining our own individual leadership styles, and pinpointing what we should change to become better leaders. I'm struggling with the *change* part, though. In my experience, people just don't change. They talk about change, sometimes they go through the motions of change, but that's about as far as it goes. Eventually, be it weeks, months or years later, we revert back to our old (bad) habits.

Case in point: Jamie. Three separate attempts at rehabilitation, some of the best counsellors and addiction experts in the country, thousands and thousands of euros (his mother's money, of course), all leading to a few months' sobriety (three months is his record), before he reverts. In fact, after each attempt to change, after each — inevitable — fall off the wagon, his addiction seems to become more ingrained, more irreversible. So as I half-listen to the instructor on this Saturday morning, this expert on change, I must admit to being unconvinced. And really quite sleepy.

Isla was in her pyjamas when I left this morning. She could hardly contain her excitement, hopping up and down on the bed as I tried to kiss her goodbye.

'How many hours till Katie comes?'

'Four. Now don't be all over her. Make sure you give her space. And be good. Be *very, very* good.'

Despite everything, Katie didn't cancel. She's a saint, she really is. There was no positive spin I could put on it, no way I could reasonably explain how even though I *said* I wanted to shake her, I didn't really *mean* it. Anything I said would have made the situation worse. So I said nothing, and neither did she. Ever since, I've been extra friendly, hoping to make it up to her, hoping that she realises it was something I said in the heat of the moment, and not a reflection of how I truly feel … at least not how I feel now that I know her. Katie has been pleasant but distinctly aloof. I hope Isla will charm her today, and coax her into liking us once again. Because Katie *did* genuinely like us, all of us, Isla and Eddie and me. I could feel it. She wasn't just being polite.

Tuning back into what's going on around me, I hear the instructor mention something about role-play.

'I have a script for you to work with,' he says, using an irritating jovial tone, 'outlining a difficult conversation between a leader and a nonperforming employee. Look at the background information before you read the script. You'll notice that some of the messages are better delivered in an indirect manner, and the script is in fact only part of the solution. In other words, being a good leader sometimes involves holding your silence. If you think the script can be improved, feel free to workshop within your group and add your own suggestions.'

He splits us into groups. 'Emma, Vincent, Ciara and Mairead.'

This is going to be torture. Ciara and Mairead are investment bankers, and Vincent's a corporate lawyer. All three of them are completely up themselves. Whoever came up with this model — throwing random people together for a week while they learn the intricacies of leadership — needs to have a serious rethink.

'This is a great networking opportunity for you all,' the main instructor spouted on the first day. 'We hope that you continue to keep in contact after the course.'

I can tell you now I have no bloody intention of seeing any of them again after today. Not Ciara or Mairead, with their sleek hair and perfectly pressed white shirts. Not Vincent, with his know-it-all smirk and sailor-like casual clothes. And not any of the others either.

The girls throw themselves into the role-playing, carrying on as though they've just won the leading parts in the school musical.

'I loved drama at school,' Ciara titters.

'Me too,' Mairead chimes in.

I try my best. In fact, it takes all my acting skills to disguise how bloody stupid I think this is. We all take a turn at being the leader having 'the difficult conversation', and then at being the belligerent employee. Actually, I'm quite good at playing the employee: getting into character by shouting and swearing, even chewing gum to make myself seem more aggressive. Even so, morning tea is a very welcome diversion. They're constantly feeding us: fruit, cakes, sandwiches, wraps, pies, quiches, biscuits, more fruit, and bowls of mints perched invitingly on the desks should we feel peckish while we're working. The food's the only good thing about the course.

Badly in need of a boost of some sort, I have two coffees in quick succession, and a sticky bun from the huge platter of cakes. My class-mates cluster together in small groups, daintily sipping their coffees. They steer clear of the cakes. It seems that the future leaders of the business world are on a diet.

After my caffeine and sugar hit, I slip away to the bathroom. Just a few more hours to endure before I get my certificate. They'll probably ask for feedback, and I'll be honest. Yeah, some of the course material's interesting, but most of it's ordinary and not remotely groundbreaking, as the brochure claims it to be. Plus, a little suggestion for the section on leadership qualities. Leaders should be able to relate to people from all walks of life. Being 'stuck-up' is big no-no. Everyone in the room take note.

I'm just about to come out of the cubicle when I hear the outer door of the bathroom swing open and a familiar shrill voice.

'She's embarrassing ...' Ciara. Or is it Mairead? It's hard to tell one from the other when I can't see them face to face.

'There should be some sort of filter ... not just anyone should be allowed in.' This is definitely Mairead — her voice is slightly more plaintive. So that was Ciara who spoke first.

'I'm going to complain.' Ciara sounds decisive.

'I will too.' Mairead clearly doesn't want to be left out of the action.

'I mean, she's clearly not of the appropriate standard. What is she? Some low-level accountant? You know, I bet she isn't even qualified.'

It's *me*. They're talking about *me*. I'm 'embarrassing', not of the 'appropriate standard'. No, I'm not qualified, I want to yell out, but I somehow contain myself.

'Her accent, it's grating ...'

My accent? I almost laugh. Really, they should have a good listen to how *they* sound.

Mairead sniggers. At least I think it's Mairead. I'm so stunned to discover that they're gossiping about *me*, I've lost track.

'She even looks rough. Did you see her neck?'

'Yeah, I wonder what happened there ...'

'A fight, I'd say.'

Rough? A fight? I don't know which of these insults I should be more indignant about. Enough.

The cubicle door crashes against the wall when I yank it open with too much force. Words are rushing up my throat. Angry come-backs rise one after the other, making it hard to take a proper breath.

The horror on their prissy faces stalls me.

I won't retaliate. It's like the instructor said: sometimes silence can make a more effective statement than words.

Except it's not that easy.

'It was a car accident,' I say to their reflections in the mirror, unable to look at them directly. 'It wasn't a fight. Just so you know.'

They look even more horrified, if that's possible.

That's it. Zip it. Not another bloody word.

I take my time washing and drying my hands. Then I walk out, my head high.

Back in the classroom, I change seats so that I'm as far away from Ciara and Mairead as possible. Sitting at the back, I can observe them without them observing me. They're subdued, chastened. I wonder if I'm the only one who notices this.

She even looks rough …

That one hurt the most. Because of Isla. I don't want anyone thinking that her mother looks rough.

When Brendan asks me what I learned from this course, I will tell him that I learned what qualities a leader should aspire to having, and what deficiencies I identified in my own leadership style, and how I intend to rectify those deficiencies, temporarily disregarding the fact that I don't believe in permanent behavioural change.

But the biggest lesson was something that happened outside the classroom. In the bathroom, of all places. I was calm and to the point, even though I wanted nothing more than to lash out. And I'm so very proud of myself for holding it together.

'How was the course?' Katie asks when I finally get home.

I pull a face. 'Actually, I wasn't that impressed.'

'Me neither,' she says, wrinkling her nose. 'Most of the stuff I knew already, we covered it in university. And the people I did the course with were really painful …'

I laugh, pulling Isla close for a hug. 'We must have had the same group. I can categorically say that I never want to lay eyes on *any of them* ever again.'

'Same here.' Katie is just as vehement.

'Thanks for today. Here.' I hand her an envelope. It's a voucher for a clothes shop I think she'll like. 'This is a small thank you.'

She blushes. 'Oh, Emma, I don't need anything … It was my pleasure.'

'Take it. I'm really grateful. I — ' For the second time today, words clog up my throat, though for an entirely different reason.

I know exactly what I want to say: *Katie, I want us to be friends. Not just work colleagues, real friends. The more I get to know you, the more I like you. I want you to be a role model for my daughter. I don't want anyone to mock her accent when she gets older, or to think she looks rough, or to regard her as not of the 'appropriate standard'. I want Isla to have all the right qualifications, all the right social kudos. You can help me with that, I know you can. Now I'm making it sound as if I want to be friends only because of Isla, and that's not the case. You're good for me, too. I could learn a lot from you if we were friends.*

Of course I don't say any of this aloud.

'See ya Monday,' is all that comes out.

Chapter 23

Louise

Analiese phones again a few days later. She sounds a little breathless, as though she's excited. 'Louise, sorry for interrupting you again … It's just that I've been thinking …'

'About the painting?' Balancing the phone between my ear and my shoulder, I continue to dab with my swab of cotton wool. I'm on the last stretch. I should invite Analiese to come and see it. While she's here, I could seek her advice on repairing the damage. Of course Tom, Heidi and Peter have all given their professional input, but Analiese seems to care about this painting in a more personal way.

'Karen Brooks,' she says. 'I think you should go to see her.'

'Karen Brooks lives in the country,' I point out pleasantly. 'And I don't have a car.'

'I do,' Analiese replies.

'I can't borrow your car. I don't even have a licence.'

'I meant that I could drive you.'

It's very kind of Analiese, it really is, but she clearly hasn't thought it through.

'What about Stella?'

'I could ask my mother to take her. Just for a day. That would be okay, wouldn't it?'

She's asking my approval. There seems to be a thread of desperation in her voice.

'Yes, I'm sure it would,' I reply, even though it's really not my place to say.

We arrange for Analiese to pick me up from home on Thursday morning.

'Expect me at nine-thirty,' she says firmly. 'That way we should miss the worst of rush hour.'

Analiese is forty minutes late and flustered by the time she pulls up outside my place on Thursday morning.

'Sorry, Louise.' Her curly hair is still wet, and there was obviously not enough time to iron her top. She chucks a clean nappy and a teething ring into the back seat to make room for me to sit in the front. 'I can't seem to manage any semblance of punctuality these days.'

'Don't worry. We have plenty of time.' Bowral, Heidi informed me yesterday, is about a two-hour drive from Sydney. We should get there before lunchtime. That leaves an hour or two with Karen before we embark on the drive home. This is assuming that Karen is home, and willing to speak to us. I tried calling her again, and eventually resorted to a voice message, letting her know we would be dropping by and what we want to speak to her about.

Analiese manoeuvres the car through the side streets until she hits the main road. At the first set of lights, she turns up the radio.

'I like this song,' she declares, sitting a little straighter behind the wheel. 'Do you know who it is?'

'Ed Sheeran.'

'Thanks.' She pulls a face. 'I feel like I've been on a different planet the last couple of months.'

I laugh politely. She takes off when the lights turn green, and for a while the only conversation is the song.

'This feels weird,' she says eventually, glancing around at the empty baby seat in the back. 'I keep expecting Stella to start babbling, or fussing … I hope she's alright with Mum …'

Realising that she needs some distraction, I direct the conversation to work. 'How did you end up at the Sydney City Art Gallery?'

She takes her eyes off the road to shoot me a smile. 'I come from an arty family. My mother's an art historian. Dad is a part-time artist. So art was all around me when I was growing up … How about you?'

My own question boomerangs back at me and I'm ill-prepared for it. 'Oh, a teacher encouraged my love of art.'

It wasn't a teacher, it was my social worker, Natasha. She saw how much I enjoyed drawing, and went out of her way to foster that love, to give me something to focus on when times were tough. Natasha brought me to my first gallery, and walked around with me for hours and hours while I gazed in wonder at each piece. Natasha arranged some free lessons with a local artist. Natasha advised me when it came to choosing subjects for my leaving certificate, and later at college when I realised the boundaries of my talent and became more interested in the history and science of art than in drawing. I owe everything to Natasha, and God knows where I would be today without her encouragement. This train of thought reminds me to send her an email, or maybe a postcard. She still likes to know how I'm doing.

'You're my success story,' she revealed the last time we met.

This made me feel both proud and profoundly sad. Yes, there's a thrill in being the stand-out success, but at the same time I shudder to think where some of her other charges have ended up. Natasha looked worn out that day, as though the job was getting too much for her. I suppose social work can burn you out: too many sad endings, often before a life is even properly begun.

'I couldn't get enough of drawing when I was a little girl,' Analiese says now. We're in the tunnel going under the harbour. A truck rumbles past in the lane next to us. 'Some paper and colouring pencils, and I was as happy as Larry.'

'Yes, me too.'

A memory gushes forth. My mother shoving some spare paper at me: *'Be quiet, Louise … Here, do some drawing.'*

Did I love art simply because I loved art? Or did I come to love it because I had no choice, because my mother was forever suggesting it as a way to keep me occupied, and quiet?

'Ssshhh … Go and draw, Louise.'

She was obsessed with keeping me quiet. Maybe these particular memories occurred in the aftermath of some massive argument with Simon, when she wanted both of us to be as invisible and silent as possible. But maybe she herself had little tolerance for noise — for her own child, even — and it was nothing at all to do with Simon's tempers.

'Ssshhh.'

Afterwards, when I would proudly show her my creation, she would barely glance at it. *'You haven't coloured in the sky… Go and do that now … '*

My memories are blurred, but of this I am quite certain. When she wasn't in the throes of an argument with Simon, she was distant, on the peripheries of family life, uninvolved, as though she might up and leave at any moment … which she did.

Analiese begins to talk about her early career in London.

'I lived there too,' I exclaim. 'Where were you?'

The rest of the journey flies as we compare careers, what we've worked on and where we've lived. It turns out we have a lot in common, Analiese and me.

Other than our families, of course. Analiese, like Dan, comes from a solid, three-kids, devoted-parents home. So removed from my own upbringing, it could be a fairytale.

'It looks a bit derelict.' Analiese puts words to my own first impressions of Karen Brooks' house.

The house is on one of the picturesque streets off Bowral's town centre, with charming country cottages and well-tended gardens all around it. Maybe this is why I'm so shocked by how unkempt it looks. The gate is falling off its hinges, there is no other way to describe the garden than wild, and a black cat slinks around the letterbox — which, incidentally, is overflowing with mail — adding a touch of spookiness to the blatant neglect.

Feeling as uncertain as young children running an errand to the local 'haunted' house, we negotiate the broken gate, the overgrown pathway, and knock on the door, all while the cat regards us with his luminous eyes.

'She's not home,' Analiese states when no one answers our knock.

I decide it's worth another, more insistent knock. After all, we've come a long way, I've taken the day off work, and Analiese went to the trouble of organising her mother to babysit Stella. It's not as if we can call back tomorrow.

There's a sound from inside, the click of a door, followed by slow, seemingly reluctant footsteps.

The woman who answers the door matches the house. Her hair is blonde-grey, and as unkempt as her front garden. She's wearing a black fleece sweater and heavy cords, totally at odds with the sunshine beaming down on us as we stand on the small patio at the front of the house. Two obviously well-fed cats sidle around her stockinged feet.

'Karen Brooks?' I feel compelled to check, because this woman looks so far removed from the cultured voice on her voicemail message, and from the images I had in my mind of what the heiress of a valuable painting would look like.

'Yes, that's me.'

'I'm Louise ...' As I offer my hand to shake, I can't help but notice the cat hair speckled on her black sweater. 'And this is Analiese ...' Analiese also proffers her hand. Karen looks bemused and so I prompt, 'We're from the Sydney City Art Gallery.'

Karen looks none the wiser, as though this is genuinely the first time she has heard of us. Now that I've met her, I realise it's entirely possible that she doesn't listen to the messages on her phone, and going by the letterbox behind me, it's fair to assume that she doesn't keep up to date with her mail either.

'Come inside,' she offers with a vague smile, stepping back to let us in, the cats squealing in protest when she gently nudges them out of the way with her foot.

'Treasure, Sparkles, move!'

Analiese and I follow Karen down the hallway to the kitchen, where there's a sour smell … and another couple of cats padding nonchalantly along the countertop.

'Can I get you some tea?' Karen offers.

'No thanks,' Analiese and I say in unison. I suspect Analiese, like me, would love a cup of tea after the long drive, but not in this kitchen. The cats, *the smell*. It's overpowering, yet Karen seems oblivious.

We sit around the circular kitchen table. One of the cats launches itself from the countertop onto Karen's lap.

'Coming to say hello, Pearlie?' She smiles at it in delight, her hand stroking its arched back.

'Karen …' I begin.

'Call me Kitten,' she murmurs. 'I prefer it.'

'Kitten,' I say, trying to remain unfazed. 'Kitten, we've been doing a lot of work on the painting, the one donated from your father's estate …'

'I didn't get along with my father,' Karen — Kitten — reveals, a faraway look in her eyes.

I pause, not sure if she expects me to comment on this.

'He was horribly strict,' she continues, her hand methodically stroking Pearlie, who has curled into a sleek ball on her lap. 'And cruel, both to humans and to animals. I can't understand cruelty to animals. Humans can hurt you, yes, but not animals …' She shakes her head, clearly perplexed by her father.

'Did the painting originate from his side of the family?' I ask, trying to bring her back to the reason for our visit.

She nods. 'My grandparents were Dutch. I believe the painting came here when they did, in the 1940s.'

Analiese and I already know this. The executor, on donating the painting to the gallery, informed us of the family's heritage. We've come here today to see if we can uncover more details.

'Was your grandparents' surname the same as yours?'

'No, Brooks is my married name.' Kitten pauses, and from the look on her face it appears that her marriage is another sad story. My eyes inadvertently flick to her hand. She isn't wearing a wedding ring, and the house, from what I've seen, doesn't have signs of another resident, at least not a human resident. 'My grandparents' surname was Verbeck. Willem and Inge Verbeck.'

Analiese leans forward. This is good information. With any luck, we may be able to find records of this family in The Netherlands.

'Do you know exactly where they came from?' she asks.

'Rotterdam … My grandfather had a warehouse of some description and, by all accounts, they were rich. They had a big house and servants, and my father certainly had all the traits of a spoiled little rich boy. The family fell on hard times in the war. Their house was badly damaged in the bombings of 1940, and my grandfather's warehouse was wiped out completely. He salvaged what he could from the house — some paintings and some silver cutlery that I still have — and used the money he had left to pay for the family's passage to Australia and a house in Wahroonga. They never regained the wealth they lost in the war. My grandparents and my father were quite bitter about this.' Kitten shakes her head disapprovingly. 'Money means nothing in the end.' She unfurls Pearlie, hugging the cat to her bosom. 'It's all about love.'

Analiese and I share a quick glance, silently conferring on what else we should ask this strange woman. A phone begins to ring in another room. We both look back to Kitten, who seems to have no intention whatsoever of getting up to answer it.

'Do you remember your father or grandparents ever speaking of the painting?' I ask, as the phone rings on in the background. I can see now how my calls went unanswered. 'Sometimes even small bits of seemingly inconsequential information can tell us a lot.'

'No.' Kitten shakes her head. 'It was put in our garage after my grandparents passed on, along with some of their other belongings. My mother wanted the whole lot to be sent to the dump, but she didn't have any say in things. My father was the boss. He made all the decisions. She didn't have a very happy life, my mother …'

And neither, it seems, has her daughter. There's something damaged about Kitten, something that's not quite right. Her excessive affection for her cats, her obliviousness to everyday chores such as housekeeping and checking her mail, and her obvious isolation from the community in which she lives. Her face, when you look closely, could be striking; the right clothes, a comb run through her hair, and she would be immediately less tragic. This is no way for someone of her age — early fifties, at most — or of any age, to be living.

'Can you remember when the painting became damaged?' Analiese's question juts into my thoughts.

'As far as I know, it was always like that. The other paintings were hung in my grandparents' dining room, but I don't remember that particular painting ever being displayed. I think it went directly from their garage to our garage. I'm not sure why they even bothered to bring it to Australia with them …' Kitten shrugs, then suggests, 'Perhaps they knew it had a certain value but didn't have the will, or later on the money, to pay for it to be restored.'

'Where are those other paintings now?' I ask, realising that this is a question we should have asked earlier on. 'You mentioned that your grandfather salvaged some other artworks?'

'One of them is here, in my sitting room. My brother has another. And we sold one to pay for my father's funeral.' Cradling the cat like a baby, Kitten stands up. 'Here, I'll show you the one I have. I'm rather fond of it.'

Kitten leads the way to her sitting room, which is directly off the kitchen. Like the rest of the house, the room has seen better days. The couch is an ugly shade of green, and covered with cat hairs. The carpet looks plain filthy. The smell in here is worse, and it soon becomes apparent why: there are several cat litters, which evidently haven't been cleaned out anytime recently, in the corner of the room. In fact, the smell is so overwhelming it's hard to appreciate the painting hanging over the dusty buffet. It's a portrait, not dissimilar in style to our girl, except that the subject is male. The same pale skin and quirk around the mouth. Is he from the same family? And is it the same artist?

Analiese and I scan for similarities, but a more detailed and considered study is required.

'Do you know who the subject is?' I ask Kitten.

'My father believed he was a relative. Obviously, a long way back.'

The smell. I can feel my stomach rising. Analiese, bless her quick thinking, comes up with the perfect solution to facilitate a quick exit.

'Do you mind if I take some photos?' she asks Kitten.

'Of course not.'

'Make sure you get the signature in,' I remind Analiese. There's a small squiggle in the bottom right-hand corner that could be the key to the artist of our painting, too.

Analiese takes a couple of hurried shots with her phone. Then we thank Kitten for her time, and almost fall over ourselves in our haste to get out of the house and into the fresh country air.

Analiese and I take in deep gulps of oxygen, the sunshine and the scent from next door's garden restoring some of our equilibrium. Both of us are too stunned to speak. It's hard to find a way to sum up the experience we've just had, to come to grips with Kitten and how she lives. Even the big picture defies words. From a grand house in Rotterdam to squalor — there's no other word for it — in a country town in New South Wales, Australia. From maids and expensive artworks and a spoiled little rich boy, to dust and cat hair and a sad, mentally disturbed woman who goes by a name akin to the cats she so identifies with.

Analiese seems every bit as lost for words as I am.

Chapter 24

Emma

'Fuck.'

The curse is sharp, rising above the piano music, and we all turn our heads to its source: Margaret, the oldest student in our beginner's ballet class and, I would have thought, the most unlikely to swear in such a vehement manner. As usual, she's in full costume, a silver-haired ballerina. She's normally the most elegant of us, her chin held at the perfect angle, her arms in a graceful arc, but right now her face is screwed up in pain, and her hands are clutching her leg.

'What's wrong?' Trish tentatively touches the older woman on the arm. We're all a bit wary of Margaret. I think she must have had an important job in her day, perhaps an executive of some sort: she looks as though she might snap an instruction to you at any moment.

'My knee …' Margaret replies through gritted teeth. 'I've pulled something.'

There's an injury of some description every week. Trish had to miss a few classes when she twisted her ankle. Another lady hurt her back.

I'm beginning to realise that ballet is more about brute strength than elegance.

Margaret tries to hobble towards a seat, but her leg is having none of it. 'Ouch. Fuck. Fuck. *Fuck.*'

It's quite difficult not to laugh out loud each time she swears, it sounds so *wrong* coming from her seemingly prim mouth.

'Here, let me help.' I hook one of her arms around my shoulders. 'Trish, you take the other side.'

Using the both of us as crutches, Margaret limps her way towards one of the plastic chairs. We manoeuvre her into sitting position, her injured leg jutting out in front.

'Thank you, ladies,' she barks. 'This is *so* annoying.'

'Can we call someone for you?' Miss Sophia enquires, looking anxious. All the other injuries sustained in her class have been relatively minor. This is the first time someone has needed to be helped off the dance floor.

'My husband.' Margaret indicates a light-coloured leather handbag propped on one of the other chairs. 'If someone can get my bag, I'll call him myself.'

I go and get her bag. It's really quite beautiful, Margaret's bag. Soft platinum-coloured leather. Gucci. I've never held a Gucci handbag before, not even a knock-off one. It's surprisingly squashy, yet at the same time it feels solid and enduring, as though it will last forever.

'Nice bag,' Trish breathes in admiration.

'I've always wanted one.' Margaret's shrug is brusque. 'So I treated myself for my sixtieth birthday. Every woman my age should have a handbag she loves. I use it every day, no point in leaving it to gather dust when I waited all my life to afford it.'

A designer handbag, coveted for years before finally being purchased. We're all enthralled.

Plucking out her phone, she calls her husband. We all stand and wait. It hasn't occurred to anyone, not even Miss Sophia, to resume dancing.

'I've hurt my leg,' Margaret informs her husband. 'I can't bear weight. No, I don't need an ambulance, I'm sure it will be fine in a few days. A torn muscle, I'd say. I need you to come and get me. What? Oh, for God's sake, Frank, it's always the same story with you. Okay, I'll try to get a lift from someone.' She terminates the call, and addresses all of us. 'Does anyone have a car?'

One by one, we shake our heads.

Maybe it's not so odd that nobody has a car. The single twenty-somethings probably can't afford one, not with the horrendous insurance for young drivers. Trish is within walking distance. I live a short bus ride away. And this is inner-city Dublin; it's easy to get by without a car.

'I suppose I'll have to get a taxi, then,' Margaret concludes in a matter-of-fact tone.

'I'll go home with you,' I offer, feeling sorry for her. 'You'll need some help.'

'Thank you, Emma.'

Miss Sophia phones the taxi company, and finally resumes class while Trish and I help Margaret outside.

Rain is beginning to spatter the footpath. Luckily, the taxi doesn't take long and we help Margaret into the back seat before the rain really starts to bucket. Poor Trish gets soaked on her way back inside.

'Done yourself an injury, love?' the cabbie enquires cheerfully, as he pulls away from the kerb.

Margaret snorts. She's probably thinking about the inconvenience of the next few days. I know I would be.

'She's hurt her leg,' I reply on her behalf.

For a while we say nothing, the cab driver, Margaret and me. The wipers are screeching against the windscreen, the rubber obviously needing to be replaced. The noise makes me wince each time. Margaret must find it highly irritating, too.

'Was your husband at work?' I ask after a few minutes.

'Yes.'

'My husband works shifts too. It's a pain.' Eddie isn't my husband, but I know he wouldn't mind me describing him as such: quite the opposite, in fact.

'It's not shift work. He's on call all hours of the day and night. It's ridiculous, Emma, and bloody dangerous too.'

'Where does he work?' I ask, intrigued.

'The National Drugs Unit.'

'Oh.' I blush. God knows why. It's not like *I'm* on drugs. Guilt by association, I suppose.

I wonder if Margaret's husband — Frank, I think she said his name was — has ever come across Jamie. Jamie has had so many convictions, it's quite possible. I wonder what Margaret would say if she knew that my ex, the father of my child, is one of the addicts who cause her husband to work all hours and put himself in needless danger.

'Want some gum?' I ask, completely at a loss as to what else to say.

She nods, helping herself to the fresh packet I'm holding out. 'Thank you.'

We chew through the few minutes it takes to get to Margaret's house — a charming terrace a few suburbs away.

'Can you help me get her inside?' I ask the driver.

'No problems, love.' He unbuckles himself and jumps out into the rain.

Together we support Margaret as she hops up the short pathway, wait while she finds her keys, and make sure she is alright before we leave.

'Where to now, love?'

Back in the taxi, I realise the driver has kept the meter running.

'Turn back the way you came,' I reply, feeling slightly sick at the thought of what this good deed is going to cost.

By the time he drops me home, the fare is almost seventy euros.

I don't have enough on me, and once again the meter stays running as I rush inside to get the extra cash.

Chapter 25

Louise

I've made friends with Analiese. All that time together in the car, the mutual — totally bizarre — experience of Kitten, the nice lunch we had in the town centre afterwards, followed by the extra favour I asked of her before we left for home.

'There's someone in the area I know. Do you mind if we drop by quickly?'

Analiese didn't hesitate. 'Sure. Do you have the address?'

'Yes.' I reeled off the house number and street name from memory, and Analiese put the details into her SatNav.

It was only a five-minute drive from the town centre. As Analiese followed the voice prompts, turning through the neat grid of streets on the edges of the town, my knees began to knock. What was I thinking, dropping by like this? What if the woman thought I was harassing her? What if she got offended, or frightened? Called the police? But how could I be this close — *five minutes away* — and not try? Just one look was all I needed. Then I could strike her off the list.

By the time we got there — a single-storey cottage on a square block — and I emerged from the car, my legs could barely support me.

'I won't be long,' I promised Analiese weakly.

The house looked normal. Not neglected, like Kitten's. Not too pristine and magazine-like, a look the neighbouring house was obviously trying to achieve. As I went to knock on the door, it whisked open, and a woman — obviously on her way out somewhere — came unexpectedly face to face with me. We both jumped.

'Sorry.' My voice was shaky as I apologised. 'I was about to knock. I'm looking for Janet Mitchell.'

'I'm Janet Mitchell.' She raised her chin a fraction, and I had a proper look at her.

She could have been my mother. The right age, the right physique. Even her hair was similar: copper, cut to her jaw line. But her face was wrong. Too narrow. Her eyes, her nose, her chin, all those features were wrong too.

'Sorry, Mrs Mitchell,' I apologised again. 'I'm Louise—'

Recognition dawned. 'Oh, you're the girl who wrote looking for her mother.'

'Yes. I was in the area …' I looked over my shoulder at Analiese's car, goodness knows why. A nervous reaction, I suppose. Analiese was doing something on her phone. Checking on baby Stella, no doubt. 'I hope you don't mind me calling in out of the blue like this …'

She shook her head, this woman who, from a distance at least, could have been my mother. 'Of course not … I should have responded to your letter. It's been a busy few weeks. I feel terrible now to have kept you waiting, wondering …'

'No, no, it's fine.' It wasn't fine. It was excruciatingly awkward.

Both of us apologising inanely, and still standing a little bit too close to each other. 'I'd better go. My friend is waiting.'

She stayed there at the door, Janet Mitchell, and watched me retrace my steps down her front path, and into the passenger seat of the car. I didn't need to turn around to see the pity written all over her too-narrow face.

'Who was that?' Analiese asked in a friendly tone as she turned the key in the ignition.

She caught me at a bad moment. If I hadn't felt so suddenly and utterly despondent, and so terribly stupid for calling unannounced on the woman (who had quite simply been too busy to respond to my letter, hardly a crime), I might not have answered so honestly.

'It was someone I thought could be my mother ...'

'Really?' Analiese cast me a shocked glance before fixing her eyes back on the road. 'So you don't know where you mother is?'

'No ... She left when I was eight.'

It took the entire journey back to Sydney, the best part of two hours, to tell Analiese everything. The day my mother left, what had gone on before, the debilitating confusion afterwards, Simon and all his contradictions, the private investigator, the whole lot. I'm not used to telling people my life story, and so I haven't yet mastered a short version. I've told Dan, and Mary to a lesser extent, over numerous sittings. With Analiese it all whooshed out at once. Like air from a balloon, only slower. Analiese asked some questions, but mostly she listened, all the way up the freeway, through the outskirts of Sydney, whizzing through the harbour tunnel.

'I'm glad I know this about you,' she said when we were minutes away from home.

'I'm sorry I monopolised the conversation.' I felt quite sheepish in the aftermath of my outpouring. 'You must be looking forward to getting back to Stella.'

'I am. I can't wait to see her.' Analiese smiled, excitement lighting up her plump face. 'I enjoyed today, don't get me wrong. But I miss her now. I can't wait to get my hands on her.' She pulled into my street, parking neatly outside my apartment block. Before I could unbuckle my belt, she leaned over and hugged me. She felt squashy and warm, and seemed to be completely unaware of how embarrassed I was.

'You've got to be strong, Louise. I never realised just how strong you have to be ... To be a mother, that is ... Maybe your mum simply wasn't strong enough.'

And so we're friends, Analiese and me. In just one day, one car trip, we became friends. I don't make friends easily. Neither, incidentally, does Emma. We're bad for each other in that way. Living next door, she saw everything that happened to me, and I saw everything that happened to her. We never had to divulge something the other knew absolutely nothing about, never had to master the skill of getting past that initial politeness you have with a stranger. We never learnt how to find out what makes someone tick, or how and when to reveal your true self, getting the timing right. She was always there for me. I was always there for her. Even when I was in London and New York, I still felt I had that close-range view into her life, that intimacy. But now, with an eleven-hour time difference and 17,000 kilometres between us, it's not the same.

When I got inside after Analiese's hug, I didn't quite know what to do with myself. I opened my worksheet and deleted Janet Mitchell from Bowral. I made a cup of coffee I had no interest in drinking. Then, because I couldn't help myself, I rang Emma. It was early in the morning, too early for her to be up for work for at least another hour.

She pretended to be cross with me.

'For fuck's sake, Lou, do you know what time it is?'

I laughed. God, it was good to hear her voice.

Chapter 26

Emma

Someone is knocking on our door. I'm in the bedroom, half-dressed.

'Eddie, can you get that?' I holler.

He doesn't respond. I hear water running in the bathroom. Damn it, he must be shaving.

'Isla?' I call out next, increasing my volume because I can hear music playing in her bedroom. I've noticed that she's been doing this more often, playing music alone in her room. It seems awfully grown up for a five-year-old. It's consoling, though, that she alternates the pop music with more age-appropriate make-believe games.

'Yeah, Mammy?' She comes to the door of her bedroom as I come to the door of mine. We confer across the hallway. She's wearing a turquoise top and bright green jeans. It's her third outfit so far this afternoon, not counting her school uniform.

'Did you hear the door, love?'

'Oh, is someone there?' Her small face brightens with excitement, and just like that she's a little girl once more.

'Can you go and see who it is? If it looks like someone selling some-thing, pretend we're not here.'

Isla skips down the hallway, rising on her tiptoes to peek through the peephole.

'It's a man with flowers, Mammy. A big, big bunch of them.'

Then, completely forgetting to check with me first, she turns the key in the lock and begins to open the door.

'Isla!' I squeal as I dive into the bedroom for cover. Whoever is dropping off flowers — it must be the wrong address — doesn't need to be confronted by my half-naked body.

Grabbing a blouse from the wardrobe — not the one I was search-ing for when I was interrupted by the knocking — and quickly buttoning it up, I can hear Isla conducting a conversation. Quite obviously, I still can't trust her when it comes to strangers!

By the time I emerge, she is in the process of closing the door while trying to keep hold of one of the biggest bouquets I've ever seen in my life.

'They're not for us.' I shake my head ruefully as I relieve her of them.

'They are,' she insists. 'The man knew your name.'

'He did?' I'm surprised.

'He said he was Margaret's husband. Who's Margaret, Mammy?'

Oh, that makes more sense. 'Margaret is a lady from my ballet class.' I bury my face in the flowers, inhaling their scent. An extravagant yet traditional combination of roses, carnations and lilies, whites and yellows fresh against dark green foliage. 'I helped her out last week. I think this is her way of saying thanks.'

In a sudden, quite inexplicable, burst of curiosity, I dart towards the living room, to the window. A few doors down, there's a man getting into his car, a white new-model Mercedes. He has a neat haircut and a suit. Is this Margaret's overworked drug-busting husband? He seems to glance my way, and I step back from view, flushing guiltily.

Eddie comes out of the bathroom, a lovely waft of after-shave following him.

'A secret admirer?' he asks, raising one dark brow at the flowers in my arms.

Isla answers before I can. 'They're from Margaret to say thank you to Mammy for helping her.'

'Let's hope they're a good omen,' Eddie says, and reaches for his jacket, hanging on the back of one of the dining chairs. 'Are you two ready?'

We're going to the bank, the three of us, to see if they'll give us a mortgage. I've taken a half day off work, Eddie is wearing his one and only suit, and even Isla seems to realise this is a big thing.

'I'll turn off the music and get my coat,' she says obligingly.

'I just need to put these in water,' I reply in turn. 'And run a comb through my hair.'

In the kitchen, as I unwrap the flowers from their cellophane, I discover a business card in their midst. On the back, in scrawling writing: *Thank you from both of us.*

Turning the card over, I read the navy-blue font on the front.

Frank Hurley, Sergeant, National Drugs Unit. 01 9854 5582

Well, there's a number I won't ever be calling. All the same, I keep the card, tucking it into the pocket of my skirt.

'Isla, you wait out here … Look, they have colouring pencils …'

'But I want to come inside and listen …' Isla's lower lip thickens. She has a lot invested in this house, too. I regret now that we took her to see it, and that we told her about today; how we were going to ask the bank for a loan so we could buy the house. She knows far too much.

I whisper in her ear. 'Sorry, pet ... this discussion is for grown-ups only ... You'll have more fun out here, you really will.'

She sits petulantly, pulling the colouring paper close so she can assess what she is required to colour in. Reassured that she will stay put, I walk into the meeting room where Eddie and the loan officer, Dermot Fitzgerald, are waiting.

'Sorry to keep you. My daughter believes she should be involved in everything.' Smiling wryly, I stick out my hand for Dermot to shake, and exchange a nervous glance with Eddie before sitting down. The three of us are in a circle around a table. The room is characterless and very small — space is clearly at a premium here. Dermot has a copy of our loan application on the table in front of him. My handwriting looks nice and neat from this angle. I spent a lot of time on that application form, not to mention all the supporting paperwork that had to go with it. Payslips, bank statements, identification (which proved a pain as neither of us has a passport or a current driver's licence). It's all there, everything the bank asked for, bound together with a pink paperclip from Isla's stationery set.

Dermot clears his throat. 'We've assessed your application ...' His voice gives him away. It has that nervous thread that creeps in when one has to impart bad news. 'I'm sorry, but we're not in a position to offer you a loan at this point in time ...'

I shouldn't be so shocked. After all, I knew there was a fair chance of this outcome. I remember reading somewhere, a couple of months ago, that forty per cent of mortgage applications are turned down these days. Credit of any description is becoming a rare commodity.

'I took a half day from work for this,' I tell him, a dangerous wobble in my own voice. 'Why the hell didn't you phone and spare us the effort of coming in here?'

'We have a policy to speak to our customers face to face, to explain the reasoning behind our decisions …'

'I couldn't care less about your stupid bloody policies—'

Eddie reaches out his hand and takes mine, in an obvious effort to calm me. 'As per your policy, Dermot,' he says carefully, 'can you let us know exactly where our application didn't hold up?'

Dermot nods, clearly relieved to have one of us reacting in a sensible manner. 'Of course. There were two things, really … One in relation to you, Mr McCarthy, and one in relation to Miss Kelleher.' He regards Eddie with his pale blue eyes which, I decide nastily, are too small in his slightly pudgy face. 'Your income seems to be largely comprised of shift allowance rather than base pay, and the bank views this as high risk.'

Eddie's jaw sets in a tight line. 'My income has stayed the same for virtually the last six years. *Despite* all the economic turmoil. In fact, I would regard my income as quite *low risk.*'

Dermot, obviously not wanting to get into a detailed discussion about the bank's approach to risk, nervously turns his eyes to me.

'Through our standard background checks, we discovered a number of concerning matters in relation to Miss Kelleher, too. A shoplifting conviction, a number of unpaid phone bills …'

Heat rushes to my face. 'That was a long time ago,' I mumble. 'I was a teenager … I'm a different person now, I have a good job, I'm a *mother* …'

'Nevertheless, the question mark is there, and combined with the composition of Mr McCarthy's income …'

Well, there we are. It's not one of us, it's both. There's a certain comfort in this.

There's nothing more to be said. When we open the door of the meeting room, Isla, having no real concept of failure, jumps to her feet.

'Are we buying the house?' she squeals.

Even Dermot winces at thought of disappointing her.

'No,' Eddie replies flatly, and takes her by the hand. I can see he wants to get out of here as fast as he can.

As I hurry after him, I glance distractedly at the table where Isla was sitting, and I see her picture lying there, almost complete but for an uncoloured patch of grass. It's a house, of course. With red bricks, windows filled in yellow, and a garden full of flowers.

The kind of place that, because of Eddie's shift work and my inability to say no to Jamie, we will never own.

Chapter 27

Louise

'It's not the same artist,' Analiese declares.

'No, it's not.'

The technique is quite different. We can both see this now that we've blown up the photographs of Kitten's painting and carefully compared them with our unidentified girl.

'I wonder, though,' Analiese tilts her head, her eyes flicking once again from the photograph in her hand to the girl in the painting, 'if the subjects are from the same family.'

'There *seems* to be a resemblance,' I agree. It's hard to tell for sure, though. The look — pale skin, thin lips, frizzy hair — is common for the era, and we're both aware of this.

Stella makes a gurgling sound, as though to say 'look over here at me'. She is propped in her stroller, her eyes bright in her chubby face. Her hands and feet are in motion, waving and kicking. She is quite obviously enjoying her new surroundings.

'Are you trying to talk to us, Stella?' Analiese coos.

Stella responds with a dimpled smile and another gurgle. She really is quite gorgeous. Analiese is lucky to have such a beautiful, good-natured baby, and Stella is even luckier with her clearly devoted mother. That mysterious bond between mothers and daughters. Is it nature, nurture ... or sheer luck?

'I have a contact in Amsterdam,' I say, getting back to the job at hand. 'Jacquie's been very responsive so far. She didn't come up with anything on our girl, but it wasn't for want of trying. I'll send these photos to her, along with the names of Kitten's grandparents, and see if she uncovers anything.' My eyes fix on the signature in the bottom right-hand corner of the painting. 'Who knows, Jacquie might recognise that squiggle.'

Analiese is thoughtful. 'We should contact Kitten's brother, too ... I'd really like to see the painting he inherited ...'

'I suppose we can *try* to get his contact details from Kitten ...' I trail off. Kitten obviously has an aversion to answering her phone — though she must pay the bill, because she's still connected — and despite the fact that landing on her doorstep proved to be rather effective, I really don't have the time to take another day off work.

'Leave Kitten to me,' Analiese says airily. 'I have all the time in the world. I'll ring and ring and ring until she answers.'

'Are you sure you want to do this? I mean, you're meant to be on maternity leave ...'

'I'm very sure.' Analiese smiles at her daughter. 'It will keep Mummy sane, won't it darling?' Then she looks back at the painting. 'By the way, our girl is looking good, Louise. You're almost there, I see.'

'Yes, just another few days. Then I have to repair that poor face of hers.'

'Are you going to line the back?'

'That's the plan. Give the new inset something to adhere to, make the whole thing more sturdy. Hopefully, it will last another couple of hundred years.'

Analiese goes closer, her fingers running along the edges of the canvas. 'There's not a lot of margin to take the inset from.'

'No. But I think I can manage it. Just.'

'Yes …' Analiese nods slowly. 'And it would be such a shame to have to use a different canvas for the inset.' She turns to face me. 'I feel a little jealous, to be honest. I can happily do without the drudgery of the cleaning, but I love this part. Trying to repair the damage as best you can. Seeing, and knowing you are responsible for achieving, the end result.'

'Come in any time, Analiese.' I touch her on the arm to convey my sincerity. 'I could do with a second opinion. And bring Stella. She seems perfectly at home here.'

'I might do. You know, today wasn't as hard as I thought it would be.' She pulls a face. 'I'll never forget that first trip. Just trying to get from the car park to here. What a nightmare! I'm so glad I traded in that huge unwieldy pram for this stroller. It's so much easier to get around with.'

Quite suddenly I remember having a similar conversation with Emma about Isla's pram. It must have been three or four years ago — Isla was about one at the time — and Emma was so thrilled with her new stroller, it could have been a brand-new car that she'd bought.

Shortly afterwards they leave, Analiese pushing Stella in her stroller, the baby's eyes wide and darting from side to side, taking everything in. As they go, they are stopped every few steps. Everyone needs one last baby fix: Gabriella, Peter, even Heidi, whom I wouldn't put down as particularly maternal. They tickle Stella's chin, pull on her bare little toes, and oohh and aahh over her. It's touching to watch.

They are lovely people. All of them. In fact, I've never worked with such a nice group, never felt so much at home, or so integral to the team. My contract is already three months in. Suddenly, it seems far too short, this twelve-month contract. It's going to be hard to leave when it's up. To wrench myself away from these people and start all over again, in some other gallery in some other city, who knows where.

Dan is away on a business trip, following up a story in Perth, which I was stunned to discover is the best part of a five-hour flight from Sydney. It is vast, this country.

Dan's been gone three days already and won't be home until late on Friday night. I miss him. Physically. Emotionally. In every way. I keep thinking of things I want to tell him. About work. About my mother. Small things. Big things. They're building up in my head. But I seem to lose track as soon as he phones. It's only afterwards that I think of them, all the things I meant to tell him.

Joe emerges from his bedroom. I am sitting on the sofa in the living room, in the middle of making phone calls to Elizabeth Mitchells.

'I'm getting a beer,' he says. 'Want one?'

I put down my phone. 'That would be lovely, Joe. Thanks.'

Sounds emanate from the kitchen: cupboard doors opening and closing, the clink of glass, the roll of bottle tops on the counter. A few seconds later, Joe reappears, a bottle in each hand.

'Here.' Carefully, he hands mine over.

I thank him and he sits down next to me. He seems tired, even a little downcast.

'How's the writing going?' I ask, taking a sip. It's icy cold, just the way I like it.

'It's not,' Joe replies shortly.

'Hard day at the office?' I flash him a sympathetic smile.

'It's been a hard week.' He sighs and runs a hand through his hair, making it stick up at the front, the same way Dan's hair is inclined to stick up first thing in the morning. 'Sometimes I don't really know why I do this job. It's so frustrating, so bloody *laborious* ...'

'You do it because you're good at it,' I tell him in a chirpy tone, because he is clearly in need of cheering up. 'And because you love what you do ...'

'I don't love it.' He scowls at me. 'Some days I actually *hate* it. And I'm not good at it, Louise. I've just spent an entire day labouring over one *stupid* page. Bloody hell, I think I wasted an hour this morning on a *stupid* word ... one word, that was all, a whole hour gone ...'

He has surprised me. It never occurred to me it could take him that long — a full hour — to find the right word. Me, yes, it could take that long. Because I've never been good with words or anything to do with reading or writing. Him, no. He's an author, for goodness sake.

'I think you're a perfectionist,' I say eventually, having given it some thought. 'You're not just looking for any old ordinary word. You're looking for the perfect word, a word that will say more than it needs to say, a *super* word. The rest of us would just make do. Not Joe Connolly, though.'

He doesn't return my smile. Quite obviously, nothing I can say will coax him out of this negative mood, so I switch on the TV, surfing the channels until I settle on a program that I know we both like. Joe, like Emma and me, is a reality TV fan. To be brutally honest, I watch it so I can feel good about myself. *Secret Family, Intervention,* even *Wife Swap.* Watching how people live, witnessing their mistakes, their failures and just how much they can hurt each other, makes me feel that my own situation isn't so bad after all. It's terrible of me, I know, but I can't seem to help it. Joe, on the other hand, watches reality TV for an entirely different reason.

'You just couldn't make up stuff like this,' he often says, busily scribbling in his notebook.

We've spent many contented evenings in front of the box, me feeling progressively relieved that I'm not some kind of addict or about to be evicted or lose my job, and Joe happily harnessing idea after idea for his writing.

He doesn't take any notes tonight but the beer relaxes him and he seems to be in a slightly better mood by the time he says goodnight. I watch TV for another half hour, but bed beckons. I'm tired from work, and from all the dead-end phone calls I made before Joe interrupted me. Most of all I'm tired from missing Dan. Everything seems so much harder when he's not here.

Just as I'm about to fall asleep, my phone beeps with a message.

She's not your mum. Will check the other one tomorrow. Sweet dreams.

Before leaving for Perth, Dan reviewed my spreadsheet to check the status of the Janet and Elizabeth Mitchells living there. Most of them had replied to my letter. All but four, which was an astoundingly good response, all things considered. Two of the four lived too far away from the city for Dan to call on them, but the other two were relatively accessible, or so he said. He insisted on dropping in on them, even when I said it was too much to ask of him, too much trouble.

Never mind. Better luck tomorrow. Love you.

For a few moments I stare at the last two words of my response, before replacing them with *Thank you.*

I do love Dan. I love the sharpness of his mind, his unwavering generosity, his sexy smile, the timbre and articulateness of his voice, his boisterous in-your-face family, absolutely everything about him.

And I know he cares about me, too. I know he misses me as much as I miss him. I know that he's terribly busy with this story he's following up, all the loose ends that need to be tied up before he jumps on the plane back to Sydney, but yet he has made the time to call on a complete stranger in order to help me with my search. This speaks volumes to me.

But, in the same way as my job at the gallery and my lovely working relationship with my colleagues will come to an end, so too will this relationship — love, or whatever it is — with Dan.

It won't be for months yet, but already I feel quite frightened at the thought.

Chapter 28

Emma

I'm still furious. Eddie has calmed down: he's subdued but resigned. I've only got angrier. With Eddie, for planting the idea in my head in the first place. With myself, for falling in love with the house, and for being so damned stupid as to think we had a chance. With Dermot, the mortgage officer who so flippantly wasted our time, and his thick-headed adherence to policy. And with Jamie. That shoplifting charge was *his* fault. I was doing it for *him*. Four packets of paracetamol, hidden up my jacket sleeve. I would have got away with it too, had Jamie not been hanging around outside, looking suspicious. The security guard recognised him, and when he saw me come out of the chemist's, and realised I was with Jamie, he stopped me. I bet Jamie can't even remember. He's had so many altercations with the police, security guards, every authority figure you can imagine, I bet he doesn't remember I got charged because of him. His memory is riddled anyway, thanks to all the drugs. *I remember.* The guilt. The shame. My mother's shocked expression when she came to collect me from the police station. Jamie's selfish fury that I hadn't been successful. I can recall every excruciating detail.

Isla comes out of her room, holding her backpack. 'Mammy, I've got one pair of jeans, one skirt, one T-shirt, one top, two knickers ...'

She's done well, for a five-year-old. In fact, she's a dab hand at packing. Every fortnight. Winter and summer. It's relentless. 'Very good. But what are you going to wear to bed?'

'Oh.' She claps her hand over her mouth. 'My pyjamas.'

She rushes back to her bedroom. 'And don't forget your toothbrush,' I call after her.

There has been a shift these past few weeks. She is not as anxious about the visits as she used to be. I suppose it's because Jamie has been making an effort. I glean some details of this from Isla, but mostly from Sue, his mother, who phones me periodically to keep me up to date.

'He's been sober two months.'

'He's seeing an excellent counsellor. Very knowledgeable and supportive.'

'He's looking for a job, Emma.'

She's deluding herself. That he'll stay sober. That anyone will employ him. I suppose mothers are the most susceptible of creatures. They so badly want to believe the best of their children. They lay all their hopes on the slightest improvement. They truly believe they can love their children out of any fix. Poor Sue. The harsh truth is that she has enabled Jamie more than helped him. She has paid his bills. She welcomes him into her home, embraces him in the family, no matter how badly or how often he lets her down.

'He's my son,' I've heard her cry. 'I can't turn my back on him.'

You have to. Turn your back on them. Because otherwise they'll drag you down, too. You have to walk away, not have them ruin your life along with their own. This is what all the experts say.

There's a knock on the door. It's him. My anger surges again. Isla and I arrive at the door together.

'Your toothbrush?' I double-check.

'Oh golly, I forgot again!' She scoots off in the direction of the bathroom.

I open the door. He's standing there, hands in his pockets. He looks neater, cleaner. His skin is brighter. No, I will not be sucked in like his mother.

I have no intention of speaking to him, but suddenly the anger is there again, and I can't contain it, can't help myself.

'Do you remember the day I got charged with shoplifting?' My voice is shrill, nasty. 'The day you asked me to get you the paracetamol? The chemist's in Templebar ... Remember?'

His face is completely blank. Just as I suspected.

'They charged me because I was *with you*. If I had been on my own, I would have only got a caution, not that I would have dreamt of stealing in the first place without *you* to egg me on. But because of you and your history, *I was charged*.' I stop to take in a sharp breath. 'I just got turned down for a mortgage because of that day ... *And you can't even fuckin' remember!*'

I'm hot. The weather has changed, and quite suddenly my winter clothes are suffocating. God, I hate this time of year. There's no other option: I will have to strip off a layer of clothes. Or else I'll collapse and be the next casualty in Miss Sophia's ballet class for beginners.

When there's a break in the music, I leave the barre, where we have been doing a rather gruelling series of exercises, and hurry towards my sports bag. Quickly, I shuffle out of my long-sleeved T-shirt. I have a white tank top underneath. Not ideal, but then nothing is. Nothing can hide it.

As the music starts again, I slip back into my spot, holding onto the barre lightly with my right hand while lifting my left leg up and out, up and out, again and again. All the time I stare steadfastly ahead, concentrating fiercely, on the movement, on the music, on not giving into the temptation to look in the mirror.

'Face a partner, please,' Miss Sophia calls, twiddling once more with the music system.

Nine times out of ten Trish is my partner. She twirls around to face me. Her smile slips when she sees this version of me, the 'summer me', the one who cannot always wear high-necked, long-sleeved tops. I don't need to look in the mirror to appreciate how shocking it is for her. The angry, mottled red against my otherwise pale skin. My right arm, my chest, the base of my neck, marred and hideous.

Trish is too polite to say anything. They all are. Quite obviously the others have noticed, too. How could they not? Their quick, furtive glances make my skin burn anew. It's hot and tight and very scratchy.

'Step one, two, three ... turn ...'

I try to listen to Miss Sophia's instructions, to time my movements to Trish's, but all I can hear, all I can see, is Jamie.

He could make me do anything. Half the time he didn't even need to ask. All it took was a look.

'Stretch high ... higher ...' Miss Sophia commands.

It hurts when I stretch, an uncomfortable pinching sensation. The doctors said it would. The skin has lost its suppleness, its elasticity. It has been grafted in from elsewhere, and it's resentful, unco-operative.

'Look at me,' I hiss at Jamie, this time in my head, my arms and legs doing ballet movements independently, it seems, of my brain. 'Just look at me. This is your fault, too. And I bet, just like everything else you've fucked up, you don't give it more than a moment's thought.'

Chapter 29

Louise

Dan texts me. He's outside. I slip out of bed and tiptoe through the shadowy apartment, anxious not to wake Joe. Actually, I'm surprised Joe didn't go out tonight — he's a Friday night clubber. Then again, Dan wasn't going to come over, given that his flight was getting in so late, so Joe's social plans were irrelevant. Until I texted Dan: *I'm still awake if you want to call around.*

We were going to catch up tomorrow. That was the plan. Then I realised that I was aching for him so much I wouldn't sleep a wink.

His reply came within seconds: *I've asked the taxi driver to do a U turn.*

Wearing my pink and blue stripy cotton pyjamas, I open the front door as quietly as I can, and there he is in his dark suit and white shirt, looking a little crumpled from the flight. I fling myself into his arms. Neither of us says a word, we just stand there, hugging so tightly it's quite hard to breathe.

'Joe's here …' I whisper.

'Typical,' he retorts, his voice too loud.

'Ssshhh ...'

He comes inside, softly closing the door behind him. Holding hands, stifling giggles, we stealthily make our way to my room. As soon as the bedroom door is shut, we're in each other's arms again. Which one of us thought it was feasible to wait until tomorrow?

'I missed you so much,' he says between kisses. His hands, cool from the outside air, slide inside the top of my pyjamas.

'Me too.' It seems lacking, my response, but I can't think of anything else to say, anything that would adequately describe just how desperately I missed him.

His fingers find my nipples, teasing them until they're hard little buttons, and it's all I can do not to moan out loud.

'I missed your breasts.' His breath is hot in my ear. It sends a spike of desire right through the centre of my body. 'And I missed this.' His hand slips inside the waistband of my pyjamas, between my legs. This time I can't help it, I moan, a wanton sound in the stillness of the night. God, I hope Joe cannot hear.

Within moments we're in bed, naked, our clothes on the floor, to be recovered sometime tomorrow. Greedily, I luxuriate in his body, the solidness of his torso, his narrow hips as they fuse with mine. I missed the smell of him, the mix of his own Dan smell and the traces of sandalwood in his aftershave. I missed the leathery feel of the skin on his thighs. I missed how my muscles inadvertently squeeze when he's inside me, how that makes *him* the one who can't help moaning, the frenzy, the complete loss of self as we both hurtle towards a climax.

Afterwards, lying spooned in his arms, I smile as I whisper, 'I would be quite amazed if Joe didn't hear that.'

'The only way to wake that boy is to whack him with a boot,' Dan replies dryly.

'You tired?'

'Exhausted.' He yawns. I can't see his face, but I think he may have closed his eyes.

'Before you go to sleep ... Did you manage to see her?'

'Her' is the Elizabeth Mitchell he was going to try to call on today.

'Yes. She was lovely. Again, very apologetic that she hadn't replied to your letter. But she wasn't your mother.'

I'm curious for more detail. Living, breathing Janet and Elizabeth Mitchells fascinate me. 'What did she look like?'

'Blonde hair. Well-dressed. She's an executive in a mining company. Busy job, which is why she didn't have time to reply.' Dan pulls his arm tighter around my midriff. 'Sorry, Louise. Another disappointment.'

'Not so much.' I'm more philosophical than disappointed. I can't imagine my mother in Perth. I don't know precisely why, I just can't see her there. Not big enough? Too remote? Despite being born into a rural family, she wasn't a country girl. She liked people and bustle and action. For some reason I remember this aspect of her personality quite clearly.

Anyway, Dan is back. I feel relieved, elated, quite the opposite of disappointed.

Dan and I spend a great part of the weekend in bed. We get up late on Saturday morning, have a passionate encounter mid afternoon, retire early, and follow a similar pattern on Sunday. Joe gives us a wide berth. I am certain he heard us on Friday night, though Dan remains adamant he didn't.

Monday dawns with blue skies and I wake feeling insanely happy.

Dan finally went home late last night, and his smell, his presence lingers. As I walk into work, I fear it's obvious from the glow of my skin, the sway of my body, exactly how I have spent the weekend.

'Morning, Louise.' I like the way Gabriella says my name, the way she rolls it in her mouth, as though it's something tasty she's eating. 'How was your weekend?'

'Lovely.' A blush accompanies my reply. 'How about you?'

'Yes. A good weekend. Everyone happy in the family.'

I'm under the impression that there are many spats and quarrels in Gabriella's extended family, violent disagreements with overzealous European-style gesturing, and that everyone being happy and peaceful is a rare occurrence.

'I have food,' she continues.

I don't know why she announces this fact as though it's a great surprise. Gabriella always has food on Monday mornings. Leftovers. Her quarrel-prone, food-loving family needs to learn not to over-cater. I mean this in the nicest possible way. Actually, I take that back. My stomach is already wondering what this 'food' is.

'Fruit cake,' Gabriella supplies. 'I'll bring it around at morning tea.'

A few minutes later, after a quick hello to Heidi, and a diversion to the kitchen to make myself a cup of coffee, I'm sitting at my desk, going through my email. Amid all the group messages and junk mail that arrived over the weekend, there's a message from Jacquie, my contact in Amsterdam.

Dear Louise,

I am pleased to say that I have identified the signature on your painting. I am sure that it is the mark of Jean-Baptiste Chevalier, a French painter known for both portraits and landscapes. Cheva-lier mainly worked and lived in Paris. I have also been successful in finding records of Mrs Brooks' grandparents, Willem and Inge Verbeck, and I am in the process of trying to trace the family history, to establish if their ancestors lived in Paris at any stage. This, I am sure you will appreciate, will take some time as well as the co-opera-tion of experts in other fields. I will contact you as I receive updates.

Kindest regards,

Jacquie

Oh my God. A breakthrough! At least one of the paintings that Kitten's grandparents brought with them to Australia — the painting that now hangs in Kitten's squalid sitting room — originally comes from France. Does that mean the family also originates from France, somewhere back along the line? Or did these paintings come into the possession of the Verbecks in some other manner, and have nothing at all to do with their ancestors?

The message was sent late Friday night. It has been sitting here all weekend, while I've been in bed with Dan.

I run next door to tell Gabriella, who has been labouring over the frame for even longer than I've been working on the painting.

'France!' she exclaims. Then she frowns down at the partially restored frame, the reconstructed parts white and unpainted next to the bronze colour of the rest. 'Well, I suppose that is possible, given the design and technique. It can be hard to distinguish at times, as you know … How very interesting!'

Back at my desk, I hesitate before calling Tom, who as curator should be top of the pecking order for breaking news like this. I call Analiese instead.

Her phone rings and rings. She must be feeding Stella, or settling her down for a nap. I leave her a voice message, my words tripping over each other in sheer excitement. 'The artist of Kitten's painting is Jean-Baptiste Chevalier. He's French. And if the male he painted is indeed related to our girl, that suggests she's French too.'

Tom is next. He answers his phone, listens, and then proceeds to ask lots of questions, questions I would have thought of myself if I weren't so keyed up. Specifics on the artist's life, his works, even the social circles he moved in. I take down all Tom's queries, and draft them into a comprehensive email back to Jacquie.

In reality, we've raised more questions than we've answered. We're a long way off proving anything; after all, it's not as if Jean-Baptiste Chevalier painted our girl. It was clearly someone else. Still, though, I'm delighted, thrilled even, at this small development.

When you've been searching long and hard with virtually no success, finding the smallest clue is redeeming in ways you cannot imagine.

A fresh possibility can keep you going for months, years even.

Chapter 30

Emma

Isla is excited. *I'm* excited. We're meeting Katie in Grafton Street this afternoon. We don't normally go into the city centre on Saturdays. Maybe it's the nicer weather that has prompted this change of plans. It was my idea, so I should really have a better grasp on what brought it about.

'What are you doing this weekend?' Katie asked the other day.

'Nothing. How about you?'

'I have some shopping to do,' she said in that airy voice of hers. 'I'll hit Grafton Street, I think.'

And in that instant, I wanted to go to Grafton Street too. The busy shops, the buzz on the street, the smell of coffee and food, the promise of buskers on the corners. I just wanted to go, it was that bloody simple.

'We'll meet you. Isla and me. Just for a milkshake. If that's alright.'

'Sure.'

Poor Katie. I ambushed her plans, forced myself and Isla upon her, and I can't even explain why. On the weekends Isla is in my care, we tend to hunker down, pottering, playing games, not venturing outside too much. I tend to cosset her, because always at the back of my mind there's the weekend after, when she's with Jamie and could be exposed to things no child should ever see.

Isla is trying on her third outfit for our little excursion.

'How about this one, Mammy?'

It's a glittery number Jamie's mother bought for her, more suited to a New Year's Eve party than an ordinary Saturday afternoon.

'Slightly too dressed up,' I say tactfully.

Finally she settles on a white and red top, and black leggings. Her total ensemble is quite similar to my white shirt, black jeans and red pumps.

'Look, we're matching,' Isla exclaims in a proud tone that implies she has done this on purpose.

Grafton Street is busier than I imagined, and I keep a tight hold of her hand. It's a predominantly young crowd: teenage girls with short skirts, high shoes and shopping bags swinging from their hands; teenage boys with T-shirts, Converse sneakers, and phones glued to their palms. Isla and I walk slowly, somewhat in awe.

'There's Katie,' Isla squeals, and slips out of my grip. For a moment she disappears and panic overwhelms me until I spot her, hanging off Katie, the two of them already laughing about something.

'Don't run off like that,' I chastise her as soon as I catch up. 'You could get lost.'

She's instantly contrite. 'I'm sorry, Mammy.'

I give Katie a sheepish smile. 'And I'm sorry we're a bit late ... We had a few wardrobe issues.'

'Oh, I only just got here,' she says. 'Let's go inside.'

The tables are packed with people, the volume of voices deafening, and I'm about to suggest we try somewhere else when the table right next to where we're standing is freed up. Katie and Isla pounce on the empty seats, laughing gleefully at our good luck, and I take their orders — milkshakes all round — and join the long queue at the counter.

'What are you two jabbering about?' I ask when I finally get back, balancing the milkshakes and a plate of oversized chocolate-chip cookies on a tray.

'I told Katie about the mean man at the bank who won't loan us the money,' Isla declares with a mutinous edge to her voice.

Oh dear. I really need to have a word with my daughter about keeping certain matters private, particularly when she's around Katie.

'He wasn't mean,' I say, giving Dermot Fitzgerald the benefit of the doubt. 'He was just keeping to the rules.'

Katie is looking at me. She's wearing one of her helpful expressions — I recognise it from work.

'My brother is a mortgage broker,' she says. 'I'll give you his card on Monday.'

That's nice of her, and it would be wise to get a second opinion, but I suspect Katie's brother will come to the same conclusion as Dermot Fitzgerald.

Eddie McCarthy: Shift Worker: Declined.

Emma Kelleher: Shoplifter: Declined.

'Thanks.' I force a smile, as though I really believe her brother could make any difference, and then take a big gulp of liquidised ice-cream and strawberry flavouring. 'Mmm … This is good …'

On Monday morning Katie's brother's card is perched on my keyboard: *William O'Mahony, Independent Mortgage Broker.*

I'll show it to Eddie when I get home, ask him what he thinks, if he's willing to be humiliated all over again. This morning I'm not in the right frame of mind for houses or mortgages: I'm too preoccupied with my annual performance review, which is scheduled to start in ten minutes. I have no idea what Brendan is planning to say, or what kind of performance rating he will give me, but I already feel defensive, and this is not good.

Soon I'm rapping on his office door, and summoning a smile as he calls me in.

'Well, Emma …' he begins officiously. 'You've done well this year … worked hard … had some challenges, some successes …'

This all sounds remarkably similar to last year. Really, I don't need to hear this waffle: I just want to know the end result, the rating he's given me. Here's how it works. All employees are rated one to five. One means you're fabulous. Five means they want to get rid of you.

'So …' At last he's getting to the point, the rating. 'I've given you a three. This means you're doing your job to the high standard we expect.'

The same result as last year, and all the years before that. Bastard. Why am I so upset? I should have seen this coming. Brendan sees me as average, and nothing I do — no matter how hard or long I work — will change this.

Swallowing the saliva that has built up in my mouth, I ask, 'And my salary?'

He smiles brightly. 'A one per cent increase.'

One per cent. Last year it was nothing. The year before it was a staggering — not — two per cent. In short, my salary, like me, is going nowhere.

'So that's it,' he concludes, shuffling the papers he's pretended to read from. 'Let's look forward to another successful year, eh?'

I stand up, because he expects me to take my leave now, perfectly happy to be rated as average, yet ready to put in an above-average effort, if you please. My hand is on the door handle. One of the few things I learned from that stupid leadership course was when to speak out, and when not to. This, I think, is one of those occasions where I must. Speak out. Take him to task. The thought of holding my tongue for another twelve months, and finding myself in precisely the same position this time next year, is motivation enough.

Turning around to face him, I enunciate my words clearly, so there's no mistake. 'I want you to know, Brendan, that I'm very disappointed with the rating you've given me, and with your proposed salary increase … I'm quite sure I'm worth more than that …'

Then I allow a few moments to lapse, so he has time to absorb what I've said, and the fact that I've considered it rather than blabbed it in the heat of the moment, before I open the door and make what I hope is a dignified exit.

I'm shaking. God, I really despise that man. Maybe I should look for something else. Qualifications aren't the be all and end all, and surely my experience will count for something out there in what the media is calling a 'seriously depressed job market'. I'll call some recruitment agencies, maybe tomorrow when I've calmed down. Yes, even if nothing comes of it, at least I'll feel I haven't taken this latest insult lying down.

Katie is hovering outside. She's obviously next in line.

'How did you go?' she asks breathlessly.

'Prick,' I mutter, then give her a half-apologetic smile before walking on. Even though none of this is her fault, I can't help some of my resentment spurting in her direction too. Undoubtedly, Brendan will give Katie a one or two. And a decent salary increase. Before I know it, I'll be reporting to Katie, not the other way around.

Still fuming, I try to do some work, my fingers banging the keyboard viciously as I answer some messages. I'm in full flight when my mobile phone beeps with an incoming text message. Probably Eddie checking how I got on.

The new message isn't from Eddie, it's from Jamie.

I need to talk to you. Can you call over tonight?

My mood changes instantly. From anger to fear, like the flick of a switch. Jamie never initiates contact outside Isla's drop-offs and pick-ups. This request isn't good. My fear is sharp and authentic, eclipsing the petty gripes about Brendan and my performance review.

Why? My fingers, so fast and furious a few moments ago, feel clumsy and slow. *What do you want?*

His reply comes moments later. I can hardly breathe while I wait for the beep.

Tell you when you get here.

No, it's not good. I have this sixth sense when it comes to Jamie. I always know when something bad is about to happen.

There's Katie walking by, on her way back from Brendan's office. She has a slight smile on her face. Yes, she's obviously pleased with how her review went, but she's trying not to show it because she's aware mine didn't go so well.

Lucky Katie. On the up and up in her job. With no drug addict ex to worry about. Lucky girl.

Chapter 31

Louise

There's a letter for me. On the table, where Joe leaves my post. That's not odd in itself — I have a fairly constant stream of mail, and most days there's at least one envelope with my name on it. What's odd is the yellow sticker indicating that this particular letter has been forwarded from the post office box I set up when I first came to Sydney, and the stamp, which has a picture of the Queen and evidently cost 87 pence. It must be from Bob. Yes, now that I've had a closer look I can see that the postmark is from his area. Yet, when I tear it open, I don't find Bob's looping scrawl but an official-looking letterhead and type.

Dear Miss Mitchell,

I'm writing in the capacity of executor to the last will and testament of Mr Bob K. Mitchell. Given my knowledge of Bob's personal situation, specifically his lack of close family and friends, I am aware that his death may be news to you and apologise for announcing it in this manner. Bob suffered a heart attack while he was shopping in the local village. He collapsed, an ambulance was called, but sadly the paramedics could not revive him.

As Bob's solicitor and executor, it is my job to settle his estate as per the instructions in his will. You are listed as the main beneficiary. However, I should point out that Bob's farm and home were under lease, and it appears, from a cursory examination of his finances, that he did not own any assets of major value. In the interests of transparency, I feel that it is appropriate to advise you that I do not expect your inheritance to be more than a few hundred pounds.

I will contact you again soon, probably within a month, to give you more information about Bob's assets and liabilities and the net worth of his estate. I apologise again if this letter is your only notification of his passing.

Yours sincerely,

Edward Ramshaw

Solicitor

Bob is dead.

Quite suddenly, my knees are too weak to support me and I slide down against the wall, the letter from Edward Ramshaw, Solicitor, fluttering from my grasp before landing wrong-side-up on my knees. Bob, *my only relative*, is dead.

We met only the once. At his farm, a rundown jumble of buildings deep in the Dorset countryside. He made me tea, and then took me for a walk over the hills so he could point out the house where my mother had grown up: a plain stone cottage set in the stunning countryside.

'She was a pretty little thing, your mother,' Bob recollected as we stood at our vantage point looking down at the house. 'But I found it hard to engage with her, even as a small child. She was restless, holding her attention was difficult, drawing conversation from her worse again. But I put it down to myself … being a bachelor, I didn't have much experience with children.'

The family didn't know that Janet was pregnant when she left — my existence was a complete shock to Bob, as it would have been to my grandparents if they'd still been alive.

'I don't remember Janet going around with anyone,' said Bob, squinting his watery eyes as he tried to see into the past. 'I have no idea at all who your father might be.'

I send Bob a card every Christmas, and he sends one to me. In my last card I told him I was coming to Sydney, and gave the post office box address. Bob, my mother's uncle, the only relative that I know of, a bachelor farmer in his seventies whom I met just once, is dead. He has left me a few hundred pounds, all that he had to his name.

Tears roll down my face. My sobs are loud and startling in the otherwise silent apartment.

I'm not sure if I'm crying for me or Bob.

Both of us, I decide.

Dan can tell that something has happened as soon as I open the door. A couple of hours have passed, I've peeled myself off the floor, had some crackers and cheese to eat — I couldn't face a full meal — and turned on the TV.

'Hey, are you okay?' he asks, peering closely at me.

'No …' Tears well once more, and the sense of grief is so overwhelming I need to lean against him or I'll fall down again.

'What is it?' His face is sober with concern for me.

'Bob …' I've already described to Dan how much it meant to me to meet Bob, to listen to his recounting — however sketchy — of my mother's childhood, just to lay eyes on the cottage where she grew up, and to take in the simplicity of the surrounding countryside, a simplicity that must have been reflected in her early life, before it became so complicated she felt compelled to walk out on it.

'Bob has died …'

'Oh, Louise.' He pulls me tight against him, his hands pressing my shoulder blades, and I cry into his shirt. This grief is completely out of proportion.

'I'm just shocked …' I say between sobs. 'I didn't expect this, that's all. It's come out of nowhere.'

'Did you get a phone call?' he asks.

'No, a letter from his solicitor. It happened last month, and I've only found out now.'

Would I have gone back for the funeral if I'd known earlier? I'd like to think I would have. Who was there to see him off? His immediate neighbours, I suppose, as well as some farmers from further afield who knew his face from market day. The local busybodies, the ones who attend every funeral in the area, treating them as social occasions. Perhaps an ex-girlfriend who read of his death in the local newspaper, and came to the funeral because she still held a torch for him. Now I'm being fanciful.

Dan stays a few hours, sits on the couch with me, keeps one arm slung over my shoulders, and talks intermittently but not too much.

'Do you want me to stay?'

It's getting late. He's tired, I can tell from his voice. I haven't asked him about his day. I know I should, but I can't summon the will. Shaking my head, I say, 'Sorry, I'm terrible company. I'm better off alone tonight.'

I walk him to the door, and as we're saying goodbye Joe arrives home.

'Hello, people.'

Joe's had a few drinks. His cheery voice and slightly bleary eyes would make me smile on any other night. He punches Dan on the arm as a special greeting, Dan instinctively strikes back, and suddenly I have an image of them as young boys, rumbling and wrestling at every given opportunity.

'Goodnight,' I say quickly and slip away, leaving the brothers alone.

In my room I can hear the murmur of their voices as they talk, and I can't help feeling a stab of resentment. Dan, Joe and Samuel have each other, as well as their parents, and a plethora of aunts and uncles in Ireland and Australia. It seems too much, what they have. Far too much.

The homesickness is sudden and violent. What I wouldn't give right now to see Emma's slightly sarcastic smile, to hear Ann-Marie's motherly tones, to feel Isla's skinny arms hugging me close. I even miss Eddie, I realise with a start. Solid, uncomplicated Eddie. No, I cannot just jump out of bed and phone them. Emma's at work. Isla's at school. Eddie will be catching up on sleep.

For what seems like hours, I lie totally still, trying to let go of the loneliness and homesickness, trying to sleep. Eventually I give up, turn on the bedside lamp, and rummage in the drawer for pen and paper.

Dear Mr Ramshaw,

I was very sad to receive your letter about my grand-uncle Bob. As you suspected, I had not heard of his death and feel quite terrible that I was not there for the funeral. I'm sorry to ask something of you, something clearly outside your role as his solicitor — I don't know who else I can ask. I would be grateful if you could send me a copy of the obituary, if there was one, from the local newspaper, and any information you have on the funeral. Maybe there was a guestbook or perhaps someone spoke during the service, a friend or acquaintance? Bob may have told you that my mother disappeared more than sixteen years ago, and that he was my only living relative (at least that I know of). This may be difficult for you to organise, and puts yet another burden on you that is above and beyond your role, but I would like to keep whatever I can of Bob's belongings: photographs, letters, things that were of personal value to him. I'm happy to pay for the postage of these items to the above address. Again, I am sorry for the inconvenience and hope that you understand my motivation and sentimentality given our family situation.

Kindest regards,

Louise Mitchell

I wrote the letter to ease my mind, to enable myself to sleep. Towards the start of it, I thought that perhaps it could be a draft of something I would type up and send by email tomorrow. But as I reached the end, I knew I couldn't face writing it all again, or even waiting until tomorrow to send it off. Skimming down through it, I can see its faults. It should be longer, better worded, and I dread to think how many spelling mistakes it may have. Words have never been my strength. Slipping on a sweater over my pyjamas, I creep out of the apartment, into the coolish night outside, and walk to the post box in the next block.

There, it's gone.

I feel marginally better. At least I've done *something*, made an effort to conserve some of Bob, the last of my family.

Chapter 32

Emma

'I want to have Isla fifty per cent of the time.'

I'm sitting on Jamie's sofa (a seen-better-days two-seater with matching rips on the armrests) having refused a drink (I wouldn't put my lips near anything from his kitchen, and the knowledge that Isla does so keeps me awake at night), when he drops this bombshell on me.

'*What?*' I splutter, as though my mouth is full of the drink he offered me moments ago.

'I want to see Isla during the week.' His voice is tinny. He's nervous. I notice this even through my rapidly escalating alarm. 'For her to stay here some week nights. Whatever nights agreed with you, of course.'

Dear God. *Dear God, help me.* I will not, *cannot* agree to any such thing.

'Isla has *school* during the week,' I say haughtily, because it's the easiest veto. All the other reasons, the *real* reasons, are more difficult, painful to vocalise. Anyway, he knows. He knows he's a drug addict, and always will be, despite this latest attempt to kick the habit. He knows his flat is dirty — having said this, it's looking remarkably tidy today — and that he has neglected Isla in the past, putting his need for drugs before her safety, her care, even her sustenance. And he must know it's only a matter of time before he relapses again, and that having Isla here during the week only increases her chances of seeing it happen.

'I want to be involved in her schooling, in her weekly routine,' is his shrugged reply. 'Seeing her only every second weekend makes me feel as though I'm on the periphery, not part of her real life.'

That's the point, Jamie. I don't want you to be part of her *real life*. Every second weekend is bad enough, thank you.

I try to inject a note of reasonableness into my voice. 'Jamie, *you know* I can't agree to this.'

'*I know* that you don't trust me. And with good cause. But things are changed now. I'm changed.' He's doing a lot better at sounding reasonable than I am. This isn't right.

'I don't trust you,' I snap. 'Not one little bit, Jamie. You're not changed, drug addicts never are … there's always the risk, a big risk if you ask me …'

'I promise you, Emma. I promise you I won't let Isla down.'

'Your promises mean fuckin' nothing to me.'

It's time to go. I can't listen to any more of this.

'I'm sorry I've upset you.' When he sees me get up, he stands too. Though there's a reasonable distance between us — reasonable, the word of the day — he feels too close. I duck my head, unable to bear looking at the face that has broken my heart in so many ways.

'I'm not going to agree to this,' I declare, just so he's perfectly clear. 'I will never, *ever* agree to this.'

'I'm sorry,' he says again. 'But I'm her dad. She's all I have. The only reason I keep going.'

'I've told you before, Isla is not some step in a rehab program. You can't use her to keep yourself on the straight and narrow. She's just a little girl.'

'*Our* little girl. As much mine as yours. Half and half.'

There's no talking to him. So I leave, slamming the door behind me, the noise adding to the racket that's building in my head. This can't be happening. Isla spending as much time with Jamie as with me? No way. No bloody way.

The problem is that there *is* a way. At least Jamie always seems to find one. Showing his best side to the social workers so that they give him another chance. Taking advantage of the loopholes, playing to the sympathies and apathies of the relevant decision-makers. Outside, as I walk down the street towards the bus stop, my eyes burn with unshed tears.

He isn't doing this to spite me. Jamie isn't petty or mean just for the sake of it. He genuinely loves Isla, even I can see that. If he were motivated by something other than love — by money, or spite, or some personal advantage — I'd find this much easier to deal with, less frightening.

A bus comes, and I get on, flashing my pass to the driver, more scared than I've ever been in my life.

I'm not going to work today. I'm having a sick day, or a mental health day as my colleagues like to call it. I need a break from Brendan, and even from Katie, his star employee, but the real reason is that I'm still so upset over Jamie I'm liable to lash out if anyone so much as looks at me.

Isla is excited that I'm taking her to school and Eddie is thrilled to be relieved of school drop off and to be able to sleep in properly after his shift. Maybe I should have mental health days more often.

During the fifteen-minute walk to Isla's school, we talk about her teacher (Mrs Tobin), a particularly naughty boy in her class (Ryan), and what sports they are doing today (rounders, apparently). I do not mention her father, but his presence is with us every step of the way, a dragging unease that makes me clutch Isla's hand a little too tightly.

'Can you stay a while?' Isla asks when I stoop to kiss her goodbye at the gate.

'Sure.'

I went to this school, too. Unbelievably, some of the teachers who taught me are still here. Mrs Tobin, for instance. She seems perfectly nice, quite kindly in fact. Nothing like the cross, unaccommodating creature of my memory.

'Isla!'

A blue uniformed blob rushes forth, attaching itself to Isla: her friend, Rosie.

'Bye, Mammy.' Isla dismisses me immediately. So much for wanting me to stick around.

'See you later, pet.' I steal a hug from her before she darts away and becomes another blur of blue.

What if Jamie gets what he wants? In what state would Isla arrive at school on the mornings he has her? Untidy hair? Her uniform dirty? Her books missing? Hungry? It would take only one of these things to make the other children notice, to make her stand out, to make her a target. Last night, when I couldn't sleep, I was mostly worrying about her spending more time with Jamie, in his flat and the risks associated with that. School is another worry. In fact, the thought of Isla arriving at the gates without breakfast and with unkempt hair and a uniform with yesterday's stains on it, is enough to make me feel genuinely ill.

At home I make a mug of strong tea and a slice of buttered toast, in a vain attempt to settle my rolling stomach. I'm sick. I really am. In my heart, the worst place. If Brendan were to see me now, hunched shoulders, the half-touched tea, hardly nibbled toast, he'd have no doubt that I'm legitimately ill.

My phone beeps. Not Jamie again. Please.

It's from Louise: *Sad news. Bob has died. Last month. Got a letter from his solicitor yesterday.*

Bob. It takes me a while to place the name. The grand-uncle in Dorset. Poor Louise. Another loss.

I swap my mobile for the house phone, and dial the long series of numbers required to get me through to her.

'It's me,' I say unnecessarily when she picks up. 'That's such sad news about Bob.'

'It was a heart attack.' Her sigh rings of finality, disillusionment. 'He died almost instantly.'

'Did you say it was last month? Did I read that right?'

'Yes …' Her voice breaks. 'Imagine dying like that, your only living relative not finding out until a month later … Imagine what it's like to be so alone … I can't stop thinking about it.'

We're both silent for a while, because really, what can you say? It's too sad for words, and I know she's frightened the same will happen to her.

'What about the farm?' I ask, to keep her talking more than anything else.

'The farm was leased. I suppose they'll rent it out to someone else.'

With that another silence stretches down the line.

'Are you calling from work?' she asks eventually.

'No. I've taken a sick day.' My reply is sotto voce, as though Brendan might get wind of it if I speak too loudly, which is silly of me. 'I'm really frustrated with work, but worse than that, Jamie is making life difficult.'

'What has he done now?' There's a fierceness to her voice, a protectiveness that reminds me instantly of the fact that she's always on my side.

'He wants to have Isla during the week. He wants fifty per cent custody. To halve her down the middle.'

'No.' Louise's denial is sharp and instant.

'Yes.' Now, it's my voice that's breaking up. I'm not a crier. I will *not* cry over this. No matter how terrifying I find it. 'I don't know what to do, Louise.'

Her reply is harsh, and exactly what I need. 'What you need to do is take control. You need to figure out what factors they consider, and you need to gather evidence and present your case.'

I'm already sitting up straighter, pulling myself together.

'I've told them ...' I begin. 'I've written to them, zillions of times, to tell them what he's like.'

'Paint a picture, Em. Don't just write. Find some photographs. Use your imagination. Writing on its own isn't enough.'

'I had forgotten just how bloody bossy you can be,' I joke, even though my brain is already processing what she has said, and how I might begin this 'picture'.

'Some people just need a shove in the right direction,' she replies, the harshness now dissolved into an altogether softer tone.

The next silence indicates it's time to say goodbye.

'I'm really sorry about Bob, Lou. Take care, alright?'

'Take care you too. And give Isla an enormous hug for me. I can't tell you how much I miss her.'

I finish my lukewarm tea, put the toast into the rubbish bin, and get to work. Louise has set me a task, and I must do it. By the time Eddie gets out of bed, dishevelled in his T-shirt and boxers, there's paper spitting from the printer.

'What are you doing?'

'Researching what the courts will take into account when they look at Jamie's case.'

He sits down next to me, a frown marring his face. 'Is it going to court?'

'Yes,' I reply confidently. 'Because there's no way I'm going to agree to mediation or counselling or any of the usual crap they put you through to try to make you compromise.'

He absorbs that for a while.

'Are we going to need a solicitor?' he enquires eventually. I can tell by his tone that he's behind me. No matter what the cost, financial or emotional, he's willing to bear it.

'Maybe we'll qualify for legal aid ...'

Then I hug him, because I really don't know what I would do without him, supporting me no matter what, making me stronger than I actually am. His face is bristly, his T-shirt soft under my hands, his skin still warm from bed. His lips find mine and we kiss. A gentle kiss that quickly becomes more heated.

'I'm busy,' I say primly.

'I know. But when you're finished ...'

Grinning at each other, we pull apart.

It takes a while to refocus on what I was reading before he came in.

Chapter 33

Louise

Two major things happen in the one week. The first from Dan. He bounces into the pub where we've agreed to meet after work. Hair untidy, jacket open, tie loose, and with an energy about him that draws everyone's eye, not just the group of girls standing near the doorway, who openly stare. Seeing my wave, his face cracks in a smile.

'I have some news.' His lips are cool as they kiss mine. The weather is changing, getting progressively colder in the mornings and evenings. Our relationship is a season old. It's hard to believe we started it in a heatwave.

'What?'

He sits down, though he looks as if he might jump up again at any moment, he is so excited. 'I've had a call. Just fifteen minutes ago. From Elizabeth Mitchell in Perth.'

'One of the ones who specifically told you she wasn't my mother? Has she changed her mind?'

My sardonic tone doesn't curb his excitement. 'She has recalled something since. She used to live in South Australia, before moving to

Perth. Apparently, there was a receptionist at the local doctor's surgery who had the same name as her. Elizabeth crossed paths with her a few times, and they shared a laugh about the coincidence. It was all a long time ago, but I guess it isn't every day you meet someone with the same name and it stuck in the back of her mind.'

I should have got drinks as soon as I came in. If I had done so, this would be the point at which I would take a sip and collect my thoughts, or rather my reservations.

'There were no Elizabeth Mitchells who matched our criteria in South Australia.'

Dan takes my hand and strokes it in the same way he might placate a disgruntled child. 'She had an English accent. Elizabeth remembers this quite distinctly. She said that the receptionist's accent was like "a breath of fresh air in the stuffy waiting room". Those were her exact words.'

This stuns me. Because I remember my mother's voice, and how it was so different from the flat accents of the other mothers at school. Her voice had something special, a feel-good factor that's hard to describe. All I can say is that her voice could make you smile, no matter what she was saying.

'Are we getting drinks?' My question has an underlying quiver.

'Yes. I'm onto it.' Dan gets up. Before departing for the bar, he leans down and informs me, 'I'm going to email a photograph of your mother, to see if it jogs Elizabeth's memory. And I'm going to look a lot closer at South Australia, particularly Adelaide, where the doctor's surgery was.'

'It could be her.' Apparently, that's what Elizabeth Mitchell, Perth, said when she saw my mother's photograph. 'It could be her.'

I'm a little annoyed, to be honest. How did we even start looking at

Elizabeth Mitchells? Who suggested my mother went by her second name? Dan, that's who, and I'm not convinced, not at all. And now Adelaide. Much like Perth, I cannot visualise my mother in Adelaide. I know it is meant to be a nice city, very cultural and pretty, but he seems to have forgotten that my mother was attracted to big, noisy, gritty places. She ran away from Dorset, for God's sake. How could she end up somewhere as sedate as Adelaide?

I'm working on my girl. After all these months of cleaning, repairing and other preparation work, I can finally begin to inpaint the right side of her face. Dipping my brush into a mixture of ground pigment and resin, which has been colour matched, I dab on tiny flecks of colour. The pigmented resin has the same optical qualities as oil but it's soluble in white spirits and is — unlike oil — easily removable. Everything we do is reversible. Nothing is permanent. It's odd to think that we go to all this effort, months and months of work, undertaking something that can be so effortlessly undone.

My thoughts gradually move away from Dan and this new — and unlikely, if you ask me — possibility. For a while, it's just me and the girl, the sheer exhilaration of this new stage, each delicate movement of my brush bringing her a step closer to being less damaged, less tragic.

There. Enough for now. Better let it dry before adding more texture.

The second major event of the week is waiting for me in my inbox, after I've washed my hands and made a cup of coffee. It's a message from Amsterdam, from Jacquie.

Dear Louise,

I have good news to report. Our researchers have traced the Verbeck family history all the way back (through many generations and marriages) to the Auguste family who lived in the Montparnasse area of Paris in the late 1700s. A detailed family tree is attached for your reference. From the civil registers, we have been able to garner the following information about the Augustes. Parents: Jacques, Marguerite. Children: Nicolas, Victor, Mathilde and Geneviève. According to a certain social publication at the time, Nicolas and Victor were similar in looks, and thus Jean-Baptiste Chevalier's portrait could have been of either one. We will continue to see if we can find out more information to determine which brother he painted. Regarding the sisters, Mathilde is regularly referred to in the social columns, and one article in particular specifically mentions her dark hair. On this basis, we can assume that Mathilde is not the subject of the portrait you are working on. What is unusual is that we cannot, at this stage, find any reference to the youngest sister, Geneviève. With just over a year's age difference, Geneviève should have been on the social scene at a similar time to Mathilde. We will continue to investigate.

In the meantime, if you have any further photographs of the work in its current state, please send them on.

Kindest regards,

Jacquie

Geneviève. It's an educated guess, and may never be proved conclusively, but that doesn't stop me from being momentarily overwhelmed by a surge of pure excitement. *Geneviève.* The name actually suits my girl. Mischievous. Weightless. A flight of the imagination.

Yes, it could be her.

There are those words again: *It could be her.*

Frustrating and inconclusive, yet at the same time compelling and full of excruciating hope.

I pick up the phone and call Analiese. We need to find Kitten's brother. The painting he kept after his father's death could very well be the final piece of the jigsaw.

Chapter 34

Emma

The child's welfare is the primary consideration. According to my research, this includes the religious, moral, intellectual, physical and social welfare of the child. Funny how they put religious first, as though it's more important than everything else. Mum would be pleased with that.

After much deliberation, I've concluded that the driving factor must be the child's physical welfare. Will they be safe? Will they be clean and well cared for? Will they be fed appropriately? Will the environment around them be hygienic and well maintained? All the tangible stuff, really, because all the other things — moral, intellectual, social — are much harder to pin down.

So I'm painting a picture, as Louise told me to. A list of all Jamie's unsavoury friends who are liable to drop by his flat at any time. A log of previous visits when Isla wasn't fed or bathed, and was left unsupervised for long periods of time: I drew from all the notes I've made over the years, knowing this day would come. I've outlined the lack of maintenance and cleanliness in his home, the garbage bags outside the front door, the mouldy bread Isla reported back to me (*it had green fluffy stuff on it, Mammy*), the rank smell from the bathroom. The fact that his place looked relatively clean the other night — no obvious garbage or smells or dirty dishes — is worrying me, though. To tell the truth, I'm also worried about space. Jamie's flat is a ground-floor one with a small garden. Our place has no outdoor area at all. Will this be a mark in his favour?

With this concern in mind, I've formulated a back-up plan. Yesterday I called Katie's brother to make an appointment. He knew instantly who I was.

'Katie said you might call.'

Eddie and I are going to see William next week. Isla isn't coming with us this time. I've asked Katie to watch her.

You see, the house is my back-up plan, my secret weapon. It gazumps Jamie's place any day. The modern kitchen, the newly carpeted bedrooms, the grassy garden: all of it screams clean, well cared for, safe.

You know the best thing about the house? It's not close to Jamie's place. It won't be as easy for him to commute (the journey involves two buses with timetables that don't sync). Right now, we're too close to him, we've made it all *too easy*. Another thing, another *big* thing, is if we live in Clondalkin Isla will have to change schools. That will be the deal-breaker for Jamie. It will be a nightmare getting her to and from her new school. Unless he moves too, which he won't, I'm quite sure.

I can't resist any longer. I haven't looked at the website since Dermot Fitzgerald turned us down for the mortgage. Now, like a child stealing chocolate from the fridge, I indulge myself in a virtual tour, the luscious photographs filling up my screen. There's the kitchen, the living area, from lots of different angles. And the garden, for which we'll buy a swing set and one of those lovely wooden cubby houses.

It's perfect. Every square inch of it. The answer to everything.

I'm in my ballet gear when Jamie knocks on the door: black leggings, black T-shirt, pale-pink hair band (for aesthetics only). My ballet slippers are in the bag slung over my shoulder — not to be worn outdoors, on Miss Sophia's instructions. I'm running slightly late for class.

'Hi.' Jamie looks wary. We haven't spoken since I walked out on him.

Isla squeezes past my legs before I can say anything. 'Hi, Dad.'

She's not exactly over the moon to see him — she never is — but I have to admit that she's considerably more relaxed than she used to be.

'Why couldn't you come last night?' she asks, hitching her backpack higher on her back.

Jamie texted yesterday to say he couldn't have Isla last night, and would pick her up this morning instead. That was perfectly fine with me.

'I had something on,' he murmurs. Then he looks at me and adds, 'A job interview.'

Well, that's a first.

'Where?' I ask abruptly.

'In a garage.'

'Behind the counter?'

'Yeah.'

Ha! Bet he hasn't thought this through. The hours wouldn't be child-friendly. What will he do with Isla when he's at work?

'My mother would have to help out. Just like Eddie helps you.'

It's like a punch to the stomach. He *has* thought it through, and he has an answer. Sue would help. Of course she would. More time with her granddaughter and her son finally getting his life on track, she'd be thrilled to help in any way.

'Bye, Mammy.'

Isla blows me a kiss, and they set off. Jamie has his hood down. It's usually shrouding his face, and I'm used to seeing the back of it when he walks away. I'm not used to seeing his head, the vulnerability of his shaved skull. It's like he's come out of hiding. The request for joint custody, the improved cleanliness of his flat, this job interview at the garage, is he really changing?

I'm being stupid. Getting sucked in again. Like his poor mother.

Locking the door behind me, I stride off in the opposite direction.

I'm ten minutes late by the time I get to class, and I'm surprised to find it hasn't started. Miss Sophia is usually a stickler for time. Instead everyone is standing around, talking in high, excited voices.

'Ah, Emma,' Miss Sophia greets me in the broad country accent I still find difficult to marry to her sophisticated appearance. 'We're just discussing the performance.'

The performance? What performance?

Miss Sophia thrusts a leaflet at me. 'It's *The Wizard of Oz*. Obviously, we're not doing a full production, just a cut-down version, mainly for family and friends.'

Oh, for fuck's sake. She's not serious, is she? I'm only just coming to terms with doing ballet — okay, I'm more than coming to terms with it, I'm actually enjoying it — but now a concert? In front of people? Family and friends, and other people's family and friends, as in *strangers*?

'All the proceeds go to charity,' Margaret supplies. This is the first time I've seen her since her accident. She has a support bandage wrapped around her knee. 'I've suggested the local outreach centre that Frank works with.'

A performance in front of strangers with all the proceeds going to drug addicts. Bloody great!

'I'm the Wicked Witch,' Trish cackles.

'And I'm the Tin Man,' Margaret adds dryly. 'The benefits of having a stiff knee ...'

'What's Emma?' someone asks.

'Emma is Glinda, the Good Witch of the South,' Miss Sophia states in a no-nonsense tone.

What? I snort in laughter. That's a miscasting if ever I heard one. Surely one of the younger, prettier girls would be more suitable? I could be the scarecrow or the lion, something incognito ... if anything at all, because I really think this is the most stupid idea I've heard in a long time.

'Who's Dorothy?' I ask to switch the focus. I'll deal with the casting later, have a quiet word with Miss Sophia when everyone else isn't listening in.

'That's me,' Miss Sophia says, looking slightly abashed. 'It's a difficult role, even in our simplified version ...'

Well, as she is the only one of us who can *actually dance*, it makes sense that she takes the lead role and deflects the attention away from everyone else.

Finally, we get underway, doing some stretches at the barre. Then as soon as we're warmed up, we jump directly into rehearsals, working on the first scene, which is largely Dorothy. Miss Sophia obviously lives for this, the chance to perform, even if it is only in the church hall in front of family and friends. At the end of class, I wait until everyone has left before I go to see her.

'I don't think I'm suitable for that particular part.'

'I think you're perfect for the Good Witch,' Miss Sophia shoots back quickly, too quickly, as if she were expecting this resistance from me.

'Regardless of the dancing, there's this …' I finish the sentence by gesturing the right side of my body, the ugly, red-purple skin. 'I don't want to turn your lovely production into a freak show.'

'Oh that?' says Miss Sophia. 'That's nothing that can't be hidden by some clever costume design and stage make-up.'

She's stumped me. How can she dismiss my concerns so easily, as though they're only in my mind and not for everyone — an entire audience in this case — to see? *Oh, that!* Is she blind? Hopelessly optimistic? She gathers her stuff and switches off the lights, and I follow her to the door, where she turns the key in the deadlock, pulls the bolt across, and clicks another padlock in place (this area is shocking for break-ins). She turns to me again, her eyes knowing under all the mascara and kohl.

'Someday, over a glass of wine, you can tell me how it happened.'

Chapter 35

Louise

This is what happened. It was Jamie's fault, of course. And ours too, because until that night we were totally under his spell. Me as much as Emma.

I'm fuzzy on some of the details. We were at Sean's house, I know that for sure. His parents were away. I think it was their wedding anniversary. Yes, I remember Sean mocking them. *Twenty years of bliss, what a fuckin' joke.* We were at that age, you see, when we mocked everyone. Nothing and nobody was safe from our contempt.

Sean's goody-two-shoes older brother was at his girlfriend's place, so we had a free house. There were about eight of us in the front room, some slouched on the sofas, some — including me — sitting on the floor. The room stank of cigarettes, alcohol and pot.

Sean's friend — I can't remember his name — was hitting on me, his hand had crept around my waist, and I was contemplating whether or not I was interested in him when I heard Jamie's raised voice.

'What do you mean you won't fucking come here? ... *What?* ... For *fuck's sake* ...'

Pacing angrily, I could only catch some of what he was saying over the blare of the music, but I didn't need to hear it all. I knew what he was doing, we all did, and our eyes were riveted on him, in awe.

Hanging up abruptly, he addressed all of us. 'He says I have to fucking go there and get it.'

He didn't specify what 'it' was. He didn't need to. Jamie was our leader, the one forging the way, deciding when and what we experimented with. In hindsight, it was probably cocaine. Jamie didn't move onto the harder stuff until afterwards (without the restraint we must have inadvertently provided, he quickly climbed the ladder to hard drugs).

'I'll go with you,' Emma said, standing up, a little unsteady on her feet. 'It's not a long walk.'

'I'm not fucking walking,' he snapped. 'It's pouring.'

He strode out to the hallway and yanked open the front door, with the rest of us flocking after him.

He was right. It was pouring, the rain pinging off the driveway, and off the family's red Ford Fiesta, which was parked directly in Jamie's line of sight, as though waiting for him.

'Gimme the keys to your old man's car,' Jamie demanded, his eyes on Sean.

Sean gave a nervous laugh. 'No way, Jamie. Dad would fucking kill me.'

Jamie glared at him. 'I'm only fucking borrowing it.'

Someone, I can't remember who, asked, 'Can you even fucking drive?'

I remember exchanging a look with Emma. Could Jamie drive? She shook her head. No, he couldn't.

But that didn't deter him, or us. Sean didn't put up much of a fight, and in the end Jamie ran out into the rain with the car keys.

'Who wants to come for a ride?' There he was, quickly getting wet and alluringly more dangerous. How could we resist him?

Emma got in the front next to Jamie, and I sat in the back, between Sean and the friend who was still — full marks for perseverance — trying to hit on me. I wish I could say I hesitated before getting in, that I had the intelligence to stop and think, at least for a moment, but in all honesty I don't think I did.

We took off, the tyres spinning wildly. Sean's shoulder bumped against me, and I laughed hysterically even though it hurt. His friend nuzzled my neck as we skidded around a corner, then his hand slid inside my top. The sensation of his fingers brushing my nipple only added to the thrill.

'Slow down, man,' Sean called out, with the same jokey-nervous tone from earlier. Deep down Sean was sensible, but he didn't have the self-possession to refuse Jamie, or to take him to task in more than a half-hearted manner.

'What did you say?' Jamie yelled back, putting his foot down further on the accelerator, and causing more hysterical laughter. Sean, ironically, was laughing the hardest.

This is the fuzzy bit. I don't know how long we were in the car: it could have been two minutes or twenty. All I can remember is screeching laughter and tyres, my stomach rolling with the sharp corners, rain streaking the windows. At first I thought the jerks were deliberate. Maybe they were. Jerk left. Jerk right. Then we must have clipped something, because Sean's shoulder hit me really hard, and I didn't laugh this time.

'Slow down,' I screamed, far too late.

'Jamie!' I heard Emma's voice, shrill and ominously clear as the car spun out of control. 'Jamie, stop it.'

But he couldn't. Of course he couldn't. For God's sake, he didn't even know how to drive properly. Despite the fuzziness of what went before, I distinctly remember those last few seconds, before we hit whatever it was we were inevitably going to hit, and I remember thinking: this is it, the end. And I was sad, because despite everything, my defecting mother, my shitty life with Simon, I didn't want this to be the end. I was starting university next month. Art History and Science. Me. Going to university. A whole new life that I couldn't bear the thought of missing out on. And Natasha, who had done so much work to get me into that course, would be so disappointed …

'Stop,' someone screamed, maybe me.

Then we did stop, with an almighty bang, one that reverberated through every bone in my body, and made my stomach jolt upwards, as though it was inside my throat. Sean was on top of me, a dead weight. Nobody spoke in those first few seconds, and I thought we were all dead, even me.

'Get me out. Get me out.' I was relieved to find my voice, that I could thrash my arms and legs. 'Get me out of here.'

Sean's friend got me out — I wish I could remember his name — edging me from under Sean, across the back seat. Tiny shards of glass fell from me when I finally stood up straight, like droplets of rain dripping from the creases of my clothes, even my hair. My jeans were torn and bloody, but I couldn't feel anything other than terror, sheer utter terror. What had we done? Jesus, what had we done?

'Emma,' I screeched. 'Emma, Jamie …'

A faraway grunt seemed to reply. Jamie?

'No, Sean first,' the friend insisted, probably because Sean was more accessible. The passenger side of the car was totally mangled — Emma and Sean had clearly taken the worst of the impact. Sean was the tallest and heaviest of the boys. We yanked him by the under-arms and hoped for the best. It was claustrophobic being back in the car, which had never been big in the first place, but now that it was collapsed in on itself it seemed nothing more than a jumble of misplaced seats. Eventually we got Sean out, laid him on the roadside, his ginger hair matted with dark blood, his big body lifeless.

'Jesus.' The friend sounded as though he was on the verge of tears. 'Jesus Christ.'

It sounds terrible, but I felt that we had wasted enough time on Sean.

'Emma? Jamie?' I called as I tried to open the driver's door. It wasn't budging. The friend attempted it too, then Jamie, who realised what we were trying to do and applied some pressure from his side with his shoulder. It gave way.

At this stage other people were starting to come, from the houses across the street. I saw their figures in the distance, dark silhouettes descending on us.

Jamie, dazed, bleeding, like an alien version of his usual self, turned to Emma.

'Come on, Em ...' He shook her shoulder to rouse her. 'Em ... *Emma ...*'

'Petrol,' someone shouted from behind us, one of the newcomers. 'I can smell it. Get out. *Get out now.*'

In the face of all the panic that ensued, Jamie was quietly resolute. 'I'm not leaving her.' As ever, he was oblivious to danger.

Despite everything, all the grief he's caused Emma over the years, I can't accuse him of deserting her that night. He could have left her to burn, but he didn't. In fact, he risked his own life to save her. That might sound incredibly brave, and maybe it was, but you must take into account that Jamie doesn't place much value on his life, otherwise he wouldn't live the way he does.

'You grab her arms ...' Jamie instructed the friend just as there was another bang. Flames flew up from the back of the car, hot orange against the dark background of the sky. 'Hold on. I just need to manoeuvre her legs ...'

'Fucking hurry.' The friend, more rational than Jamie, and a lot less reckless, was finding it harder to be brave. 'Hurry. Jesus. *Jesus.*'

Emma was on fire by the time they got her out, flames greedily licking her purple viscose top. She wasn't conscious, and didn't appear to feel the pain, and that was the only reason I could stay standing and participate in what was going on.

'Roll her on the ground,' I screamed, knowing this first-aid basic from somewhere. 'Roll her.'

So we rolled her on the wet dirty road. It worked. It put out the fire. But her clothes were melted into her skin — purple on white — and I'll never forget the smell as long as I live. What had we done? Whatever we had been trying to prove, we had gone too far, way too far.

Sean's father, who will have bad memories of his wedding anniversary for the rest of his life, didn't press charges. The burns, the concussions, the broken ribs, the cuts — I escaped relatively lightly with a long gash to my thigh, which required fifteen stitches and left the scar I have today — Sean's father thought we had learnt our lesson well enough.

The police weren't as forgiving. Jamie was charged with a series of criminal offences, which resulted in the first of his many stints in prison.

Sean's head injuries left him with some permanent brain damage. Just enough to make him different, a little bit strange, and, for the most part, unemployable. My heart breaks whenever I think of him.

As for Emma and me, it was a turning point. We grew up that night, morphed from silly, selfish teenagers into adults with an understanding of life and death, responsibilities and consequences. Finally, when Emma was conscious and they allowed me in to see her — with her bandages and drips and monitors — we looked each other in the eye. Neither of us needed to say it. We just knew. That this was the end of Jamie and us.

But despite our resolve, our remorse, the sheer shock and disbelief about the path down which Jamie had led us, it wasn't the end.

Because Isla was already inside Emma.

Emma didn't know it yet, but a baby, not even the size of a jelly bean at that stage, would tie her to Jamie forever.

Chapter 36

Emma

William, Katie's brother, says we have a lot of work to do. He doesn't bullshit us or give us false hope (like Dermot Fitzgerald did), and I like that. He's practical, helpful, a bit like Katie in that regard, but quite a lot older — maybe seven, eight years? — and obviously very experienced at his job.

'We need a letter from your employer,' he instructs Eddie, 'indicating the permanent nature of the shift work.' After supplying Eddie with more specifics on what the letter needs to contain, he then turns his blue eyes — the same shade as Katie's — to me. 'Emma, you also need a letter from your employer, detailing the responsibility and trust that's placed in you at work. We want to negate all that stuff from your past, make it clear that you're in a position of authority now. Do you have a budget you're in charge of?'

'Yes.'

'And you have an authority limit for approval of expenditure?'

'Yes ... Actually, I have more than that.' For some bizarre reason,

I'm blushing. 'I'm a signatory on all the company's bank accounts. And I handle the day-to-day liaison, too.'

'Excellent.' William smiles, revealing a set of white even teeth. On his desk there's a photo of him with that same smile, and a blond-haired child on either side — Katie's niece and nephew. 'On my part, I will approach lenders who are less conservative than your own bank. Don't be mistaken, it is very tough out there, but institutions *are* lending, and some of them aren't such *sticklers* ...'

William gives the impression that our particular bank isn't one of his favourites. Well, I don't bloody like them either, so that's one thing we have in common.

After agreeing to meet him again next week, he comes around his desk to shake my hand, then Eddie's. Nice manners, like Katie.

'What d'you think?' I ask Eddie when we get outside.

'Let's not get our hopes up,' he replies. Then he swings my hand in his and we stroll towards the bus stop, a few blocks away. It's Saturday (I was happily surprised to discover that William's office opens on Saturday mornings) and the street has a busy yet relaxed feel. The sun is trying to come out and for some reason this feels symbolic. William's flexible opening hours, his quiet confidence and targeted questions, even his dislike for our current bank, all these factors result in the very thing Eddie has just cautioned against: my hopes creeping upwards.

At home we find Katie, Isla and *my mother* in the kitchen, having tea, Isla's cup consisting mostly of milk.

Bemused, I survey the cosy scene before me. 'Mum, what're you doing here?'

She smiles warmly at Katie. 'I was dropping something in to you. I didn't know you were out. Katie offered me some tea, which was very kind of her.'

It's official. The whole family is now in love with Katie.

'I'll pour you both a cup.' Katie jumps up to get more mugs.

'Not for me, thanks,' Eddie declines. 'I'd better go and get changed for work.'

Anyone else would roll their eyes at the thought of work, especially on a Saturday, but not Eddie. He wants to get in there, dirty his hands, earn the extra shift allowance, see our bank balance go up.

'Did you meet Katie's brother?' Isla asks excitedly when Eddie's gone.

'Yes, we did,' I tell her, careful with my words because she already knows too much. 'He was very helpful. He's given us some homework to do.' Mum is looking confused, so I explain, 'Katie's brother is a mortgage broker.'

'Oh.' Mum takes a sip of tea. 'So you're trying again?'

'Yeah,' I reply, before changing the subject because Isla is all ears. 'What did you need to drop around, Mum?'

'Oh, yes.' She picks up her bag from the floor, a battered beige tote she's had forever, and rummages in it. Margaret's Gucci handbag pops into my head, and suddenly I feel quite sad because my mother wouldn't even know what Gucci is. I should buy her a new handbag for her birthday. Obviously not a designer one, but something good, leather. As Margaret said, every woman of her age should have a handbag she loves.

Mum finally locates what she was looking for. 'It's a mass card for Louise's grand-uncle. God love him, I don't know if he was Christian or not, but I felt I should do something ...'

'Thanks, Mum. I'll send it on to her.'

Louise will be touched, I know she will. Mum is always sending her religious tokens. Rosary beads from retreats she's been on, wallet-sized pictures of saints, bookmarks with prayers on them. She sends them via me (she's under the impression I post things regularly, and is trying to be economical by combining the postage). Louise is genuinely appreciative of all the trinkets and prayers that come her way. *I need all the help I can get*, she says whenever I bring it up.

Eddie reappears, wearing his overalls, boots and fluoro vest.

'Sorry, I left my phone in here,' he mutters, obviously a little embarrassed to have Katie see him in his work gear. He needn't be. I think Katie knows who we are now, and she hasn't run for the hills yet.

'Will you do it, Eddie?' Isla squeals. 'Will you? Please, please.'

'Do what?' asks Mum, confused again.

Eddie looks to me for permission. I grin at him.

'See you later, folks,' he says, opening the window wide.

He vaults over the sill, raises one hand as goodbye and disappears from view.

'Mother of God,' Mum exclaims.

We laugh, quite hysterically, for a long time afterwards.

Chapter 37

Louise

'It's Mathilde.' Analiese sounds very certain. 'It has to be.'

A girl on the cusp of womanhood, porcelain skin, dark hair pinned in an elaborate up-style that was fashionable in the era, smiles beguilingly at us. I have to look hard in order to find a family resemblance, but I think it's there. The forehead and nose are not dissimilar to Geneviève's (the name has attached itself even though the evidence to back it up is not complete, and may never be so).

'I seem to remember, in the most recent email from Jacquie, a reference to Mathilde's dark hair,' I muse. 'I think it was from one of the social publications at the time.'

George, Kitten's brother, clears his throat. He's a well-groomed man in his late fifties, wearing crisply ironed pants and a formal shirt. His house, from what we've seen so far, seems every bit as immaculate as his appearance. It's safe to say he's the polar opposite of his sister. We're standing in his spare bedroom, having recovered the portrait from where it was stored in one of the built-in wardrobes.

'My wife doesn't like old things,' he offered by way of explanation. 'She prefers modern art.'

Now the portrait is propped against the foot of the bed, and Analiese and I crouch down for a closer look.

'Jean-Baptiste Chevalier,' I state for clarity. Analiese, like me, would have instantly noticed the signature, the now-familiar squiggle on the bottom right-hand corner of the canvas.

Analiese straightens and addresses George. 'It's a lovely painting. In excellent condition, considering its age and how far it has travelled. It's a pity your wife doesn't like it.'

He clears his throat again. So far, he hasn't said much at all.

'Did you handle the sale of the other painting?' I ask.

'Pardon me?'

'Kitten told us that another painting was sold in order to pay for your father's funeral. I wondered if you were involved in the sale.'

He flicks his hand, as though such a task — the sale of a valuable painting! — is beneath him. 'Karen directed the executor. I was overseas at the time.'

So *the executor* sold the fourth painting. The very same executor who handled the donation of our painting to the gallery. He should have disclosed his involvement in this other, obviously related, sale from the outset, but recalling his self-important tone on the phone, and his misguided notions on privacy, I can see how the omission occurred.

'It was another portrait, right?' I check.

'Yes.'

'Male?'

'Yes. Quite similar to the painting Karen kept,' he replies, referring again to his sister by her proper name.

'It would be either Nicolas or Victor, then,' Analiese presumes. 'The executor should have retained photographs and other records. We'll ask to see his files.'

'Speaking of photographs,' I say to George, 'do you mind if we take a snap or two before we go?'

This time I've come prepared with a proper camera. He nods and watches rigidly while I compile a portfolio of shots.

'She's mentally ill, you know,' he announces suddenly, his voice so harsh it makes me lower the camera from my face.

'Sorry?'

'My sister is mentally ill. The cats, the house, her personal hygiene, it's quite … *disgusting.*' He spits out the last word.

Kitten's home was disgusting, but it feels wrong to be so derogatory, so scathing. Yes, she is disturbed, but at the same time she seems to be an essentially kind-hearted woman. Unlike her brother. Suddenly, I feel quite protective of Kitten, and I can see by Analiese's demeanour she feels the same way. She's standing straighter, a defensive set to her usually soft face.

'Thank you for your time today, George,' I say coldly. 'We'll be in touch.'

'What a horrible, horrible man,' Analiese declares when we get back to the car.

Shaking my head, I click my seatbelt into place. 'He's her *brother.* You'd think he'd be at least a little understanding about her problems, a little bit supportive. Instead he seems to hate her for it. As though she can help the way she is.'

'And her father was mean to her, too,' Analiese adds, jerking the car into gear. 'Poor Kitten. No wonder she prefers cats.'

Analiese pulls up outside my place at the same time as Dan. He jumps out of his car, spots me in Analiese's hatchback, smiles and comes our way. I roll down the window.

'Dan, Analiese. Analiese, Dan.' I make the introductions in a perfunctory manner — they already know of each other — then I turn to Analiese. 'Want to come inside for a drink?'

She looks momentarily tempted. 'I'd love to … but I really can't. I have to get back to Stella.'

I knew she wouldn't be able to come in, but I also know she appreciates being asked.

'I'll call you tomorrow,' I promise. 'After I've had a word with that thick-headed executor.'

Dan and I wave her off, and then go inside together. I've just closed the door behind us when my phone beeps with a text. It's from Analiese: *He's gorgeous. Lucky you!*

Lucky me indeed. Dan *is* looking particularly gorgeous today. His trousers have a really nice cut, and the blue of his shirt complements his skin and hair. He wears a lot of blue. Someone — his mother, maybe, or one of his ex-girlfriends — must have told him how well it suits him.

'Tea, coffee, beer?' I throw at him.

'Anything else on the menu?' he enquires, putting his arms around me.

I laugh, and right at that moment I see it. Propped against the fruit bowl on the dining table. Even from this distance, I recognise the stamp.

'Nope,' I answer, pirouetting out of his embrace, snatching up the envelope. 'It looks like Bob's solicitor has replied to my letter.'

What am I expecting? Some reference to Bob's belongings and what can and can't be sent to me. Something dry and officious, solicitor-like. Instead, this is what I read:

Dear Louise,

I knew your mother …

I can't read on. There are too many words. It's two pages long, this letter, far too dense. And I'm too emotional to make sense of it. I'm always worse when I'm emotional.

'Read it for me.' I thrust it at Dan. 'Please.' Weakly, I remember my manners.

'What's wrong?' he asks, glancing from the letter to my face, seeking clues to explain this drastic change of mood.

'Just read it for me. Please.'

He complies. 'Dear Louise, I knew your mother …' He pauses at the same juncture as I did, every bit as shocked.

'Go on,' I urge, a little frantic by now.

He casts me another worried glance before steering his eyes back on the page.

I knew your mother. She was in the year above me at high school, in the same class as my sister. I hope you don't mind me saying this, Janet was the most beautiful girl in the school and almost all the boys, including yours truly, had a crush on her. She was aloof, a bit of an enigma, and we found that even more captivating than her looks. One particular memory stands out for me, when I bumped into her one Saturday afternoon in the village. She was with a boy who was a few years older, obviously her boyfriend, and I was devastated. The fact that she was barely aware of my existence didn't lessen my heartbreak. Being happily married with three children of my own, I'm pleased to say my "heartbreak" didn't have any long-term effects.

I hope I have not taken further liberties here, but I also asked my sister, Viv, for her recollections of Janet. These are Viv's words, taken directly from an email she sent me. 'Despite being beautiful, Janet was a strange girl. She would float in and out of class, always on her own, she had no close friends. Though she was in my year group the whole way through school, she never felt part of us, and we never really got to know her. She was secretive, almost compulsively so. She didn't talk much, not about herself, or her family, or boys, or anything at all. If ever questioned directly, she was so elusive with her answers, so untrusting of us, that we felt frustrated by her. Looking back, I think there was something not quite right about her.'

Dan pauses to check my reaction. I gesture at him to keep reading. There will be plenty of time later to see how I feel about this. Right now, knowing is more important than feeling.

Louise, I took from your letter that you are desperately seeking details of your family history, and even though my schoolboy recollections are embarrassingly trivial, and my sister's are not exactly flattering, I'm taking a gamble that they're better than nothing at all. Please forgive me if this isn't so. Offending you is far from my intention.

Regarding your grand-uncle's estate, my assistant is working through his belongings and will send a package in the coming weeks. The postage is on us … All best, Edward Ramshaw.

Dan says nothing when he finishes. For a few moments we're frozen in silence. Then words begin to build up in my throat. Things I should say at this point. Firstly, that I'm grateful to Edward, *hugely grateful*, that he told me this stuff. Strangely, I don't find it creepy that he had a crush on her; in fact his teenage heartbreak has a certain poignancy to it. And neither am I hurt by Viv's comments, because I, better than anyone else, know just how detached my mother was from the people who were supposed to be close to her. Who was the older boy she was with in the village that day? Was he my father? Given how secretive she was, it's anyone's guess. Another thing I want to say — or ask — is for Dan to hand back the letter now he has finished reading it. I can't bear for it to be out of my possession a moment longer, because it's precious and needs to be preserved and kept safe. I'll put it in the box, with her other things.

Instead of all this, something entirely unpredictable pops out of my mouth. 'I'm dyslexic.'

'What?'

'I'm dyslexic … I think it's time you knew that about me.'

'Jesus, Louise. Isn't this something I should already know?' Dan is rattled and this gives me a weird sense of satisfaction. 'Why are you only telling me this now?'

'The letter …' I shrug. 'It seemed relevant.'

'*Relevant?*' he splutters. 'It was relevant *months ago*, when we were getting to know one another.'

My response is another shrug, which only infuriates him further.

'It didn't have to be a big secret. Grow up, Louise.'

'Ha! You're only annoyed because you don't know me as well as you think you do.'

'Exactly,' he says coldly.

'Well, what can I say? I can be secretive. Just like my mother.' I laugh sourly.

He levels a look at me, a look that says that I'm being childish and perhaps a little spiteful and he's had quite enough of me. 'Apparently so.'

Chapter 38

Emma

Here's a secret about Louise that nobody knows but me. She has trouble reading and writing. School was a nightmare for her, until the social worker, Natasha, figured out what was wrong and got her some support. Poor Louise stood out at school for two excruciating reasons: she was the girl whose mother had walked out, as well as the girl who was so far behind that she needed to be whisked out of class a few times a week for special one-on-one support. Louise had the last laugh, though. She worked her guts out, ended up with a decent leaving certificate, and went on to do a degree, which is more than can be said for most of her peers, including me.

One thing in my life I am most proud of is that I helped Louise get her degree. I proofread all her assignments, corrected all the spelling mistakes and missing words (of which there were many). That was my contribution. It doesn't sound like much but I know she really appreciated my help, and that it gave her extra confidence whenever she had a paper to submit. I just wish I'd had the drive and determination to do a degree myself. Too late now, though.

The dyslexia makes me wonder about Louise and Dan, and how compatible they really are. He's a writer — from a family of writers and avid readers, I hear — and she fundamentally doesn't trust or enjoy the written word. Despite what she's achieved, despite the fact that most people can't even tell she's dyslexic and is a slower-than-average reader and would be bloody lost without Spell Check, Louise doesn't relate to words, or books, or even that newspaper Dan writes for, in the same way she relates to art and everything visual. Essentially, it's as if she speaks a different language from most of the rest of us.

As I said, it makes me wonder, and worry, about Dan and her. Then again, I suspect I'm casting around for faults in their relationship, for reasons why it won't work out. Everyone knows that opposites attract. This possessiveness over Louise needs to stop. I don't like it in myself. The ever-increasing possibility of losing her to Dan, *to Australia*, is no excuse.

Here's another secret. About me, this time. A much more trivial secret than Louise's dyslexia. Something altogether more light-hearted, yet totally surprising. I'm enjoying the rehearsals for the show. In fact, I'm more than enjoying them, I'm loving them. It's a bit like a jigsaw, I've discovered, all the various scenes and how they interlock. The choreography, the soundtrack, the visual effects of the costumes and set, how they all come together, the fact that you think they *never will* come together, but then you master whatever it was that was holding things up (the difficult steps, the ever-so tricky timing), and suddenly you have a glimpse of what the finished production will be like, and *wow!*

The Wizard of Oz. It's a good story, a timeless tale with solid morals (at the risk of sounding like my mother). We all have an inner strength, a power within us. Instead of always looking outward for answers, we should first look inwards.

I've bought the DVD for Isla so that she'll have some idea of the story before she goes to see me in the show. She's watched it five times already, half-terrified and half-besotted with the Wicked Witch of the West.

'Ding, dong the witch is dead …'

Both Isla and I go around the house singing the songs, Eddie's baritone sometimes joining in. The neighbours must think we're bloody mad.

'Your dress is going to be so pretty, Mammy.'

Isla is dying to see my costume. So am I, although I'm more curious than enthralled. Miss Sophia's friend, a seamstress, is in charge of costumes. Some are being hired, others are being made from scratch. Mine, for obvious reasons, falls into the latter category, with the neckline needing to be as high as possible.

'It's for a good cause, Brendan.'

I've hit my ever-stingy boss for four tickets, as well as one of the raffle prizes. It feels good to get something off him, seeing that a proper pay rise seems out of the question. All in all, I've sold about twenty tickets to my work colleagues and my mother's church friends, and I can't contain my proud grin as I inform Miss Sophia of my sales efforts at our weekly production meeting.

Who would have thought that *The Wizard of Oz* could make a grown woman — especially me, a hardwired cynic — so happy.

'Because, because, because, because, becauuuuuuse …'

Such a monumental surprise. A secret that I'm probably not disguising all that well.

Chapter 39

Louise

Things aren't the same with Dan. I've hurt him. The way I flung my dyslexia at him, totally out of the blue like that, was both horrible and unnecessary. I don't know what brought it about. I really believed I was taking the contents of Edward's letter quite well, being philosophical about the not-so-nice revelations about my mother, and then, *bam*, I've struck out at Dan, which makes me suspect I wasn't taking things as well as I thought I was.

'Delivery for you.' Peter drops a package on my desk.

'Thanks,' I call after him as he heads off to his end of the room.

Inside the package there are a number of blown-up photographs of the painting that was sold, a copy of the auction records, and a pompous letter from the executor, who is infuriatingly unapologetic for not disclosing this information sooner, and, from the belligerent tone of the letter, unappreciative of the lecture I gave him yesterday on the intricacies, and common misinterpretations, of privacy laws.

A quick glance at the photographs confirms that it's one of the brothers, either Nicolas or Victor. The resemblance between this young man and the one in Kitten's painting can't be denied. And here's a close-up of Jean-Baptiste Chevalier's signature, another irrefutable link between the paintings. At least three of them, anyway.

So that's Nicolas, Victor and Mathilde all painted by a prominent artist of the time, and all in excellent condition today. If my girl is indeed Geneviève, the youngest daughter, I need to find out why she was treated so differently. Specifically, why she was painted by a different artist, and why she was allowed to deteriorate, to become so damaged, while her siblings' portraits have been so well maintained.

I swing around on my seat to study her again. She's so much less tragic now that she has the markings of a second eye, so much more pleasing to look at. I like her. I've liked her from the start, but whenever I looked at her for extended periods all I could see was the damage. Her humour, her soul, overtaken by her imperfections.

What was different about you? I ask silently.

Of course she can't answer that question. It's for me to find out.

I'm typing a letter to Jacquie, outlining all these developments, guesses and further questions, when my mobile rings.

'It's Mary. Can you talk?'

Hearing her voice in my ear, with its undertones of bossiness (which for some reason I find quite endearing), makes me smile.

'Of course. What is it?'

'Dan asked me to trawl through some records for him. He's been busy, as you know, and I have time on my hands, not to mention the fact that I enjoy the sleuthing around ...' Mary pauses to catch her breath. She talks so quickly, she often runs out of steam. It's more noticeable on the phone.

'What has Dan asked you to do this time?' I ask with a mix of suspicion and resignation. Dan, with Mary's assistance, has been running the show for the last few weeks. Sometimes I feel quite superfluous.

'The archives of the local paper, *The Portside Messenger*. It covers all the northern beach suburbs of Adelaide, where that other Elizabeth Mitchell lived. The thing is …' Mary sucks in a big breath. 'I think I've found something.'

'What?'

'An engagement notice,' she declares, sounding both proud and very excited. 'Elizabeth Mitchell and Anthony Russo. In April 2003.'

It takes me a while to gather my thoughts. Okay, so we have established that an Elizabeth Mitchell lived in Adelaide around ten years ago, and that she got engaged to be married. Big deal. It's just another Elizabeth Mitchell to add to our list, that's all. Or maybe Elizabeth Russo, if she goes by her married name.

'Louise, did you hear me?' Mary prompts, clearly expecting a more instantaneous reaction.

My sigh has a touch of exasperation. 'Look, Mary, I've said to Dan numerous times that I can't see my mother living in Adelaide. To be perfectly honest, I can't see her getting married either. And I'm still not convinced that she would be going by her middle name. It's interesting that we've apparently found an Elizabeth Mitchell in Adelaide, but overall I think we're going down a rat hole here, wasting everyone's time on *the wrong person in the wrong place.*'

'But the English accent …' Mary protests.

'*So what about the accent!*' My exasperation explodes into my voice. 'There are thousands of English in this country, Mary. This connection is flimsy, the recollections of some woman in Perth, the name, an accent, for goodness sake … I mean, I'm grateful for your help, for everything you've done and everything Dan has done, but I have to use some reason here, and trust my instincts. And my gut is telling me this is wrong, and we need to stop right now. Immediately, in fact.'

I finish to silence and the horrible feeling I've gone too far.

'I've upset you,' she says in a voice that is quiet for her. 'I'm sorry.'

Oh God, she isn't the one who should be sorry. Shame fills me. Shame and weariness. 'No, I'm sorry. I shouldn't have snapped. You're just trying to help. Please forgive me, Mary.'

Another silence follows. Bloody great. Now I've hurt Mary, too.

'I really am sorry, Mary,' I say again, close to tears. Maybe it's time to give up. I've tried and failed. Everyone should know when to quit. Otherwise I risk ending up angry and bitter and totally alone.

'I know you're sorry, love. Don't worry about it, now.' Her voice has such warmth, such understanding, that it's nearly my undoing. 'Look, is everything okay between you and Dan?'

I'm caught off guard. 'Why do you ask?'

'Because I spoke to him earlier and he wasn't himself either. He was, well, a bit like you … a little *tetchy*.'

Closing my eyes, I see Dan, the way his mouth tightens when he gets annoyed, the frown that creases his forehead.

'We're fine,' I say resolutely, even though I'm not at all sure that we are.

Dan doesn't know I'm here. We didn't make arrangements to meet after work. Men and women spill from the building, and I crane my neck, searching for him. He might not even be in the office today. He could be on the road, chasing down a story. Or at an important meeting somewhere else in the city. It was presumptuous of me to want to surprise him like this.

After a half hour of waiting, I have no choice but to text him: *I'm outside. Are you still at work?*

His reply comes moments later: *Be there in ten.*

I use the ten minutes to secure a spot on the low wall that encircles the front of the building, and to rehearse what I want to say. But when he finally emerges, I wave to catch his attention and the words I so carefully chose fly straight out of my head.

Our greeting is an awkward embrace. Everything has been awkward, stilted, *not right*, since that argument.

'Do you want to go somewhere?' He looks weary. A hard day at work? Not sleeping well? Stressed about me, about us?

'Let's just sit here.' Now that I've psyched myself up to do this, I want to get it over with.

He sits down next to me, his leg brushing against mine, bringing a distracting jolt of chemistry. Focus.

'I didn't tell you because it makes me feel stupid.' These aren't the exact words I practised saying, but the gist is there. 'I wasn't deliberately keeping secrets, Dan, or being immature. I've hidden it all my life, at school, at college, at work. Being dyslexic makes me feel stupid … and embarrassed … and ashamed. It's as simple as that.'

A few moments of silence, then he speaks.

'Okay, I get that. But you're wrong, you know. I hate that word, "stupid", but if you insist on using it, then I have to make it clear you're the least stupid person I know.'

'Oh, come on,' I counter with some impatience, 'all of you, the entire family, are so clever and accomplished and *bookish*. How can you even comprehend someone like me?'

'We *admire* someone like you.' Dan's tone is quietly adamant. 'Someone who's visual rather than literal. Everything feels more vivid with you around, less black and white.'

'Says who?'

'Me, Mum, Joe ...' He smiles. 'We talk about you nonstop behind your back.'

'I've upset your mother,' I sigh, and then I relay the details of my conversation with Mary: her good intentions, my churlish response.

He's completely unperturbed. 'Don't worry about Mum. She's hardy. She can take an argument — or two — in her stride. As can I. We might get angry or sulky for a while, but we'll bounce back. Do you get that?'

'Maybe I'm starting to.'

He smiles again. 'It would be stupid not to.'

Then he hugs me, drawing me tight against his shirt, warm from his skin beneath. And the sheer relief that we're okay, that we seem to have found our way past this stumbling block, is something I cannot even begin to put words to.

Chapter 40

Emma

Three days ago I got a letter from the district court, formalising Jamie's application for increased access. I knew it was coming, but it was still a shock seeing it in black and white, dauntingly official.

I've spent the last few nights finalising my response, outlining all Jamie's transgressions over the past five years, which is Isla's entire life. I responded in a similar fashion when he first requested weekend access four years ago, but I realise now I could have done more, *should* have done more. My only defence is that I still had faith in the system back then. It was like a slap in the face when they granted the access. The shock, the outrage, the bloody unfairness of it, still stings today. This time round I'm relying on me, not the system. My submission includes eight pages of text, five photographs (Jamie with glassy eyes, his kitchen with dirty dishes and rubbish festering on the countertop, Isla in a clear state of neglect after a weekend with her father) and two statutory declarations (from my mother and Eddie). I've painted a picture, at least I hope I have, and I posted my work of art to Family Services on the way to work today. Next on my list is a visit to the local community law centre to see if I can get legal aid. I already know what kind of solicitor I want. Someone older, with grey hair and stacks of experience. Someone who struts into court in a sharp business suit and oozes authority. I don't care if it's a male or female, as long as they can kick ass.

All this has consumed me over the last few days, so I am a little bit behind with my homework for William.

'What's this?' Brendan asks when I front up at his office midmorning with my letter, outlining my responsibilities within the company and how wonderfully trustworthy I am.

'Something I need for my mortgage application.'

He frowns. 'Is this a standard part of the process now?'

'Yeah.' If you have a history of shoplifting. 'They're very strict on who they give loans to these days.'

He frowns again, before reluctantly signing his name. 'How's the board report coming along?'

'Grand.' I haven't even started it.

Back at my desk, I find myself staring into space when I should be making a start on the report. It's not easy to put the Jamie situation to one side, even though I've done all I can for now. Anxiety rolls around my stomach, making me feel both full and empty all at once. I have a plan. A two-part plan. The comprehensive reply I sent to Family Services this morning, and my secret weapon: the house in Clondalkin. So why does my plan suddenly seem so insubstantial? Maybe because Family Services are a bit like Jamie's mother, Sue. Eternally hopeful that the drug addicts of the world will be cured, and that their families will live happily ever after. And maybe because the house still feels like a long shot.

The letter I typed up for Brendan is still open on my screen.

Emma Kelleher has been employed by me as an Accounts Supervisor for the last four years. Emma's role encompasses financial reporting, management reporting, treasury and taxation. She is a bank signatory, a liaison for internal and external auditors, and she manages the day-to-day relationship with our bank. Emma's role requires a high level of responsibility and trust ...

It's true. A lot of trust is placed in me. I can sign cheques and make bank transfers — not on my own, mind you, but that's almost irrelevant. You see, I know my way around the accounting system well enough to create the supporting paperwork, and the other bank signatories *trust* me and hardly look at what I submit for their signature. If I wanted to, I could siphon off some money. Easily a few thousand. It happens every day, employees stealing money and disappearing into thin air.

Of course I'm not going to steal money from the company. I'm just saying I could, if I wanted to. Just like I could disappear, if I wanted to, if I *needed* to. Strange that this has only dawned on me now. There was I, praying that Jamie would disappear, the alternative never once occurring to me. *I can go instead.* Vanish. Like Louise's mother did, except that I would obviously take Isla with me. And Eddie. And Mum. We could all move far away — England, France, Italy, somewhere we wouldn't need a visa — and start a new life.

Would they really come with me, Mum and Eddie? Uproot their lives just so I can get Isla away from Jamie? I hope so, I really do. Anyway, it would be strictly last-resort, if all else fails. If Family Services doesn't pay any regard to my submission, if we don't get the mortgage, if Jamie continues not to self-destruct.

259

That's a lot of 'ifs'.

Still, if it comes down to it, I'll do it, I'll go and never come back. I've lost a lot because of Jamie. My youth, my reputation, my confidence, even my looks. I *will not* lose Isla too. She's everything to me, a loss I simply cannot survive.

Chapter 41

Louise

Oh my God. *Oh my God, it's her.*

I am almost 100 per cent sure of it. She's not as slender as the woman in my memories. Her hair is lighter, possibly because of the Australian sun. But she has the same stance, the same tilt of her head, and despite the poor quality of the photograph, that same wistful, strangely compelling smile.

Oh my God. It really *is* her.

I don't know what to say to Dan. He found her for me. Dan *and* Mary. Mainly Dan (after all, Mary was acting under his direction), but who cares who was acting for whom, or who was in the driving seat: *they found her.* She's here, in my hand. Weightless, still distant, but *right here.* Can you believe it? They were right, and I was wrong. My mother *was* in Adelaide. She *did* get married. Here's the evidence. She's wearing a simple white knee-length dress, holding a modest bouquet of flowers, and there's a groom standing next to her. My eyes flick over him — slightly shorter than the bride, dark skin, pleased-with-himself grin — but he cannot hold my attention for more than a moment when *she* is standing right next to him. See how little I knew about her? I was wrong on all accounts. If Dan and Mary had listened to me, my mother would have remained lost forever.

'Louise?' Dan is looking at me intently.

'It's her,' I breathe. I'm in shock. All my brain can do is regurgitate the same phrases over and over. 'It's *really* her. I just can't believe it.'

This is how it happened. Mary, undeterred by my outburst on the phone, continued to trawl through the newspaper archives, specifically searching for marriages. Six or seven months later, in October 2003, she found this photograph under the heading *Couple tie the knot in soccer stadium.* Apparently, Anthony Russo, my mother's new husband, an amateur yet highly enthusiastic soccer player, arranged to have his wedding ceremony in what he regarded as the most sacred of places: the local soccer stadium. According to the article, this was the first ever wedding ceremony to be held at these grounds. 'We are unsure if this is a one-off or the start of a trend,' commented the bemused groundsman when interviewed by the journalist. In the background of the photograph is the scoreboard, 'Congratulations Anthony and Elizabeth' in lights.

'Dan, I don't know what to say, how to thank you, or Mary.'

He shrugs. 'Don't thank us yet. Not until we have your mother right in front of you. In the flesh. Which I am determined to do.'

He puts his arms around me and I'm grateful because I'm shaking so much I'm barely able to hold myself up.

'I need to tell Emma,' I tell him weakly. 'I should call her.'

He nods, steers me towards the couch, and then proceeds to locate my phone.

'All part of the service,' he jokes when I shoot him a grateful smile.

Emma's phone rings out. I try again. And again. Until I'm left with the decision: whether or not to leave a message. *I have to tell her. Right now.* She was there with me the day my mother left. I stayed in her flat, eating biscuits, nervously watching telly, while Simon rang around friends and acquaintances and, finally, the Garda. It's imperative that Emma's here — if not next to me then at least at the end of the line — on the day my mother has been found.

'Emma ... Dan has found her.' My voice, disjointed at first, slowly gathers momentum. 'He found my mother ... She calls herself Elizabeth ... *She got married.* If I hadn't seen the photo with my own eyes, I wouldn't have believed it ... Oh my God, you know what this means? I could have brothers and sisters ... I honestly don't know how I feel about that. Now, I'm going off on a tangent ... The photograph we have was taken a while ago, in 2003, so we still have to find out where she is today. Dan thinks it will be relatively fast from here. We have two names to go on, two people to track down, double the chance of success. Elizabeth *and* Anthony. Oh my God, I don't know whether to laugh or cry. Call me. *Call me as soon as you get this.*'

Hanging up, I stare down at the phone, hoping that it will ring, hoping that Emma was unavailable only for a few moments, and is ready now to hear this breaking, monumental news. But my phone stays silent, and Emma, for the first time in my life, feels achingly out of reach.

Once again, with that mind-reading ability he seems to have, Dan pulls me into a hug.

'I love you,' I blurt into his shirt.

Did I just say that out loud? There's a weird disconnect between my brain and my mouth. My timing, it has to be said, is way off.

'I love you, Dan. I really do.'

There it is again. My voice speaking. Definitely me. And it's not like I'm telling a lie. How could I not love this man? He found her. He found my mother for me. No one else could have achieved it but my brilliant, dogged, not to mention utterly gorgeous, Dan.

He pulls me closer again. 'I love you, too.' I can feel his lips move against my hair as he speaks. 'And I feel privileged to share this journey with you.'

Privileged. The word sticks in my otherwise fuzzy brain. I'm privileged, too. To have Dan. To have Mary. And, with their assistance, to have — finally, after all these uncertain years — found concrete evidence of my mother's existence after she left us. My body feels as if it's going into shutdown. My arms are heavy, my lips so numb I can hardly speak. It seems that in order to process this extraordinary development any further, my body will first need to sleep.

'I think I need an early night.'

'Good idea.' He helps me up from the couch. 'Come on. Bed.'

'That wasn't a proposition, you know,' I say, and he laughs in the loud, unself-conscious way all the Connollys laugh.

Then Dan, who has done so much for me, more than anyone else in my life, leads me to the bedroom, finds my pyjamas, and puts a blanket over me. I fall asleep, certain of the fact that he will be there in the morning when I wake up.

Chapter 42

Emma

'It's beautiful.' Margaret's praise is delivered in her usual barking style. 'Such lovely detail. A perfect fit.'

Looking at myself in the practice mirror, I have to agree. Heavily sequinned pale-pink satin corset, dramatic bulbous sleeves, layer upon layer of tulle jutting out above the knee — the costume is like something from one of Isla's fairy books. Thinking of Isla brings a gush of the usual anxiety. She's with Jamie again. How is it that the weeks go by so quickly? I've barely got over our last separation when the dread of the next one is upon me. It's relentless.

In the mirror I crane my neck, trying to see how much of the scarring is visible above the specially designed neckline.

'Stop doing that,' Margaret snaps. 'You look like an ostrich.'

I giggle, and then she giggles, which is so surprising I giggle even harder. She's dressed in a silver tunic and tights. On the night of the concert her face will be sprayed with silver wash-off paint, but we're not doing makeup at today's rehearsal for fear we'll get the costumes dirty. Margaret's angular face and steel hair are perfect for Tin Man, but her dancing ability — if she didn't have that problem with her knee — is wasted on the role. She's the most elegant dancer of all of us, and if we were ever to do a production like this again I'm pretty sure she would have a more prominent role.

'If I only had a brain …' I sing, teasing her.

'It's a heart!' she says crossly. 'The Tin Man needs a *heart*, not a brain, you twit.'

We laugh even harder, on the verge of becoming hysterical when Miss Sophia calls us to order.

'Ladies, are you ready over there?'

Adopting our respective characters, Margaret stiffly marches to her nominated place, and I tiptoe elegantly towards mine. Miss Sophia, her black hair in two Dorothy-style pigtails, imparts some last-minute instructions before turning on the music. It's the first scene after the tornado, when Dorothy arrives in Oz.

'That's wonderful, Emma. Lovely, graceful entry. Raise your wand a little higher. Use your posture and expression to tell the story.'

Miss Sophia directs and dances seamlessly, although today she's more director than Dorothy.

'Beautiful, Emma. Or should I say Glinda. Very regal.'

Praise like this is rare from Miss Sophia. This costume must have some magic in it. I do feel like an entirely different person. Infinitely more elegant and poised, and it's obviously showing in my dancing.

The hours fly, three of them, and all too soon it's time to pack up.

'Put your costumes back in their bags, please.' I'm surprised Miss Sophia has any vocal cords left. She's been talking nonstop since we started. 'We'll hang them here in the storeroom to keep them safe.'

'Margaret, hold on a sec.' Reaching out, I touch the older woman on the arm to catch her attention.

'Yes?'

'Can you take a photo for me? I want to show Isla.'

'Of course,' she says.

As I'm taking my phone out of my bag, I see two missed calls, from Louise.

'Over there, next to the mirror,' Margaret instructs, swiping the phone from my hand and frowning furiously while she works out how to operate the camera. 'Isla will be able to see the dress from all angles with the reflection ... Good ... Now smile ... Let me get a close up ...'

By the time Margaret relinquishes my phone, I've already forgotten about the missed calls. We get changed together, putting our costumes back in their protective plastic before hanging them in the storeroom.

'Frank is picking me up,' Margaret announces suddenly. 'We're going for a late lunch.'

As we emerge from the confines of the hall, we see her husband's white Mercedes parked directly outside.

'Wonders will never cease,' Margaret exclaims. 'He's actually here, and on time too ... Do you want a lift anywhere?'

'No, thanks ... Enjoy your lunch.'

'I will,' she declares in a determined tone. She gets into the Mercedes, they pull out, and I find myself smiling at the back of the car until it turns out of sight. Where will they go for lunch? A traditional pub in their local suburb? A glitzy place with posh waiters and a view of the city? Or maybe they'll drive to Malahide or somewhere else near the sea and have fish and chips sitting at a weather-beaten picnic table. That's what I'd choose, if it were me and Eddie going out for lunch. I hope they have a nice time, Margaret and her husband. I'm half-scared of them — especially Frank and what he does for a living — but I like them, too. They have their struggles, their domestic spats, but they seem to be essentially honest. No pretending, no pussy-footing around, and that's very appealing to me.

Approaching the bus stop, I impulsively decide to keep going and walk the rest of the way home. It's a relatively nice day, I'm fit and healthy, and I'm still on a high after this morning's rehearsal. I feel *happy*, but how can that be? I'm never happy when Isla is with Jamie. He picked her up last night at the usual time, trying to make small talk as he stood at the door, acting as though we're on friendly terms, as though he's not turning my life upside down with this stupid request for joint access.

'Don't forget to feed her,' was all I said.

Funny how I can set aside all these bad feelings about Jamie, and the almost constant anxiety about the custody issue, while I'm dancing.

Eddie has already left for work and the flat feels sombre. Taking my bag from my shoulder, I switch on the kettle, and it's only then I remember the missed calls from Louise. I check my phone and see that she's left a message. While the kettle hisses in one ear, her voice quivers in the other.

'Emma ... Dan has found her ...'

What?

'She got married ...'

Oh my God. Oh my God. Oh my God.

After the initial shock, I find myself overcome by doubt. Are they sure it's Louise's mother? One hundred per cent certain?

Replaying the message, I listen hard to each and every word.

This wedding photograph she mentions is more than ten years old. I wish I could see it for myself. You see, Louise can't be trusted.

She wants this too badly to be objective. It might not be Janet, just someone who looks similar enough to fool Louise.

Sitting down on one of the rickety kitchen chairs, I call her back. It rings out.

I try again. No luck. Of course it's late over there, very late. She's obviously fast asleep, exhausted from all the drama. Just like her, I'll have to resort to leaving a message, which feels utterly inadequate in the circumstances.

'Louise, I can't believe it … Call me … I don't care if it's day or night, call me as soon as you can. And send me the photo. Scan it and email it to me. As soon as you can.'

For an indeterminate length of time, I sit there in the kitchen, fully expecting her to call me back.

She doesn't.

This is bloody excruciating. Louise couldn't speak to me when she needed to, and now I can't speak to her. Fuck! If I could just see the photograph. For now I'm assuming it's not Janet … But what if it is? Well, that's a whole new ball game. Let's be clear here, we're talking about a woman who walked out on her eight-year-old daughter, who left her in the care of a volatile, alcoholic man who wasn't even her father. What kind of woman would do that? Does she deserve a second chance? No, not in my book.

Maybe this is the real reason I've never really helped Louise with her search. This is something of a revelation to me, one that sends me into another spiral of thought. If Janet is as selfish and cruel as I believe she is, why would Louise risk bringing her back into her life? To give her the chance to let her down all over again? Okay, I understand *some* of Janet's desperation, her helplessness, and how walking out can seem like the only answer. But this is where we differ: I would take Isla with me. Without Isla, there would be no point.

My phone remains silent. It will be hours before I can speak to Louise, and I'll just have to find ways to fill that time. I wish Isla was here with me, and that I could hug her to show how much I love her and will never leave her. If Isla were here, I could while away some time playing games with her, or going to the park.

Mum. I need to tell Mum. Like me, she was there that awful day Janet left, and was deeply affected by the confusion, the sense of dread, the lack of an outcome throughout all these years. Relieved to have something to do, someone to talk to, I quickly call her up.

'Mum, you're *not* going to believe this …'

Mum is completely speechless as I impart the news.

'Good Lord,' she gasps when she finally finds her voice. 'Good Lord in heaven. I need to sit down before I fall down …'

If we feel like this, deeply shocked, beyond stunned, borderline disbelieving, I cannot begin to imagine how Louise feels.

Wake up, Louise. Wake up so I can talk to you. Warn you.

Chapter 43

Louise

Emma's reaction to my news is a mix of hardwired cynicism and over-the-top protectiveness. Typical Emma.

'Send me the photo,' she commands, obviously cranky that I haven't done so already.

'I don't have a scanner at home,' I reply, still in my pyjamas and feeling somewhat disoriented after my marathon sleep. 'You'll have to wait until I get into work tomorrow.'

'For God's sake, take a photograph with your phone,' she snaps.

'Okay. But don't complain about the quality.'

That's exactly what she'll do, complain about the quality, as though this conversation never happened. Emma has high standards. She can be difficult, exacting. I often wonder how she gets along with her work colleagues.

'Louise, don't meet her on your own,' she's saying now. 'Make sure someone is with you. Dan would be best.'

Dan is in the kitchen, cooking breakfast, completely unaware that he's being cast in the role of bodyguard.

'You don't know this woman,' she continues, her voice insistent in my ear. 'If she really *is* your mother, you don't know who she is *today* …'

'I'm nowhere near meeting anyone,' I tell her, picking some fluff off the brushed cotton of my pyjamas. 'We don't even know where she is, at least not yet. Anyway, you shouldn't assume the worst …'

'And you shouldn't assume the best,' she counters stubbornly.

She's afraid that my mother will hurt me in some way.

'Stop worrying, Em. I'm not worried, so you shouldn't be.' It feels like the right time to change the subject. 'How's Isla?'

There's a pause, and I can tell even before she says anything that Isla's with Jamie.

'I won't see her till dinnertime tomorrow. Imagine if he gets joint custody, Lou. It will be like this half the time. I'll go bloody crazy with worry.'

'He won't get custody,' I say, aiming for a confident tone. 'That would be too dumb for words.'

Now I'm the one being protective. I feel her pain, the full extent of her worry as though it were my own, and I want to shield her from it, even if only through my flimsy reassurances. I wish I knew more about the technicalities of custody disputes. Then I could really help her. Maybe I should do some research.

'I won't let it happen,' Emma says just as Dan emerges from the kitchen bearing two plates laden with bacon, eggs and heavily buttered toast. My brain fleetingly thinks of the calories at the exact same moment my stomach jumps with traitorous delight. 'It's not going to bloody happen. *Never.*'

Something in her voice sends a chill down my spine.

'I'd better go,' I say reluctantly. 'I'll call you during the week when we can talk properly. Give Isla a kiss for me.'

Dan and I sit down opposite each other and tuck in. The food settles comfortingly in my stomach. It makes me feel cared for and safe, which only adds to the happy mood I seem to have woken up with.

Dan, his hair endearingly ruffled and wearing yesterday's clothes, asks how I would like to spend the rest of the day.

'I want to do some internet searches …' Sighing, I add, 'It's a pity I can't go to the AEC office …'

The AEC office is closed at weekends. All the listings of Anthony and Elizabeth Russos are in lock-down until tomorrow morning.

Dan leers at the mere mention of the AEC office. It's one of our in-jokes now.

'And I want to get started on the phone directories,' I add, smiling but not losing focus.

I've decided that I'm taking back the reins. This search started with me, and will end with me. I'm thankful for Dan and Mary's continued help, but I'm driving it, not them. I'm motivated now, spurred on by their success.

Imagine all the free time I'll have when it's over. No more trawling the internet, phone directories or electoral rolls. No more spreadsheet jockeying or typing up endless letters of enquiry. I suppose that some of this free time will be taken up with my relationship with her, phone calls, meeting up, getting to know her again. But I can certainly direct some of my free time to Emma's cause, too. Get online and see what I can find out.

'I won't let it happen … Never.'

What, exactly, did Emma mean by that? The mutinous edge to her voice has stayed in my head. It's the only downer on an altogether wonderful morning.

Dan's leer is still in place, and he has a certain look in his eye. Something tells me we'll go back to bed after breakfast. My internet searches may be slightly delayed.

Emma

The photo. I hate saying this, but I think it *is* Janet. The essence of someone is not their hairstyle or their figure or even their facial features. It's an aura, and when that grainy picture finally arrived on the screen of my phone, my instincts screamed recognition. I've dissected every aspect of the image since, dismissed each feature on its own merits, but when I put it away for a while and then surprise myself by suddenly picking it up again, I can't deny that feeling of recognition: the same one you get when you — unexpectedly, completely out of context — see someone you know.

Mum thinks it's Janet, too. I texted her the photo and then spent ten minutes explaining how to open it (Mum hardly knows how to operate her mobile — the battery is flat half the time).

'She's put on weight.' Mum sounded far away on the other end of the phone. I could almost see her frown, her eyes squinting down at the screen. 'Then again, I suppose we all have. And her hair is different, but mine is too … I think it's her. Dear God in heaven, I think it's Janet …'

Mum's validation means something. After all, she was an adult when Janet disappeared, whereas Louise and I were just kids. Mum was her neighbour, the closest thing Janet had to a friend (though Mum has often said it was hard to get close to her).

I send Louise a text: *Mum thinks it's her.*

A few minutes later she responds: *Good, because I do too. Dan and I are on the internet, searching for Anthony and Elizabeth Russos. Exciting.*

Why is it exciting? Bloody hell, this woman walked out on you, Louise. Have you forgotten that? She cold-heartedly walked out the door, leaving you in the care of a man she didn't want to live with herself. How can you be excited about finding her? Why are missing parents so special anyway? I see it all the time on TV and in magazines, how 'incomplete' people feel when a parent isn't in their lives for whatever reason (never good). It baffles me, to be honest, how these careless, cruel, essentially *selfish* mothers and fathers are glorified in the minds of their children. If I run away with Isla, will she feel like this about Jamie? Will she idolise him, turn him into a hero, into a far better person than he is? Will she — ten or twenty years from now — suddenly become obsessed with searching for him, and get *excited* at the prospect of meeting the drug-addicted father who neglected her and constantly put her in danger when she was too young to defend herself?

Speaking of Jamie and drugs, it occurs to me that perhaps Janet had a drug problem too. Maybe that's why she left as abruptly and weirdly as she did. Of course the thought has crossed my mind before now, but this time it gels, really gels. Drug addicts are fundamentally selfish. When it comes to a choice between their child's needs and drugs, there isn't a contest. It would explain a lot about Janet: her vagueness, her detachment from life, how she could bear to walk away from her daughter.

My phone beeps again. This time it's Eddie. *Going for a beer with the boys after work. OK?*

He doesn't do this very often because of his anti-social work hours. Also, there's the money factor. Eddie doesn't want to whittle away cash on rounds of drinks. He's not mean — not at all — he's just focused on our savings and desperate to get that mortgage. Me too. I want the mortgage more than I've ever wanted anything in my life. I want that house, with its safe garden and clean, new kitchen. Eddie's dream has become mine. I've taken it over.

I text him back: *Of course.*

So ironic that I really need him tonight. Only Eddie, with his solidness, his calmness, his maturity, can ease some of the anxiety I've been feeling since I saw that photo. I have this persistent bad feeling about Louise's mother, similar to the bad feeling I get about Jamie. I need one of Eddie's thick arms around my shoulders, reminding me that I can be strong too.

9pm. Is Isla in bed? Bloody hell, I hope so. Has Jamie fed her, showered her? Has he cuddled her, kissed her goodnight, told her that he loves her? Probably yes to all the above. Jamie's trying really hard, and Isla's responding. It's almost worse than when he's not trying at all. The more she trusts him, opens up to him, responds to him, the further she'll fall when he eventually lets her down ... which he will. Jamie is destined to break Isla's heart, just like he broke mine.

At ten, after two lonely beers and another hour of skittering thoughts, I decide to call an end to this strange, unsettling day. The rehearsal this morning now feels like an irrelevant memory, the sense of happiness afterwards a foolish anomaly.

In bed, staring into the dark, my hands join of their own volition.

Dear God ... Louise first ... Please don't let her get hurt all over again. Protect her from her mother... Now Isla. Please return my beautiful daughter safely to me tomorrow. Watch over her. Don't let her come to any harm ... Now Jamie. Dear God, forgive me yet again for asking this of you, but please, please take him somewhere far, far away from us. We can't have him in our lives. You know how dangerous he is. Yes, I can be the one who goes away, but would that be fair on Eddie and Mum, asking them to leave everything behind, Eddie's job, Mum's friends? Would they do that for me? For Isla? Shouldn't Jamie be the one who goes? Wouldn't that be fairer? Please, God, please don't give him any more custody than he already has. And please, oh please, have our mortgage approved, because that alone could solve a lot. Thank you, God. Amen.

Chapter 44

Louise

Anticipation wakes me up early on Monday morning. Dan is still asleep, his head turned towards me. For a while I study his face, the strong lines of his cheek bones and jaw softened by the grey early morning light. It's tempting to run my fingers across his face, but that would wake him. Dan, in my opinion, doesn't sleep enough. He goes to bed later than me, and generally — this morning is an exception — wakes up earlier. Sometimes I worry that he'll burn out, that his energy — which is so vital to who he is — will be overcome by exhaustion. Then I laugh at myself for being over-protective, like Emma.

Carefully, so as not to wake him, I slip out of bed. The chill in the room takes me by surprise, and I dart towards the bathroom and the promise of a steaming hot shower.

Dan gets up about thirty minutes later. By this stage my hair is blow-dried, my make-up has been applied, and I'm trying to steady my fluttering stomach with a strong cup of tea.

'Someone is being an early bird,' he comments, dropping a kiss on my head.

'Butterflies.' I smile back at him. 'My body seems to think something is going to happen today.'

'I don't think it's quite that imminent,' he says, looking over his shoulder as he waits for the kettle to re-boil.

'I know. But my body is not in line with my brain.'

By the time I get to work, I'm in a very good mood. I stop to chat to the security guard, call hello to the receptionist, and pop my head around Gabriella's door to say good morning. Like me, Gabriella is in the last stages of the restoration. In a couple of weeks, Geneviève will be reunited with her frame and exhibited downstairs in the gallery alongside other portraits of the same era. I suspect Geneviève will be quite popular with the hordes of visitors.

Heidi and Peter aren't in yet, and our shared work area is silent. Geneviève regards me noncommittally as I type in my password. It will be strange when they take her downstairs — I'm quite used to her watchful presence. My oversize computer screen comes to life and I double-click on my inbox. A dozen or so new messages. The one from Jacquie stands out immediately, and I open it first. Straight away I see that this message is longer than her others, and I'm conscious once again of that weird, fluttery sensation I woke up with. Pulling my chair in closer to the desk, I read slowly and carefully through the dense text.

Dear Louise,

We have found something significant: a record of Geneviève Auguste at La Bicêtre Hôpital in Paris. (FYI, Civil Registers for that period are not reliable, and hospital records are considered a useful additional source of information.) Our investigations have revealed that Geneviève was admitted on at least two separate occasions to La Bicêtre, which was an asylum for the mentally ill. We can assume, therefore, that she suffered from a mental illness of some description. This would explain her absence from the Parisian social scene, and why it has been so difficult to find any trace of her at all. The conditions at La Bicêtre were particularly horrific, with written accounts of patients being shackled to the wall in dark, cramped cells, and unable to even lie down to sleep. It was common at the time for families to be unsympathetic, and to dissociate themselves from the family member, abandoning them to the deplorable living conditions and abusive 'care' of the asylums. Families were deeply ashamed, and often considered the sufferer's behaviour to be wilful or plain evil. It is quite possible that Geneviève may have had a relatively common, treatable disorder in today's world — autism or perhaps bi-polar — but sadly all mental illnesses were treated as one back then. Actually, not 'treated', more like 'punished'.

Interestingly, La Bicêtre Hôpital made history in the late 1700s, when Philippe Pinel took charge. Pinel believed that patients would improve when treated with kindness and consideration, and on his orders the patients were unchained, provided with sunny rooms, and allowed to exercise on the grounds. We cannot determine if Geneviève benefited from these improved conditions. Oddly, there are no records of either her discharge from the hospital, or of her death, either at the hospital or elsewhere.

I trust that this information is useful. As I am sure you know, it is hard to prove conclusively that Geneviève is the subject of your portrait, but I, for one, am confident of our 'educated guess'.

Regarding the artist, I have several new leads to follow up and will write to you again in due course.

With kindest regards,

Jacquie

I should care about the artist, but I don't.

Poor, poor Geneviève.

This is not the happy ending I had wished for. When we started out, I imagined the best for my girl: competing suitors, glorious children, a rich and happy life. Not this. Never this. This is wrong, so wrong. You only have to look at her face to see she wasn't mad. Her poise, the mischievous twist to her mouth, her intelligent bearing. Didn't they see this? Her family and the doctors? Were they totally blind? How could they have sent a beautiful young girl to that terrible place?

'You've done a wonderful job.'

I jump at the sound of Tom's voice. 'Oh.'

'Sorry. I didn't mean to startle you.' He stands in front of Geneviève, studying her with his expert eye. 'I'm very pleased with how she's turned out. This has been an extraordinary transformation. You are to be congratulated, Louise.'

This is high praise indeed. Curators can be the harshest critics, and Tom is no exception. I'm pleased that he's pleased, proud of what I've managed to achieve, but Jacquie's email message has put a terrible cloud over everything.

'Apparently, she ended up in a lunatic asylum,' I tell him sadly. 'I just can't believe it.'

I indicate Jacquie's message, still open on my screen, and Tom leans across me to read it.

That lovely sense of anticipation I woke up with has gone, replaced by a heavier, altogether darker feeling. I was sure something would happen today, confident I would get another step closer to finding my mother. Instead, the development has come from Geneviève and it has a bitter, helpless note to it. Is this some kind of omen regarding my mother?

However crazy and fanciful it seems, the two of them — my mother and poor Geneviève — seem to be linked in some way.

Chapter 45

Emma

You know the way you can tell something is going to happen? You get this funny feeling in the pit of your stomach, as though your body knows something, and is waiting for your brain to catch up.

All morning I've had this feeling. I'm a little late for work because it's hard to rush when you have butterflies. I'm vague with Katie when she asks me a question (quite a relevant question, I'm happy to say) because it's hard to be specific when your stomach is fluttering.

Butterflies: I've never thought about it before, but I like the term, the imagery it evokes. I don't think Isla has experienced butterflies yet. She can be a little shy (at least for the first few minutes of meeting someone new), but I don't think she's ever actually been nervous. Then again, butterflies aren't exactly the same as nervousness. They're altogether nicer, more anticipatory, *more positive.*

My phone rings just before lunchtime, and I instantly know: this is what I've been waiting for. The number is an unfamiliar one.

'Emma, it's William,' the voice says, before adding, quite unnecessarily, 'Katie's brother.'

'Hello, William,' I reply, suddenly feeling more wary than hopeful.

There's a small silence. Here it comes. *Sorry, none of the banks are willing to lend you money. You and Eddie are a bad credit risk. Shoplifting, shift allowance, blah, blah, blah ...*

'Your mortgage application has been approved.'

What?

'Say again?'

'I said your mortgage application has been approved. Congratulations.'

'But ... but ... how ... fuck ... sorry ...'

'Is there a problem?' he asks, sounding perplexed. 'Have you changed your mind?'

'No,' I shriek. 'We have *not* changed our minds, *not at all* ... We had kind of given up hope, at least I had, so you've taken me by surprise ... Thank you, William. Thank you so much. What do I need to do? Do I need to sign something? I'll come over right away ...'

'No need to sign anything,' he says, now in an amused tone of voice. 'Not until you've had your offer accepted.'

Bloody hell. An offer. Eddie and I are in a position to make an *offer*. On a house of our own. We will be *house-owners, mortgagees*. Who would have thought those words could be so downright thrilling?

'Thank you, William. You're obviously very good at what you do.'

One thing's for sure, he's a million times better than that unimaginative twat Dermot Fitzgerald, who turned us down the first time, and I'm going to sing his praises to everyone I know. *Need a mortgage? Katie's brother is the best in the business.*

After thanking William another few times, I finally hang up. What now? Eddie. He'll be chuffed. I can see his smile, slow at first before it transforms into an outright grin. He's the one who started this, who planted the seed (as outrageous and unachievable it seemed to me at the time). In all fairness, Eddie should have been the first to know.

My call goes straight to Eddie's voice message.

'This is Eddie,' he states sombrely. 'Leave a message.'

'Ring me,' I hiss down the line.

Of course, Eddie's still sleeping — that's why his phone is switched off. In an hour or so he'll get out of bed, have a shower and then have a strange breakfast-cum-lunch before collecting Isla from school. This is agony, not being able to speak to him, not being able to divulge that his dream is about to come true.

I can't just sit here waiting for him to wake up and call me back. Suddenly it's imperative that I deliver the news in person, just to see the look on his face. I log off my computer, slip on my jacket, check that I have my house keys. Katie is on the missing list so I scribble a note and stick it on her monitor.

'Something has come up at school,' I announce to Brendan from the doorway of his office. My voice is appropriately urgent, my fingers crossed (in my head, at least). 'Isla's not feeling well.'

He frowns. 'Will you be back this afternoon?'

'I doubt it. They only phone the parents if it's serious.' God, I hope this lie doesn't come back to haunt me, and that Isla is not suddenly struck down with an out-of-the-blue sickness.

Brendan can't say no. Sick children are a water-tight excuse. 'Call me and let me know if you'll be in tomorrow,' he says with a distinct lack of graciousness.

'Alright. See ya.' My response sounds a little too airy for a mother who has been urgently called to school to pick up her ill child.

Moments later, I'm walking through the revolving door towards the rather lovely day outside: pale blue sky, hazy sun, coolish breeze, a day to remember. In a flamboyant, celebratory gesture, I discard the notion of waiting for a bus and flag down a taxi.

'Eddie! Eddie!' When he doesn't respond to my voice, I shake him — rather roughly — by the shoulder. 'Wake up. *Wake up.*'

'Huh?' Finally, he turns his head a fraction and peers at me through half-open eyes.

'Wake up. I've something to tell you. Something super important.'

'What?' he asks, reluctantly propping himself up on one elbow. 'Hey, aren't you meant to be at work?'

'I came home to tell you in person … We've been approved.'

He blinks. 'For what?'

'For a mortgage, stupid.' I grin at him.

He sits up straighter, the sheet falling away to reveal his bare chest and its snarl of dark hair. At the start of our relationship, I found Eddie's hairy chest quite fascinating. He felt like an entirely different species from Jamie, who seemed boyish and underdeveloped by comparison.

Eddie's not saying anything. His brain is obviously not functioning properly.

I spell it out to him. 'We can make an offer on the house, Eddie. We can ring the agent right now and make an offer.'

Still he's dumbfounded.

'*Eddie, say something.*'

'I don't know what to say …' His voice trails away. 'Only that this is brilliant, bloody brilliant.'

He grabs hold of me, pulls me onto the bed, and we roll over a few times, Eddie laughing at my squeals.

'Stop fooling around,' I say, going all prim on him. 'Call the agent now. Let's make an offer on this stupid house. Come on.'

'What do I say?' Suddenly Eddie looks very unsure of himself.

'How would I bloody know?'

We laugh again, equal parts excited and daunted.

'How much?' he asks next.

What did the agent say at the viewing? Offers over one hundred and eighty-five?

'One seventy-one,' I whisper.

Is it too much? Too little? It's not as if we know what we're doing here!

Eddie makes the call in his boxer shorts, sitting on the side of the bed. 'It's Eddie McCarthy … It's about that house we viewed …' The agent obviously can't place us (so much for the immediate connection Eddie had with him!) and Eddie proceeds to explain which house he's referring to. 'The one in Clondalkin. Cherrybrook. Yes, that one. I'd like to make an offer…'

'Well?' I demand when he hangs up a few moments later.

'He's going to take the offer to the vendor.'

'When will he get back to us?'

'I don't know.' Eddie is matter of fact. 'Couple of hours. Tomorrow at the latest.'

'*Tomorrow?*'

'We've placed our offer.' Eddie shrugs his broad, bare shoulders. 'There's nothing we can do now but wait.'

A few facts become apparent at once. We're on a bed. Eddie is almost naked. We have nowhere else to be. I can think of an excellent way to distract the both of us while we wait.

'Nothing?' I enquire in a suggestive tone, slipping my arms around him.

'Maybe one thing,' he corrects himself, pulling me down with him so we're both horizontal. 'Let's seal our end of the deal.'

Sealing the deal involves me shedding my clothes (Eddie is extremely helpful in this regard). It also involves lots of kissing, before hot, noisy, illicit, middle-of-the-day-when-I-should-really-be-at-work sex.

I'm lying in Eddie's arms, feeling sleepy, satiated and quite pleasantly naughty, when his phone rings. Both of us jump to sitting position.

'Yes.' Eddie's voice is husky when he answers. Post-sex husky. I wonder if the agent has any idea. 'Okay. Just a minute ...'

Eddie puts his hand over the speaker to consult me. 'It's ours for one seventy-five,' he imparts in a grave tone.

'One seventy-three,' I shoot back, while at the same time thinking, *What am I bloody-well doing? I don't want to scare them off.*

'One seventy-three,' Eddie relays back to the agent.

Silence. Oh, that didn't work. I'm about to grab Eddie by the arm to get his attention, and mime to him that we'll pay the one seventy-five, when he says the most magic three words I've heard in my life. 'It's a deal.'

He ends the call. We stare at each other, Eddie every bit as stupefied as me.

'I think we just bought a house.'

'Jesus Christ,' is all I can think of saying.

A few moments later he says it again, louder. 'We've just bought a house, Emma. Fucking hell.'

He hugs me. I feel numb, caught somewhere between thrilled and terrified.

Eddie drops kisses on my face. 'The agent wants us to go around there to sign the paperwork.'

I let out a whimper that turns into a squeal.

'Let's get Isla out of school early,' he decides. 'We can get the paper-work signed, and then go for a celebratory pizza together in town.'

That's another thing I love about Eddie: he never forgets Isla.

'It's a deal,' I say. It seems to be the phrase of the day.

Chapter 46

Louise

This is the message I sent to all the Anthony Russos on Facebook.

Hello,

My name is Louise Mitchell. I am searching for my mother, Janet Elizabeth Mitchell, who was born in Dorset in 1973. I believe that Janet moved to Australia in 1997/1998 and went by her second name, Elizabeth. She married Anthony Russo in October 2003 at a football stadium in Adelaide. Are you that Anthony Russo? If you are, it would be wonderful if you got in contact. If you aren't, a simple response saying so would greatly assist as I can then eliminate you from my enquiries.

Many thanks,

Louise Mitchell

Of course I sent this after contacting all the Elizabeth Russos I could find on Facebook, and in conjunction with the letters I posted to everyone of either name on the electoral roll. I'm also plodding through the phone directory — there's nothing quite as direct as verbal contact. I have two new Excel worksheets to keep track of everything. Operation Elizabeth and Anthony Russo, as Dan calls it, is well underway.

The first response arrives just before lunchtime on Wednesday, as a Facebook message.

Dear Louise,

I married Elizabeth Mitchell in Hindmarsh Stadium on October 6, 2003. My marriage to Elizabeth was short-lived, and we divorced less than two years later. I don't know where she lives now and therefore cannot help you contact her. She never mentioned that she had a daughter. Good luck in finding her.

Regards,

Anthony

My first reaction? Shock: this is the man who married my mother. For once I have actually found the right person. And disappointment: there isn't a horde of stepbrothers and stepsisters for me to meet and get to know, or even a family home to visit — there's nothing left of the marriage, nothing at all.

Dan is away at a conference for a few days. This morning, as he kissed me goodbye, he said he would be uncontactable for most of the day. Still, I can't seem to stop myself reaching for the phone.

'I'm just about to go into another session,' he half-whispers when he picks up. 'Is it urgent?'

'Not urgent,' I reassure him. 'I just wanted you to know that I've heard from Anthony Russo through Facebook. The marriage didn't last very long. They got divorced.' I'm astounded that I sound so matter-of-fact. Is it really as cut and dried as that?

There's a pause. I imagine Dan standing outside a conference room, wearing one of the charcoal suits and blue business shirts that look so flattering on him, his face creased in concentration, other delegates milling noisily around.

'Does he know where she is?' he asks eventually.

'No, he doesn't.'

'Ask if you can see him.' Sometimes Dan can sound a little abrupt, but I know him well enough to tell that his clipped tone is caused by a combination of his natural decisiveness and the session at the conference being about to start.

'I don't know where he lives. His profile is private. What if he's still in Adelaide?'

'Wherever he is, we'll fly there,' Dan states. The extent of his commitment takes my breath away. He makes it sound so easy, as though Adelaide's nothing more than a short drive away. 'I've got to run. They're starting inside. Talk later, okay?'

'Okay,' I reply.

I read Anthony's message again, and again, my shock lessening and my disappointment increasing on each reading.

I thought I had practically found her. I had hard evidence: her wedding photograph, her husband's name, the date she got married.

But the wedding wasn't a happy-ever-after one, there was a quick — ugly? — divorce, and her ex-husband doesn't even know where she is today. Now I can't help feeling as if I've lost her all over again. What if she's married someone else since? Changed her name yet again? Gone to another country? Is this ever, ever going to end?

My phone rings. It's Analiese, and I remember, with a rush of guilt, that I'm meant to be meeting her for lunch.

'Where are you?' she demands, sounding fraught.

'I'm so sorry. I got distracted. I'll explain when I get there.'

Ten minutes later I've arrived at the café and apologised again. Leaning in close to Stella, I tickle the underside of her double chin.

'Ouch.' I untangle her strong fingers from my gold hoop earring, trying not to split my ear open in the process.

'Here.' Analiese produces a toy from somewhere. 'Quick, let's order before all hell breaks loose. Now that she's rolling around, she hates being in her stroller.'

As soon as we've placed our order, Analiese doesn't miss a moment. 'So what was it you were going to explain?'

I return her gaze as steadily as I can. 'Just before lunch, I received a message from my mother's ex-husband.'

Analiese's mouth drops open. 'Really? Oh my God. You are absolved, *totally absolved* for being late. Tell me everything.'

'Here.' I take out my phone and open Facebook. 'You can read it for yourself.'

I watch her face — plump, open as a book — as she reads.

'It's short,' she says.

'Yes. As was the marriage.'

'He didn't even know you existed,' is her next comment.

'Yes,' is all I can say.

Forget the actual shock of finding Anthony so easily, and the disappointment that the marriage was a nothing. It's the fact that he didn't know about me that suddenly feels the most devastating. It's as if someone has taken the butterknife from the table and plunged it into my heart, turning it slowly so as to induce the most pain.

By the time our meals arrive, Stella is in serious 'get me out of here' mode, bracing her chunky legs against the stroller, twisting her body this way and that and letting out sharp intermittent cries, rather like a warning bell before a major explosion. Analiese gobbles down her meal, unbuckles her daughter and jiggles her on her knee.

'There's something wrong,' she declares. 'If your mother was in the depths of despair, I could — at a stretch, and only because I've had some fairly dark moments myself — understand her walking away, and convincing herself that it was better for everyone if she didn't return. But then she married this man, and never even mentioned you. I mean, it's not as if you were going to live with them. She could have easily said, "I have a daughter who lives in Ireland with her father—"'

'Stepfather,' I correct, but even that is stretching the technicalities of my relationship with Simon. He was never actually married to my mother. Unlike Anthony.

'Stepfather,' Analiese repeats distractedly. 'Oh Stella, what did you do that for?' She bends to pick up the plastic toy Stella threw away in frustration. Her face is flushed when she resumes. 'What I'm saying is that it just isn't *normal*, any of it, and whatever was bothering her when she walked away clearly wasn't some one-off thing … Ssshhh, Stella. Oh dear. Sorry, Louise. I think it's time for a quick exit.'

While Analiese puts Stella back in her stroller and attempts to buckle in her wailing squirming little body, I pay the bill.

Outside we exchange a quick hug.

'I'm going to ask Tom if I can come back to work,' Analiese announces unexpectedly. 'Twelve months' maternity leave is too long — I'm yearning for my job. Maybe I'll come back part-time — I wanted to discuss it with you today but we've had so much else to talk about …' She shrugs and smiles. 'Next time …'

And with that, she's gone, pushing the stroller through the lunchtime crowds, Stella's wails eventually swallowed by the traffic and noise of Sydney.

Back at my desk, I waste no time.

Thank you, Anthony, for your reply. I am sorry that your marriage broke up. I appreciate that you don't know where my mother is, but I would still like to meet you. I haven't seen my mother since I was eight years old. Anything you can tell me about her, no matter how small or seemingly inconsequential, is of huge importance to me. As you can see from my profile, I live in Sydney. If you can let me know your whereabouts, I could organise to come and see you.

There. That will do. Send.

Now, I'd better get some work done. Geneviève is waiting for me. I've neglected her so far today. 'Sorry,' I say to her in my head.

Tom hasn't mentioned anything about another project. Maybe he has been hedging his bets, suspecting all along that Analiese would come back early. Maybe he doesn't have enough work or funding for both of us. Is this the only painting I'll work on for the Sydney City Art Gallery? The butterknife is back in my heart, twisting in slow callous circles, but I know the last thing Analiese intended was to make me feel worse.

Dipping my brush in the resin, I begin — with incredible sadness and an undeniable sense of finality — the delicate, close to invisible strokes that will render Geneviève ready to re-enter this cruel, cruel world.

Chapter 47

Emma

I'm going to fuckin' kill Eddie. I *specifically* told him I didn't want Isla to see the dress rehearsal. Wait for me outside, I said.

The two of them are standing at the back of the hall, trying to look unobtrusive and totally failing. Isla is bouncing from foot to foot. She keeps turning to Eddie to check that he is finding it all as wondrous as she is.

'She twisted my arm,' I can already hear his protest.

'She walks all over you,' I'll chide in response.

Maybe it's not so bad they're here. At least my part is over. I want that to be a surprise. I want them both to be proud of me, but I can see from their faces that they already are. I sneak Isla a little wave.

Dorothy clicks her heels. 'There's no place like home.'

Isla mouths the words as the lights dim, a bed is wheeled out from the wings, the lights come on again, and Dorothy wakes to find it has all been a dream.

I feel a bit like Dorothy at the moment, as though I'm stuck in a dream, or a movie, with good bits (our new house), and evil bits

(Jamie). But good is about to prevail over evil, at least I hope it is, and we — Eddie, Isla and me — are going to live happily ever after.

The soundtrack stops and the cast, including me, rush forward to form a bunched-up line. Our bow is low and theatrical, and Isla is rapt. Once she gets the nod from Eddie, she bounds over to me.

'Mammy, you look so … *pretty* …'

I laugh. I don't think anyone has called me 'pretty' before, not even my own mother. It's the costume.

Isla fingers the material, her eyes wide with wonder. 'Are these real diamonds?'

'Of course they are,' Margaret pipes up. 'Now, you must be Isla.'

'Yes,' Isla replies shyly, stepping back a little.

'I'm Tin Man. Otherwise known as Margaret.'

There's a pause. Isla's shy side grapples with her social side. 'Mammy helped you when you hurt your leg,' she says eventually.

'She certainly did. And now, thanks to my wonky leg, I can do a very convincing march, just like Tin Man. Will I show you how to do it?'

'Yes, please.'

Margaret marches around me, Isla follows, and Eddie comes to join the fanfare.

'This is Eddie,' I say to the marching Margaret.

'Nice to meet you, Eddie,' she puffs in time to her marching. Then she looks back at Isla. 'I'll look out for you in the front row next week.'

'Third row,' I answer for Isla. 'The front was sold out.'

'My Daddy is bringing me.' Isla pauses, thinks a little, then adds (because she is an accurate little creature), 'Eddie is not my daddy.'

Yes, Eddie is not her daddy. Her daddy is Jamie, one of the drug addicts who plague your husband, Margaret, but let's not delve into that now. Needless to say, I bought Jamie's ticket for the show. They should have a relatively unhindered view from the third row, and I can keep a close watch on Jamie.

'Okay, Isla,' I interject brightly. 'I'd better get out of my costume so we can hit the road.'

'We're going to see our new house,' Isla tells Margaret in a confidential tone. 'It has two bathrooms and a *garden*.'

'Has it?' Margaret looks suitably impressed. 'Well, isn't that absolutely wonderful.'

Eddie distracts Isla while Margaret and I go to get changed.

'Your daughter is simply delightful,' Margaret comments in a tone that's significantly softer than her usual voice.

Pride shoots through me. 'Yes, she is.'

With sports bags over our shoulders, we come back out to the main hall.

'See you next week, Isla,' Margaret promises. 'I'll be looking out for you when I'm on stage.'

'See you, Margaret,' Isla sings.

It's the only blight on the show: the fact that Isla will be with Jamie. Of course, I asked him if he could wait until the following weekend to have her.

'Sorry, Emma,' he said. 'I'd miss her too much.'

He sounded as if he meant it, so I didn't push.

Eddie has his tape measure out. 'We'll put the dining table here … and the sofa by the window.'

With some difficulty, I try to imagine our cheap, scratched, too-small table in the space he has indicated.

'We'll need to buy a new table and chairs,' he says gently, as though being the bearer of bad news.

Yes, we will. I can see that now.

'What about the telly?' I ask, my eyes flitting around. 'Where will we put that?'

'Only one place for it, the back wall ...' He thrusts the measuring tape at me. 'Hold that end.'

Between us, we measure each wall, and Eddie jots down the numbers in a special notebook he has bought for the purpose.

Upstairs, we measure and consult, starting off in the smallest bedroom and ending up in the master.

'Our bed will fit in easily ...' Eddie looks pensive. 'Actually, there's enough space for a queen size ...'

I frown at him. 'Are you saying that we should buy a new bed, too?'

He shrugs. 'If we can afford it ... We can put our double in the spare room. Your mother can sleep there when she stays over.'

He incorporates Mum and Isla into everything. I love that about him, and his thoughtfulness defuses some of the financial worry. The costs are adding up, though. I'll need to rework the numbers when I get home.

'So a new bed and a new dining set ... We can't get anything else. Not for now, at least. Our old sofas will have to do.'

'Our old sofas are perfectly fine,' he agrees.

He takes my hand in his and we go downstairs. Isla is out in the garden.

'I think we should build a small patio here ...' Eddie has dropped my hand for his measuring tape.

'Stop,' I say sharply. 'We can't afford to spend any more money.'

He squats, measures, writes, stands. 'Second-hand pavers. I'll lay them myself. Next to no cost. Trust me, Emma, you'll love it.'

He's right, a patio would make the garden. We could eat outside in the summer. Oh God, I am so excited about this. I almost need to pinch myself. This is ours. This garden. This beautiful house. Well, not ours yet. The completion date isn't for another six weeks. The vendors could change their mind, or we could, and all that would be lost is the deposit, *all* being the operative word.

'I love you,' Eddie says unexpectedly.

'I love you too,' I reply with a quick kiss.

We're not usually lovey-dovey like this. We don't feel the need to constantly declare our feelings. But I kiss him again, slower, with more feeling this time. Maybe we'll be more demonstrative in this house. It's hard to believe that just a week ago I was considering leaving the country, running away. I didn't want to — that goes without saying — but I would have done it. This house has saved me. The undoubted stability and respectability in the eyes of the court. Being on the other side of the city (if not in another country) from Jamie.

Thank you, house. Thank you, God. Thank you, thank you, thank you.

Chapter 48

Louise

Sydney Airport is Friday-night busy, the vibe fast and efficient. Striding commuters, businesslike staff, minimal chatter. Everyone seems extraordinarily focused.

'I missed you.' Dan's hug is so enthusiastic it lifts me right off the ground.

'I missed you too … Now put me down.'

Obediently, he lowers me, still squeezing so tightly that my body is moulded to his as the crowds move around us.

'I can't believe we're doing this. Going to Adelaide.' I'm quite short of breath. Partly due to the shoot of pure lust at the feel of his body pressing against mine, and partly because of the terrible nervousness that has been plaguing me ever since I booked these flights.

'Try not to worry,' Dan says cheerfully. 'Just think of this as a romantic weekend getaway.'

He must be so tired, away at the conference all week, barely enough time to dart home and throw some clothes in a bag. Yet he's here. He insisted on it. As soon as I got permission of sorts from Anthony, Dan pushed me into booking flights.

'Why wait until next weekend?' he challenged.

Why indeed? To give me some time to get used to the idea. To give Dan the chance to get over a particularly gruelling week. To give Anthony time to prepare for a visit from his ex-wife's daughter, whose very existence was unknown to him until a few days ago.

Dan and I check in at one of the self-service kiosks, and proceed to the security gate with our carry-on bags. Forgetting that I have some loose coins in my jeans' pocket, I set off the alarm. Dan smirks and shakes his head at me as I retrace my steps, empty my pockets, then go back through.

'I need a drink,' I declare when I'm proven not to be a security threat.

'Brilliant idea.' He slings one arm around my waist. 'We can use all that loose change to buy them.'

'Ha, ha.'

I pay for the drinks, to make a point.

So here we are. Sitting on stools in one of those trendy bars that tries — unsuccessfully, if you ask me — to disguise the fact that it's smack bang in the middle of an airport.

Dan takes my hand in his and quite suddenly I do feel an unexpected sense of romance. Our first weekend away together. Two days and nights in a new city. And I really did miss him this week. In fact, each time he has to go away for work, I feel his absence more keenly.

'Analiese is coming back to work early.' I have a lot to fill Dan in on. Our phone conversations this week were short, centred around Anthony and the details of this last-minute trip. Dan's behind on all the other developments in my life.

'Oh, really? That's a surprise.'

I sigh. 'I think she finds fulltime motherhood difficult. And she loves her job. She misses it terribly, so I understand where she's coming from, even if it doesn't bode well for me.'

'What do you mean?' Dan looks serious now. 'Aren't you on contract?'

I pull a face. 'Yes, but like most contracts, it can be terminated.'

'But with notice, right?'

'Six weeks.'

He's quiet for a while. 'Are you saying that there's a chance you'll have to go back home in six weeks?'

'Yes ... If Tom doesn't come up with another project for me.'

I've killed the mood. Dan doesn't look quite so happy now. Just as I'm thinking of a way to restore some light-heartedness to the occasion, there's an announcement over the speakers.

'Qantas Flight 688 to Melbourne and Adelaide ...'

'That's us,' I say brightly, reaching for my bag.

'This aircraft has been delayed on arrival ...'

'Oh, not us, then.' I drop my bag back down. 'More drinks? I still have some change left!'

This quip earns a smile from him, and by the time I come back with two more beers we're back on track.

'Emma is buying a house.' This is another piece of news I forgot to impart on the phone. Of course Dan's never met Emma, but he always listens as though he has. He gets that she's the closest thing I have to family.

'You really do sound surprised now,' he says, taking a long sip of beer.

It's true, I am surprised. Don't get me wrong, I'm delighted for her, and proud of her, but the idea of it — Emma having a mortgage, rates to pay, *a lawn to mow* — takes a bit of getting used to.

'Only because it's hard to equate the old Emma with the Emma of today ...'

'Which version do you prefer?' Dan asks, astute as ever.

I don't have to think to answer. 'Today's Emma ... Isla and Eddie have been so good for her ... Now this house. She's beside herself with excitement ...'

About a half hour later, there's another announcement, another delay, and so we have another drink.

It's Dan's turn to update me on all the things I missed out on. 'It looks like Samuel is going to be offered a permanent job at work ... which couldn't be better timing as I reckon Mum is about to throw him out on his ear ...'

I snort with laughter. I can picture it: Mary hoisting Samuel into the air, her face red with exasperation.

'And Mum has been trying her hand at book marketing. She's persuaded the priest to put a mention of Joe's latest novel in the parish newsletter. I think the priest is completely unaware of the explicit sex scenes and violence ...'

Even funnier. My beer gets caught in my throat, and now I'm half-choking, half-laughing. I love Mary. Her sheer conviction. Her fighting spirit. Her many flaws.

I love Dan too, and all the Connollys. To be honest, I'm a little tipsy. Three drinks, no food, a rollercoaster few days, and suddenly I'm fond of everybody, even the grandfatherly man sitting at the table next to us. He catches my glance and responds with a quiet smile.

'No more drinks,' I say to Dan. 'I just wish we could go now.'

Right on cue, we hear the ding-dong that precedes an announcement.

Dan and I listen, warily at first, before exchanging smiles of relief when our flight is finally declared ready for boarding.

He jumps up. 'Adelaide, here we come.'

Our seats are towards the back of the plane. Taking the window one, I buckle up, trying to contain my nervousness and excitement.

This is it. By the end of this weekend I will finally have some answers. All my earlier misgivings, the sinking feeling that I'd lost my mother all over again, seem to have dissipated. My hopes have stealthily crept up again. They're sky-high now, as high as this plane will go when it soars into the air. Maybe even higher.

Yes, Anthony is clearly a man of few words. A monosyllabic affirmative response when I suggested meeting at his house. Later on, a one-liner with his home address and phone number. No frills.

I don't need frills, I need information. Pure and simple facts about my mother. Her personality. The things she cares about. What makes her laugh, what makes her irritated. For instance, does she still hate noise?

Be quiet, Louise … Ssshhh …

All these things I will find out from Anthony, the man who married my mother, who lived with her for two years, and whose memories of her will be so much sharper and truer than my blurred childhood recollections.

I'm clutching Dan's hand as the plane takes off.

Chapter 49

Emma

My knees are knocking. There is no way I can dance. Absolutely no fuckin' way. The hall is filling rapidly, and I'm peering through the crack in the curtains — checking yet again for Jamie and Isla — when Margaret slips me something. It's cold and smooth in my hand, and I look down to see a stainless steel hip flask.

'You look like you could do with some of this,' she whispers.

'Is this *alcohol*?' My shock temporarily usurps my nerves.

'Whiskey,' she confirms.

'Margaret!'

She fixes me with her no-nonsense stare. 'I'm shitting myself. Aren't you?'

Margaret's uncharacteristic crassness makes me laugh. It's a thin, wheezy sound, and not at all like my usual laugh.

The whiskey sears my throat. The taste of it melds with the smell — malt, smoke and wood — and brings me back to another place and time. Louise and Jamie and me. The drinks cabinet in someone's house. An old man's drink, Jamie said, guzzling it back before passing the bottle to me. Who cared? The whiskey was there, it had an instant effect, and so we were up for it.

The best part about whiskey is the warmth in your belly, and the slight numb sensation all over. I'd forgotten that.

I decide to take one more swig before passing the flask back to Margaret, who does the same, the stainless steel blending momentarily with the silver paint on her neck and face. Will I see her after tonight? For some reason this concert feels like the climax, the end of something. My ballet lessons, my friendship with Margaret and Trish. Of course it doesn't have to be, it just feels as if it is.

'I don't know where Jamie is.' I take one last peek through the curtains.

Mum is there, next to Eddie, who has got off work especially. Mum's checking her watch, glancing anxiously over her shoulder, obviously wondering about Isla. Bloody Jamie. So typical of him to be late. To worry everyone. He'll never change.

'Don't worry,' Margaret says. 'Isla won't let him miss it.'

Margaret's right. Isla wouldn't miss this concert for the world. She knows all the songs off by heart. I can see her jumping up and down, pulling on Jamie's sleeve.

Hurry, Daddy. We can't be late.

It's probably the bus. They never run on time, and Jamie wouldn't have factored in any buffer time because he never thinks of things like that.

My phone. I should check it. Maybe Jamie has tried to call me. Do I have time for a quick look? The curtain should have gone up five minutes ago.

'I'm just going to check my phone,' I hiss to Margaret, before scampering away.

My bag is under a chair — no fancy lockers or change rooms for this show — and I quickly determine, from the blank screen on my phone, that Jamie hasn't tried to call.

'Phones away, *please.*' Miss Sophia has spotted me. She has been a little bit terse this evening, and seeing me with my phone hasn't improved her mood. 'And please make sure they are properly switched off.'

'Sorry,' I mouth, obediently switching it off.

Back to the wings.

'Any messages?' Margaret asks.

'No.'

The lights dim, the music begins, the curtains inch back, and Jamie and Isla's third-row seats are still empty.

Louise

I have never in my life been this nervous. Not at my graduation ceremony. Nor my first day at work. Not even when I had to speak before a few hundred art patrons at an exhibition opening in London.

'I'm so nervous I could be sick,' I tell Dan as we sit in the back of a taxi, finally on our way to see my mother's ex-husband.

'Ugh. Not on me.' He recoils, in an obvious bid to get me to laugh. He succeeds.

Joke over, he slides back across the seat, puts his arm around my shoulders, and goes into tourist mode to distract me.

'Next time we come here I want to take you to the Barossa.'

I like the idea of coming here again. Nerves aside, it has been a lovely couple of days. Friday night was room service and a passionate reunion between the crisp sheets of the hotel bed. On Saturday we ventured outside, strolling hand in hand around the city, visiting the cathedrals and museums and shops.

'We might even be married by then,' Dan adds, and yet again he coaxes a laugh from me.

Last night, after another discussion about Analiese's early return to work, Dan issued me with a very drunken, last-resort marriage proposal.

'If Tom doesn't keep you on, we can always get married,' he said magnanimously. 'Then you can stay here under a spousal visa.'

I spluttered into my drink. 'I think that's the most unromantic marriage proposal I've ever heard.'

'And how many have you heard?' he enquired, slipping into interrogation mode.

'No comment,' I replied, adopting one of his favourite phrases. 'And if Tom *does* get me another project?'

'Then we'll just live in sin.' His shrug implied that the answer was obvious. 'And have dozens of children out of wedlock. The children will have Irish names that nobody can pronounce properly. And they'll all be great writers and artists.'

I woke with a smile on my face this morning, despite being more than a little hung over. After a buffet breakfast at the hotel and a walk around the Botanic Garden, it was time to hail a taxi and get down to the real purpose of our visit.

Now we're here. The taxi has stopped. I get out and gulp in some fresh air while Dan pays the fare. We're outside a modest house. Red brick with cream trim. Built in the 1950s. A neat, unambitious garden. All in all, not too different from Dan's family home.

Dan joins me, and without further ado takes my hand. He leads me up the path. He is the one who knocks on the door.

Anthony Russo opens it. He's taller in real life than his wedding photograph suggests. First impressions are of tanned skin, thick grey-black hair and a lithe body — he must still play soccer or keep fit in some other way. Yes, I can see why my mother married this man.

'Lovely to meet you at last,' I say, sticking out my hand, summoning a smile even though my stomach is doing loops.

'Hello, Louise,' he replies.

As he takes my outstretched hand in his, I can't help noticing that he hasn't returned my smile.

Emma

At times during the show, I actually forget about Jamie and Isla. It's all-consuming: the lights, the action, the sheer concentration required. My performance demands 100 per cent, and I have no choice other than to throw myself into it. In the end, adrenaline takes precedence over stage fright and the nagging worry about Isla. Of course I make a couple of mistakes (minor ones, mainly skipped steps which — hopefully — the audience don't notice), but overall I'm pleased. While I'm performing, I'm looking at my fellow dancers, the positioning of my arms, my feet. It's only when I retire to the wings that I can check for Isla and Jamie. The lighting is very low, the audience dark and blurry, but as far as I can tell their seats are still empty.

The audience is laughing and clapping and gasping in all the right places.

'It's a hit,' Margaret whispers as we near the end.

Miss Sophia is, of course, the star of the show, her dancing exquisite and of a standard high above the rest of us. I can see why she lives for this. It might be just the church hall and a friendly bunch of family and friends — hardly discerning critics — but making people happy like this, entertaining them, transporting them to another world, tapping into their emotions could be very addictive.

There's no place like home … There's no place like home …

A child's voice rises above Dorothy's. People laugh.

It's over. We've done it. Margaret and I hug before joining everyone on stage for what turns out to be a standing ovation. We could be in the Gaiety Theatre. The audience is clapping wildly, being over-exuberant in their response.

Lights pop on around the hall and suddenly it's fully illuminated. There's Eddie and Mum. Isla is definitely not there. She has missed the show.

All the joy drains out of me.

Backstage is chaos. Hugging, squealing, bodies and costumes everywhere.

Mum and Eddie seek me out before I can make it to my phone.

'Where are they?' Mum asks frantically. 'Doesn't Jamie know the show is tonight?'

Poor Mum. Jamie has ruined her night too. I bet she spent the entire time looking over her shoulder, conferring with Eddie on possible explanations, instead of enjoying the performance, maybe even being proud of me.

'Of course he knew,' I snap back at her. 'I don't know where the fuck he is …'

No public transport mishap could make them this late. Isla has missed the entire show, the whole one-off performance. Unbelievable, yet not. I shouldn't have trusted Jamie with something so important. Isla will be devastated. *I'm devastated.* I'm going to fuckin' kill him. If he walked in right now, I'd launch myself at him, dig my fingernails into his skin, inflict as much hurt as I could. He always, *always* ruins everything.

I am so frustrated, angry, disappointed, I think I could actually cry.

Margaret comes over and hovers at the edge of our group. I don't need to tell her what's wrong. My face, I am quite sure, speaks for itself. I should introduce her to Mum — they haven't met, after all — but I can't trust myself to speak. Blinking away the threat of tears, I locate my phone and switch it back on.

The screen fills with missed calls. Dozens of them. All from Jamie's number.

'He's been trying to call me,' I tell Mum and Margaret and Eddie. 'I don't care what his excuses are.'

Jamming the phone to my ear, I wait for my return call to get through.

'It's ringing,' I tell them.

I'm literally bursting with things to say to Jamie. Words like 'unreliable', 'useless', 'disgusting', fill my mouth, ready to spew out when he answers.

But to my astonishment, Jamie doesn't answer the phone.

Isla does.

Louise

The inside of Anthony Russo's house, the little we see of it, is as modest as the outside. The three of us go into the front room and sit down on matching beige sofas, old-fashioned but well maintained. Dan and I perch on one, Anthony on the other. The silence that falls is quite excruciating. Clearly, refreshments are not going to be offered. I'm realising, too late, that Anthony Russo is genuinely reluctant to meet me.

Information, I remind myself. I'm here for information. Which is fine in theory, except that I can't think of a single question to ask this man.

When it becomes evident that neither Anthony nor I seem capable of taking the lead, Dan tries to facilitate.

'Thank you for seeing us,' he says, taking my hand in his. 'Louise hasn't seen her mother since she was eight years old. Maybe if she starts with her story, you can take over with yours, and we'll all get a fuller picture.'

Of course. That's the logical way to proceed. Clever Dan.

His hand squeezes mine, prompting me to begin.

'My mother grew up in Dorset. She was sixteen and pregnant with me when she ran away from home. I don't know who my father is ...'

Anthony says absolutely nothing as I give a brief outline of my childhood: my mother's volatile relationship with Simon, her unhappiness — obvious even to a child — the lack of money and hope, the suddenness and shock of her departure. Then I'm done. Louise and Janet Mitchell: the ten-minute version.

'Your turn,' I say, wishing I had something to drink, even water.

I wait for Anthony to speak. This feels like one of those perpetual stories, where one person starts off, and then hands over to someone else for the next instalment. Anthony leans forward in his seat, then jerks back again. His hands are clenched together. His face is contorted. And it's suddenly clear to me: this isn't about a lack of friendliness or graciousness, this is genuinely painful for him.

Just as I come to the realisation that I am not going to like what he is going to say, he finally opens his mouth.

'I wish I'd never set eyes on your mother.'

Chapter 50

Emma

'Mammy? Mammy?' Isla's voice is so unexpected and small, I'm caught completely off guard.

'Isla?' It takes me a moment to adjust. This isn't Jamie. It's Isla. I'm not angry with her. I *love* her, more than anything in the world. I'm *worried sick* about her. 'Where are you? Why aren't you here? Where's Daddy?' Even though I know that asking more than one question at a time is only going to confuse her, I can't seem to stop myself.

'I don't know,' she replies, but I'm not sure which question she's answering. Despite all the background noise on my end — the chatter and laughter and post-show buzz — I can hear the fear in her voice. Isla sounds the way she does when she wakes from a nightmare: young, vulnerable, disproportionately scared.

She's alone. He's left her alone. I just know it. *I'm going to fuckin' kill him.*

Stay calm, I tell myself in the next breath. Be logical. Find out what happened and where she is. Don't let her know how scared you are. Feeling Eddie's, Mum's and Margaret's eyes on me, I resist the urge to look at them. I need to focus on Isla. Covering my left ear with my hand in order to block out the noise, I ask, once again, 'Where's Daddy?' My tone is remarkably controlled, considering how I feel.

'Some men punched him and knocked him down ...'

Oh Jesus. Sweet Jesus. Jamie, what have you done? Where have you taken our daughter?

'Where are you?' Any pretence at calmness has gone out the window. How can I be calm hearing this? No mother in the world would be calm knowing her little girl was left alone, having witnessed her father — who is supposed to *protect* her, to keep her safe — being punched to the ground.

'I don't know this place, Mammy,' she replies, my panic reverberating in her voice. 'I'm lost.'

Calm. Calm. Don't panic her again.

'Are you inside or outside?' I try once again for a more normal tone.

'Outside. Daddy told me to run.'

He told her to run. Bloody hell. He was getting drugs, I'd put money on it, and something went wrong. He told her to run. If they haven't killed him, I will. Taking my daughter — my beautiful innocent Isla — out with him to get drugs.

'Are you on a street somewhere? Are there houses?'

'There's garage doors and big buildings, but I don't think anyone lives here.'

Oh Christ. It sounds as if she's in an industrial park somewhere. Probably in the middle of nowhere. So exposed. So young. Anyone could come along and take advantage of her. The thought chills my heart.

'I want you to walk until you get to a street corner. Stay on the phone, keep talking to me while you walk. Good girl. Stop when you get to a corner ...'

Only now do I risk looking at them. Mum is totally stricken. Eddie is hopping from foot to foot, ready to jump into action. Margaret is less up to speed, but clearly concerned. She's still in costume, as am I. The Tin Man and The Good Witch.

'I'm at a corner, Mammy.'

'Great, Isla. Now, look up. Can you see a street sign? Good girl. Can you tell me the letters? … Sammy Snake. What's next? Clever Cat … Annie Apple … Noisy Nic … Lucy Lamp …'

Eddie has cottoned on. He has his phone out. Thank God for Google Maps.

'Oscar Orange … Noisy Nic again … What's next Isla? Peter Puppy and Lucy Lamp. Good girl. Now wait a minute, pet …' I lock eyes with Eddie. 'Scanlon Place. She's somewhere called Scanlon Place.'

While he fiddles with his phone, I glance at Mum and Margaret, who shake their heads. They have no idea where it is either. Our eyes focus back on Eddie.

'I have it,' he says, looking up from his phone. 'It's in Crumlin. Tell her I'm on my way …'

Then he's gone, jogging through the backstage chaos. Everyone but our small group is unaware of the real-life drama that's unfolding. Hurry, Eddie, hurry.

'Isla? Eddie's coming to get you. Stay where you are … Don't move … Keep talking to Mammy until Eddie gets there … Yes, the show is over, don't worry about it, it doesn't matter now … I love you so much. You know that, don't you?' My face is wet. I'm crying. Jamie has done it. He has finally reduced me to tears.

Someone's hand is on my arm.

'Tell me what I can do to help,' Margaret says.

I'm about to brush her off, when suddenly the obvious occurs to me. The police. Her husband.

'Is Frank in the audience?' I ask.

'Yes. He's taken the night off work.'

'Tell him there's an emergency. We need him.'

Louise

'I wish I'd never set eyes on your mother,' Anthony says again. 'For Lauren's sake more than my own ...'

Lauren? An unexpected twist in the story. A surprise character.

'Who's Lauren?' Dan asks the question before I can.

'Lauren is my daughter.' Anthony's voice has a disquieting rawness to it. 'From my first marriage ... I was a widower when I met Liz. Lauren was two. It was one of those whirlwind romances. Both Lauren and I fell madly in love.'

Liz. He knew my mother as Liz. Not as Janet, or even Elizabeth. Liz sounds like a stranger, someone I don't know the first thing about. Anthony has stalled. Even if the subject matter weren't so painful, it's obvious he's not a natural storyteller. Dan and I will have to continue to ask questions in order to keep him going.

First things first. 'How did you meet?'

'At the doctor's surgery. Lauren had cut open her chin. Liz was extremely helpful, letting us go to the front of the queue. Lauren took to her immediately, and so did I. Beautiful, obviously good with children — or so I thought. I was instantly infatuated. Later that day, I returned with a thank-you bunch of flowers. It went from there. We were married within six months. All too fast ... These are the mistakes you make when you're lonely.'

He stops dead again. A few seconds elapse. It's clear that we are about to begin another chapter of this story.

'And then?' I prompt.

'Then we bought a house together. As with all marriages, I began to see another side to Liz. Her moods, which seemed particularly extreme. One day full of joy, the next withdrawn. As the months passed, she became more argumentative and secretive. And at times she showed a certain disregard for Lauren. She was not as affectionate or attentive as she could have been. But Liz wasn't Lauren's natural mother, so I excused some of this behaviour. In hindsight, I excused far too much. My first marriage had been happy, uncomplicated. Carolyn died in a car accident. It was sudden, and heartbreaking, but I understood where I was at every juncture of our marriage, even the end. The longer I was with Liz, the less I understood her, and the less I understood *us*. Our marriage was crumbling around us, yet no one had died. We were destroying it ourselves … or rather Liz was.'

He stops again, and this time I don't feel the urge to hurry him on. I need a break too. My eyes search the room, seeking out the minutiae. There are a few framed photographs scattered around. I get up and walk towards one: it's a teenage girl, with brown skin like her father, and a thick plait of almost-black hair resting on one shoulder.

'This is Lauren?'

'Yes … The problem with Lauren is that she isn't confident the way other fourteen-year-olds are. She clings to me, when at this age she should be pushing me away. She's overly anxious, easily upset. Her psychologist says that childhood trauma can have long-lasting effects.'

Trauma. Just hearing the word is enough to bring my hangover back, the weight in my head, the sickness in my stomach. I'm afraid to look at Anthony or Dan, so I fix my eyes on Lauren.

'What did my mother do?'

One second. Two seconds. Three seconds.

'She walked out, disappeared on us …'

The room is spinning. Anthony's voice sounds far away.

'One day I came home from work and found Lauren alone in the house, hysterical. She had wet her pants and hadn't eaten for hours. Liz was gone. She'd taken her purse and some clothes. She'd left a four-year-old child unattended and walked out of our lives.'

Last night's drinks rise up in my throat. I am going to be sick. Oh God, I need to get out of here. Now.

Dashing through the house, flinging open the front door, I barely make it in time. Retching into the flowerbeds in Anthony Russo's front garden, I've reached a new low.

She did it again.

Incredible but true. My mother found a new family, and when the going got tough she walked out on them too.

She did it again.

This was the last possibility on my mind. Worst-case scenario, in my clearly wildly naive opinion, was that she would have a new family, whom she adored and would never dream of abandoning. Of course that scenario wasn't really a bad one; it would have caused me the most hurt, that's all.

This is the worst possible outcome. It hadn't occurred to me that she would do it again. And, worse, to a four-year-old. At least I was older, and at school that day. To think she left a defenceless child alone in the house like that. I'm ashamed, deeply ashamed, to be related to her.

'Are you alright?' Dan is crouched down next to me.

My stomach is still heaving but nothing more is coming out. A cold, defeated sweat settles over my skin.

'She did it again,' is all I can say.

Chapter 51

Emma

Frank, Margaret's husband, drives like a teenage joy-rider, squealing around corners, putting his foot to the floor on the straight stretches of road, completely fearless. I'm vaguely aware of the spectacle we're creating — pedestrians are stopping to watch us whiz past, children are excited by the screaming siren, other vehicles are hurriedly getting out of the way.

'Nearly there,' Frank says. 'Another ten minutes at most.'

'We're almost there,' I repeat to Isla, who has been waiting on the line this whole time. 'Margaret's husband is driving super fast—'

Isla cuts me off. 'I see Eddie … Eddie's here … Eddieeeee!'

'He's there,' I relay to Margaret and Mum, squashed on either side of me in the back seat. 'He has her. He has her.'

I start bawling again. I don't know why. The nightmare is over. Isla's safe with Eddie.

'Shush, now.' Margaret tries to console me. 'It's okay. Everything is fine.'

Mum, on my other side, links her fingers through mine. She's crying, too. 'Thank God,' she breathes. She's been quiet for most of the journey. Praying, I realise now. What strange car companions we make. Margaret, still in her Tin Man costume. Me, Glinda, pink and glittery. Mum, praying, praying, praying.

Though the emergency is strictly over, Frank barges through a few more red lights, and almost goes on two wheels around one particularly sharp corner.

'Frank!' Margaret admonishes.

He says nothing, but for some reason I can picture him rolling his eyes.

'Scanlon Place,' he announces a short while later.

There she is. I can see her through the windscreen, through the dusk. Eddie has her high in his arms. She's safe. Thank God. Thank God. Thank God. Thank God.

Scrambling out of the car, I run to them at full speed — the two people I love most in the world. As we huddle together, I kiss every part of her I can find: her face, the freckles on her nose, her hair (badly in need of a comb), the hollow of her neck, each of her slender fingers.

Only when I finally stop kissing her do I notice the disapproving expression on her face.

'Oh, Mammy. You know you're not meant to wear your ballet slippers outside. They'll be ruined.'

Louise

My mother's ex-husband takes pity on me and drives us back to our hotel.

'Good luck,' he says, and I think neither of us knows what he means by this.

'Thank you, Anthony,' I say, polite and just as meaningless.

In our hotel room, I change my clothes, brush my teeth thoroughly and repack my bag. My stomach, my whole body, feels empty and tender. Dan tries to talk to me but I cannot string more than a few words together. What is there to say? My mother is a horrible, callous human being. I've wasted all this time, all these years, trying to find someone who isn't worthy of love, or of a family.

'It's over.' I finally find my voice as we wait outside the hotel for our taxi to the airport. 'I'm giving up — I don't want to find her.'

He reaches over to take my hand. 'Don't make any decisions yet. Wait until you gain some perspective on this.'

Furious, I snatch my hand away. 'It's nothing to do with you. This is my mother, my story, and this is where it ends.'

Dan gets the message that I want to be left alone and we hardly speak on the return flight. He puts on his earphones, reads a little, closes his eyes for a catnap, all while I stare unseeingly out the window. The magic of the weekend is gone — the romance, the sightseeing, the drunken proposal — obliterated. That woman was a different person. She had hope, though she should have known better.

We touch down in Sydney to a cold rainy night. Another taxi.

'Will you be alright?' Dan asks worriedly when we pull up outside my apartment block.

'I'll be fine,' I lie.

We exchange a brief clumsy embrace.

He lingers. 'I don't like leaving you this way.'

I can see that, but there's no question of him staying the night.

'I just need to be on my own. Goodnight, Dan.'

Emma

This is what happened. From what I can piece together from Isla and Frank, who found Jamie down the side of a deserted factory with two stab wounds to his torso, lucky — Frank's choice of adjective, not mine — to be alive.

Jamie relapsed, as I knew he would. A dealer phoned him to say he had some cheap drugs, and Jamie's three-month sobriety imploded. Just like that. One phone call was all it took. He brought my beautiful, innocent daughter with him to the agreed meeting place, that rundown business park. He gave her his phone to play with, and told her to wait a short distance away, literally a few steps from the planned exchange. But the dealer had set a trap for Jamie. Apparently Jamie had a longstanding debt and the dealer wanted to teach him a lesson. When he drew his knife, and Jamie belatedly realised there were no drugs to be had, and that he had in fact been set up, he screamed at Isla to run.

The only saving grace was that she had his phone.

And she knew how to make a phone call, clever girl.

But I didn't answer her calls. There was a period of time — about an hour — when she was alone, completely defenceless, while I was being Glinda, pirouetting across the stage with my stupid bloody wand.

What could have happened chills me to the bone.

If she didn't have his phone.

If she didn't know how to make a call.

If the battery had gone dead by the time I eventually called back.

If that low-life drug dealer had come after her.

Later that night, when she's washed and fed and safely in bed with her treasured Koala, I locate Frank's business card — the one he left with the thank-you flowers, a lifetime ago — and I call him.

'You need to help me protect my daughter. You need to report this to Family Services, because I've been trying and trying and trying, and they just won't bloody listen. He can't get equal custody. He shouldn't have any custody at all, anyone can see that. Please, help me, Frank. Please.'

Louise

Once I'm inside the flat, I know what I have to do. I start with the intangible stuff. The spreadsheets and Word documents. Delete, delete, delete. Purging, that's the technical word, and it's wonderful. Everything is gone so quickly and easily. Years and years of files and pain. Poof. Gone.

Next come the hardcopy files. Written requests for information. Responses received. Contact names and numbers. Useless, all of them. I carry the files downstairs, to the recycling bin, and rip the documents into tiny shreds until my fingers ache from the motion.

'What are you doing?'

It's Joe, coming in from a night on the town.

'None of your business,' I snap at him.

He looks at me for a moment, then shrugs and walks off. I go inside a few minutes later, after I've judged he's had enough time to find his way to bed.

Good. He's in his room. Now, the box. The old letters, photographs and other random pieces. For sixteen years I've treasured everything in that box. I've used all my skills to preserve its contents. It goes against the grain to destroy it. I stall.

She has done nothing to merit being remembered. She didn't treasure me or Simon or Lauren or Anthony. Or even her own parents, whom she ran away from first. Why should I treasure anything of hers?

This line of thought propels me back downstairs. I throw the box, in its entirety, into the recycling bin. There are things in there that aren't recyclable: a pen, a necklace, a scarf. I don't care.

It hits me then. The grief. I'm doubled over with it, until I collapse to the ground, cold and wet from the earlier rain. My body convulses with each sob.

It feels as if somebody has died.

Chapter 52

Emma

Patients in fluffy dressing gowns and slippers are puffing cigarettes outside the front of the hospital. It's a bleak scene, and my mood darkens even further.

'He's in intensive care,' the hard-faced blonde behind the information desk tells me when I enquire about Jamie. 'Close family only.'

'I'm his girlfriend.' I knew I would have to tell some lies in order to see him, but the words still stick in my throat, and take me back to when I *was* his girlfriend, and he was my whole life.

I share the oversized lift with an orderly and a trolley of toilet rolls. Maybe my job *isn't* the most dead-end one in the world. Which reminds me: tomorrow is Monday, and I will have to go to work. My job, my desk, Katie, Brendan — I feel as though they all exist in another universe.

The intensive care unit is on the third floor. There's another reception desk to get past, and a security door.

'I'm his girlfriend,' I explain to the nurse, the lie no easier the second time round.

'He's in a serious condition.' She accepts the lie and buzzes the door open for me to enter. 'Ten minutes only.'

Ten minutes is more than enough for what I need to say. All last night I was awake, fury, relief, helplessness, fury again, churning inside me. I got up at least five times to check on Isla. Long before morning came I knew I needed to come here.

Sue, his Mum, is sitting with him. She spots me through the glass window, and comes outside before I can go in.

'He's in a bad way,' she whispers, even though there's no risk Jamie can hear anything through the glass.

'Do you expect me to feel sympathy?'

She touches my arm. 'Don't go in if you're angry. Come back tomorrow.'

'I just need to get a few things off my chest.'

'You'll only upset him,' she says, quite unbelievably.

'Hang on a minute,' I splutter. 'Do you know what he *did*? Where he took Isla? The danger he put her in?'

'I know *everything*.' Her voice has risen. She hears herself and takes a more conciliatory tone. 'But he's in a bad way, Emma. There will be time enough for recriminations later.'

'You're always letting him off the hook,' I cry. 'No matter what he does. You're part of the reason he is the way he is ...'

'Not here,' she cuts me off. 'Not here. There are other sick people to consider. *Please.*'

She's infuriating, completely infuriating. I can't listen to any more of these excuses. Years and years and years of them. *Jamie this. Jamie that. My poor boy.* Turning abruptly, I shove open the heavy door to the ward.

My anger falters when I see him. The oxygen mask. The

colourlessness of his face. His bare, scrawny chest. Dressings, drips, tubes, monitors.

His eyes are red, wet. Jamie is crying. Like me, he is not a crier. A memory. Watching a sad movie in someone's house. The others blinking back tears, Jamie and I rolling our eyes, sneering. Tough: that's how we liked to think of ourselves.

Criers are die-ers. Was that my saying or his?

He fiddles with his oxygen mask, lifting it to the side so he can speak. 'I'm sorry,' he breathes, and then breaks down completely, sobs racking his thin body, inflicting further pain.

I came here to verbally tear strips off him. To tell him that he was never ever going to see Isla again. To tell him that Frank and the Drugs Unit and Family Services are onto him. I can't. I would need a heart of stone to go into attack while he's in this state.

Before I know what I'm doing, I take his limp hand in mine.

And I realise something.

I am no better than Sue. No matter how many times he fails, or how many times he lets all of us down, or how hard I pray for him to disappear from Isla's life, or even how much I adore Eddie, there will always be a part of me that loves Jamie.

It's bloody heartbreaking. For everyone.

Louise

When I wake, the first thing I see is the box. It's on the bedside locker. Slowly, last night comes back to me. Joe lifting me off the ground, helping me up the stairs, putting me to bed. He must have retrieved the box from the recycling bin. I don't know how I feel about this.

I can hear voices from the living room. Dan's here. Mary, too. Her voice is clearly distinguishable from the lower tones of her sons. She's bossing them around about something. Me. It's *me* they're talking about. The Connolly family are on the other side of the wall, conferring about *me*.

I lie there for a long time, too weary, too defeated, to get out of bed and face them.

The Connolly family.

They argue and bicker and annoy one another. But when the chips are down, they draw close and show their true strength: their unity. I'm not one of them. Despite how fond I am of them, despite how much I love Dan, despite the serious undertones to his joke marriage proposal, I realise now that I will never fit into that unit. The place I come from, my family — if that's what you can call my mother and Simon — is simply too dysfunctional, too far out of their orbit.

Time passes. A half hour? They're not showing any signs of leaving. Sighing, I heave myself into an upright position. God, I'm weak. The last time I felt like this was after a bad bout of flu in New York. It was winter and bitterly cold in my loft apartment. I shiver at the memory and reach for some clothes: jeans and an old long-sleeved top. They've fallen quiet out there, so they can obviously hear me moving around. Next the bathroom. I need to pee and brush my teeth before facing them.

Finally, I emerge.

They're sitting in a semi-circle. It's not unlike walking into a job interview.

'We've come to a decision,' Dan announces.

'What?'

'We're going to hire a private investigator. With the information we already have, a professional should be able to find your mother within days.'

'I don't want to find her.' I've already told him this. Before we left Adelaide. Jesus, what will it take to get him to listen?

'You need to, Louise.' Mary has spoken. Then she waits until I switch my angry, why-don't-you-listen gaze from Dan to her. 'It's quite clear to all of us that you need closure.'

Closure. Ha! Mary has been watching too much *Dr Phil*, I think.

'So you can go on with your life,' she adds.

Just like that, I swerve from derision to quite the opposite. Yes, I do need to go on with my life. I need to stop looking back. Forward is where I need to look. Mary is *absolutely right*. I'll find my mother. Tell her what I know. Tell her what I think of her. Then it will be over. I'll put it behind me and never look back again.

'Do you know someone?' I ask all of them.

Dan answers. 'Of course.'

Chapter 53

Emma

Here are some things about Jamie that most people don't know.

He comes from a well-to-do family. His mum, Sue, lives in a beautiful old house in a posh suburb. No gangs on the street corners, no drug deals outside her front door. Unlike my poor mother.

When he was young Jamie wanted to be an architect. He was a good student, particularly strong in maths and art — until getting high became his one and only ambition in life. The really sad thing is that his mother still thinks there's some hope of him going to university and completing a five-year degree in architecture. Yes, she is that deluded.

It was Jamie's older brother who got him into drugs. Roy used to smoke pot with his friends some days after school. Jamie was only thirteen when Roy allowed him to try a few puffs. Within a matter of months, both boys were smoking every day, after school and at home. As the addiction and taste for risk took a firmer hold, they began to experiment with harder drugs. When he was twenty Roy met a 'nice' girl and moderated his drug use, eventually stopping altogether. He's married now, with one kid, and works as a computer technician. Sue thinks her first son is a paragon of virtue.

'If it wasn't for Roy …' she often says, in a sad, disappointed voice.

She has no idea that her darling Roy started Jamie off. God forgive me, but I'd love to tell her. It would change nothing, though. It would only upset her even further, and rob her of the pride she has in at least one of her boys.

Another thing that's quite unexpected about Jamie is his kindness, and his loyalty to his friends. After the car accident, he was the only one of us who kept in contact with Sean. Poor slow Sean, who still lives with his parents, who will never have a proper job. Jamie, when he's sober, calls in to see him. From what I understand, they play Go Fish and listen to old CDs together.

And he's affectionate, too. Jamie is surprisingly affectionate. He likes to kiss and hug: Isla, his mum, me when I was his girlfriend.

On Monday, during my lunchbreak, I go to the hospital again. I know the score, and whiz through all the questions and security.

Sue isn't here, thank God. It's not that I don't like Sue, or she doesn't like me. It's just the blame thing. I blame her for enabling him: for paying his bills, for listening to his bloody excuses, for trying to love him into recovery, for making his drug use our problem instead of his. She blames me. Maybe if I was a nicer girl — like Roy's wife? — he would have given up years ago.

Jamie's sleeping. His skin is grey, his breathing shallow. Even though he's off the oxygen, he looks almost dead.

Another thing that nobody knows is that I've planned his funeral a thousand times. As clear as day, I can see his coffin at the church, Sue and Roy and the rest of us dressed in black, the horrible inevitability that shrouds the whole scene. What precedes the funeral varies.

Jamie dying at home from an overdose and not being found for days. Or dying in some dirty flat belonging to one of his so-called friends after a dodgy batch of drugs. Or in the toilets of some club, or in the dank laneway outside, his thin curled-up body a gruesome discovery that would cause nightmares for the poor person who happened upon him. At the start I was trying to brace myself, as though by imagining his death in advance I could mitigate some small part of the shock and sadness. Later, when faced with the reality, and terrible risk, of his access rights to Isla, I imagined his funeral as a convenient way out. I'm ashamed to admit that now, ashamed that I actually *prayed* for him to die.

His eyes flicker open.

'This is what's going to happen,' I tell him sternly. 'You're going to get treatment *again* …'

He nods wearily. How many times has he been in rehab now? Four? Five? I bet he, like me, has lost count, and hope.

Once again, in an impulse that feels almost primal, I find myself taking hold of his limp hand. 'I must be mad, completely off my fuckin' head, but I'm going to allow you to continue to see Isla. *Not* on your own … Me, Mum, Eddie or your mother must be there too. And no overnight stays. If you can't agree to that, then you're not going to see her at all. Family Services know exactly what's going on now. Margaret's husband has filed a report and a recommendation. So I call the shots. It's my way or no way. Understand?'

He nods again. It seems he's too weary, too broken, too rock bottom to even speak.

I squeeze his hand. 'It'll be alright,' I tell him, and for the tiniest moment I allow myself to believe it.

Louise

Geneviève is gone. Having been revarnished twice, the final steps in her treatment, this morning she was taken away for the exhibition, which is opening in a few days. Later, when she has been replaced in her frame and hung against the clean white walls of the gallery, I will go down to admire her. In the meantime, Tom has asked me to work with Peter on a massive landscape painting that needs a thorough clean. Peter works on one end, and I work on the other. He doesn't talk much while he works, which suits my present frame of mind. Every now and then he hums under his breath, and I find myself listening, trying to place the tune, and becoming distracted from the job at hand.

'So Analiese is coming back next month,' he comments after a long silence.

I glance across at him, but his eyes are trained on his section of the painting. 'Yes, three days a week — Wednesday, Thursday and Friday.'

Analiese and I spoke on the phone yesterday. She was in serious organisational mode: spring cleaning the house, making and freezing casseroles, sprucing up the garden. Housework, cooking and gardening are obviously going to present a challenge once she's back in the workforce.

'Stella is at Mum's,' she told me, efficiency brimming in her voice. 'They're having a trial run today. I've typed up a schedule for them. Not that Mum doesn't know how to mind a baby — she's had four of her own, for God's sake — but best practice has changed, and Stella's routine, the food I want her to eat, how much sleep she should have, what games are good for her development … they're all important to me.'

Analiese has such a scrupulous approach to mothering. She's only going to be missing three days a week, but still feels the need to type up copious instructions. My mother left forever and didn't even think to scribble a note. No guidelines on food, or sleep, or my development. Okay, so I was eight, not a baby, but still so young and defenceless. Some guidance, any guidance, would have been good. Even if it was just to say, *I'm not coming back, ever. And please don't bother to find me. Save your energy for something more worthwhile.*

'Has Tom mentioned any upcoming projects to you?' I ask Peter, wondering again how the workload will be divvied up when Analiese returns.

'Oh, there are always plenty of projects in the pipeline,' Peter replies dryly. 'The problem is getting the funding for them.'

Funding. Yes, that would be a stumbling block.

As it was for Dan and me last night. Funding for the private investigator. He wants to pay. In fact, the whole Connolly family wants to chip in.

'We want to do this for you. All of us. Consider it a gift.'

'A gift,' I spluttered incredulously to Emma, whom I called as soon as Dan left.

'I think it's a wonderful gift,' she said. 'I can't think of anything you need more.'

Her response surprised me. Her cynicism is something I've come to rely on. It's my reality check should I get too excited or happy or hopeful. But Emma has been off kilter since this latest incident with Jamie. She's very shaken by it, subdued when I would have expected her to be enraged. To be honest, it's hard to get to the bottom of how either of us feels over the phone. I really wish she was here. Just for a few days. She's the only one who can come close to understanding how angry and disappointed and deeply ashamed I am about my mother. And I suspect I'm the only one who can begin to understand the complexity of her feelings for Jamie.

As the silence stretches on with Peter, my thoughts slip from Emma back to Dan. He's already hired the investigator. It's a woman, Leanne somebody or other. I feel too disassociated from the process to commit her full name to memory. Dan has briefed her — I didn't want any part of that either. Apparently she's very experienced and does this kind of work all the time.

'I don't want updates,' I told Dan tersely. 'I don't want to hear anything until you've found her.'

This might sound ungrateful of me, but I've quite simply reached my limit. I can't handle all the new possibilities, the inevitable false leads or any of the other ups and downs that come with searching. The only way I can take any more is to keep my distance from it, and leave the whole sorry mess in Dan's very capable hands.

Around eleven, Peter offers to go across the road and get some coffees, and while he's gone I take a break from the cleaning and catch up on some emails. I'm surprised to see that Jacquie, from Amsterdam, has been in touch again, and even more surprised to read her latest update.

We've found your artist. His name is Sebastian Therien, and we believe he painted Geneviève while he was a student at The Royal Academy of Painting and Sculpture. Sebastian Therien went on to become a sculptor, and had a great deal of talent, but he never reached the heights of Jean-Baptiste Chevalier in terms of fame or success.

So this begs the question why the portraits of Nicolas, Victor and Mathilde were all painted by a prominent artist of the time, while

Geneviève's was painted by a student (albeit a very talented one). We can only conclude that the reasons were monetary based. Perhaps the Auguste family had fallen on hard times. Or perhaps, given Geneviève's 'mental issues', her parents deemed her portrait to be of lesser value, and so opted for a cheaper alternative to their other children.

I skim the rest of Jacquie's message. So that's it. Mystery solved. Artist: check. Identity of subject: check. And lots of ancillary information too, information that won't make it onto the printed card that will be displayed next to the portrait. Why Geneviève was painted by an artist much less renowned than the one who painted her siblings. Why her portrait was left to deteriorate while the others were so well taken care of. Why she wasn't mentioned in the social publications of the time. Her stints at La Bicêtre Hôpital, asylum for the mentally ill. The fact that there is no record of either her discharge from the hospital, or her death there. Beautiful, intriguing Geneviève Auguste, discarded by her family, discarded by society.

Automatically, I pick up the phone to share the news with Analiese. No answer. She's probably elbow deep in garden soil, or standing on a chair wiping the tops of her wardrobes, or busy typing up further babysitting instructions for her mother.

'Call me when you get a chance,' I tell her voicemail.

On impulse, I decide to go downstairs and see Geneviève, even though I suspect they're still deciding on the exact placing and the lighting for her.

To my surprise, she has been mounted on the wall, and her smile is one of the first things I see as soon as I enter the series of rooms dedicated to the exhibition.

She looks amazing. The bright magenta of her gown against the whiteness of the wall. The pale yet warm tones of her skin. The flecks of green in her brown eyes, her right eye painted by *me*.

'I've missed you,' I tell her, under my breath.

Now I know why I've become so attached to this painting, why my emotional connection to it is so strong. We're the same, Geneviève and me: we both know what it feels like to be 'thrown away'.

Chapter 54

Emma

Here we are. Back in the church hall. All of us in full regalia once again. A one-off repeat performance of *The Wizard of Oz* in honour of Isla.

I didn't ask for this. Margaret thought of it, and she was the one who put the idea to Miss Sophia, who, of course, could not pass up the opportunity to perform, even if only to a handful of people. Isla, guest of honour, has the best seat. Mum, who can hardly remember the first performance because she was so sick with worry, is on one side of her, and Katie, who couldn't attend because of a nasty stomach bug, is on the other. Katie's sitting on the very edge of her seat, her face lit up. She seems even more excited than Isla. There are a few others in today's audience, family and friends of the cast who for one reason or another missed the first show, or decided that they wanted to see it again.

Margaret is standing next to me in the wings. We're both gazing at Isla, whose legs are swinging back and forth while she waits for this much-anticipated show to begin.

'Thank you for organising this,' I whisper. Of course I've thanked Margaret before now, and will again. She has become a close friend. An unexpected friend, because I never imagined a friendship with a woman more than thirty years older than me. Frank, too. Margaret's husband — despite her frequent complaints about him — is practical, brave, extraordinarily committed, and essentially kind. While I was raging at Jamie and didn't care if he died on the side of the road, Frank held his hand until the ambulance came, and reassured instead of berated him. That awful evening, when everything had gone wrong, when Frank's rare day off was commandeered by my emergency, he treated Jamie like a real person, not just an irritation, or a hopeless case — which I was guilty of doing. Jamie has told me that Frank has been to see him in hospital, and has left leaflets on the various treatment programs and other support that is available to him.

'Just thank God she's here,' Margaret replies now. 'Sitting there safely.'

Katie is holding one of Isla's hands. Dear, helpful Katie. Another unexpected friend.

Neither Margaret nor Katie will ever take the place of Louise, but I'm grateful to have them in my life. Tomorrow, when this tumultuous week is finally behind me, I will call Louise for a long talk. Our last phone conversation felt unsatisfactory, unfinished. So much has happened. For both of us. I know she has Dan, and her new friend from work — Analiese, I think her name is — but I want her to know that I'm here too. I've *always* been here, and always will be.

The music starts.

'Emma!' Trish hisses at me.

Oh fuck! I'm meant to be on props until my first appearance on stage. I hurry forward to help Trish.

It's not a perfect performance. There are many mishaps, missteps, and very obvious mistakes. But the mood is joyous. As I pirouette across the stage, and point and flex and go through all my steps (plus my fair share of mistakes), I feel happy and strong, and almost elegant.

At the end of the performance, after a quick informal bow, I rush off stage to seek Isla's feedback.

'You were brilliant, Mammy,' she tells me, her little face so earnest I can't resist kissing it.

Katie adds her congratulations.

Taking a bow, as though I'm receiving an Oscar, I begin, 'I'd like to thank all my supporters. My beautiful daughter, Isla. My good friend, Katie. My wonderful mother, who paid for my first dance lessons …'

Mum and I exchange a grin. Her eyes are a little teary.

'Katie recorded some bits on her phone,' Isla beams. 'Maybe we can show them to Daddy.'

Isla misses Jamie. I've tried to explain what happened as honestly and kindly as I can. Daddy was hurt by some bad people and is very sick in hospital. After hospital, he'll have to go to another place to get better, so it will be a while before she can see him again. I suggested to her that she should make him a very special get-well card. Her creation is on the kitchen table, a flamboyant display of glitter, bright markers and uneven bubble writing. I'll take it in to him tomorrow.

'That's a good idea,' I say, my happiness making me more accom-modating. 'Katie can send the video clips to me and I'll forward them on to Daddy. Now, I'd better get changed.'

'We'll wait in the playground down the road,' Mum decides, putting her hand on Isla's shoulder and pointing her towards the door.

I change out of my costume, depositing it into the dry-cleaning bag. Then I help pack up the props and set. When everything is tidied away, I say my goodbyes. I'm on my way out the door — visualising Isla at the playground, Katie pushing as she swings high into the air — when I switch on my phone.

Just like the last time, I have numerous missed calls.

Not from Jamie. From Louise.

There's a text, too, embedded in the middle of the missed calls: *My mother died last year. It's over.*

Shock scrambles the words until they're nonsense. I stop in my tracks, reading each word slowly, searching for a different meaning, a different outcome, until the truth hits me straight in the gut.

Janet is dead. The search is over. She was never found.

Chapter 55

Louise

Dan found out first, of course, because he was the one who engaged the private investigator. She phoned him and broke the bad news, and then followed up with an email which contained more detail.

Despite its practical, economic use of language, I couldn't read the email, couldn't progress past the first few sentences. It was as if I was back at school, before I got help, and the words looked both familiar and utterly foreign. Seeing my panic, my helplessness, Dan took over, reading it to me slowly.

His voice, sounding very far away, told me that my mother, Janet Elizabeth Russo (apparently, she continued to use her married name after the divorce) had passed away after a short illness. Liz, as she was known to her friends, lived in a group home in Cremorne (ironically, walking distance from Joe's flat). She had been diagnosed with border-line personality disorder and was on medication for her illness and associated depression, but she died from other causes: an aggressive cancer of the stomach. Her friends at the home were aware that she had a daughter (the fact that she finally acknowledged my existence is of no consequence to me). Liz had moved into the home after a suicide attempt, which — according to the unofficial enquiries made by the investigator — had not been her first. However, she responded well to mood stabilisers and worked on a casual basis at a local garden centre, as well as doing various jobs around the home. In fact, she was considering moving out of the home when she began to feel stomach pain. When made aware that her cancer was terminal, she decided to donate her body to science. She died at Mater Maria Hospice on August 4, 2013, two days before her fortieth birthday.

So, as I said in my text to Emma, it's over. My mother, Janet, Liz, whatever she called herself, is over, dead, gone forever. And I was wrong, totally wrong. I fully believed she was alive, that I would 'feel it' if she had died, that somewhere deep inside me I would know this fundamental truth. How laughable. She died, and I knew nothing, didn't feel a thing. August 4, 2013: I was living in New York then. I would have thought of her on her birthday, I always do. But she was already two days dead, and there was I, completely oblivious.

It just goes to show how little I knew about anything.

Hearing of my mother's death has made me sick. My body has gone into shutdown, and I have no strength. It's much worse than when I found out what she had done to Anthony and Lauren. Throwing up in Anthony's flower beds, collapsing near the recycling bin downstairs, is nothing compared to this. This time I can't get back up. Strong arms, genuine concern, a good night's sleep — nothing, nobody, can help me this time round.

Borderline personality disorder. Mood swings. Zoning out of family life. Feeling overwhelmed. Most significantly, *not being able to control the urge to flee.* Dan says it explains a lot and I suppose it does. Maybe if my mother had been diagnosed earlier things could have been different. After all, it seems she responded well to treatment when she finally got some. Back when she was a schoolgirl, when it was obvious to Edward Ramshaw's sister that Janet Mitchell was rather 'strange', perhaps her parents could have sought a medical opinion, and perhaps a teenage pregnancy — me — could have been avoided. Later in the piece, maybe if Simon hadn't been such an alcoholic bully himself, he might have been more aware that my mother's behaviour was far from normal. He could have urged her to 'see someone'. Even later again, if Anthony hadn't been so confused by the apparent personality change in his new wife, and helpless in the face of her changeable moods, maybe he could have intervened before she ran away for the third time in her life, leaving poor Lauren, a defenceless child, alone in the house for hours on end, by far the worst of her transgressions.

It's not like the possibility of mental illness didn't cross my mind. Of course it did. But I was overly simplistic in my approach, trawling my memories for 'classic' signs of depression. Did I remember her not wanting to get out of bed? Being unduly sad? Crying a lot? No, I didn't. Of course depression is much more complicated than that, and borderline personality disorder even more complex again. I simply didn't have enough information to lead me there, and even if I did, I'd have needed a degree in psychology to make sense of it.

But all this surmising doesn't alter what actually happened, or in any way change my feelings about her, or cancel out all the things I still need to say to her. Things I have saved up for sixteen years, conversations banked up inside me. Not nice things, mind you. I admit that they're angry, hurtful, ugly things. Now I can never say them, never let them out. If I can't get them out, they'll fester. They're already festering. I can practically feel the poison seeping into my blood ...

There's something I haven't told anyone.

My mother phoned. Once. About eighteen months after she 'left'. On my birthday. She asked me how I was.

I said I was fine.

Yes, that's what I said. 'Fine.' The most inane, wishy-washy of words.

She wished me a happy birthday and then hung up.

I stood there with the phone in my hand, wondering if I had imagined it.

'Who is it?' Simon yelled out.

'No one,' I called back, my face burning at the magnitude of the lie.

I never told a soul. Not even Emma.

It was shame that made me mute. My mother hadn't come to any harm. She wasn't ill in some hospital, or kidnapped by a psycho, or murdered by Simon, or dead due to some freak, tragic accident. She was very much alive. She had left me. It was as simple as that.

All the things I've wanted to say have been building up ever since that phone call. A thousand other words I should have said instead of 'fine'. Now I'll never have the chance to say those other words, never have a right of reply, never be able to state, 'I'm not *fine*. Not at all. And *you're* to blame.'

As I've said, those unspoken words are like poison inside me.

That must be why I feel so sick.

Chapter 56

Emma

'Emma!' Brendan roars from his office.

I've been waiting for this. He has obviously read the letter I propped against his keyboard before he sauntered in this morning.

'Emma. In here. *Now.*'

Katie looks scared on my behalf. 'What have you done?'

Standing up, smoothing down my trousers, I give her a wobbly smile. 'I've resigned.'

Her mouth is still open as I walk past her desk. I'll talk to her later, once I've got through this, and explain everything.

'Yes, Brendan.' I've purposefully closed the door behind me. I don't want Katie or anyone else to hear anything further. Especially not if this doesn't go the way I planned, and there's every chance of that.

'What is this about?' he splutters, the letter in his hand.

'I believe it's called a letter of resignation,' I reply with more than a hint of sarcasm. I don't want him to know that my knees are knocking, or that I feel a lot closer to petrified than sardonic.

'You can't resign,' he declares, his face hot with outrage. 'Not out of the blue like this. Not without *talking* to me first.'

'We have talked.' I shrug as a show of nonchalance. 'Lots of times, Brendan. I've asked you to consider me for promotion. I've asked to be paid a salary equivalent to the market value for my role. I've asked for more flexible work hours ...'

'Not all at once,' is all he can say. 'I don't ever recall you asking for all these ... *improvements* ... all at once.'

'No, not all at once,' I concede. 'I've tried not to be too demanding, but in the end I think I've let you take terrible advantage of me.'

'No ...' he protests. 'No.'

'Yes. Definitely, yes.'

There's silence as we regard each other across his desk. I meet his gaze as squarely as I can.

'Do you have another job to go to?'

'Yes.' The lie comes easily, and sounds confident, almost aggressive. Deliberately softening my tone, I add, 'But that isn't to say I won't change my mind. Despite being underpaid, underappreciated and under-trained, I like working here ...' My lips stretch in a small smile, showing him — I hope — that I'm confident enough to display a sense of humour, even when everything's on the line.

'What are you asking for?' he frowns, suspicious now.

'Twenty per cent salary increase for each of the next three years. A new job description which acknowledges the fact that I manage this department. I'd like to finish at three on Fridays ... and I need two weeks' leave immediately to attend to some personal issues.'

He weighs it up, then latches on to the last — and ironically the least costly — of my demands.

'You can't take holidays just like that,' he cries. 'The board reports will be due, for a start.'

'I'll train Katie on how to do the reports, and anything else that can't wait. As you already know, Katie is very capable, real leadership material ... I have the leave accrued, Brendan. I just want to take what's due to me, that's all.'

It's a stand-off. His eyes flicker from the letter to me. It was a gamble, resigning like this, a huge gamble. Please, please don't bloody backfire on me.

'Okay,' he says after a very long pause.

For a moment I'm confused. Does he mean 'Okay I accept your resignation' or 'Okay I accept your new working conditions'.

'Okay what?' I ask, my voice breaking a little.

'I accept all these requests. I'll get the paperwork rolling. And you'd better start training Katie.'

'Will do.' I flash him a smile — this time a genuine one — which he doesn't return. Brendan doesn't like being held over a barrel. It will take him a long time to forgive me for this. Maybe he never will.

'What happened?' Katie asks urgently as I pass by her desk again.

'I'll tell you later,' I say with a smile.

First, I need to make some calls.

Eddie. I should let him know it paid off. I risked everything — our new house, his dreams, our future — and it worked. Thank God, thank God, thank God.

And Louise. I need to talk to her as soon as possible. She'll be so surprised. Actually, what I'm really hoping is that the surprise will knock some of her sadness aside.

But first, before I speak to anyone else, I need to call Mum.

Chapter 57

Louise

I have a stream of visitors. It appears that they seek prior permission from Dan or Joe — God forbid they should ask me directly — before they descend with gifts, sympathy and well-meant advice.

Gabriella calls on her way home from the gallery, one hand dangling a bag of get-well biscotti.

'Tom passes on his condolences,' she states, the bed sinking as she sits down on it, her rear end uncomfortably close to my thigh. I shimmy away to create some distance. 'He said to take as long as you need. There's an exciting new exhibition on the cards. It's all top secret, but he gave me permission to discreetly mention it to you. Apparently, some of the pieces are in an awful state, and we're all going to be very, very busy.'

Despite my sickness, my overwhelming sadness, my general inertia, a spark of gratitude ignites inside me. Tom has work. When I'm feeling better, I'll have a job to go to. I'll be busy, and this is good, something I can look forward to.

Mary comes every day. She brings a variety of homemade soups and a need for cleanliness. She shoos me out of bed so she can make hospital corners with the sheets. She turns on the shower and stares me down until I relent and get in. (If I refuse, I fear she'll strip off my clothes herself, and give me a smack on the bare bottom to help me on my way.) She vacuums my room, pulls back the curtains, and lets in some air.

'You're going to be fine,' she declares as she puffs pillows and straightens whatever it is that's askew. 'You've been knocked for six, that's all. Of course, it'll take you a few days to recover.'

I hope so, I really do.

Then there's Joe. He coaxes me from the bed to the couch so we can watch reality TV together. He makes endless cups of tea and coffee. Despite being at a critical point of his new novel, he stops and checks up on me.

'Alright, Louise?'

'Yes,' I reply, even though I'm not alright at all. I've fallen apart.

Analiese visits too. She doesn't bring anything, and apologises — totally unnecessarily — for this.

Her advice comes from a different angle.

'Your mother is just like Geneviève,' she says.

'No, Geneviève is *me*,' I tell her. 'I'm the one who got thrown away.'

She shakes her head, her dark curls in need of a comb. 'You're wrong. You've got your health, a career you enjoy and people who love and understand and are worried about you. You haven't been thrown away. But your mother has ... or was. She fell through the cracks of school, her family and society. She lived most of her life without her illness being properly diagnosed. Don't throw *her* away, Louise. Cherish what you had of her. Love her no matter what.'

Analiese has reached me in a way the others haven't. There is some truth in what she's saying. If I turn my back on my mother, remove her from my thoughts and my life, am I no better than Geneviève's family? Or — another relevant example — does it make me the same as George, Kitten's brother, who didn't have a shred of empathy for his mentally disturbed sister? I need some time to mull this over, to cast myself in this other role, and try to channel the support, understanding and unconditional love I fully expected of Geneviève's and Kitten's families in similar circumstances.

Amidst all these visitors — who each bring me something valuable, something to make me a little bit stronger — there's Dan. My constant. Every morning. Every night. Dan, who is doing absolutely everything he can to help me.

He says that the news of my mother's death has plunged me back into crisis mode. He assures me this is a common reaction. All the confusion, hurt, shame, helplessness and devastation of those early days is dredged up and re-experienced. New to the mix is grief. According to Dan's sources, when someone goes missing, those who are left behind experience trauma more than grief. They don't know the why, where or how, and the uncertainty is more distressing than anything else. But now that I finally know the truth, I can grieve. This is all according to Dan, investigative journalist and amateur psychologist.

Crisis, trauma, grief, whatever. All I know is that I feel sick.

'I need to see her death certificate,' I state, three days into my sickness.

Dan nods. He understands. He will get it for me, no questions asked.

It seems that where I was once looking for evidence of life, I'm now in desperate need of evidence of death.

Am I coming closer to acceptance? To being able to get back on my feet? I hope so.

Despite my confusion and sadness and ultimate need for proof, there's one thing that's clear.

I'm not alone.

Gabriella, Analiese, Mary, Joe, Dan, and of course Emma.

I might *feel* hopelessly alone and thrown away, but the fact is, I'm not.

Chapter 58

Emma

It's a first time, for all of us: me, Mum and Isla. Twenty-four, fifty-four and six years old respectively, and not one of us has ever been on a plane, or abroad, for that matter. It's laughable, sad. Bloody unbelievable in this day and age.

Emergency passports were required, and obtained — at a price. In addition to the cost of the flights and our spending money, the trip comes with a price tag that makes me feel queasy if I think about it for too long. Hopefully, my pay increase will eventually compensate, but for now there's a big hole in our house budget. Eddie and I had set a little aside for new furniture — that money was the first to be pilfered. Isla had some cash in her bank account, which I hated withdrawing, but justified on the basis that this experience has to be worth more than any fad toy she could have chosen to spend her money on. The rest of the money came from our current account, the very same account from which our first mortgage payment will be debited in a few weeks' time. Mum and I had quite a big argument about the cost of her flight, which I insisted on paying. It's important to me, my payback for all I've put her through, even though I can hardly afford it.

So here we are. Three generations of women, three modest cabin bags, three brand-new passports in hand, about to join the queue for security.

'Time for me to say goodbye,' Eddie says, stopping at the QUEUE HERE sign.

Isla flings herself at him. 'Bye, Eddie. We'll phone you as soon as we land.'

He picks her up — with new coloured jeans and a funky top, she looks very mature today — and plants a kiss on her head. 'Be good for your mammy.' Then he turns to me, and gives me a kiss too — like Isla's, on the head. 'Take care, alright? And don't forget to enjoy yourself.'

I don't think I've ever loved him as much as I do at this minute. Here, in the middle of a busy Monday afternoon at Dublin airport, wearing his favourite faded jeans and a new black T-shirt that makes his eyes seem darker than they are, I'm so proud that he is my boyfriend, my partner, my *co-mortgagee*. And I don't think I've ever felt so grateful to anyone either. For understanding how important this is to me, for allowing me to spend some — quite a lot, actually — of the money we so badly need for our new house on this impulsive dash to the other side of the world. He's going to work his ass off while we're away, take on every possible extra shift, and hopefully we'll be able to scrape enough together to make that first mortgage payment when it's due.

The rush of undiluted love and gratitude has made me quite emotional. 'Thank you,' I say, and then worry it hasn't conveyed enough.

He kisses me again, this time on the lips, and steals a kiss from Mum too, who is wearing red soft-soled shoes and beige chinos — all purchased especially for the occasion — and looks like the consummate traveller.

'Have fun, girls.' With a wave, Eddie's gone, and for a moment I'm close to crying.

We proceed through the security checkpoint, Isla highly excited, Mum slightly nervous, me in a growing state of disbelief.

I'm doing this. I'm really doing this. Going somewhere. *Sydney*.

Mum tries to strike up a conversation with the security personnel, but they aren't really interested in the fact that this is her first trip abroad, or how wonderful it is that she's travelling with her daughter and granddaughter, or that she's read all about Sydney and what a fabulous city it is for tourists.

With security done, we follow the crowds to Duty Free, and Isla's eyes light up when she sees all the goodies. I say no each time she shows me something she likes — cuddly toys, model airplanes, jumbo boxes of sweets — but Mum eventually gives in and buys her a shamrock key ring.

'You're meant to buy souvenirs in Australia, not Ireland,' I tell them both in exasperation. 'We're not tourists *here*.'

Neither of them seems to get my point.

As I turn around, I notice someone staring at me. She looks familiar: sleek hair, crisp white shirt with jeans.

'Hello, Emma.' When she realises that I can't quite place her, she briskly supplies her name. 'Mairead. From the leadership course.'

Of course. How could I forget that superior expression, that grating plaintive voice?

I nod at her expensive looking wheelie bag. 'Where are you off to?'
'Manchester. You?'

'Australia. Family holiday.' I proudly glance towards Mum and Isla, who both look very well-to-do (not remotely 'rough') in their new clothes. 'Are you going to Manchester for work?'

'Not exactly.' Mairead looks uncomfortable. 'It's an interview, actually … I'm between jobs at the moment.'

'Well, good luck,' I say graciously.

'Nice meeting you again,' she lies, and then she and her wheelie bag continue on their way.

'Who's she?' Isla asks, following Mairead's progress with wide eyes.

'Nobody important …' I'm interrupted by an announcement over the intercom.

'That's us,' Mum says, looking startled.

She's right. Our flight is about to board. This is it.

Of course, I thought about doing this trip alone, and leaving Isla at home in the combined care of Eddie, Mum and Sue. It would have saved a lot of money, but I couldn't do it. I suppose it's one of the ways in which Janet has affected me. I don't ever want to leave my daughter behind, not even for the shortest while, not even for the soundest reason. Wherever I go, she goes, and the recent scare with Jamie has only confirmed my stance on this.

I didn't need to invite Mum either. But it felt right. I'll never be able to buy her a Gucci handbag like Margaret's, but I'll have done this: flown her to the other side of the world, given her the trip of a lifetime. More importantly, Mum was the closest thing Louise had to a mother for many years, and I think it will mean an awful lot to Louise to see her.

And so, with renewed resolve, my heart quickening with equal parts excitement and nerves, I take Isla's small hand in mine, and hold onto Mum's arm with my other hand.

'Let's go,' I say, and we hurry to the departure gate.

Chapter 59

Louise: Cremorne Point, Sydney Harbour

July, technically the middle of winter, yet a perfect blue sky and a sun with a nurturing warmth.

'This is *winter*?' Emma said incredulously when she arrived last week. 'No wonder you don't bloody well want to go home.'

I never actually said I didn't want to go home but I don't need to vocalise everything with Emma. She just knows me.

'Ready?' Dan asks now. 'Looks like everyone is here.'

'Yes.' We're a small group: all the members of Dan's family; Analiese, Gabriella and Tom from work; and Kathy, Glynnis and Tony, friends of my mother from the group home. In fact, Kathy suggested this location for the memorial service. Apparently, my mother used to walk along the foreshore every other day, and this was one of her favourite spots to sit. Today, I've borrowed Mary and Richie's outdoor furniture so everyone has a seat. Light refreshments sit on a table to the side, for afterwards.

I nod at Emma, who is manning my iPod docking station — her nominated job — and she presses 'play'.

Whitney Houston, *I will always love you*. Haunting, heart-breaking, tragic. Apparently, it was Mum's party piece. She sang it once, at one of the 'block' Christmas parties. I had to take Ann-Marie at her word on this: I don't remember.

The song finishes and I stand up and walk to the front, where I can see everyone.

'Thank you for coming today.' The breeze coming in from the harbour tickles my face and hair. 'We're here to mark the life of my mother, Janet Elizabeth Mitchell, who died last year ...'

I thought I'd have closure when Dan supplied me with a copy of the death certificate. I didn't. Despite the distraction of Emma, Isla and Ann-Marie arriving in Sydney, full of enthusiasm and empathy and support, everything still felt hopelessly unresolved.

'How can I put it behind me?' I asked Emma one night over a glass of wine.

She thought for a while. 'Maybe you need to have a funeral. Or a memorial service of some description. Some kind of line in the sand.'

Emma is different. More mature, wiser, and softer — *much* softer. She's always been a good mother, but I can see more than ever how much she cherishes Isla. Her relationship with Ann-Marie seems different too. Not once has she rolled her eyes, given a tart response, or lost her temper with her mother. There's a new warmth between them, understanding, *respect*.

What she said about the funeral made immediate sense. A ceremony, so obvious in hindsight. Of course I needed a ritual to mark the end. A way to acknowledge the loss of my mother.

Now I had purpose. And a small army of willing helpers. Mary organised the food. Joe put together the beautiful memorial booklet. Analiese, Gabriella and Tom helped just by insisting that they be present. Anthony declined to attend, and I understand why. Kathy gathered some of my mother's belongings that were still in the house — gardening gloves, a book, some earrings. I've put these mementos with my own, on a small table with the framed photograph that is usually next to my bed, and some fresh flowers: it's a shrine of sorts.

'It's been a long journey to get to this point. Sixteen years, three continents, and many people who helped me along the way ...'

Emma, Ann-Marie, Dan, Mary, Joe, Analiese. Then, on an entirely different level, Geneviève and Kitten, who were just as important in helping me come to this hard-fought understanding — of mental illness, its many guises, the shunned sufferers, and the tragic toll on families.

'My memories of my mother are mostly blurred, but some things are distinct. Her voice, how musical it was. The flash of her smile, the red of her lipstick, the swish of her skirt. I remember the warmth of her arms around me ...'

Positive things only, as per Dan's advice. The simmering tension and resultant shouting matches, the soft sound of her breathing while I lay awake on the thin mattress on the floor, her general disassociation and constant requests to me to be quiet, none of these memories have a place in today's proceedings.

Ann-Marie is going to speak after me. She's very nervous, and trying not to show it. I've been touched by the fact that she's here, that she has come all this way, taken her very first trip abroad, to see me. She's *always* been there for me. Right from the first day my mother went missing, Ann-Marie has been watching out for me, praying for me, doing whatever she could to fill the gaps. I'm terribly, terribly grateful to her.

After Ann-Marie, Kathy will speak. I'm looking forward to hearing what she has to say. She's a gentle, kind woman. Like me, I am sure she will include only the positive things. Kathy is a community counsellor. She monitors the group home, and provides support to its residents, who do daily battle with the constant and very varied challenges of mental illness.

In a strange alignment of timing, I got a letter and a cheque from Edward Ramshaw yesterday. My inheritance from Bob: £4,000, quite a bit more than expected. I'm going to give the money to Kathy, for the home. Maybe she can use it to make some improvements — an overhaul of the garden, or new coat of paint — a legacy from my mother.

Dan is in the process of writing a feature article about my journey, the early confusion and embarrassment, followed by the anger and rebellion, then the obsession with searching for her, the grief at learning the truth, and finally something closer to acceptance and a sort of peace. His editor at the paper is very interested and says he will probably run it in the Lifestyle section. If reading my story helps someone somewhere, lessens the trauma and pain in any way, that will be a good thing.

When I get back to my seat, I see that Isla has clambered onto Dan's lap. She's very taken with him, and he with her. He's good with children. Fun yet firm. Generous with his time and his attention. It's no wonder Isla has fallen for him.

Emma likes Dan too. She hasn't said so outright — that's not her style — but I can tell. Typical Emma, she was standoffish at first. Dan was himself: honest, helpful, and smart enough to know not to push it. Yesterday I heard them laughing together, some joke, probably about me, and I smiled to myself.

I will marry Dan. In a few weeks' time, when everything has settled down, the subject will come up again, we won't be half joking this time, and I'll say yes. Mary will be ecstatic. I don't know if we'll get married here or in Ireland. Maybe Ireland. I need to show Dan some things: the bleakness of the flats where I grew up (perhaps Ann-Marie's new neighbours will allow us inside for a look), and the school where I had so many struggles. I'd like him to meet Natasha. I've seen where he comes from, the warm encompassing landscape of his home and family, so it will be his turn to experience mine, though it is altogether more desolate.

Ann-Marie's eulogy starts off shakily but she gains confidence as she goes along. As I sit and listen, amongst these beautiful supportive people, in this stunning part of Sydney Harbour, that terrible unrelenting loss loosens its grip on my heart. With each phrase, each gentle puff of wind, each ray of sunlight that catches the frame of Mum's photograph, it loosens further still, until — finally — it lifts away completely. It's no longer part of me. In fact, for a few moments The Loss feels as though it's alongside me, a presence of sorts, before it is carried away by Ann-Marie's words and the breeze, out into the vastness of the sparkling harbour.

Acknowledgements

A few years ago I came across an article 'Missing Mums' in *Australian Women's Weekly*, and that was the very moment this book began its life. Since then, many people have helped in many ways to turn that spark of an idea into a fully fledged novel.

Immense thanks to Analiese and Simon for your assistance with the technical aspects of this book and for providing such a wonderful insight into your work, which is so very different from my own. I should state that all the paintings referred to in this novel are completely fictional, as is the Sydney City Art Gallery.

Thank you, Brian Cook, for your heartfelt response to *Once Lost* and for being the most wonderful agent on the planet. I really don't know what I would do without you.

Thank you Di Blacklock and Liane Moriarty for being there every step of the way, cheering me on, helping me make all the important decisions, and supplying me with potent cocktails. Actually, the latter gave me terrible hangovers and didn't help at all, but I know you both meant well.

Thanks to my early readers, Rob and Erin, who read the entire novel and provided excellent feedback. Then there's Conor and Ashling who picked up the odd stray page and declared that they wanted to read more. It's always nice to get a stamp of approval from your children.

This novel would not be what it is without the meticulous input of Julia Stiles and Sarah Shrubb, my wonderful editors.

Thank you, Siobhain Harvey, for sharing your ballet experiences and making me laugh.

And, finally, a huge thank you to all my readers. It means the world to me that you take the time to read my novels.

ALSO BY BER CARROLL

Worlds Apart

Erin and Laura are cousins and best friends who share a love of languages and travel.

Erin, a French teacher in Dublin, reaches crisis point and drops everything to move to Australia. In Sydney, not only does she land the perfect job, but she meets the perfect man. Finally, her life is falling into place. Except Sydney isn't home, and never can be.

Back in Ireland, Laura is struggling. Her husband appears distant, her work life is spinning out of control and her daughter's strange new nanny is undermining her at every turn. She longs to travel in Erin's footsteps, to drop everything and run far away. But these are dangerous thoughts for a mother and wife.

As Erin and Laura desperately try to find their place in the world, a shocking family secret comes to light, and nothing will ever be the same again.

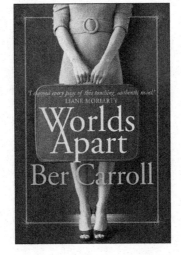

Less Than Perfect

Can we ever really leave our past behind?

From an early age, Caitlin O'Reilly was taught by her father to strive for nothing short of perfection. Growing up in a small town in the North of Ireland, she tries to live up to his expectations, and when she goes to university and falls in love for the first time, she thinks everything really is perfect. Until one day when the town, her love and her family, are completely destroyed.

Ten years later, Caitlin has created a new life for herself in Melbourne, leaving her past and her family firmly behind. But when she meets Matthew and finds herself falling in love again, what happened in Ireland is suddenly closer and more relevant than ever, unearthing all the hurts and betrayals and secrets she has tried so hard to bury. As Caitlin's life reaches another crisis point, it seems that there is nothing she can do to keep her past and her present from colliding …

This is an emotionally gripping story about love, forgiveness and less-than-perfect families.

The Better Woman

Sarah Ryan grows up in her grandmother's house in a small Irish village. Sarah is clever and ambitious and eager to move away from the sleepy village. She fully believes that John Delaney, the boy-next-door and her first love, will be right by her side ... until he breaks her heart.

Jodi Tyler is raised on Sydney's northern beaches amidst a close and loving family. But Jodi has a secret, a tragic secret which leaves her determined to make a success of her life. Like Sarah, Jodi's grandmother ends up providing her with a home. And when Jodi falls head over heels in love, she too ends up with a broken heart.

This is a story of two remarkable women who face all life's challenges head on — and those they love and lose on their journey. Set in Ireland, Australia, London and New York, Sarah and Jodi make their way in the world unaware that their lives are running in parallel. It is only when they both want the same thing that their paths will finally cross ...

High Potential

Katie Horgan is going places: soon she'll be a partner in the prestigious law firm where she works. But her love life is going nowhere — until she meets Jim Donnelly. Jim is brilliant, handsome and, like her parents, Irish. The only problem is that he already has a girlfriend.

When Katie is sent to Ireland as part of her training, she happily settles into life in Dublin where she works in a clinic that provides free legal advice to the homeless. She befriends Mags, who makes it her business to initiate Katie into Dublin's social scene. Then Jim Donnelly comes home on a visit, their relationship deepens, but everything begins to unravel ...

Bit by bit, the truth comes out, about Jim, Mags, and the reason that Katie's parents left Ireland — and Katie learns that life and love are not as black and white as she always thought.

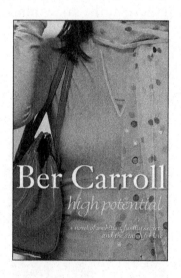

Just Business

Niamh Lynch appears to have it all: a high-flying career, a handsome, successful husband and a loving family. But looks can be deceiving.

From the moment she has to deliver the terrible news that there will be heavy redundancies at her workplace, her marriage crumbles and her life falls apart.

Certain cracks have been there for a long time, since her family left Ireland. Others are new. Who will catch her as she falls? Her mother whom she can't forgive? Her father from his grave? Or Scott, a man who has just lost his job, but who seems to understand her in a way nobody else does?

Executive Affair

Claire Quinlan is unlucky in love and fed up with her life in Dublin. So when an opportunity arises to transfer to the Sydney office of her company, she grabs it. She sets up house in Bondi with her old friend Fiona, finds a new boyfriend Paul, and is sure that her life has changed for the better.

But her new job and boyfriend are more challenging than she imagined. She finds herself falling for the handsome American vice-president, Robert Pozos. Robert is sophisticated and charming and very complicated. He spells another broken heart, but she just can't seem to stop herself ...

Then Claire uncovers a corporate fraud and she suddenly doesn't know who she can trust. Everyone has something to lose: Robert, Fiona, Paul. But Claire, who always played it safe, is risking the most.

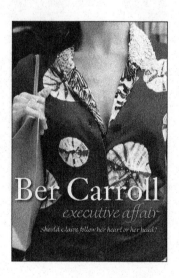

Ber Carroll was born in Blarney, County Cork, and moved to Australia in 1995. Her first novel, *Executive Affair*, was inspired by her initial impressions of Sydney, and her exciting, dynamic work environment at the time. Ber now lives in Sydney's northern beaches with her husband and two children. *Once Lost* is her seventh novel. Incidentally, Ber is short for Bernadette, but please don't call her Bernadette: this is what her mother calls her when she is in trouble for something.

Ber's novels have been published in five countries, including Ireland. If you would like to know more about Ber and her novels, you can visit her website at www.bercarroll.com, or you can subscribe to her newsletter (Book Chat) with fellow authors Dianne Blacklock and Liane Moriarty (see Ber's website for a link to the newsletter).